READER'S DIGEST

CONDENSED BOOKS

FIRST EDITION

THE READER'S DIGEST ASSOCIATION LIMITED
25 Berkeley Square, London W1X 6AB

**THE READER'S DIGEST ASSOCIATION
SOUTH AFRICA (PTY) LTD**
Nedbank Centre, Strand Street, Cape Town

Printed in Great Britain by Petty & Sons Ltd, Leeds

Original cover design by Jeffery Matthews F.S.I.A.D.

ISBN 0 340 27009 8

Reader's Digest
CONDENSED BOOKS

REFLEX
Dick Francis

ONE CHILD
Torey L. Hayden

RANDOM WINDS
Belva Plain

IN THE
SIGN OF THE BEAR
R. D. Symons

COLLECTOR'S LIBRARY
EDITION

In this Volume:

Reflex

by Dick Francis *(p. 9)*

Philip Nore, steeplechase jockey and amateur photographer, is the hero of Dick Francis's latest action-packed thriller. Philip finds himself involved in two mysteries. The first takes him back into his lost childhood to discover some surprising truths about himself and his family. The second, in which he unravels the intriguing secrets of a dead photographer's box of discarded film, leads him deep into the dangerous underworld of racing.

ONE CHILD
by Torey L. Hayden *(p. 149)*

Though Torey Hayden was experienced in teaching emotionally disturbed children, she had never before encountered a little girl like Sheila. Severely abused both emotionally and physically, the six-year-old was violently hostile, and her teacher despaired of ever gaining her confidence. But patiently Torey built up a fragile bridge of trust and love, and discovered inside the tormented child a very special person, perceptive, responsive and highly intelligent.

A deeply moving true story of a sensitive teacher and a desperately unhappy child.

RANDOM WINDS

by Belva Plain (p. 269)

Martin Farrell has two dreams: to be a doctor like his father and to marry the beautiful Mary Fern. Though he achieves some of his ambitions, fate has surprises in store, and Martin is swept away from his American home to England, then back again to a celebrated career as a surgeon. But the woman he marries is not Mary Fern, and it is not until Martin faces the truth about his own family that he can come to terms with his life and its unfulfilled longings. *Random Winds* is a memorable love story—powerful, tender and tempestuous.

IN THE SIGN OF THE BEAR

by R. D. Symons (p. 453)

A small child, sole survivor of a plane crash in the Canadian Arctic, is brought up by a wandering tribe of Eskimos. But, happy as he is, the boy knows he does not belong, and embarks on a search for himself and his roots. The hazards and hardships of the frozen wilderness test the young man to the utmost, but in the end his journey comes to a triumphant conclusion.

The author's love for the magnificent unspoiled vastness of northern Canada and his understanding of its human and animal inhabitants combine in an unforgettable story, justly hailed as a modern classic.

Reflex

A CONDENSATION OF THE BOOK BY
Dick Francis

ILLUSTRATED BY WALTER RANE
PUBLISHED BY MICHAEL JOSEPH

To Philip Nore, jockey and amateur photographer, the contents of the small box looked harmless: some blank-looking film and several spoiled photos. But the owner of the box had been a fine photographer. Why had he kept these failures around? And why had his widow's home been ransacked? Philip found it all a fascinating puzzle. And Philip loved puzzles. Almost as much as he loved steeplechasing. And almost as much as he was to love Clare, the girl who bullied her way so sweetly into his life. As he begins to unravel the dead photographer's secrets, Philip is plunged into a dangerous conspiracy that threatens to end more than one career in the racing world—perhaps even his own.

Chapter 1

Winded and coughing, I lay on one elbow and spat out a mouthful of grass and mud. The horse I'd been riding raised its weight off my ankle, scrambled untidily to its feet, and departed at an unfeeling gallop. I waited for things to settle: chest heaving, bones still rattling from the bang, sense of balance recovering from a thirty-mile-an-hour somersault and a few tumbling rolls. No harm done. Nothing broken. Just another fall.

Time and place: sixteenth fence, three-mile steeplechase, Sandown Park racecourse, Friday, November, in thin, cold persistent rain. I stood up wearily and thought that this was a damn silly way for a grown man to be spending his life.

The thought was a jolt. Not one I'd ever thought before. Riding horses at high speed over jumps was the only way I knew to make a living, and it was a job one couldn't do if one's heart wasn't in it. The chilling flicker of disillusion nudged like the first twinge of a toothache. But I reassured myself. I loved the life. Nothing was wrong except the weather, the fall, the lost race.

Squelching uphill to the stands in my paper-thin racing boots, I thought only about the horse I'd started out on, sorting out what I might say to its trainer. Discarded "How do you expect it to jump if you don't school it properly?" in favour of "Might try him in blinkers." The trainer, anyway, would blame me for the fall and tell the owner I'd misjudged the pace. He was that sort. I thanked heaven I didn't ride often for that stable, and had been engaged on that day only because Steve Millace, its usual jockey, had gone to his father's funeral. Spare rides were not lightly to be turned down. Not if you needed the money, which I did.

The only good thing about my descent was that Steve Millace's father wasn't there to record it. George Millace, pitiless photographer of moments all jockeys preferred to ignore, was at that moment being lowered underground. And good riddance, I thought. Goodbye to the snide pleasure George got from delivering to owners the irrefutable evidence of their jockey's failings. Goodbye to the motorized camera catching one's balance in the wrong place, one's arms in the air, one's face in the mud.

Where other photographers played fair and shot you winning from time to time, George trafficked exclusively in ignominy and humiliation. There had been little sorrow in the changing room the day Steve told us his father had driven into a tree. Out of liking for Steve himself, no one had said much. But he knew. He had been anxiously defending his father for years.

Trudging back in the rain, it seemed odd to think that we wouldn't be seeing George Millace again. His image came sharply to mind: bright clever eyes, long nose, drooping moustache, twisted mouth sourly smiling. A terrific photographer, one had to admit, with exceptional timing, always pointing his lens in the right direction at the right moment.

When I finally reached the shelter of the veranda outside the changing room, the trainer and owner were waiting.

"Misjudged things, didn't you?" said the trainer.

"He took off a stride too soon. Might try him in blinkers."

"*I'll* decide about that," he said sharply, as he led the owner away from me and the danger that I might say something truthful about the horse not being schooled properly. I turned towards the changing-room door.

"I say," said a young man, stepping in front of me. "Are you Philip Nore?"

"That's right."

"Could I have a word with you?" He was about twenty-five, tall as a stork, and earnest, with office-coloured skin. Charcoal flannel suit, striped tie.

10

"Sure," I said. "If you'll wait while I get into something dry."

When I went out again, warmed and in street clothes, he was still on the veranda. "I . . . er . . . my name is Jeremy Folk." He produced a card: Folk, Langley, Son and Folk, Solicitors, St. Albans, Hertfordshire.

"That last Folk," said Jeremy, "is me." He cleared his throat. "I've been sent to ask you to . . . er . . ." He stopped, looking helpless.

"To what?" I said encouragingly.

"To go and see your grandmother." The words came out in a rush. "She's dying. She wants to see you."

"I'm not going."

"But you must." He looked troubled. "I mean . . . if I don't persuade you, my uncle . . . that's Son" —he pointed to the card, getting flustered— "er . . . . Folk is my grandfather and Langley is my great-uncle, and . . . er . . . they sent me . . ." He swallowed. "They think I'm frightfully useless, to be honest."

A glint in his eyes told me he wasn't as silly as he made out.

"I don't want to see her," I said.

"But she is dying," he said.

"I'll bet she isn't. If she wants to see me, she would say she was dying just to fetch me, because nothing else would."

He looked shocked. "She's seventy-eight, after all."

I stared gloomily out at the rain. I had never met my grand-mother and I didn't want to, dying or dead. I didn't approve of deathbed repentances. It was too late. "The answer is no."

He shrugged and seemed to give up. Walked a few steps out into the rain, bareheaded, vulnerable. Turned around and came back again. "Look . . . she really needs you, my uncle says."

"Where is she?"

He brightened. "In a nursing home. I'll lead you there if you'll come. It's in St. Albans. You live in Lambourn, don't you? So it isn't so terribly far out of your way, is it?"

I sighed. The options were rotten. That she had dished out stony rejection from my birth gave me no excuse, I supposed, for doing it to her at her death.

The winter afternoon was already fading. I thought of my empty cottage; of nothing much to fill the evening; of two eggs, a piece of cheese, and black coffee for supper; of fighting the impulse to eat more. If I went, it would at least take my mind off food. "All right," I said resignedly. "Lead on."

THE OLD WOMAN sat upright in bed staring at me, and if she was dying, it wasn't going to be on that evening, for sure. The life-force was strong in the dark eyes. "Philip," she said, looking me up and down. "Hah." The explosive sound contained both triumph and contempt and was everything I expected. Her ramrod will had devastated my childhood and done worse damage to her own daughter, and there was to be, I was relieved to see, no maudlin plea for forgiveness.

"I knew you'd come running," she said, "when you heard about the hundred thousand pounds."

"No one mentioned any money."

"Don't lie. Why else would you come?"

"They said you were dying."

She gave me a malevolent look. "So I am. So are we all."

She was no one's idea of a sweet little pink-cheeked granny. A strong, stubborn face with disapproval lines cut deep around the mouth. Iron-grey hair. Dark, ridged veins on the backs of the hands. A thin, gaunt woman.

"I instructed Mr. Folk to make you the offer. I told him to get you here. And he did."

I turned away and sat unasked in an armchair. She stared at me steadily with no sign of affection, and I stared as steadily back. I was repelled by her contempt and mistrusted her intentions.

"I will leave you a hundred thousand pounds in my will, upon certain conditions," she said.

"No, you won't," I said. "No money. No conditions."

"You haven't heard my proposition." I said nothing. I felt the first stirrings of curiosity, but I was not going to let her see it. The silence lengthened. Finally she said, "You're taller than I expected. And tougher. Where is your mother?"

My mother, her daughter. "I think she's dead."

"*Think!* Don't you *know?*"

"She didn't exactly write to me to say she'd died. No."

12

"Your flippancy is disgraceful."

"Your behaviour since before my birth," I said, "gives you no right to say so."

Her mouth opened, and stayed open for fully five seconds. Then it shut tight and she stared at me darkly. I saw in that expression what my young mother had had to face, and felt a great uprush of sympathy for the feckless butterfly who'd borne me.

There had been a day, when I was quite small, that I had been dressed in new clothes and told to be exceptionally good as I was going to see my grandmother. My mother had collected me from where I was living and we had travelled by car to a large house, where I was left alone in the hall, to wait. Behind a closed door there had been a lot of shouting. Then my mother had come out, crying, grabbed my hand, and pulled me after her to the car.

"Come on, Philip. We'll never ask her for anything, ever again. She wouldn't even see you. Don't you ever forget, Philip, that your grandmother's a hateful *beast*."

I had never actually lived with my mother, except for a traumatic week or two now and then. We had had no house, no permanent address. Herself always on the move, she had solved the problem of what to do with me by simply dumping me for varying periods on a long succession of astonished friends.

"Do look after Philip for me for a few days, darling," she would say, giving me a push towards yet another strange lady. "Life is so unutterably *cluttered* just now and I'm at my wit's end to know what to do with him, so, darling Deborah (or Miranda or Chloe or Samantha or anyone else under the sun), do be an absolute *sweetie*, and I'll pick him up on Saturday, I promise."

Saturdays came and my mother didn't, but she always turned up in the end, full of flutter and laughter and gushing thanks, retrieving her parcel, so to speak, from the left-luggage office.

She was deliciously pretty, to the extent that people hugged her and indulged her and lit up when she was around. Only later, when they were left literally holding the baby, did the doubts creep in. I became a bewildered, silent child, for ever tiptoeing around so as not to give offence, perennially frightened that someone, one day, would abandon me altogether out in the street.

13

Looking back, I knew I owed a great deal to Samantha, Deborah, Chloe, et al. I never went hungry, nor was I ever totally rejected. But it was a disorienting existence from which I emerged at twelve, when I was dumped in my first long-stay home, able to do almost any job around the house and unable to love.

She left me with two photographers, Duncan and Charlie, standing in their big bare-floored studio that had a darkroom, a bathroom, a gas ring, and a bed behind a curtain.

"Just look after him until Saturday, there's a sweet pair of lambs." And although birthday cards arrived, and presents at Christmas, I didn't see her again for three years. During those years, Duncan and Charlie taught me all I could learn about photography. I started by cleaning up in the darkroom and finished by doing all of their printing. "Our lab assistant", Charlie called me.

After Duncan departed, my mother swooped in one day and took me away from Charlie, and drove me down to a racehorse trainer and his wife in Hampshire, telling those bemused friends, "It's only until Saturday, darlings, and he's fifteen and strong, and he'll muck out the stables for you. . . ."

Cards and presents arrived for two years or so, always without an address to reply to. On my eighteenth birthday there was no card, no present the following Christmas, and I'd never heard from her again. She must have died, I had come to understand, from drugs. There was a great deal, as I grew older, that I'd sorted out and understood.

The old woman glared across the room, as unforgiving and destructive as ever, and still angry at what I'd said. I stood up. "This visit is pointless. If you wanted to find your daughter, you should have looked twenty years ago. And as for me . . . I wouldn't find her for you, even if I could."

"I don't want you to find Caroline. I daresay you're right, that she's dead." The idea clearly caused her no grief. "I want you to find your sister."

"My *what?*"

The hostile dark eyes assessed me shrewdly. "You didn't know you had a sister? Well, you have. I'll leave you a hundred thousand pounds in my will if you find her and bring her here to me."

I felt an intense thrust of shock, a stinging jealousy that my mother had had another child. Now I had to share her memory. I thought in confusion that it was ridiculous to be experiencing displacement emotions at thirty.

"Well?" my grandmother said sharply.

"No," I said. "And if that's all, I'll be going."

"Wait," she said. "Don't you want to see her picture? There's a photograph of your sister over there on the chest."

Without wanting to, but impelled by curiosity, I walked over to the chest. There was a snapshot lying there and I picked it up. A little girl, three or four years old, on a pony, with shoulder-length brown hair, wearing a striped T-shirt and jeans. Photographed in what was evidently a stable yard, but the photographer had been standing too far away to bring out much detail in the child's face. I turned the print over, but there was nothing to indicate where it had come from.

Vaguely disappointed, I put it down and saw, with a wince of nostalgia, an envelope lying on the chest with my mother's hand-writing on it. Addressed to my grandmother, Mrs. Lavinia Nore, at the old house in Northamptonshire where I'd had to wait in the hall. In the envelope, a letter. I took it out.

"What are you doing?" said my grandmother in alarm. "That letter shouldn't be there. Put it down."

I ignored her. The letter was dated October 2, with no year.

Dear Mother,

I know I said I would never ask you for anything again but I'm having one more try, silly me. I am sending you a photograph of my daughter, Amanda, your granddaughter. She is very sweet and she's three now, and she needs a proper home and to go to school and everything. I know you wouldn't want a child around, but if you'd just give her an allowance, she could live with some perfectly angelic people who love her and want to keep her but simply can't afford another child. She hasn't the same father as Philip, so you couldn't hate her for the same reasons. Please, Mother, look after her. Please, please, answer this letter.

Caroline

Staying at Pine Woods Lodge, Mindle Bridge, Sussex.

I looked up at the hard old woman. "You didn't reply?"

"No."

It was no good getting angry over so old a tragedy. I looked at the envelope to try to see the date of the postmark, but it was smudged and undecipherable. How long, I wondered, had my mother waited at Pine Woods Lodge, hoping and desperate?

I put the letter, the envelope, and the photograph in my jacket pocket. I felt in an obscure way that they belonged to me, and not to her.

"So you'll do it," she said.

"No. If you want Amanda found, hire a private detective."

"I did. Three detectives. They were all useless."

"If three failed, there's no way I could succeed."

"You'll try harder. For that sort of money."

"You're wrong. If I took any money from you, I'd vomit." I walked over to the door and opened it without hesitation.

To my departing back she said, "Amanda shall have my money . . . if you find her."

WHEN I WENT BACK to Sandown Park the next day the letter and photograph were still in my pocket, but the emotions they had engendered had subsided. It was the present, in the shape of Steve Millace, that claimed everyone's attention. He came steaming into the changing room half an hour before the first race with drizzle on his hair and fury in his eyes. His mother's house, he said, had been burgled while they were out at his father's funeral.

We sat in rows on the benches, listening with shock. I looked at the scene. Jockeys in all stages of dress—in underpants, bare-chested, in silks, pulling on boots—and all of them listening with open mouths and with eyes turned towards Steve. Automatically, I reached for my Nikon and took a couple of photographs. They were all so accustomed to me doing that sort of thing that no one took any notice.

"It was awful," Steve said. "Mum had made some cakes and things for the aunts and everyone, for when we got back from the cremation, and they were all thrown around the place, squashed flat, jam and such, onto the walls. And all those things taken."

16

He went on. "They stripped Dad's darkroom. Just ripped everything out. It was senseless . . . like I told the police. They didn't just take things you could sell, like the enlarger and the developing stuff, but all his work—all those pictures taken over the years, they're all gone. Mum's just sitting there, crying."

He stopped suddenly and swallowed, as if it was all too much for him. At twenty-three, although he no longer lived with them, he was still very much his parents' child. George Millace might have been widely disliked, but he had never been belittled by his son.

Slight in build, Steve had bright dark eyes and ears that stuck out widely, giving him a slightly comic look, but he was more intense than humorous and apt to keep on returning obsessively to things that upset him.

"The police said that burglars do it for spite," Steve said. "Mess up people's houses and steal their photographs. They told Mum it's always happening." He went on, talking to anyone who would listen. I finished changing and went out to ride in the first race.

It was a day I had been looking forward to. I was to ride Daylight in the Sandown Handicap Pattern Steeplechase. A big race, a good horse, and a great chance of winning. Such combinations came my way rarely enough to be prized. There was just the first race, a novice hurdle, to come back from unscathed, and then, perhaps, I would win the big race with Daylight, and half a dozen people would fall over themselves to offer me their horse for the Gold Cup.

Two races a day was my usual mark, and if I ended a season in the top twenty on the jockeys' list, I was happy. For years I'd been able to kid myself that the modesty of my success was due to being too tall and heavy. Even with constant semi-starvation I weighed ten stone seven. Most seasons I rode in about two hundred races with forty or so winners, and knew that I was considered "strong" and "reliable" but "not first class in a close finish."

At around twenty-six I'd come to terms with knowing I wasn't going to the top, and oddly, far from depressing me, the realization had been a relief. All the same, I'd no objection to having Gold Cup winners thrust upon me, so to speak.

On that afternoon at Sandown I completed the novice hurdle fifth out of eighteen runners. Not too bad. I changed into Daylight's colours and in due course walked out to the parade ring. Daylight's trainer, for whom I rode regularly, was waiting there, and also Daylight's owner, who said without preamble, "You'll lose this one today, Philip."

I smiled. "Not if I can help it."

"Indeed you will. My money's on the other way."

I don't suppose I kept much of the dismay and anger out of my face. Victor Briggs, Daylight's owner, had done this sort of thing before, but not for about three years, and he knew I didn't like it. A sturdily built man in his forties, unsociable, secretive, he came to the races with a closed, unsmiling face. He always wore a heavy navy-blue overcoat, a black broad-rimmed hat, and thick black leather gloves. He had been, in the past, an aggressive gambler, and in riding for him I had the choice of doing what he said or losing my job with the stable. So I had lost races I might have won. I needed to eat and to pay off the mortgage on the cottage. For that I needed a good big stable to ride for.

Back at the beginning, Victor Briggs had offered me a fair-sized cash present for losing. I'd said I didn't want it; I would lose if I had to, but I wouldn't be paid. He said I was a pompous fool, but after I'd refused his offer a second time he'd kept his bribes in his pocket. And since I'd been free of the dilemma for three years, it was all the more infuriating to be faced with it again.

"I can't lose," I protested. "Daylight's the best of the bunch."

"Just do it," Victor Briggs said. "And lower your voice, unless you want the stewards to hear you."

I looked at Harold Osborne, Daylight's trainer. "Victor's right," he said. "The money's on the other way. You'll cost us a packet if you win, so don't."

"Us?"

He nodded. "Us. That's right. Fall off, if you have to. Come in second if you like. But not first. Understood?"

I understood. Back in the old pincers.

I cantered Daylight down to the start with reality winning out over rebellion, as before. I'd been with Osborne seven years. If he

18

chucked me out, all I'd get would be other stables' odds and ends: a one-way track to oblivion.

I was angry. I didn't want to lose the race; I hated to be dishonest. And the ten per cent of the winner's purse I would lose was big enough to make me even angrier. Why had Briggs gone back to this caper after all this time?

While the starter called the roll, I looked at the four horses ranged against Daylight. There wasn't one among them that could defeat my gelding, which was why people were staking four pounds on Daylight to win one. Four to one on.

Far from risking his own money at those odds, Victor Briggs in some subterranean way had taken bets from other people, and would have to pay out if his horse won. And so, it seemed, would Harold. However I might feel, I did owe him some allegiance.

After seven years of a working relationship, I had come to regard Harold Osborne as a friend. He was a man of rages and charms, of tyrannical decisions and generous gifts. He could outshout anyone on the Berkshire Downs, and stable lads left his employ in droves. But he had trusted me always, and had defended me against criticism when many a trainer would not. He assumed that I would be, for my part, totally committed to him and his stable, and for the past three years that had been easy.

The starter called the horses into line, and I wheeled Daylight around to point his nose in the right direction. No starting stalls were used for jump racing. A gate of elastic tapes instead.

In misery I decided that the race, from Daylight's point of view, would have to be over as near the start as possible. Losing would be hard enough, and practically suicidal if I waited until it was clear that Daylight would win. Then, if I just fell off in the last half mile for not much reason, there would be an inquiry and I might lose my licence; and it would be no comfort to know that I deserved to.

The starter put his hand on the lever, the tapes flew up, and I kicked Daylight forward. Cheat the horse. Cheat the public. Cheat. Damn it, I thought.

I did it at the third fence, on the decline from the top of the hill, round the sharpish bend, going away from the stands. It was the least visible place to the crowd and the most likely place for an accident. The fence had claimed many a victim during the year. Daylight, confused by getting the wrong signals from me, and perhaps feeling my turmoil in the telepathic way that horses do, put in a jerky extra stride before take-off, where none was needed.

I'm sorry, boy, but down you go; and I kicked him at the wrong moment, and twitched hard on his bit while he was in mid-air, and shifted my weight forward in front of his shoulder.

He landed awkwardly and stumbled slightly, dipping his head to recover his balance. I whisked my right foot out of the stirrup and over his back, so that I was entirely on his left side, out of the saddle. I clung to his neck for about three bucking strides and then slid down his chest, losing my grip and bouncing onto the grass under his feet. A flurry of thuds from his hoofs, a roll, and the noise and the galloping horses were gone. I sat on the ground, unbuckled my helmet, and felt absolutely wretched.

"BAD LUCK," THEY SAID in the changing room. I wondered if any of them guessed, but no one nudged or winked. It was my own sense of shame that kept me staring mostly at the floor.

"Cheer up," Steve Millace said, buttoning some orange and blue colours. "It's not the end of the world." He went off to ride, and I changed gloomily back into street clothes. So much, I thought, for winning, for trainers climbing over themselves to secure my services for the Gold Cup. So much for a boost to the finances. I went out to watch the race.

Steve Millace, with more courage than sense, drove his horse at leg-tangling pace into the second-to-last fence and crashed on landing. It was the sort of hard, fast fall that cracked bones, and one could see that Steve was in trouble. He struggled up as far as his knees, then sat on his heels with his head bent forward and his arms wrapped around his body, hugging himself. Arm, shoulder, ribs . . . something had gone.

Two first-aid men helped him into an ambulance. A bad day for Steve, too, I thought, on top of all his family troubles. What on earth made us do it, disregarding injury and risk and disappointment, when we could earn as much sitting in an office?

20

I met him later in the changing room. His shoulder was bandaged, his arm in a sling. "Collarbone," he said crossly. "Bloody nuisance."

His valet helped him dress, touching him gently. "Could you possibly drive me home?" Steve asked me. "To my mother's house? Near Ascot."

"Yes, I should think so," I said. I took a photograph of him and his valet, who was smoothly pulling off his boots.

"What do you do with all them snapshots?" the valet said.

"Put them in a drawer."

He gave a heaven-help-us jerk of the head. "Waste of time."

Steve glanced at the Nikon. "Dad said once he'd seen some of your pics. You'd put him out of business one day, he said."

"He was laughing at me."

George Millace had seen some of my pictures, catching me looking through them as I sat in my car one day waiting for a friend. "Let's have a look," he had said. "Well, well," he remarked, going through them. "Keep it up. One of these days you might take a photograph." He was the only photographer I knew with whom I didn't feel at home.

The valet helped Steve into his jacket, and we went at Steve's tender pace out to my car and drove off in the direction of Ascot.

"I can't get used to Dad's not being there," Steve said.

"What happened? You said he drove into a tree."

"Yes." He sighed. "He went to sleep. At least, that's what everyone reckons. There weren't any other cars. There was a bend, and he just drove straight ahead. He must have had his foot on the accelerator. The front of the car was smashed right in." He shivered. "He had stopped for half an hour at a friend's house. And they'd had a couple of whiskies. It was all so stupid. Just going to sleep . . . Turn left here."

We drove for a long way in silence and came finally to a road bordered by neat houses set in shadowy gardens. There, in the middle distance, things were happening. An ambulance with its doors open, blue light flashing. A police car. People hurrying in and out of one of the houses. Every window uncurtained, spilling out light.

21

"No!" Steve said. "That's our house."

I pulled up outside, and he sat unmoving, staring, stricken.

"It's Mum," he said. "It must be. It's Mum."

There was something near the cracking point in his voice. His face was twisted with terrible anxiety.

"Stay here," I said practically. "I'll go and see."

Chapter 2

His mum lay on the sofa in the sitting room, quivering and coughing and bleeding. Someone had attacked her pretty nastily, splitting her nose and mouth and eyelid. Her clothes were torn, her shoes were off, and her hair stuck out in straggly wisps. I had seen her at the races from time to time—a pleasant, well-dressed woman nearing fifty, secure and happy, plainly proud of her husband and son. As the grief-stricken, burgled, beaten-up person on the sofa, she was unrecognizable.

There was a policeman sitting on a stool beside her, and a policewoman, standing, holding a bloodstained cloth. A neighbourly-looking woman stood around with a worried expression on her face. The room was a shambles, papers and smashed furniture littering the floor. On the walls, the signs of jam and cakes, as Steve had said. The policeman turned his head. "Are you the doctor?"

"No." I explained who I was.

"Steve's hurt!" his mother said, fear for her son overshadowing everything else.

"It's not bad, I promise you," I said hastily. "He's here, outside." I went and told him, and helped him out of the car.

"Why?" he said, going up the path. "Why did it happen?"

Indoors, the policeman was asking, "There were two of them, with stockings over their faces?"

Marie Millace nodded. "Young," she said. The word came out distorted through her swollen lips. She saw Steve and held out her hand.

"What were they wearing?" the policeman said.

"Jeans."

"Gloves?"

She closed her eyes and whispered, "Yes."

"What did they want?"

"Safe," she said, mumbling. " 'We haven't got a safe,' I told them. 'Where's the safe?' they said. One smashed things. The other hit me."

"I'd like to kill them," Steve said furiously.

"Just keep quiet, sir, if you wouldn't mind," the policeman said.

"I suppose you know," I said to him, "that this house was also burgled yesterday?"

"Yes, I do, sir. I was here yesterday myself." He looked at me assessingly for a few seconds and turned back to Steve's mother. "Did these two young men mention being here yesterday?"

She was silent for a long interval. Poor lady, I thought. Too much pain, too much grief, too much outrage. At last she said, "They were like bulls. They shouted. I opened the front door. They shoved in, pushed me in here. Started smashing things. Shouting, 'Tell us, where is the safe?' " She paused. "I don't think they said anything . . . about yesterday."

"I'd like to *kill* them," Steve said.

"Third time burgled," mumbled his mother. "Happened two years ago."

"You can't just let her lie here," Steve said violently. "Asking all these questions. Haven't you got a doctor?"

"It's all right, Steve dear," the neighbourly woman said. "I've rung Dr. Williams. He said he would come at once." Caring and bothered, she was nonetheless enjoying the drama. "I was home next door, dear, getting tea for my family, and I heard all this shouting and it seemed all wrong, so I was just coming to see, and those two dreadful young men just burst out of the house, dear, just *burst* out, so of course I came in here and rang for the police and the ambulance and Dr. Williams."

The policeman was unappreciative. He said to her, "And you still can't remember any more about the car they drove off in?"

Defensively she said, "I don't notice cars much."

I said diffidently to the policeman, "I've cameras in my car, if you want photographs of all this."

23

He raised his eyebrows and considered and said yes; so I fetched both cameras and took two sets of pictures, in colour and black and white, with close-ups of Mrs. Millace's damaged face and wide-angle shots of the room. The policeman told me where to send them and then the doctor arrived.

"Don't go yet," Steve said to me, and I looked at the desperation in his face, and stayed through all the ensuing bustle.

In fact I stayed the night, because after they took Mrs. Millace to the hospital, Steve looked so exhausted that I simply couldn't leave him. I made us a couple of omelettes and then picked up some of the mess: magazines, newspapers, old letters, and also the base and lid of a flat eight-by-ten-inch box that had once held photographic printing paper.

"What shall I do with all this?" I asked Steve.

He sat on the edge of the sofa, looking strained, not mentioning that his fractured collarbone was obviously hurting quite a bit. "Oh, just pile it anywhere," he said vaguely. "Some of it came out of that rack over there by the television."

A wooden magazine rack, empty, lay on its side on the carpet.

"That old orange thing beside it is Dad's rubbish box. He kept it in that rack with the papers. Just left it there, year after year. Funny really."

I picked up a small batch of odds and ends—a transparent piece of film about three inches wide by eight long, several strips of 35-mm colour negatives, developed but blank, and an otherwise pleasant picture of Mrs. Millace that had been spoiled by splashes of chemical.

"Those were in Dad's rubbish box, I think," Steve said, yawning. "You might as well throw them away."

I put them in the wastepaper basket, and added a nearly black black-and-white print that had been torn in half, some more colour negatives covered in magenta blotches, and another very dark print in a folder, showing a shadowy man sitting at a table.

"He kept those things to remind himself of his worst mistakes," Steve said. "It doesn't seem *possible* that he isn't coming back."

The bulk of the mess on the floor was broken china, the remnants of a sewing box, and a bureau, tipped on its side, its contents

24

falling out of the drawers. None of the damage seemed to have had any purpose: it was a rampage designed to confuse and bewilder.

"Why would they think your mother had a safe?" I asked.

"Who knows? If she'd had one, she'd have told them where it was, wouldn't she? After losing Dad like that. And yesterday's burglary, while we were at the funeral. Such dreadful shocks. She can't take any more." There were tears in his voice. It was he, I thought, who was closest to the edge.

"Time for bed," I said abruptly. "I'll help you undress."

I WOKE EARLY after an uneasy night and lay watching the dingy November dawn creep through the window. There was a good deal about life that I didn't want to get up and face. Wouldn't it be marvellous, I thought dimly, not to have to think about mean-minded grandmothers and one's own depressing dishonesty? Normally fairly happy-go-lucky, I disliked being backed into corners from which escape meant action.

Things had just happened to me all my life. I'd never gone out looking. Like photography, because of Duncan and Charlie. And like riding, because of my mother's dumping me in a racing stable. Survival for so many years had been a matter of accepting what I was given, of making myself useful, of being quiet and agreeable and no trouble. I had made no major decisions. What I had, had simply come.

I understood why I was as I was. I knew why I was passive, but I felt no desire to change, to be master of my fate. I didn't want to look for my half-sister, and I didn't want to lose my job.

Irritated, I put my clothes on and went downstairs, peering in at Steve on the way and finding him sound asleep. To pass the time, I wandered around, just looking.

George Millace's darkroom would have been the most interesting, but the burglary there had been the most thorough. All that was left was a wide bench down one side, two deep sinks down the other, and rows of empty shelves. Grubby outlines and smudges on the walls showed where the equipment had stood, and stains on the floor marked where he'd stored his chemicals.

He had, I knew, done a lot of his own colour developing. Most professional photographers do not. Developing colour films is difficult, and it's easier to entrust the process to commercial labs. But George Millace had been a craftsman of the first order. Pity about his unkind nature.

From the look of things he had had two enlargers, one big and one smaller, enlargers being machines that hold a negative in what is basically a box up a stick, so that a bright light can shine through the negative onto a baseboard beneath.

The head of the enlarger, holding the light and the negative, can be wound up and down the stick. The higher one winds the head above the baseboard, the larger one sees the picture. The lower the head, the smaller the picture. An enlarger is in fact a projector, and the baseboard is the screen.

Besides the enlargers, George would have had an electric box of tricks for regulating the length of exposures, a mass of developing equipment, and a dryer for drying the finished prints. He would have had various types of photographic paper, lightproof containers to store it in and files holding all his past work. The whole lot, every scrap, had been stolen.

I went into the sitting room, wondering how soon I could decently wake Steve and say I was going. Having nothing else to do, I began picking up more of the mess, retrieving bits of sewing from under the chairs.

Half under the sofa lay a large black lightproof envelope. I looked inside it. It contained a piece of clear plastic about eight by eleven inches, straight cut on three sides but wavy along the fourth. More rubbish. I put it back in the envelope and threw it in the wastepaper basket.

George Millace's rubbish box still lay open and empty on the carpet. Impelled by photographic curiosity, I picked up the wastepaper basket and sorted out all of George's worst mistakes. Why, I wondered, had he bothered to keep them? I put the spoiled prints and pieces of film back in George's rubbish box and added the large lightproof envelope. It would be instructive to learn the reason why such an expert had found these particular things interesting.

Steve came downstairs in his pyjamas, hugging his injured arm. "Thanks," he said. "You've tidied the lot." He saw the rubbish box. "For a long time he kept that box in the freezer."

"Did your father often keep things in it?"

"Masses of stuff. You know photographers, always having fits about colour dyes not being permanent. He said the only way to posterity was through the deep freeze, and even that wasn't certain."

"Did the burglars also empty the freezer?"

He looked startled. "I don't know. Why should they want his films? The policeman said what they really wanted was the equipment, which they could sell."

"Your father took a lot of pictures people didn't like."

"Only as a joke." He was defending George, the same as ever.

"We might look in the freezer," I suggested.

"Yes. All right."

He led the way into a small yard. "In there," he said, giving me a key and nodding towards the shed's green door. I went in and found a huge chest freezer standing beside a lawn mower.

I lifted the lid. Inside were three large grey metal cashboxes, each one wrapped in transparent plastic sheeting. Taped to the top one was a terse message: DO NOT REMOVE.

I shut the lid and we went back into the house. Steve looked a shade more cheerful. "One good thing, Mum still has some of his best work."

I helped him get dressed and left soon afterwards, as he said he felt better, and looked it; and I took with me George Millace's box of disasters, which Steve had said to throw in the dustbin.

"You don't mind if I take it?" I said.

"Of course not. I know you like messing about with films, same as he did. He liked that old rubbish. Don't know why."

WITH THE RUBBISH BOX stowed in the boot alongside my two camera bags, I drove the hour from Ascot to Lambourn and found a large dark car standing outside my front door.

My cottage was in the centre of a terrace of seven built in the Edwardian era: two rooms upstairs, two down, with a modern kitchen stuck on at the back. A white-painted brick front facing out onto the road, with no room for a garden. A black door, needing paint. Nothing fancy, but home.

I drove slowly past the visiting car and turned into the muddy drive at the end of the row, continuing around to the back and parking under the carport next to the kitchen. As I went in, I caught a glimpse of a man getting hastily out of the car, and I thought only that he had no business pursuing me on a Sunday.

I went through the house and opened the front door. Jeremy Folk stood there, tall, thin, as earnestly diffident as before.

"Don't solicitors sleep on Sundays?" I said.

"Well, I say, I'm awfully sorry."

"Yeah. Come on in, then." He stepped through the doorway with a hint of expectancy and took the immediate disappointment with a blink. What had been the front parlour I had divided into an entrance hall and darkroom. White walls, white floor tiles; uninformative.

"This way," I said.

I led him down the hall, past the darkroom and bathroom towards the kitchen. To the left of the kitchen lay the narrow stairs. "Which do you want," I said. "Coffee or talk?"

"Er . . . talk."

"Up here, then." I went upstairs, and he followed. I used one of the two original bedrooms as a sitting room, because it was the largest room in the house and had the best view of the Downs; the room next to it was where I slept.

The sitting room had white walls, brown carpet, blue curtains, track lighting, bookshelves, sofa, low table, and floor cushions. My guest looked around with small flickering glances, making assessments.

"Sit down," I said, gesturing towards the sofa. I sat on a beanbag floor cushion and said, "Why didn't you mention the money when I saw you at Sandown?"

He seemed almost to wriggle. "I just . . . ah . . . thought I'd try you first on blood-stronger-than-water, don't you know?"

"And if that failed, you'd try greed?"

"Sort of."

"So that you would know what you were dealing with?"

He blinked.

"Look." I sighed. "Why don't you just . . . drop the act?"

He gave me a small smile. "It gets to be a habit," he said.

He cast a fresh look around the room, and I said, "All right, say what you're thinking."

He did so, without squirming and without apology. "You like to be alone. You're emotionally cold. You don't need props. And unless you took that photograph, you've no vanity." He nodded towards the only thing hanging on the wall, a view of pale yellow sunshine falling through some leafless silver birches onto snow.

"I took it. Now what did you come for?"

"To persuade you to do what you don't want to."

"To try to find the half-sister I didn't know I had? Why?"

"Mrs. Nore is insisting on leaving a fortune to someone who can't be found. It is unsatisfactory."

"Why is she insisting?"

"I don't know."

"Three detectives couldn't find Amanda."

"They didn't know where to look."

"Nor do I."

He considered me. "Do you know who your father is?" he said.

I sat with my head turned to the window, looking out at the bare calm line of the Downs. I said, "I don't want to get tangled up in a family I don't feel I belong to. That old woman can't claw me back just because she feels like it, after all these years."

Jeremy Folk didn't answer directly. He stood up and said, "I brought the reports we received from the detectives. I can see that you don't want to be involved. But I'm afraid I'm going to plague you until you are." He pulled a long bulging envelope out of the inside pocket of his country tweed jacket and put it carefully down on the table. "They're not very long reports." He moved vaguely towards the door, ready to leave. "By the way," he said, "Mrs. Nore really is dying. She has cancer of the spine. Nothing to be done. She'll live maybe six weeks, or six months. So . . . er . . . no time to waste, don't you know?"

I spent the bulk of the day in the darkroom, developing and

printing my black-and-white shots of Mrs. Millace and her troubles. Jeremy Folk's envelope stayed upstairs where he'd put it, unopened, contents unread. At six o'clock I went to see the trainer, Harold Osborne, who lived up the road.

Sunday evenings from six to seven, Harold and I talked over what had happened in the past week and discussed plans for the week ahead. For all his unpredictable moods Harold was a man of method, and he hated anything to interrupt these sessions.

On that particular Sunday the sacrosanct hour had been interrupted before it could begin, because Harold had a visitor. I walked through his house from the stable entrance and went into the comfortable, cluttered sitting room/office, and there, in one of the armchairs, was Victor Briggs.

"Philip!" Harold said, smiling. "Pour yourself a drink. We're just going to run through the tape of yesterday's race."

Victor Briggs gave me several nods of approval and a handshake. He still wore a close-guarded expression, as if his thoughts would show, but there was overall a distinct air of satisfaction.

I opened a can of Coca-Cola and poured some into a glass.

"Don't you drink?" Victor Briggs asked.

"Champagne," Harold said. "That's what he drinks, don't you, Philip?" He was in great good humour, his voice resonant as brass.

Harold's reddish-brown hair sprang in wiry curls all over his head, as untamable as his nature. He was fifty-two and looked ten years younger, a burly six feet of muscle commanded by a strong but ambiguous face, his features more rounded than hawkish. He switched on the video machine and sat back to watch Daylight's débâcle, as pleased as if he'd won the Grand National.

The tape showed me on Daylight approaching the third fence, everything looking all right, then the screw in the air and the stumbling landing, and the figure in red and blue silks going over the horse's neck and down under the feet.

Harold switched off the machine. "Artistic," he said, beaming. "I've run through it twenty times. It's impossible to tell."

"No one suspected," Victor Briggs said. There was a laugh somewhere inside him. He picked up a large envelope, which had lain beside his gin and tonic, and held it out to me. "Here's my thank you, Philip."

I said matter-of-factly, "It's kind of you, Mr. Briggs. But nothing's changed. I don't like to be paid for losing."

Victor Briggs put the envelope down again without comment, but Harold was angry. "Don't be such a prig," he said loudly, towering above me. "You're not so squeamish when it comes to committing the crime, are you? It's just the thirty pieces of silver you turn your pious nose up at. You make me sick."

"And," I said slowly, "I don't want to do it any more."

"You'll do what you're told," Harold said.

Victor Briggs rose purposefully to his feet, and the two of them, suddenly silent, stood looking down at me. I stood up in my turn. My mouth had gone dry, but I made my voice sound as calm, as unprovoking as possible.

"Please don't ask me for a repeat of yesterday. It's the losing. You know I hate it. I know I used to do it, but yesterday was the last."

Harold said coldly, "You'd better go now, Philip. I'll talk to you in the morning," and I nodded and left.

What would they do? I wondered. I walked in the windy dark down the road from Harold's house to mine as I had on hundreds of Sundays, and wondered if it would be for the last time. He was under no obligation to give me rides. I was self-employed, paid per race by the owner, not per week by the trainer.

I suppose it was too much to hope that they would let me get away with it. It was ironic. All those races I'd thrown away in the past, not liking it, but doing it. . . . Why was it so different for me now? Why was the revulsion so strong now that I *couldn't* do a Daylight again, even if to refuse meant virtually the end of being a jockey? When had I changed? I didn't know. I just had a sense of having already travelled too far to turn back.

At home, I went upstairs and read the three reports on Amanda because it was better than thinking about Briggs and Harold.

Owing to my grandmother's vagueness about when she had received her daughter's letter, all three had scoured Somerset House for records of Amanda Nore, aged between ten and twenty-five, possibly born in Sussex. In spite of the unusual name, they had all failed to find any trace of her birth having been registered.

I sucked my teeth, thinking that I could do better than that about her age. She couldn't have been born before I went to live with Duncan and Charlie, because I'd seen my mother fairly often before that, and I would have known if she'd had a child. That meant that I was at least twelve when Amanda was born; and consequently she couldn't at present be older than eighteen. Nor could she possibly be as young as ten. My mother, I was sure, had died some time between my eighteenth birthday and Christmas. She might have been desperate enough before she died to write to her own mother and send her the photograph. Amanda in the photograph had been about three. So if she were still alive, she would be at least fifteen. Born during the three years when I'd lived with Duncan and Charlie.

I went back to the reports. All the detectives had been given my mother's last known address: Pine Woods Lodge, Mindle Bridge, Sussex, the return address on her letter to my grandmother. All had trekked there "to make inquiries".

Pine Woods Lodge, they reported, was an old Georgian mansion now gone to ruin and due to be demolished. It was owned by a family that had largely died out; distant heirs, who had no wish to keep the place up, had rented the house at first to various organizations (list attached, supplied by estate agents) but more recently it had been inhabited by squatters and vagrants.

I read through the list of tenants, none of whom had stayed long. A nursing home. A sisterhood of nuns. An artists' commune. A television film company. A musicians' cooperative. Colleagues of Supreme Grace. The Confidential Mail Order Corporation.

There were no dates attached to the tenancies, but presumably the estate agents could still furnish some details. If I was right about when my mother had written her desperate letter, I should at least be able to find out which bunch she had been staying with. If I wanted to, of course.

Sighing, I read on. Copies of the photograph of Amanda Nore had been extensively displayed in public places in the vicinity of Mindle Bridge, but no one had come forward to identify either the child, the stableyard, or the pony.

Advertisements had been inserted in various periodicals and newspapers stating that if Amanda Nore wished to hear something to her advantage, she should write to Jeremy's law firm.

A canvass of the schools around Mindle Bridge had produced no one called Amanda Nore on the registers, past or present. She was on no official list of any sort. No doctor or dentist had heard of her. She had not been confirmed, married, buried, or cremated within the county of Sussex. All the reports came to the same conclusion: that she had been, or was being, brought up elsewhere (possibly under a different name).

I returned the reports to the envelope. The detectives had tried, one had to admit. They had also indicated their willingness to continue to search for Amanda.

I still couldn't understand my grandmother's interest in her long ignored grandchildren. She'd had a son of her own, a boy my mother had called "my hateful little brother". He would have been about ten when I was born, which made him now about forty.

Uncle. Half-sister. Grandmother. I didn't want them. I didn't want to know them or be drawn into their lives. I was in no way whatever going to look for Amanda.

I stood up with decision and went down to the kitchen to do something about cheese and eggs. Then, to stave off the thought of Harold a bit longer, I fetched George Millace's box of trash in from the car and opened it on the kitchen table. It still didn't seem to make much sense that George should have kept these particular photographic odds and ends.

I picked up the folder containing the dark print of a shadowy man sitting at a table and thought it was strange that Millace had put that over-exposed mess into a mount.

I slid the print onto my hand, and it was then that I found George Millace's pot of gold.

Chapter 3

It was not, at first sight, very exciting. Taped onto the back of the print was an envelope made of the special sort of sulphur-free paper used by professionals for the long-term storage of developed film. Inside the envelope, a negative. It was the negative from which the print had been made, but whereas the print was mostly black, the negative itself was clear and sharp with many details and highlights.

I was curious. I went into the darkroom and made four four-by-five-inch prints, each at a different exposure, from one to eight seconds. Even the print made at the longest exposure did not look exactly like George's dark print. So I started again with the most suitable exposure, six seconds, and left the photograph in the developer too long, until the sharp outlines went dark, showing a grey man sitting at a table against a black background—a print almost exactly like George's.

Leaving a print too long in the developing fluid has to be one of the commonest mistakes on earth. If George had been distracted and left a print too long in the developer, he'd simply have cursed and thrown the ruin away. Why, then, had he kept it? And mounted it? And stuck the clear, sharp negative onto the back?

It wasn't until I switched on a bright light and looked more closely at the best of the four original prints I'd made that I understood why; and I stood utterly still, taking in the implications in disbelief.

I finally moved. I switched off the white light, and when my eyes had accustomed themselves again to the red safelight, I made another print, four times as large, to get as clear a result as possible.

What I got was a picture of two men talking together who had sworn on oath in a court of law that they had never met.

There wasn't the slightest possibility of a mistake. They were sitting at a table outside a café somewhere in France. The café had a name: Le Lapin d'Argent. There were advertisements for lottery tickets in its half-curtained window and a waiter was standing in the doorway. A woman was sitting inside at a cash desk in front of a mirror, looking out to the street. The detail was sharp throughout. George Millace at his expert best.

Both men were facing the camera but had their heads turned towards each other, deep in conversation. A wineglass stood in front of each of them, half full, with a bottle to one side. There

34

were coffee cups also, and an ashtray with a half-smoked cigar on the edge. All the signs of a lengthy meeting.

These two men had been involved in an affair that had shaken the racing world like a thunderclap eighteen months earlier. Elgin Yaxley, the one on the left in the photograph, had owned five expensive steeplechasers that had been trained in Lambourn. At the end of the season all five had been sent to a local farmer for a few weeks' break out at grass; and then, while in the fields, they had all been shot dead with a rifle.

Terence O'Tree, the man on the right in the photograph, had shot them. Some smart police work had tracked down O'Tree and brought him to court.

The five horses had been heavily insured. The insurance company had tried to prove that Elgin Yaxley himself had hired O'Tree to do the killing, but both men had consistently denied it, and no link between them had been found.

After threatening to sue the insurance company for defamation of character, O'Tree, saying he'd shot the horses just because he'd felt like it, had been sent to gaol for nine months with a recommendation that he should see a psychiatrist.

Elgin Yaxley had wrung the whole insured amount out of the insurance company and had then faded from the racing scene.

The insurance company, I thought, would surely have paid George Millace a great deal for his photograph, if they had known it existed.

So why hadn't George asked for a reward? And why had he so carefully hidden the negative? And why had his house been burgled three times?

For all that I'd never liked George Millace, I disliked the obvious answer to those questions even more.

IN THE MORNING I walked up to the stables and rode out at early exercise as usual. Harold behaved in his normal blustery fashion, raising his voice over the scouring wind. At one point he bellowed, "Breakfast. Be there."

I nodded, and finished my ride.

Breakfast, in Harold's wife's view, consisted of a huge fry-up accompanied by mountains of toast served on the big kitchen table with generosity and warmth. I always fell for it.

"Another sausage, Philip?" Harold's wife said, lavishly shovelling straight from the pan and smiling at me. She thought I was too thin and that I needed a wife. She told me so, often.

"You're destroying him, woman," Harold said, then turned to me. "Last night we didn't discuss the week's plans. There's Pamphlet at Kempton on Wednesday, in the two-mile hurdle; and Tishoo and Sharpener on Thursday. . . ."

He talked about the races for some time, munching vigorously all the while. "Understood?" he said finally.

"Yes." It appeared that I had not been given the sack after all, and for that I was relieved, but it was clear all the same that the precipice wasn't far away.

Harold glanced at his wife, who was stacking things in the dishwasher, and said quietly to me, "Victor doesn't like your attitude. Owners won't stand for jockeys passing moral judgments on them."

"Owners shouldn't defraud the public, then."

"Have you finished eating?" he demanded.

I sighed regretfully. "Yes."

"Then come into my office."

He led the way into the russet-coloured room. "Shut the door." I shut it. "You'll have to choose, Philip," he said as he stood by the fireplace with one foot on the hearth, a big man in riding clothes, smelling of horses and fresh air and fried eggs. "Victor will eventually want another race lost. He says if you won't do it, we'll have to get someone else."

I shook my head. "Why does he want to start this caper again? He's won a lot of prize money playing it straight these last three years."

Harold shrugged. "I don't know. What does it matter? We've all done it before. Why not again? You just work it out, boy. Whose are the best horses in the yard? Victor's. Who owns more horses in this yard than anyone else? Victor. And which owner can I least afford to lose?"

I stared at him. I hadn't realized until then that he was in the same position as I. Do what Victor wants, or else.

"I don't want to lose you, Philip," he said. "You're prickly, but we've got on all right all these years. You won't go on for ever, though. You've been racing . . . what . . . ten years? You've got at the most, five more, then. Pretty soon you won't bounce back from those falls the way you do now. So look at it straight, Philip. Who do I need most in the long term, you or Victor?"

In a sort of melancholy we walked into the yard. "Let me know," he said. "I want you to stay."

I was surprised, but also pleased. "Thanks," I said.

He gave me a clumsy buffet on the shoulder, the nearest he'd ever come to the slightest show of affection. More than all the threatening, it made me want to do what he asked—a reaction, I acknowledged flickeringly, as old as the hills. It was often kindness that finally broke the prisoner's spirit, not torture. One's defences were always defiantly angled outward to withstand aggression; it was kindness that crept around behind and stabbed you in the back. Defences against kindness were much harder to build.

I sought instinctively to change the subject and came up with the nearest thought to hand, which was George Millace and his photograph. "Um," I said. "Do you remember those five horses of Elgin Yaxley's that were shot?"

He looked bewildered. "What's that got to do with Victor?"

"Nothing at all. I was just thinking about them yesterday."

Irritation immediately cancelled out the passing moment of emotion, which was probably a relief to us both. "Philip," he said sharply. "I'm serious. Your career's at stake. You can bloody well go to hell. It's up to you." He started to turn away, then stopped. "If you're so interested in Elgin Yaxley's horses, why don't you ask Kenny?" He pointed to one of his stable lads, who was filling two buckets by the water tap. "He looked after them when he was working for Bart Underfield, Yaxley's trainer."

He strode away, anger thumping down with every foot. I walked over to Kenny, not sure what questions I wanted to ask.

Kenny was one of those people whose defences were the other way around: impervious to kindness, open to fright. He watched me come with an insolent expression. Skin reddened by the wind; eyes slightly watering; spots.

"Mr. Osborne said you used to work for Bart Underfield," I said. "And looked after some of Elgin Yaxley's horses."

"So what?"

"So were you sorry when they were shot?"

He shrugged. "Suppose so."

"What did Mr. Underfield say about it? Wasn't he angry?"

"Not as I noticed."

"He must have been," I said. "He was five horses short. No trainer with his size stable can afford that."

Kenny shrugged again. The two buckets were nearly full. He turned off the tap. "He didn't seem to care much about losing them. Something cheesed him off a bit later, though."

"What?"

Kenny picked up the buckets. "Don't know. He was right grumpy. Some of the owners got fed up and left."

"So did you," I said.

"Yeah." He started walking across the yard with water sloshing at each step. I went with him. "What's the point of staying when a place is going down the drain?" he said.

"Were Yaxley's horses in good shape?"

"Sure. They had the vet in court, you know, to say the horses were fine the day before they died. I read about it in *The Sporting Life*." He reached the row of boxes and put the buckets down. "Tell you something." He looked almost surprised at his own sudden helpfulness. "That Mr. Yaxley, you'd've thought he'd been pleased getting all that cash, even if he had lost his horses, but he came into Underfield's yard one day in a right proper rage. Come to think of it, it was after that that Underfield went sour. And Yaxley, of course, quit racing and we never saw no more of him. Not while I was there, we didn't."

I walked thoughtfully home, and when I got there the telephone was ringing. "Jeremy Folk," a familiar voice said.

"Oh, not again," I protested.

"Did you read those detectives' reports?"

"Yes, I did. And I'm not going looking for her. To get you off my back, I'll help you a bit. But you must do the looking."

"Well . . ." He sighed. "What sort of help?"

I told him my conclusions about Amanda's age, and also suggested he should get the dates of the various tenancies of Pine Woods Lodge from the estate agents.

"My mother was probably there thirteen years ago," I said. "And now it's all yours."

"But I *say* . . ." he wailed. "You simply can't stop there."

"I simply can," I said. "Now just leave me alone."

I drove into Swindon to take the colour film I'd shot at Mrs. Millace's to the processors, and on the way thought about Bart Underfield. I knew him in the way one got to know everyone in racing if one lived long enough in Lambourn. We met occasionally in the village shops and in other people's houses, as well as at the races, but I had never ridden for him.

He was a small, busy man full of importance, given to telling people confidentially what other more successful trainers had done wrong. Strangers thought him very knowledgeable. People in Lambourn thought him an ass.

No one had suggested, however, that he was such an ass as to deliver his five best horses to the slaughter. Everyone had felt sorry for him, particularly as Elgin Yaxley had not spent the insurance money on buying new animals, but had merely departed, leaving Bart a great deal worse off.

Those horses could have been sold for high prices. It was the fact that there seemed to be little profit in killing them that had finally baffled the suspicious insurers into paying up. That and no trace of a link between Elgin Yaxley and Terence O'Tree.

In Swindon, I left my film with the processors, picked up the developed negatives a couple of hours later, and went home. In the afternoon I printed the coloured versions and sent them off with the black and whites to the police; and in the evening I tried— and failed—to stop thinking about Amanda and Victor Briggs and George Millace.

By far the worst thoughts concerned Victor Briggs and Harold's ultimatum: cooperate or else. The jockey life suited me fine. I'd put off for years the thought that one day I would have to do something else. The "one day" had always been in the future, not staring me brutally in the face.

The only thing I knew anything about besides horses was photography, but there were thousands of photographers all over the place and very few full-time successful racing photographers. Fewer than ten, probably. If I tried to join their ranks, the others wouldn't hinder me, but they wouldn't help me either.

I thought violent thoughts about Victor Briggs.

Inciting jockeys to throw races was a warning-off offence, but even if I could get Briggs disqualified, the person who would suffer most would be Harold. And I'd lose my job anyway, since Harold would hardly keep me on after that, even if we didn't both lose our licences because of the races I'd thrown in the past. I couldn't prove Victor Briggs's villainy without having to admit Harold's and my own. So it was cheat or retire. A stark choice.

NOTHING MUCH happened on Tuesday, but when I went to Kempton on Wednesday to ride Pamphlet, the changing room was electric with two pieces of gossip. Ivor den Relgan had been made a member of the Jockey Club, and Mrs. Millace's house had burned down.

"Ivor den Relgan?" The name was repeated in varying tones of astonishment. "A member of the Jockey Club? Incredible!"

The Jockey Club, that exclusive and gentlemanly body, had that morning voted into its fastidious ranks a man it had been holding at arm's length for years, a rich, self-important man from no one knew where. He was supposed to be from some unspecified ex-Dutch colony. He spoke with a patronizing accent that sounded like a mixture of South African, Australian, and American. He, the voice seemed to say, was a great deal more sophisticated than the stuffy British upper crust. They, he implied, would prosper if they took his advice, and he offered it freely in letters to *The Sporting Life*.

Until that morning the Jockey Club had indeed taken his advice on several occasions while steadfastly refusing to acknowledge it. I wondered fleetingly what had brought them to such a turn-about, what had caused them suddenly to embrace the anathema.

Steve Millace walked up to me, white-faced. His arm was in a black sling and his eyes were sunken, desperate.

"Have you heard?" he said. I nodded. "It happened late Monday night. By the time anyone noticed, the whole place had gone."

"Your mother wasn't there?"

"They'd kept her in the hospital. She's still there. It's too much for her." He was trembling. "Tell me what to do, Philip. You saw Mum. All bashed about . . . without Dad . . . and now the house . . . *Please*, help me."

"When I've finished riding," I said resignedly, "we'll work something out."

He sat down on the bench as if his legs wouldn't hold him, and stared into space while I changed into my colours.

Harold came in. Since Monday he'd made no reference to the life-altering decision he'd handed me. Perhaps he took my silence for tacit acceptance of a return to things past. At any rate, it was in a normal manner that he said, "Did you hear who's been elected to the Jockey Club? They'll take Genghis Khan next."

He walked out to the parade ring, and in due course I joined him. Pamphlet was walking nonchalantly around while his pop-star owner bit his nails. Harold had gleaned some more news. "I hear that it was the Great White Chief who insisted on den Relgan joining the club."

"Lord White?" I was surprised.

"Old Driven Snow himself."

"Philip," said the pop star, who had come to the races that day with dark blue hair. "Bring this baby back for Daddy." He must have learned that out of old movies, I thought. Surely not even pop musicians talked like that any more. I got up on Pamphlet and rode out to see what I could do.

Maybe Pamphlet had winning on his mind that day as much as I did. He soared around the whole course with bursting *joie de vivre*, even passing the favourite, and we came back to bear hugs from the blue hair and an offer to me of a spare ride in the fifth race from a worried-looking small-time trainer. Stable jockey hurt. . . . Would I mind? Mind? I'd be delighted.

Steve was still brooding by my locker.

"Was the shed burned?" I asked. "Your dad's photos?"

"Oh well, yes it was. . . . But Dad's stuff wasn't in there."

I stripped off the pop star's orange and pink colours and went in search of the calmer green and brown of the spare ride.

"Where was it, then?" I asked, returning.

"I told Mum what you said about people maybe not liking Dad's pictures of them, and she reckoned that you thought all the burglaries were really aimed at the photos, so on Monday she got me to move them next door, to her neighbour's."

I buttoned the green and brown shirt, thinking it over.

"Do you want me to visit her in the hospital?" I asked. He fell on it with embarrassing fervour. He had come to the races, he said, with the pubkeeper from the village where he lived, and if I would visit his mother, he could go home with the pubkeeper, because otherwise he had no transport, because of his collarbone. I hadn't exactly meant I would see Mrs. Millace alone, but on reflection I didn't mind.

Having shifted his burden, Steve cheered up a bit.

"Did your father often go to France?" I said absently.

"France? Of course. Longchamps, St. Cloud. All the races."

"What did he spend his money on?"

"Lenses mostly. Telephotos as long as your arm. Any new equipment. What do you mean, what did he spend his money on?"

"I just wondered what he liked doing away from the races."

"He just took pictures. All the time, everywhere. He wasn't interested in anything else."

In time, I went out to ride the green and brown horse and it was one of those days which happened so seldom, when absolutely everything went right. In unqualified euphoria I dismounted once again in the winners' enclosure, and thought that I couldn't possibly give up the life; I couldn't *possibly*.

STEVE'S MOTHER was in a ward, lying on her back with two flat pillows under her head and a thin blue blanket covering her. Her eyes were shut. Her face was dreadful.

The cut eyelid, stitched, was swollen and black. The lips, also swollen, looked purple. The nose was under some shaping plaster of paris, held in place by white sticky tape. All the rest showed deep signs of bruising. I'd seen people in that state before, damaged by horses' galloping hoofs, but this injury was done out of malice to an inoffensive lady in her own home. I felt not only sympathy but anger.

She opened one eye a fraction. "Steve asked me to come," I said. "He can't drive for a day or two."

I put a chair by the bed and sat beside her. Her hand, which was lying on the blanket, slowly stretched out to me. I took it, and she held on fiercely, seeking reassurance, it seemed. After a while the spirit of need ebbed, and she let go.

"Did Steve tell you," she said, "about the house?"

"Yes, he did. I'm so sorry."

A sort of shudder shook her, and her breathing grew more troubled. "The police came here today," she said.

I put my hand over hers and said urgently, "Don't get upset. You'll make everything hurt worse. Just take three slow deep breaths. Four or five, if you need them."

She lay silent for a while until the heavy breathing slackened. Eventually she said, "You're much older than Steve."

"Eight years," I agreed, letting go of her hand.

"No. Much . . . much older." There was a pause. "The police said it was arson. Paraffin. Five-gallon drum. They found it in the hall." Another pause. "The police asked if George had any enemies. I said of course not. And they asked if he had anything someone would want enough . . . oh . . ."

"Mrs. Millace," I said matter-of-factly, "did they ask if George had any photographs worth burglary and burning?"

"George wouldn't . . ." she said intensely.

George had, I thought. "If you like," I said slowly, "I could look through the transparencies and negatives you moved to your neighbour's; and I could tell you if I think there are any that could possibly come into the category we're talking about. Then if they're OK, you can tell the police they exist. If you want to."

"George isn't a blackmailer," she said. Coming from the swollen mouth, the words sounded extraordinary, distorted but passionately meant. She hadn't much left except that instinctive faith. It was beyond me entirely to tell her it was misplaced.

I COLLECTED the three metal boxes from the neighbour. The Millaces' house itself was a shell, roofless and windowless.

I drove home with George's lifework, and spent the evening projecting his slides onto the white wall of my sitting room.

His talent had been stupendous. Seeing his pictures one after the other, not scattered in books and magazines across a canvas of years, I was struck by the speed of his vision. Over and over again he had caught life at the moment when a painter would have composed it: nothing left out, nothing disruptive let in. The best of his racing pictures were there, but there were also dozens of portraits of people. Again and again he had caught the fleeting expression that exposed the soul.

What George had photographed was a satirical baring of the essence under the external, and I was deeply aware that I was never going to see the world in quite the same way again. But George had had no compassion. The pictures were brilliant, exciting, and revealing, but none of them were kind.

None of them could have been used as a basis for blackmail.

I telephoned Marie Millace in the morning, and told her so. The relief in her voice betrayed that she had had small doubts, and she heard it herself and immediately began a cover-up.

"I mean," she said, "of course I knew George wouldn't . . ."

"Of course," I said. "What shall I do with the films?"

"Oh, dear, I don't know. What do you think?"

"Well," I said, "you can't exactly advertise that although George's work still exists no one needs to feel threatened. I'm sorry, but I agree with the police. That George did have something that someone desperately wanted destroyed. Please don't worry. Whatever it was has probably gone with the house . . . and it's all over." And God forgive me, I thought. "I think the best thing for now would be to put those transparencies and negatives into storage somewhere. Then when you feel better, you could get an agent to put on an exhibition of George's work. The collection is marvellous; it really is."

There was a long pause. Then she said, "I know I'm asking such a lot. But could you put the films into storage? I'd ask Steve, but you seem to know what to do."

I said that I would, and when we had disconnected, I took the three boxes along to the local butcher. He already kept a box of my unexposed film in his walk-in freezer room. He cheerfully agreed to lock away the extra lodgers and suggested a reasonable rental.

Back home, I looked at the negative and the print of Elgin Yaxley talking to Terence O'Tree, and wondered what I should do with them. If George had extorted from Elgin Yaxley all the profits from the shot horses, then it had to be Yaxley who was now desperate to find the photograph before anyone else did.

If I gave the photograph to the police, Elgin Yaxley would be in line for prosecution. But I would be telling the world that George Millace had been a blackmailer.

Which would Marie Millace prefer? I thought. Never to know who had attacked her, or to know for sure that George had been a villain. There was no doubt about the answer.

I had no qualms about legal justice. I put the negative and the dark print back into the box of rubbish, and I put the clear big print I'd made into a folder in the filing cabinet in the darkroom. No one knew I had them. No one would come looking. Nothing at all would happen from now on.

I locked my doors and went to the races to ride Tishoo and Sharpener and to agonize over my other thorny problem, Victor Briggs.

Chapter 4

Ivor den Relgan was again the big news, and what was more, he was there, standing outside the changing room talking to two reporters. He wore an expensive camel-coloured coat, buttoned and belted, and he stood bareheaded with greying hair neatly brushed, a stocky, slightly pugnacious-looking man with an air of expecting people to notice him. I would have been happy never to have come into his focus, but as I was passing, one of the reporters fastened a hand on my arm.

"Philip," he said. "You can tell us. You're always on the business end of a camera. How do you photograph a wild horse?"

"Point and click," I said pleasantly.

"No, Philip," he said, exasperated. "You know Mr. den Relgan, don't you? Mr. den Relgan, this is Philip Nore. Jockey, of course." The reporter was unaccustomedly obsequious; den Relgan often had that effect. "Mr. den Relgan wants photographs of all his horses, but one of them rears up all the time when he sees a camera. How would you get him to stand still?"

"I know one photographer," I said, "who got a wild horse to stand still by playing a tape of a hunt in full cry. The horse just stood and listened. The pictures were great."

Den Relgan smiled superciliously, as if he didn't want to hear good ideas that weren't his own, and I nodded with about as much fervour and went on into the changing room, thinking that the Jockey Club must have been mad. The existing members were mostly forward-looking people who put goodwill and energy into running a huge industry fairly. That they were also self-electing meant that they were almost all aristocrats, but the ideal of service bred into them worked pretty well for the good of racing. Surprising that they should have beckoned to a semi-phoney like den Relgan.

Harold was inside the changing room with Lord White, who was telling him that there were special trophies for Sharpener's race; should we happen to win it, both Harold and I, as well as the owner, would be required to put in an appearance and receive our gifts.

"It wasn't advertised as a sponsored race," Harold said.

"No. But Mr. den Relgan has generously made this gesture." Lord White nodded, turned, and left us.

"How many trophies does it take," Harold said under his breath, "to buy your way into the Jockey Club?" And in a normal voice he added, "Win that pot if you can. It would really give Victor a buzz, taking den Relgan's cup. They can't stand each other."

"I didn't know they knew—"

"Everyone knows everyone," Harold said, shrugging. He lost interest and went out of the room, and I stood for a few moments watching Lord White talking to the other trainers.

Lord White, in his fifties, was a well-built, good-looking man

47

with bright blue eyes and thick light-grey hair, which was pro-
gressively turning the colour of his name. A widely-respected man,
he was the true leader of the Jockey Club, elected not by votes
but by the natural force born in him. His nickname, Driven Snow
(spoken only behind his back) had been coined, I thought, to poke
fun at the presence of so much noticeable virtue.

I began to change into Tishoo's colours and was guiltily relieved
to find Steve Millace was not present. No beseeching eyes to
inveigle me into another round of visiting the sick.

In the race itself there were no great problems but no repeat
either of the previous day's joys. Tishoo galloped willingly enough
into fourth place, which pleased his woman owner, and I went
back to my locker and put on Victor Briggs's colours for Sharpener.
Just another day's work. Each day unique in itself, but in essence
the same. On two thousand days, or thereabouts, I had put on
colours and ridden the races. Two thousand days of hope and
sweat. More than a job: part of my fabric.

Two other races were to be run before Sharpener's, so I went
outside for a while to see what was happening; and what was
happening was Lady White with a scowl on her thin, aristocratic
face.

Lady White didn't know me especially, but I, along with most
other jump jockeys, had shaken her hand at a few parties she and
Lord White had given to the racing world. Now she was hugging
her mink around her and glaring forth from under a wide-brimmed
brown hat. I followed her gaze and found it fixed on her paragon
of a husband, who was talking to a girl.

Lord White was not simply talking to the girl but revelling in it,
radiating flirtatious fun from his sparkling eyes. I thought in
amusement that the pure, white lord would be in for a ticking off
from his lady that evening.

I gradually became aware that a man near me was also intently
watching Lord White and the girl. The man was average-looking,
not quite middle-aged, with dark thinning hair and black-framed
glasses. He was wearing grey trousers, and a green suede jacket,
well cut. When he realized I was looking at him, he gave me a
quick annoyed glance and moved away.

I joined Victor Briggs in the parade ring before Sharpener's race. He was pleasant and made no reference to the issue hanging between us. Harold had boosted himself into a state of confidence and was standing with his long legs apart, his hat tipped back, and his binoculars swinging from one hand.

"A formality," he was saying. "Sharpener's never been better, eh, Philip? He'll run the legs off 'em today."

Sharpener himself reacted to Harold's optimism in a thoroughly positive way, and ran a faultless race with energy and courage, so that for the third time in two days my mount returned to applause. Metaphorically, Harold was by this time two feet off the ground, and even Victor allowed his mouth a small smile.

Ivor den Relgan manfully shaped up to the fact that one of his fancy trophies had been won by a man he disliked, and Lord White fluttered around the girl he'd been talking to, clearing a passage for her through the throng. At the prizegiving, the scene sorted itself out. Surrounding a table with a blue cloth bearing one large silver object and two smaller ones, were Lord White, the girl, Ivor den Relgan, Victor, Harold, and I.

Lord White announced to the small crowd that Miss Dana den Relgan would present the trophies given by her father, and it cannot have been only in my mind that the cynical speculation arose. Was it the dad that Lord White wanted in the Jockey Club, or the dad's daughter? Perish the thought. Yet it was clear that Lord White was attracted to the girl beyond sober good sense.

Dana den Relgan was enough, I suppose, to excite any man. Slender and graceful, she had a lot of blonde-flecked hair curling casually onto her shoulders, a curving mouth, and wide-set eyes. Her manner was more restrained than Lord White's, and she presented the trophies to Victor and Harold and me without much conversation.

She merely said, "Well done", when she gave me the small silver object (a saddle-shaped paperweight) and had the surface smile of someone who isn't really looking at you and is going to forget you within five minutes.

While Victor and Harold and I were comparing trophies, the average-looking man in spectacles reappeared, walked quietly up to Dana den Relgan, and spoke softly into her ear. She began to move off with him, smiling a little.

This apparently harmless proceeding had the most extraordinary effect upon den Relgan. He almost ran after them, gripped the inoffensive-looking man by the shoulder, and threw him away from her with such force that the man staggered and went down on one knee.

"I've told you to keep away from her," den Relgan said, looking as if kicking a man when he was down was something he had no reservations about.

"Who is that man?" I asked of no one in particular.

Victor Briggs answered, "Film director. Fellow called Lance Kinship."

"And why the fuss?"

Briggs knew. "Cocaine," he said. "Kinship supplies the stuff. Gets asked to the parties for what he brings along."

Lance Kinship was on his feet, brushing dirt off his trousers and looking murderous. "If I want to talk to Dana, I'll talk to her," he said.

"Not while I'm there, you won't."

Kinship seemed unintimidated. "Little girls don't always have their daddies with them," he said nastily, and den Relgan hit him— a sharp, efficient crunch on the nose.

There was a good deal of blood, and Lord White, hating the whole thing, held out a huge white handkerchief. Kinship grabbed it without thanks.

"First-aid room, don't you think?" Lord White said, looking around. "Er . . . Nore," he said, his gaze alighting. "Take this gentleman to the first-aid room, would you? Awfully good of you." But when I put a hand out to guide Kinship, he jerked away.

"Bleed, then," I said.

Unfriendly eyes behind the black frames glared out at me.

"Follow if you want," I said, and set off. Not only did Kinship follow, but den Relgan also.

"If you come near Dana again, I'll break your neck," I heard him say.

There was a scuffle behind me and I looked around in time to see Kinship aim a karate kick at den Relgan's crotch and land deftly on target. Den Relgan doubled over, making choking noises. Kinship turned back to me and gave me another unfriendly stare over the reddening handkerchief.

"In there," I said, jerking my head, and he gave me a final reptilian glance as the door to the first-aid room opened.

A pity George Millace had gone to his fathers, I thought. He would have been there with his lens focused, pointing the right way, and taking inexorable notes at three point five frames a second.

Later, when I left the changing room to set off for home, I was intercepted by the tall, loitering figure of Jeremy Folk. "What do you want?" I said.

"Well . . ."

"The answer's no."

"But you don't know what I'm going to ask."

"I can see that it's something I don't want to do."

There was a pause. "I went to see your grandmother. I told her you wouldn't look for your sister for money. I told her she would have to give you something else."

I was puzzled. "Give me what?"

Jeremy looked vaguely around the racecourse from his great height. "Your grandmother agreed," he said, "that she had a flaming row with Caroline—your mother—and chucked her out when she was pregnant."

"My mother," I said, "was seventeen."

He smiled. "Funny to think of one's mother being so *young*."

Poor defenceless little butterfly. "Yes," I said.

"Your grandmother says that if you will look for Amanda, she will tell you why she threw Caroline out. And also she will tell you who your father is."

I stared at him. "Is that what you said to her? 'Tell him who his father is, and he'll do what you want.' "

"You would want to know, wouldn't you?"

"No," I said.

"I don't believe you. It's human nature to want to know."

51

I swallowed. "Did she tell you who he is?"

He shook his head. "No. She's never told anyone. If you don't go and find out, you'll never know."

"You're a real bastard, Jeremy. I thought solicitors were supposed to sit behind desks and pontificate, not go about manipulating old ladies."

"This particular old lady is a . . . a challenge."

"Why doesn't she leave her money to her son?"

"She won't say. She told my grandfather simply that she wanted to cancel her old will and leave everything to Amanda."

"Have you met her son?"

"No," he said. "Have you?"

I shook my head. Jeremy took another vague look around the racecourse and said, "Why don't we get cracking on this together? We'd turn Amanda up in no time. Then you could go back into your shell and forget the whole thing if you want."

He would persevere, I thought, with or without my help. He wanted to prove to his grandfather and uncle that when he set his mind to sorting something out, it got sorted.

As for me, the mists around my birth were there for the parting. I could know what the shouting had been about behind the door while I waited in the hall in my new clothes. I might end by detesting the man who'd fathered me. But Jeremy was right. Given the chance, one had to know. "All right," I said.

He was pleased. "That's great. Can you go tonight? I'll just tell her you're coming." He plunged towards the telephone booth and disappeared inside. The call, however, gave him no joy.

"Blast," he said, rejoining me. "I spoke to a nurse. 'Mrs. Nore had a bad day and she's asleep. Phone tomorrow.' "

Feeling a distinct sense of relief, I set off towards the car park. Jeremy followed.

"About Mrs. Nore's son, James," he said. "I just thought you might visit him. Find out why he's been disinherited." He pulled a card out of his pocket. "I brought his address." He held it out. "And you've promised to help."

"A pact is a pact," I said, and took the card. "But you're still a bastard."

JAMES NORE lived in London, and since I was more than halfway there, I drove straight to the house. The door was opened by a man of about forty, who agreed that James Nore was his name. He was astounded to find an unknown nephew standing on his door-mat, and with only a slight hesitation he invited me in, leading the way into a Victorian sitting room.

"I thought Caroline had aborted you," he said baldly.

He was nothing like my memories of my mother. He was plump, soft-muscled, and small-mouthed, and had a mournful droop to his eyes. None of her giggly lightness or grace could ever have lived in his flaccid body. I felt ill at ease with him on sight.

He listened with his small lips pouted while I explained about looking for Amanda, and he showed more and more annoyance.

"The old bag's been saying for months that she's going to cut me off," he said furiously. "Ever since she came here." He glanced around the room, but nothing there seemed to me likely to alienate a mother. "Everything was all right as long as I went to visit her in Northamptonshire. Then she came *here*. Uninvited."

A brass clock on the mantelshelf sweetly chimed the half hour.

"I'd be a fool to help you find Caroline's second child, wouldn't I?" he said. "If no one can find her, the whole estate reverts to me, anyway, will or no will, although I'd have to wait years for it. Mother's just being spiteful." He shrugged. "Are you going now? There's no point in your staying."

He started to the door, but before he reached it it was opened by a man wearing a cooking apron and limply carrying a wooden spoon. He was much younger than James, and unmistakably camp.

"Oh hello, dear," he said to me. "Are you staying for supper?"

"He's just going," James said sharply.

Suddenly it all made sense, and I said to the man in the apron, "Did you meet Mrs. Nore when she came here?"

"Sure did, dear," he said ruefully, and then caught sight of James shaking his head vigorously at him and meaning shut up. I smiled halfheartedly and went to the front door.

"I wish you bad luck," James said. "That beastly Caroline. I never did like her. Always laughing at me and tripping me up. I was glad when she went."

I nodded, and opened the door.

"Wait," he said suddenly, and I could see he had an idea that pleased him. "Mother would never leave *you* anything, of course," he began.

"Why not?" I said.

He frowned. "There was a terrible drama when Caroline got pregnant. Frightful scene. Lots of screaming. I remember it, but no one would ever explain. All I do know is that everything changed because of you. Caroline went and Mother turned into a bitter old bag. She hated you."

He peered at me expectantly, but in truth I felt nothing. The old woman's hatred hadn't troubled me for years.

"I'll give you some of the money, though," he said. "If you can prove that Amanda is dead."

ON SATURDAY morning Jeremy Folk telephoned.

"Will you be at home tomorrow?" he said.

"Yes, but . . ."

"Good. I'll pop over." He put down his receiver without giving me a chance to say I didn't want him.

Also on Saturday I ran into Bart Underfield in the post office. In place of our usual unenthusiastic good mornings, I asked him a question.

"Where is Elgin Yaxley these days, Bart?"

"He lives in Hong Kong. What's it to do with you?"

"I just thought I saw him. A week ago yesterday."

"Well, you're wrong," Bart said. "That was the day of George Millace's funeral, and Elgin sent me a cable. From Hong Kong."

"A cable of regrets, was it?"

"Are you crazy? He'd have spat on the coffin."

"Oh well," I said, shrugging, "I must say a good many people will be relieved now George is gone."

"More like down on their knees giving thanks."

"Do you ever hear anything nowadays about that chap who shot Elgin's horses? What's his name? Terence O'Tree?"

"He's still in gaol. Hit a guard and lost his chance for parole."

"How do you know?"

54

"I . . . er . . . just heard." Bart had suddenly had too much of this conversation, and began backing away.

"And did you hear that George Millace's house burned down? And that it was arson?"

He stopped in midstride. "Arson?" he said, looking surprised. "Why would anyone want . . . Oh!" He abruptly understood why; and I thought that he couldn't possibly have achieved that revelationary expression by art. He hadn't known.

Elgin Yaxley was in Hong Kong and Terence O'Tree was in gaol, and neither they nor Underfield had burgled, or bashed, or burned.

The easy explanations were all wrong.

I had jumped, I thought penitently, to conclusions. It was only because I'd disliked George Millace that I'd been so ready to believe ill of him. He had taken that incriminating photograph, but there was really nothing to prove that he'd used it. Elgin Yaxley had gone to Hong Kong instead of ploughing his insurance money back into racehorses, but that didn't make him a villain.

Yet he was a villain. He had sworn he'd never met Terence O'Tree, and he had. And it had to have been before the trial in February, since O'Tree had been in gaol ever since. Not during the winter just before the trial either, because it had been sitting-outdoors weather. I now remembered that in the photo there had been a newspaper lying on an adjacent table, on which one might possibly see a date.

As soon as I arrived home, I projected my big new print onto the sitting-room wall. The newspaper lay too flat on the table. Neither the date nor a useful headline could be seen. In the background of the picture, beside Madame at her cash desk inside the café, was a calendar hanging on a hook. The letters and numbers on it could just be discerned: it was April of the previous year. Elgin Yaxley's horses had been sent out to grass late that same month, and they had been shot on the fourth of May.

I switched off the projector and drove to the races at Windsor, puzzling over the inconsistencies.

It was a moderate day's racing at Windsor, and because of the weak opposition, one of Harold's slowest old steeplechasers finally had his day: my geriatric pal loped in first. The delight of his faithful elderly lady owner made it all well worth the effort.

"I knew he'd do it one day," she said. "It's his last season, you know. I'll have to retire him." She patted his neck. "We're all getting on a bit, old boy, aren't we? Can't go on for ever. Everything ends. But today it's been great."

Her words lingered with me. "Everything ends. But today it's been great." Most of my mind still rebelled against the thought of retirement, particularly one dictated by Victor Briggs, but somewhere the frail seedling of acceptance was stretching its first leaf in the dark. Life changes, everything ends. I didn't want it, but it was happening.

Outside the changing room one wouldn't have guessed it. I had uncharacteristically won four races that week. I was offered five rides for the following week by trainers other than Harold. If anyone had asked me in that moment about retiring, I would have said, "Oh yes. In five years' time."

THE FOLLOWING MORNING Jeremy Folk arrived, as he'd said he would, angling his storklike figure through my front door. He followed me to the kitchen.

"Champagne?" I said.

"It's . . . er . . . only ten o'clock."

"Four winners," I said, "need celebrating."

He took his first sip as if the wickedness of it would overwhelm him. He had made an effort to be casual in his clothes: wool checked shirt, woolly tie, neat pale blue sweater. Whatever he thought of my unbuttoned collar, unbuttoned cuffs and unshaven jaw, he didn't say.

"Did you see . . . ah . . . James Nore?"

"Yes, I did." I gestured to him to sit down at the kitchen table and joined him, with the bottle in reach. "Mrs. Nore visited his house unexpectedly one day," I explained. "She hadn't been there before. She met James's friend, and she realized, I suppose for the first time, that her son was homosexual."

"Oh," Jeremy said, understanding much.

I nodded. "No descendants."

56

"So she thought of Amanda." He sighed, and drank some pale gold fizz. "Are you sure he's homosexual? Did he say so?"

"As good as. Anyway, you get to know, somehow. I lived with two of them for a while."

He looked slightly shocked. "Did you? I mean, are you? . . . I shouldn't ask. Sorry."

"No, I'm not," I said, and while he buried his nose and his embarrassment in his glass, I thought of Duncan and Charlie. Charlie had been older than Duncan, solid and industrious and kind; to me he had been father, uncle, guardian, all in one. Duncan had been chatty and very good company, and neither of them had tried to teach me their way.

One day, Duncan fell in love with someone else and walked out. Charlie put his arm around my shoulders and hugged me, and wept. My mother had arrived within a week, blowing in like a whirlwind. Huge eyes, hollow cheeks, fluffy silk scarves.

"But you see, Charlie darling," she'd said, "that I can't leave Philip with you now that Duncan's gone." She'd looked at me, bright and more brittle than I remembered, and less beautiful. "Go and pack, Philip darling. We're going down to the country."

Charlie had come to my room and I'd said that I didn't want to leave him. "We must do what your mother says," he told me.

He'd helped me pack, and from the old life I'd been flung straight into the new. That evening I learned how to muck out a horse box, and the next morning I started to ride.

Charlie pined miserably for Duncan and swallowed two hundred sleeping pills. He left all his possessions to me, including his cameras and darkroom equipment. He also left a letter. "Look after your mother," he wrote. "I think she's sick. Keep on taking photographs, you already have the eye. You'll be all right, boy. So long now. Charlie."

I drank some champagne and said to Jeremy, "Did you get the list of the Pine Woods Lodge tenancies from the agents?"

"Oh gosh, yes," he said, relieved to be back on firm ground. He patted several pockets. "Here we are." He spread out the sheet of paper. "If your mother was there thirteen years ago, the people she was with would have been the boy scouts, the television

57

company, or the musicians. But the television people didn't live there, they just worked there during the day. The musicians did live there. They ruined the electric wiring and were supposed to be high all the time on drugs. Does any of that sound . . . er . . . like your mother?"

"Boy scouts don't sound like her a bit. Drugs do, musicians don't. She never left me with anyone musical. I think I'd try the television company first."

Jeremy's face showed a jumble of emotions varying from incredulity to bewilderment. "What do you mean about your mother leaving you with people, and about your mother and drugs?"

I outlined the dumping procedure and what I owed to the Deborahs, Samanthas and Chloes. Jeremy looked shattered.

"I didn't understand about the drugs," I said, "until I grew up, but certainly she was taking them for a long time. She kept me with her for a week sometimes, and there would be an acrid distinctive smell. Marijuana. She died from heroin, I think."

"Why do you think that?"

I poured refills of champagne. "Something the people at the racing stable said. Margaret and Bill. I went into the sitting room one day when they were arguing. Bill was saying, 'His place is with his mother,' and Margaret interrupted. 'She's a heroin—' Then she saw me and stopped. It's ironic, but I was so pleased they should think my mother a heroine." I smiled lopsidedly. "It was years before I realized that Margaret had really been going to say, 'She's a heroin addict.' I asked her later and she told me. She and Bill guessed, as I did, that my mother had died, and of course, long before I did, they guessed why. They didn't tell me to save me pain. Kind people."

Jeremy shook his head. "I'm so sorry," he said.

"Don't be. I never grieved for my mother." I had grieved for Charlie, though. I used his legacy almost every day, not only the photographic equipment but also the knowledge he'd given me. Any photograph I took was thanks to Charlie.

"I'll try the television people," Jeremy said. "And you'll see your grandmother?"

I said without enthusiasm, "I suppose so."

"Where else can we look for Amanda? If your mother dumped you all over the place, she must have done the same with Amanda."

"Yes, I've thought of that." All those people, so long in the past. Shadows without faces. "Still, I might try to find one place I stayed. The people there might know something."

Jeremy pounced on it. "It's a chance. Well worth trying."

I drank some champagne and looked thoughtfully across the kitchen. George Millace's box of rubbish lay on the counter, and a hovering intention suddenly crystallized. "You're welcome to stay, but I want to spend the day on a different sort of puzzle," I said. "Nothing to do with Amanda. A sort of treasure hunt, but there may be no treasure." I got up and picked the piece of clear-looking film out of the box. "Look at this against the light."

He took the piece of film and held it up. "It's got smudges on it," he said. "Very faint. You can hardly see them."

"They're pictures. Three pictures on a roll of film. If I'm careful, and lucky, we might see them."

He was puzzled. "But what's the point? Why bother?"

"I found something of great interest in that box. I think maybe some more of those bits aren't the rubbish they seem."

He followed me and watched intensely while I rummaged in one of the cupboards in the darkroom. I finally found the bottle of negative intensifier I was looking for. I carried it to the sink, where there was a water filter fixed under the tap.

"What's that?" Jeremy asked, pointing to the filter.

"You have to use ultra-clean soft water for photographic processing. And no iron pipes. Otherwise you get a lot of little black dots on the prints."

Following the instructions on the bottle, I mixed water and intensifier and poured the solution into the developing tray.

"What exactly are you going to do?" said Jeremy.

"I'm going to print this film with the faint smudges onto some photo paper and see what it looks like. Then I'm going to put the negative into this intensifying liquid, and after that I'm going to make another print to see if there's a difference."

He watched, peering into the developing tray while I worked in dim red light. "Can't see anything happening," he said.

"It's a bit trial and error," I agreed. I tried printing the clear film four times at different light exposures, but all we got on the prints was a fairly uniform black, grey, or white.

"There's nothing there," Jeremy said. "It's useless."

"Wait until we try the intensifier."

With more hope than expectation, I slid the film into the intensifying liquid and sloshed it about. Then I washed it and printed it again at the same exposures as before. This time, on the light grey print there were patchy marks and on the nearly white print, swirly shapes.

"Well, that's that," Jeremy said. "Too bad."

"I think," I said reflectively, "that we might get further if I print that negative not onto paper, but onto another film."

"Print it onto a film? I didn't know that was possible."

"Oh yes. You can print onto anything that has a photographic emulsion, and you can coat practically anything with emulsion. Glass. Or canvas. Or wood. Or the back of your hand, I daresay."

I took a new roll of high-contrast film, pulling it off its spool into a long strip and cutting it into five pieces. Onto each piece I printed the almost clear negative, exposing each one to the white light of the enlarger for different lengths of time, from one to ten seconds. After exposure, each piece went into the tray of developer.

The results, after taking each piece of film out of the developer at what looked like the best moment, then transferring it to the tray of fixer, and finally washing it, were five new positives. Taking these, I repeated the whole process, ending with negatives. Seen in bright light, all of the new negatives were much denser than the one I'd started with. On two of them there was a decipherable image. The smudges had come alive.

"What are you smiling at?" Jeremy demanded.

"Take a look," I said. "Three pictures of a girl and a man."

He held the negative strip I gave him to the light. "How can you tell? They're clearer, but they're still smudges."

"You get used to reading negatives. To be honest, I'm dead

60

pleased with myself. Let's finish the champagne and then do the next bit: positive prints from the new negatives. Black-and-white pictures. All revealed."

"What's so funny?"

"The girl's nude, more or less."

He nearly spilled his drink. "Are you sure?"

"We'll see better soon. Are you hungry?"

"Good heavens. It's one o'clock."

We ate ham and tomatoes and brown toast, and finished the champagne. Then we returned to the darkroom.

Printing onto paper from such faint negatives was still a critical business. Again one had first to judge the exposure right and then stop the developing print at exactly the best instant and switch it to the tray of fixer. It took me several tries, but I finished with three pictures which were clear enough to reveal what George had photographed. I looked at them with a magnifying glass, and there was no chance of a mistake.

The pictures were dynamite.

Chapter 5

I took Jeremy and the new pictures upstairs and switched on the epidiascope, which hummed slightly as it warmed up.

"What's that?" Jeremy said, looking at the machine.

"A kind of projector. You put things on this baseboard and the image is projected large and bright onto a screen—or in my case, a wall."

I drew the curtains against the fading afternoon light and put in the new pictures. The first one showed the top half of a girl and the head and shoulders of a man. They were facing each other, embracing. Neither of them wore clothes.

"Good heavens," Jeremy said faintly.

"Mm," I said. I projected the second picture, which was of much the same pose, except that the camera had been at a different angle, showing less of the girl and nearly all of the man's face.

"It's just pornography," Jeremy said.

"No, it isn't."

In the third picture both their faces were visible, and there wasn't much doubt about the activity they were engaged in. I switched off the epidiascope and put on the lights.

"Why do you say it isn't pornography?" Jeremy asked.

"I've met them," I said. "I know who they are." He stared and I went on. "As a lawyer, tell me. What do you do if you find out after a man's death that he may have been a blackmailer?"

He frowned. "Are you going to tell me what you're on to?"

"Yes." I told him about George Millace. About the burglaries, the attack on Marie Millace, and the burning of their house. I told him about the photograph of Elgin Yaxley and Terence O'Tree at the French café and about the five shot horses; and I told him about the lovers.

"George very carefully kept those oddments in that box," I said. "What if they are all the basis for blackmail?"

"You want to find out?"

I slowly nodded. "It's not so much the blackmail angle, but the photographic puzzles. I'd like to see if I can solve them. I enjoy that sort of thing."

Jeremy stared at the floor. Then he said abruptly, "I think you should destroy the whole lot."

"That's instinct, not reason. Someone burgled and burned George Millace's house. When I found the first picture, I thought it must have been Elgin Yaxley who'd done it, but he was in Hong Kong. And now one would think the lovers did it, but it might not be them either."

Jeremy stood up and moved restlessly around the room. "Was there any doubt," he said, "about the way George Millace died?"

I felt as if he'd punched the air out of my lungs. "I don't think so. His son said he'd stopped at a friend's house for a drink. Then he drove on towards home, went to sleep, and hit a tree."

"How did anyone know he had stopped at the friend's house? And how does anyone know he went to sleep?"

"True lawyers' questions. I don't know the answers."

"Did they do an autopsy?" he said.

"I don't know. Do they usually?"

He shrugged. "Sometimes. They'd have tested his blood for the alcohol level. They might have checked for heart attack or stroke. If there were no suspicious circumstances, that would be all. But those burglaries must have made the police think a bit."

I said weakly, "The first burglary occurred during the funeral."

"Cremation?"

I nodded. "The police did hint very broadly to Marie Millace, and upset her considerably, about George possessing photographs people might not want found. But they don't *know* he had them."

"Like we do," he said. "Burn those pictures. Stick to looking for Amanda. You could end up like Millace. Splat on a tree."

JEREMY LEFT at six, and I walked over to Harold's for the briefing. He had five runners planned for me that week, and with the five spare rides I'd been offered I would be having a busy time.

"Don't come crashing down on one of those hyenas you've accepted," Harold said. "What you take them for when you've got all my horses to ride I don't know." He never admitted that some of the biggest races I'd won had been for other stables.

"Next Saturday at Ascot I'm running two of Victor's horses," he said. "Chainmail. And Daylight."

I glanced at him quickly, but he didn't meet my eyes.

He paused and then said casually, "Chainmail might be the best bet. We'll see better what the prospects are on Friday."

"Prospects for winning?" I said. "Or losing? You tell me, Harold. Tell me early Saturday morning, if you've any feeling for me at all. I'll get an acute stomach ache. Won't be able to go racing."

"But Victor . . ."

"I'll ride my guts out for Victor as long as we're trying to win. You tell him that. And don't forget, Chainmail's still pretty wayward, for all that he's fast. He pulls like a train and tries to duck out at the hurdles, and he's not above sinking his teeth into any horse that bumps him. He's a hard ride, but he's brave, and I'm not going to help you ruin him. And you *will* ruin him if you muck him about. You'll make him a real rogue."

"I agree with you," Harold said. "And I'll say it all to Victor. But in the end it's his horse." He sighed heavily. "If necessary, I'll give you time to get sick."

I HAD an average day on Monday—a second place and a third—and Tuesday I had no racing engagements at all. I decided to placate Jeremy Folk by seeing if I could find one of the houses where my mother had left me in my childhood. A nice vague expedition, an undemanding day.

I set off for London and cruised up and down a whole lot of little streets between Chiswick and Hammersmith. I knew I'd once stayed in this area. All of the streets looked familiar: rows of tidy bow-fronted houses for middle-income people. I had lived in several like that, but I couldn't even remember the name of a road.

Buses finally triggered the memory. The house I was looking for had been just around the corner from a bus stop. I had caught the bus often there, going to the river for walks. The knowledge drifted quietly back across twenty-plus years. We'd often gone down to the river to look at the houseboats and the sea gulls; and we'd looked across to the gardens at Kew.

I drove down to Kew Bridge and started from there, following buses. A slow business and unproductive, because none of the stops were near corners. I gave it up after an hour and simply cruised around.

It was an old pub that finally orientated me. The Willing Horse. I parked the car and walked back to the dark brown doors, and simply stood there, waiting. After a while I seemed to know which way to go. Turn left, walk three hundred yards, cross the road, first turn on the right.

I walked down a street of bow-fronted terraced houses, three storeys high, narrow and neat. I walked slowly, but nothing told me which house to try. I wondered what to do next.

Four houses from the end I went up the steps, and rang the doorbell. A woman with a cigarette opened the door.

"Excuse me," I said. "Does Samantha live here?"

"Who?"

"Samantha?"

"No." She looked me up and down with the utmost suspicion, and closed the door.

I tried six more houses. No luck. At the eighth, an old lady told me I was up to no good, she'd watched me go from house to house, and if I didn't stop it she would call the police. I walked away and she came right out into the street to watch me.

It wasn't much good, I thought. I wouldn't find Samantha. She might be out, she might have moved, she might never have lived in that street in the first place. Under the old woman's baleful gaze I tried another house where no one answered, and another where a girl of about twenty opened the door.

"Excuse me," I said. "Does anyone called Samantha live here?" I'd said it so often it now sounded ridiculous.

"Samantha what? Samantha who?"

"I'm afraid I don't know."

She pursed her lips, not quite liking it. "Wait a moment. I'll go and see." She shut the door and went away. I hovered, waiting, aware of the old woman beadily watching from the road.

The door opened. There were two people there, the girl and an older woman. The woman said, "What do you want?"

"Are you," I said slowly, "Samantha?"

She looked me up and down with the suspicion I was by now used to. A comfortably-sized lady with grey-brown wavy hair.

"Would the name Nore mean anything to you? Philip Nore or Caroline Nore?"

To the girl the names meant nothing, but in the woman there was a fast sharpening of attention. "What exactly do you want?" she demanded.

"I'm Philip Nore."

The guarded expression turned to incredulity. "You'd better come in," she said. "I'm Samantha Bergen."

I stepped through the front door, and didn't have, as I'd half expected, the feeling of coming home.

"Downstairs," she said. I followed her and the girl followed me. "Sorry not to have been more welcoming," Samantha said, "but you know what it is these days. You have to be careful."

We went through a doorway into a large country kitchen. A big table, with chairs. A red-tiled floor. French windows to the garden. A basket chair hanging on a chain from the ceiling. Beams. Copper. Without thinking, I walked across the floor and sat in the

hanging basket chair, tucking my feet up under me, out of sight.

Samantha Bergen stood there looking astounded. "You *are* little Philip. He always used to sit there like that, with his feet up. I'd forgotten. But seeing you do it . . . Good gracious."

"I'm sorry," I said, standing up again. "I just . . . did it."

"My dear man," she said. "It's all right. Extraordinary to see you, that's all." She turned to the girl. "This is my daughter, Clare. She wasn't born when you stayed here." To her daughter she said, "I looked after a friend's child now and then. Heavens, it must be twenty-two years since the last time."

The girl looked a good deal more friendly. They were both attractive, wearing jeans and blouses and unpainted Tuesday afternoon faces. The girl was slimmer than her mother and had darker hair, but they both had large grey eyes, straight noses, and unaggressive chins. Both were unmistakably intelligent.

Their work lay spread out on the table. Galley proofs, the makings of a book. When I glanced at them, Clare said, "Mother's cookery book."

Samantha said, "Clare is a publisher's assistant."

We sat around the table, and I told them about looking for Amanda, and the off chance that had brought me to their door. Samantha shook her head regretfully. "I didn't even know Caroline had a daughter."

"Tell me about my mother," I said. "What was she like?"

"Caroline? So pretty you wanted to hug her. Full of light and fun. She could get anyone to do anything. But . . . she took drugs." Samantha looked at me anxiously, and seemed relieved when I nodded. "She told me she didn't want you around when she and her friends were all high. She begged me to look after you. You were such a quiet little mouse. Quite good company actually."

"How often did she bring me?" I said slowly.

"Oh, half a dozen times. You were about eight at the end. I couldn't take you the last time she asked, because Clare was imminent."

I asked if my mother had ever told her anything about my father.

"No, nothing. She was supposed to have an abortion, and didn't."

We drank some tea Clare had made, and Samantha asked what I did.

"I'm a jockey."

They were incredulous. "You're too tall," Samantha said.

"Jockeys don't have to be small."

"Extraordinary thing to be," Clare said, "Pretty pointless, isn't it?"

"Clare!" Samantha protested.

"If you mean," I said equably, "that being a jockey contributes nothing useful to society, I'm not so sure. Recreation gives health. I provide recreation."

"And betting?" Clare demanded. "Is that healthy?"

"Sublimates risk taking. Stake your money, not your life."

"But you yourself take the risks."

"I don't bet."

"Clare will tie you in knots," her mother said.

Clare shook her head. "I would think your little Philip is as easy to tie in knots as a stream of water."

Samantha gave her a surprised look and asked where I lived.

"In Lambourn. A village in Berkshire. Out on the Downs."

Clare frowned and glanced at me with sharpened concentration. "Lambourn. Isn't that where there are a lot of racing stables?"

"That's right."

"Hm." She thought for a minute. "My boss is doing a book on village life. Mind if I just give him a call?"

Before I could answer she was on her feet and at the telephone. Samantha gave her a fond motherly look. "Clare will bully you into things," she said. "She bullied me into doing this cookery book. She's got more energy than a power station. She told me when she was about six that she was going to be a publisher, and she's well on her way. She's already second-in-command to the man she's talking to."

The prodigy herself finished talking on the telephone. "He's interested. He says we'll both go down and look the place over, and then if it's OK, he'll send the writer and a photographer."

"I've taken pictures of Lambourn. If you'd like to—"

"Sorry. We'd need professional work. But my boss says if you don't mind, we'll call at your digs, or whatever, if you'd be willing to help us with directions and general information."

"Yes, I'd be willing."

"That's great." She gave me a sudden smile. She knows she's bright, I thought. But she's not as good as Jeremy Folk at concealing that she knows it. "Can we come on Friday?" she said.

Chapter 6

Lance Kinship was wandering around at the head of a retinue of cameramen and sound recordists when I arrived at Newbury racecourse the next day. We heard in the changing room that with the blessing of the management he was taking background shots for a film. I slung my Nikon around my neck and took a few pictures of the men taking pictures.

Kinship was pompously telling his crew what to do, and they listened to him tensely. I took a couple of shots of their reaction— the eyes all looking towards him from averted heads. Clearly they were men obeying someone they didn't like. At one point Kinship turned his head the instant I pressed the button, and stared straight into my lens.

He strode across to me, looking annoyed. "What are you doing?" he said, though it was obvious.

"I was just interested," I said inoffensively.

He peered through his spectacles at my camera. "A Nikon." He raised his eyes to my face and frowned with half recognition.

"How's the nose?" I asked politely.

He grunted, finally placing me. "Don't get into the film," he said. "You're not a typical jockey. I don't want Nikon-toting jocks lousing up the footage."

With a disapproving nod he went back to his crew, and presently they moved off to the parade ring.

They were down at the start when I lined up on a scatty novice chaser for Harold. They were absent, thankfully, from the eighth fence, where the novice put his forefeet into the open ditch on the takeoff side and crossed the fence almost upside down. Somewhere during this wild somersault I fell out of the saddle, but by the mercy of heaven, when the half ton of horse crashed to the ground I was not underneath it.

He lay prostrate for a few moments, winded and panting. Some horses I loved, some I didn't. This was a clumsy, stubborn delinquent with a hard mouth, just starting what was likely to be a long career of bad jumping. I waited until he was on his feet, then remounted him and trotted back to the stands.

When I was changing, someone said there was a man outside asking for the jockey with the camera. I went to see.

"Oh there you are," said Lance Kinship, as if I'd kept him waiting. "Well, what do you say? You took some photographs today. If they're any good, I'll buy them from you. How's that?"

"Well . . ." I was nonplussed. "Yes, if you like."

"Good. The crew is over by the winning post. Take some photographs of them shooting the finish. Publicity shots. Right?"

I fetched my camera and found him still waiting but definitely in a hurry. I would have to be quick, he explained, because the crew would be moving out to the car park presently to film the racegoers going home.

I would have thought that if he wanted publicity pictures, he would have brought a photographer of his own, and I asked him.

"Sure," he said. "I had one lined up. Then he died. Didn't get around to it again." We were walking fast, and his breathing grew shorter. "Then today, saw you. Some news photographers said you could do it. If your pics are no good, I don't buy, right?"

I asked him which photographer had died.

"Fellow called Millace. Died in a car crash. Here we are. Now get on with it."

He turned away to give instructions to the crew; they again listened with slightly averted heads. He wouldn't buy pictures showing that response, I thought, so I waited until he'd left and shot the crew absorbed in their work.

The horses came out onto the course and cantered down to the start. One of the crew, a frizzy-haired boy with a clapper board, who happened to be close to me, said with sudden fierceness, "You'd think this was an epic, the way he messes about. We're making commercials. A second on screen, flash off."

70

I half smiled. "What's the product?"

"Some sort of brandy."

Kinship came towards me and said it was important that he should be prominent in my photographs. The frizzy-haired boy surreptitiously raised his eyebrows into comical peaks, and I assured Lance Kinship that I would do my absolute best.

I did by good luck get one or two reasonable pictures. Kinship gave me a card with his address and told me again that he would buy the pictures if he liked them. He didn't say for how much, and I didn't like to ask. I would never be a salesman. Taking photographs for a living, I thought ruefully, would find me starving within a week.

When I reached home, I drew the curtains in my kitchen and once again went through George Millace's rubbish box, wondering just how much profit he had made from his deadly photographs.

I lifted out the large black lightproof envelope and removed its contents: the page-sized piece of clear plastic, and also, what hadn't registered before, two sheets of paper of about the same size. I looked at them briefly, then quickly replaced them, because it suddenly occurred to me that George must have stored them in a lightproof holder for a reason. That plastic and that paper might bear latent images. If they did, I didn't know how to develop them.

I sat staring vaguely at the black envelope and thinking about developers. To bring out the image on any particular type of film or paper one had to use the right type of developer, which meant that unless I knew the make and type of the plastic and of the two sheets of paper I couldn't get any further.

I pushed the black envelope aside and took up the strips of blank negatives. They were 35-mm colour negatives, some completely blank and others blank except for uneven magenta blotches. I laid the strips out end to end and made the first interesting discovery.

All the plain blank negatives had come from one roll of film, and those with magenta blotches from another, thirty-six exposures from each. I knew what make of film they were, because each manufacturer placed the frame numbers differently, but I didn't suppose that that was important. What might be important, however, was the very nature of colour negatives.

While colour transparencies appear to the eye in their true life-like colours, colour negatives appear in the reciprocal colours; to get back to the true colours one has to make a print from the negative. The primary colours of light are blue, green, and red. The reciprocal colours in which they appear on a negative are yellow, magenta, and cyan—a greenish blue. In order to get good whites and highlights, all manufacturers give their negatives an overall pale orange cast, which has the effect of masking the yellow sections.

George Millace's negatives were a pale clear orange throughout. Just suppose, I thought, that hidden under the orange was an image in yellow. If I made prints from those negatives, the invisible yellow image could turn into a visible printed image in reciprocal blue.

Worth trying, I thought. I went into the darkroom and mixed the developing chemicals, and set up the colour-print processor. I found out almost at once, by making contact prints, that under the orange masking there was indeed blue, but not blue images. Just blue.

There are so many variables in colour printing that searching for an image on blank negatives is like walking blindfold through a forest, and although I tried every way I knew, I was only partially successful. I ended with thirty-six solid blue oblongs, enlarged and printed four to a sheet, and thirty-six more with greenish blotches here and there.

I knew that George Millace wouldn't have taken seventy-two pictures of a blue oblong for nothing. When it finally dawned on me what he *had* done, I was too tired to start all over again. I cleaned up and went to bed.

JEREMY FOLK telephoned early the next morning and asked if I'd been to see my grandmother.

"I'll go," I said. "Saturday, after the race at Ascot."

"What have you been doing?" he asked. "You could have gone any day this week. Don't forget she really is dying."

"I've been working," I said. "And printing."

"From that box?" he said suspiciously.

"Uh huh."

"What have you got?"

"Blue pictures. Pure deep blue. George Millace screwed a deep blue filter onto his camera and photographed a black-and-white picture through the blue filter onto colour-negative film."

"You're talking Chinese."

"I'm talking Millace. Crafty Millace. As soon as I work out how to unscramble the blue, the next riveting Millace instalment will fall into our hands."

"Well, be careful."

I said I would. One says things like that so easily.

I WENT TO WINCANTON RACES and rode twice for Harold and three times for other people. The day was dry with a sharp wind. I booted my way around five times in safety, and in the novice chase found myself finishing in front, all alone.

There had been a time, when it was all new, that my heart had pumped madly every time I cantered to the start. Now, after ten years, my heart pumped above normal only for the big ones like the Grand National. The once fiendish excitement had turned to routine. Bad weather, long journeys, disappointments, and injuries had at first been shrugged off as part of the job. After ten years I saw that they *were* the job. The winners were the bonuses.

The tools of my trade were a liking for speed and a liking for horses. Also an ability to bounce, and to mend quickly when I didn't. None of these tools, except probably the liking for horses, would be of the slightest use to me as a photographer.

I walked irritably out to my car at the end of the afternoon. I didn't want to be a photographer. I wanted to remain a jockey. I wanted things to go on as they were, and not to change.

Early the following morning Clare Bergen appeared on my doorstep accompanied by her boss, the publisher, a dark young man whose handshake almost tingled with energy. Clare wore a bright woolly hat, sheepskin jacket, yellow ski pants, and huge fleece-lined boots. Ah well, I thought, she would only frighten half the horses. The nervous half.

I drove them up onto the Downs in a Land-Rover borrowed from Harold, and we watched a few strings of horses go through their workouts. Then I drove them back to the cottage for coffee. The publisher said he would like to poke around a little on foot, and walked off. Clare drank her second steaming cup and said, "Most of the people I know despise horse people."

"Everyone likes to feel superior," I said, uninsulted.

"And you don't mind?"

"What those people feel is their problem, not mine."

She looked straight at me. "What does hurt you?"

"People saying I fell off when it was the horse that fell, and took me with it."

"And there's a distinction?"

"Most important. What hurts you?"

"Being held to be a fool."

"That," I said, "is a piercingly truthful reply."

She looked away from me as if embarrassed, and said she liked the cottage and the kitchen and could she see the rest. I showed her the sitting room, the bedroom, and finally the darkroom.

She said slowly, "You mentioned that you took photographs, but I'd no idea . . . Can I see them?"

"If you like." I opened my filing cabinet and sorted through the folders. "Here you are, Lambourn village."

"What are all those others?" she said. She read the tags on the folders aloud. "America, France, Children, Jockey's Life. What's Jockey's Life?"

"Just everyday living, if you're a jockey."

She eased the well-filled folder out of the drawer and carried it to the kitchen. At the table she went through it, picture by picture. No comments.

"Can I see the Lambourn photos?" she said. She looked through these also in silence.

"I know they're not marvellous," I said mildly. "You don't have to rack your brains for something kind to say."

She looked up fiercely. "You know they're good." She closed the file. "I don't see why we can't use these. But it's not my decision, of course."

74

She lit a cigarette, and I noticed with surprise that her fingers were trembling. Something had disturbed her deeply; all the glittery extrovert surface had vanished.

"What's the matter?" I said at last.

She gave me a quick glance. "I've been looking for something like you."

"Something?" I echoed, puzzled.

"I want . . . I need to make a book that will establish my own personal reputation in publishing. I need to be known as the person who produced a very successful book. What I want is exceptional. And now . . . I've found it."

"But," I said, "Lambourn's not news, and, anyway, I thought it was your boss's book."

"Not that, you fool. This." She put her hand on the Jockey's Life folder. "The pictures in here. Arranged in the right order . . . presented as a way of living . . . as an autobiography, a social comment . . . as well as how an industry works . . . it'll be spectacular. You haven't had any of these photographs published before, have you?"

I shook my head. "Nowhere. I've never tried."

"You're amazing. You have this talent, and you don't use it."

"But everyone takes photographs."

"Sure they do. But not everyone takes a long series of photographs which illustrate a whole way of life. The hard work, the dedication, the bad weather, the humdrum, the triumphs, the pain. . . . Look at this last one," she said, taking it out of the folder. "This picture of a man pulling the boot off this boy with the broken shoulder. You don't need any words to say the man is doing it as gently as he can, or that it hurts. You can see it all." She replaced the picture and said seriously, "Will you give me your assurance that you won't go straight off and sell these pictures to someone else?"

"Of course," I said.

"And don't mention any of this to my boss. I want this to be my book, not his. You may have no ambition. But I have."

She thrust the folder into my hands and I put it back in the filing cabinet, so that when her boss returned, it was only the views of

Lambourn that he saw. He said that they would do well enough, and shortly afterwards he and Clare bore them away.

When they'd gone, I thought to myself that Clare's certainty about her book would evaporate. She would write apologetically and say that after all, on reflection . . . I had no expectations.

I went into Swindon to collect the films I'd left there for processing, and spent the rest of that Friday printing the shots of Lance Kinship and his crew. In the evening I captioned the prints and, feeling faintly foolish, added the words Copyright Philip Nore. Charlie seemed almost to be leaning over my shoulder, reminding me to keep control of my work.

Work. The very word filled me with disquiet. It was the first time I'd actively thought of my photographs in those terms.

No, I thought. I'm a jockey.

Saturday morning at ten Harold called. I waited for him to tell me to get sick. Instead he said, "Are you well? You'd better be. I told Victor what you said. Word for word. I said you would ride your guts out for him as long as we're trying to win. And do you know what he said? He said, 'Tell that pious idiot that's just what I expect.' "

"Do you mean . . ."

"I mean," Harold bellowed, "he's changed his mind. You can win on Chainmail, if you can. In fact you'd better. See you at Ascot." He slammed the receiver.

It seemed only too likely that Harold had promised Victor that Chainmail would win. If he had, I could be in a worse fix.

AS I TOOK OFF my street clothes in the changing room at Ascot, someone was voicing the first rumours of a major racing upheaval.

"Is it true the Jockey Club is forming a new committee for appointing *paid* stewards? No more working for the love of it?"

"I heard Lord White has agreed to the scheme," said someone else. "And Ivor den Relgan is to be chairman."

I turned to him. "That gives den Relgan an awful lot of power all of a sudden, doesn't it?"

He shrugged. "I don't know if it's true. I just heard it from one of the gossip writers."

During the afternoon one could almost see the onward march of the rumour as uneasy surprise spread from one Jockey Club face to the next. The only ones who seemed unaffected were Lord White, Lady White, Ivor den Relgan, and Dana den Relgan.

They stood near the course in weak November sunshine, the women both dressed in mink. Lady White looked gaunt and plain and unhappy. Dana den Relgan, laughing and glowing with health, twinkled her eyes at Lord White, who basked in the light of her smile, shedding years like snakeskins. Ivor den Relgan smirked at the world in general and smoked a cigar with proprietary gestures, as if Ascot were his own.

Harold appeared at my elbow. "Genghis Khan," he said acidly, "is setting out to rule the world. What they're really doing is saying to den Relgan, 'OK, you choose anyone you like as stewards, and we'll pay them.' It's incredible. Old Driven Snow is so besotted with that girl that he'll give her father *anything*."

"You really care," I said wonderingly.

"Of course I do. Racing is a great sport, and at the moment, free, its health guaranteed by having unpaid aristocrats who love the work. If den Relgan appoints paid stewards, for whom do you think those stewards will be working? For us? For racing? Or for the interests of Ivor den Relgan?"

We watched the group of four. Lord White was continually touching Dana—her arm, her shoulders, her cheek. Her father smiled indulgently and poor Lady White seemed to shrink even further into her mink.

"Someone," Harold said grimly, "has got to stop this. And before it goes too far."

I turned away, troubled, and found Lance Kinship coming slowly towards me, his gaze flicking rapidly from me to the den Relgans and back again. It struck me that he wanted to talk to me without den Relgan noticing he was there.

"I've got your pictures in the car," I said to him.

"Good, good. I'll get them after the last race. I want to talk to that girl." He glanced at Dana. "Can you give her a message? Without that man hearing?"

"I might try," I said.

"Right. Tell her that I'll meet her after the third race in one of the private boxes." He told me the number.

I nodded, and he scuttled away. He was dressed for the role of country gentleman—tweed suit, brown trilby, checked shirt—except that he'd ruined the blue-blood impression with some pale green socks. A pathetic man, I thought, buying his way into the big time with little packets of white powder.

I looked from him to den Relgan, who was using Dana for much the same purpose. Nothing pathetic, though, about Ivor den Relgan. Power hungry and complacent, a trampler of little men. I went up to him and, in an ingratiating voice, thanked him again for the silver gifts he had scattered at Kempton. "The silver saddle," I said. "Great to have."

"So glad," he said, his gaze passing over me without interest. "My daughter selected it."

"Splendid taste," Lord White said fondly.

I said directly to Dana, "Please tell me, is it unique, or is it one of many?" I moved a step or two so that to answer she had to turn away from the two men, and almost before she had finished replying that it was the only one she'd seen, I said to her quietly, "Lance Kinship is here, wanting to see you."

"Oh." She glanced quickly at the two men. "Where?"

"After the third race, in a private box." I gave her the number, and wandered away.

Daylight's race was third on the card, and Chainmail's fourth. When I went out for the third, I was stopped by a pleasant-mannered woman who I realized with shock was Marie Millace. Scarcely a trace showed of the devastation of her face. She was pale and ill-looking, but healed. "You look great," I told her.

"You said there wouldn't be a mark," she said, "and there isn't. Can I talk to you?"

"Well, how about after the fourth race? After I've changed?"

She mentioned a particular bar up in the stands, and we agreed on it, and I went on to the parade ring, where Harold and Victor Briggs waited. Neither of them said anything to me, nor I to them. Everything of importance had already been said.

I cantered down to the starting gate, thinking about courage,

78

which was not normally a word I found much in my mind. The process of getting a horse to go fast over jumps seemed to me merely natural, and something I very much liked doing. I had no preoccupation with my own safety. On the other hand I'd never been reckless, as Steve Millace was, throwing his heart over a fence and letting the horse catch up if he could. It was the latter style of riding that Victor Briggs would be expecting now. And moreover, I'd have to do it twice.

Daylight and I turned in what was for us a thoroughly uncharacteristic performance, leaving more to luck than judgment. He was accustomed to measuring his distance from a fence and altering his stride accordingly, but infected by my urgency, he began simply to take off when he was vaguely within striking distance of getting over. We hit the tops of three fences hard, and raced over the last as if it were but a shadow on the ground. But hard as we tried, we didn't win. A stronger, faster, fitter horse beat us into second place by three lengths.

In the unsaddling enclosure I unbuckled the girths while Daylight panted and rocketed around in a highly excitable state. Victor Briggs watched without letting a thought surface.

"Sorry," I said to Harold as he walked in with me to the changing room.

He merely grunted, then said, "Don't kill yourself on Chainmail. It won't prove anything except that you're a bloody fool." But I noticed that he did not instruct me to return to a more sober style for his second runner. Perhaps he, too, wanted Victor to run his horses straight, and if this was the only way to achieve that, well, so be it.

With Chainmail, things were different. The four-year-old hurdler was unstable to begin with, and what I was doing to him was like urging a juvenile delinquent to go mugging. He fought and surged and flew. I went with him to his ultimate speed, totally disregarding good sense. Without any reservation I rode my bloody guts out for Victor Briggs.

It wasn't enough. Chainmail finished third.

Victor Briggs unsmilingly watched me pull the saddle off his second stamping, tossing, hepped-up horse. I wrapped the girths

around the saddle and paused for a moment, face to face with him. He said nothing at all, nor did I. We looked with blankness into each other's eyes. I had needed two winners to save my job, and had none. Recklessness wasn't enough. He wanted winners. If he couldn't have certain winners, he wanted certain losers. Like three years ago, when I and my soul were young. With a deep feeling of weariness I went in to change and to meet Marie Millace.

SHE WAS SITTING in an armchair, deep in conversation with another woman, whom I found to my surprise to be Lady White.

"I'll come back later," I said, preparing to retreat.

"No, no," Lady White said, standing up. "I know Marie wants to talk to you." The two women smiled and kissed cheeks, and Lady White made her way out of the bar, a thin, defeated lady trying to behave as if the whole racing world were not aware of her discomfiture.

"We were at school together," Marie Millace said. "I'm very fond of her."

"You know about . . . er . . ."

"About Dana den Relgan? Yes. Would you like a drink?"

"Let me get you one." I fetched a gin and tonic for her and some Coke for me, and sat in the armchair Lady White had left.

The bar itself, an attractive place of bamboo furniture and green and white colours, was almost empty. It was a good place for talking, and it was also warm.

Marie Millace said, "Wendy—Lady White—was asking me if I thought her husband's affair with Dana would just blow over. What could I say? I said I was sure it would." She gloomily swirled the ice around in her drink. "It's so awful. Wendy thought it was all over."

"All over? I thought it had just started."

She sighed. "Wendy says her husband fell for this creature months ago, but then the wretched girl faded off the scene and Wendy thought he'd stopped seeing her. Now she's back in full view and it's obvious to everyone. I'm so sorry for Wendy. It's all so horrid."

81

"Do you know Dana den Relgan yourself?" I asked.

"No, not at all. George knew her, I think. He said when we were in St. Tropez last summer he'd seen her there one afternoon, but I don't know, he was laughing when he said it.

"Anyway, that's not what I wanted to talk to you about. I wanted to thank you for your kindness and ask you about that exhibition you suggested. And about how I might make some money out of George's work. Because I'm going to need . . . er . . ."

"Everyone needs," I said comfortingly. "But didn't George leave things like insurance policies?"

"Some. But it won't be enough to live on."

"Did he," I asked delicately, "have any . . . well . . . savings in any separate bank accounts?"

Her friendly expression began to change to suspicion. "Are you asking me the same sort of things as the police?"

"Marie. Think of the burglaries and the arson."

"George wouldn't," she said explosively. "I told you before."

I sighed, and asked if she knew which friend George had stopped for a drink with, on his way back from Doncaster.

"He wasn't a friend. Barely an acquaintance. A man called Lance Kinship. George phoned me in the morning and mentioned he'd be late as he was calling at this man's house. This Kinship wanted George to take some pictures of him working. He's a film director or something. George said he was a pernicious little egotist, but he'd pay well. That was almost the last thing he said to me."

She sniffed, fishing in her pocket for a handkerchief and wiping her eyes. "I'm so sorry. The very last thing he said was to ask me to buy some Ajax window cleaner. It's stupid, isn't it? I mean, except for saying, 'See you,' the last thing George ever said to me was, 'Get some liquid Ajax, will you?' " She gulped. "I don't even know what he wanted it for."

"Marie . . ." I held my hand out towards her and she gripped it as fiercely as in the hospital. But presently her turmoil subsided and she gave a small laugh of embarrassment. I asked her if there had been an autopsy.

"Oh . . . alcohol, do you mean? Yes, they tested his blood. They

82

said it was below the limit. He'd only had two small whiskies with that Kinship. The police asked Kinship about it after I told them that George had planned to stop there. Kinship wrote to me, you know, saying he was sorry. But it wasn't his fault. George often got dozy when he'd been driving a long way."

I told her how it happened that Lance Kinship had asked me to take photographs that George had been going to do. "George always said you'd wake up one day and steal his market," she said, and produced a wavery smile.

I asked for her address so that I could put her in touch with an agent, and she said she was staying with some friends who lived near Steve. She didn't know, she said, where she would be going from there. She had no furniture, nothing to make a home with. Much worse, she had no photograph of George.

BY THE TIME I left Marie Millace, the fifth race had been run. I went out to the car to fetch Lance Kinship's pictures, and returned towards the changing room to find Jeremy Folk standing outside the door on one leg. "You'll fall over," I said.

"Oh." He put the foot down gingerly. "I thought . . ."

"You thought if you weren't here, I might not do what you want. Well, you may be right."

"I came here by train," he said contentedly, "so can you take me with you to St. Albans?"

"I guess I'll have to."

Lance Kinship, seeing me there, came over to collect his prints. I introduced him to Jeremy, and added for Jeremy's sake that it was at Lance Kinship's house that George Millace had taken his last drink. Kinship gave each of us a sharp glance followed by a sorrowful shake of the head.

"A great fellow, George," he said. "Too bad."

He pulled the pictures out of the envelope and looked through them, his eyebrows rising high above his spectacle frames. "Well, well," he said. "I like them. How much do you want?"

I mentioned an exorbitant figure, but he merely nodded, pulled out a stuffed wallet, and paid me there and then in cash.

"Reprints?" he said. "Two sets?"

83

"Complete sets?" I said, surprised. "All of them?"

"Sure. All of them. Very nice, they are. Want to see?" He flicked them invitingly at Jeremy, who also inspected them with eyebrows rising.

"You must be," said Jeremy, "a director of great note."

Kinship positively beamed, tucked his pictures back into the envelope, and walked away. Before he'd gone ten paces he was pulling the pictures out again to show to someone else.

"He'll get you a lot of work," Jeremy said.

I didn't know whether or not I wanted to believe him, and in any case my attention was caught by something much more extraordinary. "Do you see," I said to Jeremy, "those two men over there, talking? One of them is Bart Underfield, who's a trainer in Lambourn. And the other is one of the men in that photograph I told you about of the French café. That's Elgin Yaxley . . . come home from Hong Kong."

Three weeks after George's death, two weeks after the burning of his house, and Elgin Yaxley back on the scene. I had jumped to conclusions before, but surely this time it was reasonable to suppose that Elgin Yaxley believed the incriminating photograph had safely gone up in smoke. Reasonable to suppose, watching him smiling expansively, that he felt free and secure.

Jeremy said, "It can't be coincidence. You've still got that photo?"

"I sure have. And tomorrow I'm going to have a go at the blue oblongs."

"So you've worked out how?"

"Well, I hope so. I think if I enlarge the orange negatives through blue light onto high-contrast black-and-white paper, I might get a picture."

Jeremy blinked.

Later, as we drove towards St. Albans, he told me about his researches into the television company.

"They only filmed at Pine Woods Lodge for six weeks. I got them to show me the credits, and I asked if they could put me in touch with anyone who had worked on the programme. They told me where to find the director, who's still working in television. Very

84

dour and depressing man, all grunts and a heavy moustache. He wasn't much help. Thirteen years ago? How did I expect him to remember one crummy six weeks thirteen years ago?"

"Pity."

"After that I tracked down one of the actors, who is temporarily working in an art gallery, and got much the same answer. Thirteen years? Girl with small child? Not a chance."

I sighed. "How long were the musicians there?"

"Three months, give or take a week."

"And after them?"

"The religious fanatics." He grimaced. "It's so long ago."

"Let's try something else," I said. "Why not publish Amanda's photograph in *Horse and Hound*, and ask for an identification of the stable? The buildings are probably still standing."

He sighed. "OK, then. But I can see the final expenses of this search costing more than the inheritance."

We reached St. Albans and the nursing home; Jeremy would read magazines in the waiting room while I talked upstairs with the dying old woman. Sitting up, supported by pillows, she watched me walk into her room. The strong, harsh face was still full of stubborn life, the eyes unrelentingly fierce. She said nothing like, "Good evening," but merely, "Have you found her?"

"No."

She compressed her mouth. "Are you trying?"

"I've spent some time looking for her but not my whole life." I sat down in an armchair. "I went to see your son," I said.

Her face melted into a revealing mixture of rage and disgust, and with surprise I saw the passion of her disappointment.

"Your genes to go on," I said. "Is that what you want?"

"Death is pointless otherwise."

I thought that life was pretty pointless, but I didn't say so. One woke up alive, and did what one could, and died. Perhaps she was right—that the point of life was for genes to survive, through generations of bodies. "Whether you like it or not," I said, "your genes may go on through me."

The idea still displeased her. Her jaw tightened. "That young solicitor thinks I should tell you who your father was."

I stood up at once, unable to stay calm. Although I had come to find out, I now didn't want to hear.

"Are you afraid?" She was scornful. Sneering.

I simply stood there, not answering, wanting to know and not wanting, afraid and not afraid. In an absolute muddle.

"I have hated your father since before you were born," she said bitterly. "I can hardly bear even now to look at you, because you're like he was at your age. Thin . . . and physical . . . and with the same eyes."

I swallowed and waited and felt numb.

"I loved him," she said, spitting the words out. "I doted on him. He was thirty and I was forty-four. I'd been a widow for five years. I was lonely. We were going to marry."

She stopped. There really was no need to go on. I knew the rest. The hatred she had felt for me all those years was finally explained. So simply explained . . . and forgiven.

I took a deep breath. "And what . . . was his name?"

She stared at me. "I'm not going to tell you. I don't want you seeking him out. He ruined my life. He bedded my seventeen-year-old daughter under my own roof and he was after my money. That's the sort of man your father was. The only favour I'll do you is not to tell you his name."

I nodded and said awkwardly, "I'm sorry."

Her scowl if anything deepened. "Now find Amanda for me." She closed her eyes. "I don't like you," she said. "So go away."

"WELL?" Jeremy said, downstairs.

I relayed to him the gist of what she had told me, and his reaction was the same as mine.

"Poor old woman."

"I could do with a drink," I said.

Chapter 7

In printing colour photographs, one's aim is usually to produce a result that looks natural, and this is nowhere near as easy as it sounds. For one thing, the colour itself comes out differently on

86

each make of film and on each type of photographic printing paper, the reason being that the four ultra-thin layers of light-sensitive emulsion which are laid onto colour printing paper vary slightly from batch to batch. In the same way that it is almost impossible to dye two pieces of cloth in different dye baths and produce identical results, so it is with emulsions.

To persuade all colours to look natural, one uses colour filters— pieces of coloured glass or plastic inserted between the bright light on the enlarger and the negative. Get the mixture of filters right, and in the finished print blue eyes come out blue and cherry lips, cherry.

In my enlarger, as in the majority, the three filters were the same colours as the negatives: yellow, magenta, and cyan. Used in delicate balance, the yellow and magenta filters could produce skin colours that were neither too yellow nor too pink for human faces. However, if one did not balance them properly and simply put a square of magenta-coloured glass on a square of cyan-coloured glass and shone a light through both together, the result was a deep clear blue.

I went into my darkroom on that fateful Sunday morning and adjusted the filters in the head of the enlarger so that the light that shone through the negatives would be an unheard-of combination for normal printing—full cyan and full magenta filtration, producing a deep clear blue.

Black-and-white printing paper is sensitive only to blue light. I thought that if I printed the blank-looking negatives through heavy blue filtration onto black-and-white paper, I would get rid of the blue of the oblongs and I might then get a greater contrast between the yellow dye image on the negative and the orange mask covering it. Make the image, in fact, emerge from its surroundings.

I had a feeling that whatever was hidden by the mask would not be black and white. If it were, it would have been visible in spite of the blue. What I was looking for would be grey.

I set out trays of developer, stop bath, and fixer. Then I put the first thirty-six unblotched negatives into a contact-printing frame, which held all thirty-six negatives conveniently so that they would be printed at once onto one eight-by-ten inch sheet.

Getting the exposure time right was the biggest difficulty, chiefly because the heavy blue filtration meant that the light getting to the negatives was far dimmer than I was used to. I wasted about six shots in tests, getting useless results ranging from grey to black, all the little oblongs still stubbornly looking as if there was nothing on them to see, whatever I did.

Finally, in irritation, I cut the exposure time way down and came up with a sheet of prints that was almost entirely white.

Sighing with frustration, I dipped the sheet in the stop bath, fixed it, washed it, and switched on the bright lights. The frame numbers had very palely appeared and five of the little oblongs, scattered at random through the thirty-six prints, bore grey geometric shapes. I had found them.

I smiled. George had left a puzzle; I had almost solved it.

I wrote down the frame numbers of the five grey-patterned prints. Then I took the first one numerically, and enlarged it to the full size of the eight-by-ten-inch paper. A couple more bad guesses at exposure times left me with unclear dark grey prints, but in the end I came up with one which developed into mid-grey on white. I carried it out to the kitchen.

Although the print was still wet, I could see exactly what it was— a letter typed on white paper with an old greyish ribbon. It bore no heading, date, or handwritten signature. It said:

Dear Mr. Morton,

I am sure you will be interested in the enclosed two photographs. As you will see, the first one is of your horse Amber Globe running poorly at Southwell on Monday, May 12. The second is of your horse Amber Globe winning the race at Fontwell on Wednesday, August 27.

If you look closely at the photographs you will see that they are not of the same horse. Alike but not identical.

I am sure that the Jockey Club would be interested in this difference. I will telephone you shortly, however, with an alternative suggestion.

Yours sincerely,
George Millace

I read it through six times. I felt as though I were looking into a pit. Presumably the other four grey geometric patterns would also turn out to be letters. What I had found was George's idiosyncratic filing system. If I enlarged and read the other letters, I would have to accept the moral burden of deciding what to do about them . . . and of doing it.

To postpone the decision, I went upstairs to the sitting room and looked up Amber Globe's career in the form books. On average it amounted to three or four poor showings followed by an easy win at high odds, this pattern being repeated twice a season. Amber Globe's last win had been the one on August 27 four years previously, and from then on he had run in no more races at all.

Dear Mr. Morton and his trainer had been running two horses under the name Amber Globe, switching in the good one for the big gambles, letting the poor one lengthen the odds. I wondered how George had noticed, but there was no way of knowing, as I hadn't found the two photographs in question.

I looked out of the window at the Downs for a while, waiting for the arrival of a comfortable certainty that knowledge did not involve responsibility. I waited in vain. I knew that it did.

Unsettled, fearful, I finally went down to the darkroom and printed the other four negatives one by one, and read the resulting letters in the kitchen. The sly malice of George's mind spoke out clearly. The second letter said:

Dear Bonnington Ford,

I am sure you will be interested in the enclosed series of photographs, which, as you will see, are a record of you entertaining in your training stables a person who has been 'disqualified'. I need not remind you that the racing authorities would object strongly to this continuous association, even to the extent of reviewing your licence to train.

I could of course send copies of these photographs to the Jockey Club. I will telephone shortly, however, with an alternative suggestion.

Yours sincerely,
George Millace

Bonnington Ford was a third-rate trainer who was as honest and trustworthy as a pickpocket. Again I hadn't found the photographs in question, so there was nothing I could do, even if I wanted to.

The last three letters were a different matter. The first said:

Dear Elgin Yaxley,

I am sure you will be interested in the enclosed photograph. As you will see, it clearly contradicts a statement you recently made on oath at a certain trial.

I am sure that the Jockey Club would be interested to see it, and also the police, the judge, and the insurance company. I will telephone shortly, however, with an alternative suggestion.

Yours sincerely,
George Millace

The next letter would have driven the nail right in. It said:

Dear Elgin Yaxley,

Since I wrote to you yesterday there have been further developments. I visited the farmer upon whose farm you boarded your unfortunate steeplechasers, and I showed him in confidence a copy of the photograph that I sent to you. I suggested that there might be a further inquiry, during which his own share in the tragedy might be investigated.

He responded to my promise of silence with the pleasing information that your five good horses were not after all dead. The five horses that died had been bought especially and cheaply by your farmer friend from a local auction, and it was these that were shot by Terence O'Tree at the appointed time and place. Terence O'Tree was not told of the substitution.

Your farmer friend also confirmed that you yourself arrived at the farm to supervise the good horses' removal. Your friend understood you would be shipping them out to a buyer in the Far East.

I enclose a photograph of his signed statement to this effect. I will telephone shortly with a suggestion.

Yours sincerely,
George Millace

The last letter had been written in pencil.

Dear Elgin Yaxley,
    I bought the five horses that T. O'Tree shot. You fetched your own horses away, to export them to the East. I am satisfied with what you paid me for this service.

Yours faithfully,
David Parker

I thought of Elgin Yaxley as I had seen him the previous day at Ascot, smirking complacently and believing himself safe. I thought of right and wrong, and justice; of Elgin Yaxley as the victim of George Millace; and of the insurance company as the victim of Elgin Yaxley. I couldn't decide what to do.

After a while I got up stiffly and went back to the darkroom. I put all of the magenta-splashed negatives into the contact-printing frame and made a nearly white sheet of prints as I had done with the first set. This time there were not five little grey oblongs, but fifteen. With a feeling of horror I switched off all the lights, locked the doors, and walked up the road to my briefing with Harold.

"PAY ATTENTION," Harold said sharply. "What's the matter with you? I'm talking about Coral Key at Kempton on Wednesday, and you're not listening."

I dragged my attention back to the matter at hand.

"Coral Key," I said. "For Victor Briggs. Has Victor said anything about yesterday?"

Harold shook his head. "Until he tells me you're off his horses, you're still on them."

I WENT BACK to the quiet cottage and made enlargements from the fifteen magenta-splashed negatives. To my relief, they were not all threatening letters—only the first two were.

I had expected one on the subject of the lovers, and it was there. It was the second one that left me breathless and laughing, and put me in a better frame of mind for revelations to come.

The last thirteen prints, however, turned out to be George's notes of where and when he had taken his incriminating pictures, and on what dates he had sent the frightening letters. I guessed he had kept his records in this form because it seemed safer than leaving such damaging material lying around on paper. They were fascinating, but they all failed to say what the alternative suggestions had been. There was no record of what monies George had extorted nor of where he had stashed the proceeds.

I went to bed late and couldn't sleep, and in the morning I made some telephone calls. One to the editor of *Horse and Hound*, whom I knew, begging him to include Amanda's picture in that week's issue, emphasizing that time was short. He said he would print it if I got it to his office that morning.

I said I would, and then telephoned old Driven Snow at his home in the Cotswolds.

"You want to see me?" he said. "What about?"

"About George Millace, sir."

"Photographer? Died recently?"

"Yes, sir. His wife is a friend of Lady White's."

"Yes, yes," he said impatiently. And although he wasn't overpoweringly keen on the idea, he agreed to see me the next day.

After that I telephoned Samantha and asked if I could take her and Clare out to dinner. She sounded pleased.

"I can't tonight," she said. "But I'm sure Clare would like it. What time?"

I said I would pick her up at eight. Samantha said fine and how was the search for Amanda going, and I found myself talking to her as if I'd known her all my life. As indeed, in a way, I had.

I drove to London to the *Horse and Hound* offices and arranged to have Amanda's picture run with the caption, WHERE IS THIS STABLE? TEN POUNDS REWARD FOR THE FIRST PERSON—PARTICULARLY THE FIRST CHILD—WHO CAN TELEPHONE PHILIP NORE TO TELL HIM.

"Child?" said the editor. "Do they read this paper?"

"Their mothers do."

"Subtle stuff," he said.

SAMANTHA WAS OUT when I went to fetch Clare.

"Come in for a drink first," Clare said, opening the door wide. "It's such a lousy evening."

I stepped out of the cold November wind, and she led me into a long, gently-lit sitting room.

"Do you remember this room?" Clare said.

I shook my head.

"Where's the bathroom?" she said.

I answered immediately, "Upstairs, turn right, blue bath."

She laughed. "Straight from the subconscious." She handed me a glass of wine, and we sat down in a couple of pale velvet armchairs. She wore a scarlet silk shirt and black trousers, and made a bright statement against the soft colouring of the room.

"I saw you racing on Saturday," she said. "On television. You do take some frightful risks. What happens if you're really smashed up by one of those falls?"

"You've got a problem. No rides, no income."

"What happens if you're killed?"

I smiled. "The risk is less than you'd think. But if you're really unlucky, there's always the Injured Jockeys Fund."

"What's that?"

"The racing industry's private charity. It looks after the widows and orphans of dead jockeys and gives succour to badly damaged live ones."

We went out a little later and ate in a small restaurant determinedly decorated as a French peasant kitchen with rushes on the floor and dripping candles stuck in wine bottles. While we ate, Clare turned to the subject of photographs and said she would like to come down to Lambourn again to go through the Jockey's Life file. "You haven't sold any to anyone else, have you? You did say you wouldn't."

"Not those." I told her about Lance Kinship and how odd I found it that all of a sudden people wanted to buy my work.

"The word is going around," she said. She finished her veal and sat back, looking thoughtful. "What you need is an agent."

I explained about having to find one for Marie Millace anyway; she brushed that aside. "Not *any* agent," she said. "Me."

She looked at my stunned expression and smiled. "Well?" she said. "What does any agent do? He knows the markets and sells the goods. What if I got you commissions for illustrations for other books—on any subject? Would you do them?"

"Yes, but . . ."

"No buts. There's no point in taking super photos if no one sees them." The candlelight shone on her intent grey eyes. She was a girl of certainty. She looked steadily at a future I still shied away from. I wondered what she'd say if I said I wanted to kiss her, when her thoughts were clearly more practical.

"I'd like to try," she said persuasively. "Will you let me?"

She'll bully you into things, Samantha had said.

Take what comes, and hope for the best. I said, "All right," and she said, "Great." And later, when I delivered her to her doorstep and kissed her, she didn't object.

FOUR TIMES on Tuesday morning I lifted the telephone to cancel my appointment with Lord White. Four times I put the receiver down and decided I would have to go.

Lord White's house turned out to be a weathered stone pile with more grandeur than gardeners. Noble windows raised their eyebrows above drifts of unswept leaves. A mat of dead weeds glued the gravel together. I rang the doorbell and wondered about the economics of being a baron.

Lord White received me in a small sitting room where everything was of venerable antiquity, dusted and gleaming. But there were patches on the chintz chair covers. Less money than was needed, I diagnosed. He shook hands and offered me a chair. I found it an agony to begin.

"Sir," I said. "I'm very sorry, sir, but I'm afraid what I've come about may be a great shock to you."

He frowned slightly. "About George Millace?"

"Yes, about some photographs he took."

I stopped. Too late, I wished fervently that I hadn't come. I should after all have adhered to the lifetime habit of non-involvement. But what I was there for had to be done. With foreboding I opened the large envelope I carried. I pulled out the first of the

three pictures of the lovers and put it into his outstretched hand, and, for all that I thought he was behaving foolishly over Dana den Relgan, I felt deeply sorry for him.

His first reaction was extreme anger. How dared I, he said, standing up and quivering, how dared I bring him anything so filthy and *disgusting?* I took the second and third photographs out of the envelope and rested them picture side down on the arm of my chair. "As you will see," I said, "the others are worse."

I reckoned it took a lot of courage for him to pick up the other two pictures. He looked at them in desperate silence, and slowly sank down again in his chair. His face told of his anguish. Of his horror. The man making love to Dana was Ivor den Relgan.

Several moments later Lord White said, "They can fake pictures of anything." His voice shook. "Cameras do lie."

"Not this one," I said regretfully. I took from the envelope a print of the letter George Millace had written, and gave it to him. The letter, which I knew by heart, read:

Dear Ivor den Relgan,

I am sure you will be interested in the enclosed photographs, which I was able to take a few days ago in St. Tropez. As you will see, they show you in a compromising position with the young lady who is known as your daughter. (It is surely unwise to do this sort of thing on hotel balconies where one can be seen by telephoto lenses.) There seem to be two possibilities here.

One: Dana den Relgan is your daughter, in which case this is incest. Two: Dana is not your daughter, in which case why are you pretending she is? Can it have anything to do with the ensnaring of a certain member of the Jockey Club? Are you hoping for entry to the club, and other favours?

I could of course send these photographs to the lord in question. I will telephone shortly, however, with an alternative suggestion.

Yours sincerely,
George Millace

Lord White became older before my eyes, the glow that love had given him shrinking back into deepening wrinkles. Finally he said, "Where did you get these?"

"After George Millace died, his son gave me a box with some things of his father's in it. These photos were among them."

He suffered through another silence, then said, "Why did you bring them to me? To cause me mortification?"

I swallowed. "Sir, people are worried about how much power has been given recently to Ivor den Relgan."

"And you have taken it upon yourself to try to stop it?"

"Sir. . . . Yes."

He looked grim, and as if seeking refuge in anger, he said authoritatively, "It's none of your business, Nore."

I didn't answer at once. I'd had enough trouble persuading myself that it *was* my business. But in the end, diffidently, I said, "Sir, if you are certain in your own mind that Ivor den Relgan's sudden rise to power has nothing whatever to do with your affection for Dana den Relgan, then I most abjectly beg your pardon."

He merely stared. "Please leave," he said rigidly.

"Yes, sir." I stood up and walked over to the door.

"Wait, Nore. I must think. Will you please come back and sit down?" His voice was still stern, still full of accusation and judgment and defence.

I returned to the armchair, and he went and stood by the window with his back to me, looking out at straggly rosebushes and unclipped hedges.

Finally he spoke, but without turning around. "How many people have seen these pictures?"

"I don't know how many George Millace showed them to. A friend of mine was with me when I found them. But he doesn't know the den Relgans."

"Do you intend," he said quietly, "to make jokes about this on the racecourse?"

"No." I was horrified. "I do not."

"And would you expect any reward, in service . . . or cash . . . for this silence?"

I stood up as if he had hit me. "I would not," I said. "I'm not George Millace. I think I'll go now." And go I did, impelled by a severe hurt to the vanity.

ON WEDNESDAY Harold called me with the news that Coral Key wouldn't be running that day at Kempton, after all. "Bloody animal injured itself in its box during the night," Harold said. "It won't please Victor."

On Thursday I set off to Kempton with only one ride, thinking it was a very thin week on the earning front, but almost as soon as I'd stepped through the gate I was offered spare rides by a trainer whose regular jockey had got 'flu.

His horses were no great shakes. I got one of them round into third place, and on the other I came down two fences from home; a bit of a crash but nothing broken in either him or me. The third horse, the one I'd originally gone to ride, wasn't much better: a clumsy baby with guts equal to his skill. We finished, not unexpectedly, in the middle of the pack.

The surprise of the afternoon was the presence of Clare. She was waiting for me outside the changing room.

"Hullo," she said. "I decided to come out by train and take a look at the real thing." She smiled. "Is today typical?"

I looked at the grey windy sky and the thin Thursday crowd, and thought of my three nondescript races. "Pretty much," I said. "Would you like a cup of tea? A trip to Lambourn?"

She thought it over briefly. "Lambourn," she said. "I can get a train back from near there, can't I?"

As I drove, I had an unaccustomed feeling of contentment. It felt right to have her sitting there in the car.

The cottage was cold but soon warmed. Just as I put the kettle on for tea the telephone rang. I answered it and had my eardrum half shattered by a piercing voice which shrieked, "Am I first?"

"First what?" I said, wincing and holding the receiver away.

"First!" A child's voice. Female. "I've been ringing every five minutes for *hours*. Am I first? Do say I'm first."

Realization dawned. "You're first. Have you been reading *Horse and Hound*? It isn't published until tomorrow."

"It gets to my auntie's bookshop on Thursdays. I collect it for Mummy on my way home from school. And she saw the picture, and told me to ring you. So can I have the ten pounds? Can I?"

"If you know where the stable is, yes, of course."

"Mummy knows. She'll tell you. You'd better talk to her now."

There were some background noises, and then a woman's voice, pleasant and far less excited.

"Are you the Philip Nore who rides in National Hunt races?"

"Yes," I said, and she went on without further reservation.

"I do know where that stable is, but it isn't used for horses any longer. It's in Horley, near Gatwick Airport. It's still called Zephyr Farm Stables, but it's been converted into living quarters. Do you want the address?"

"I guess so," I said. "And yours, too, please."

She read them out and I wrote them down, and then I said, "Do you happen to know the name of the people living there now?"

"Huh!" she said scornfully. "You won't get far with them, I'm afraid. They've got the place practically fortified to ward off furious parents. It's one of those commune things. Religious brain-washing. They call themselves Colleagues of Supreme Grace."

I felt breathless. "Thanks very much. I'll send your daughter the money."

"What is it?" Clare said as I slowly replaced the receiver.

"The first real lead to Amanda." I explained about the advertise-ment, and about the tenants of Pine Woods Lodge.

Clare shook her head. "If these Supreme Grace people know where Amanda is, they won't tell you. You must have heard of them. All gentle and smiling on the surface, and like steel rat-traps underneath. They lure young people with friendliness and songs and hook them into 'believing', and once they're in, the poor slobs never get out. They're in love with their prison."

"I've heard of them. But I've never seen the point."

"Money," Clare said crisply. "All the darling little Colleagues go out with saintly faces and collecting boxes, and line the pockets of their great leader."

I made the tea and we sat by the table to drink it.

Amanda in a stableyard at Horley; Caroline twenty miles away at Pine Woods Lodge. Colleagues at Pine Woods Lodge; Colleagues ditto at Horley. Too close to be a coincidence.

"You'll go looking?"

I nodded. "Tomorrow, I think, after racing."

We finished the tea and talked of her life and mine, and later in the evening we went to a good pub for a steak.

"A great day," Clare said over coffee. "Where's the train?"

"Swindon. I'll drive you there. Or you could stay."

"Is that the sort of invitation I think it is?"

"I wouldn't be surprised."

She looked down and fiddled with her spoon, paying it a lot of attention. I knew that if it took her so long to answer, she would go. "It's all right," I said easily. "If one never asks, one never gets." I paid the bill. "Come on."

She was quiet on the six-mile drive to the railway station, and not until I was waiting with her on the platform did she give any indication of what was in her mind.

"There's a board meeting in the office tomorrow," she said. "It will be the first I've been to. They made me a director a month ago."

I was most impressed, and said so. It couldn't be often that publishing houses put women of twenty-two on the board. I understood, also, why she wouldn't stay.

The train came in and she paused, before climbing aboard, to exchange kisses. Brief, unpassionate kisses. See you soon, she said, and I said yes. About contracts, she said. A lot to discuss.

"Come on Sunday," I said.

"Let you know. Goodbye."

"Goodbye."

The impatient train ground away, and I drove home to the empty cottage with a most unaccustomed feeling of loneliness.

NEWBURY RACES, Friday. Harold greeted me with mischievous amusement. "Did you hear that Genghis Khan got the boot?"

"Are you sure?" I said.

Harold nodded. "They held an emergency-type meeting of the Jockey Club this morning in London. Den Relgan was there. Lord White asked the members to cancel plans for a committee chaired by den Relgan, and as it was old Driven Snow's idea in the first place, they all agreed. It's the best about-turn since the Armada."

Harold left me, had he but known it, in a state of extreme relief. My visit to Lord White had achieved its main objective. At least I hadn't caused so much havoc in a man I liked without some good coming out of it.

That afternoon I rode a novice hurdler, which finished second, and later a sensitive mare that had no real heart for the job and finished fourth in a two-mile steeplechase.

After I changed, I found Lord White waiting outside the room. "I want to talk to you," he said. "Come into the steward's room."

I followed him and shut the door after us. He stood behind one of the chairs that surrounded the big table, grasping its back with both hands as if it gave him a shield.

"I regret," he said formally, "what I imputed to you on Tuesday. I was upset . . . but it was indefensible."

"It's all right, sir. I understand."

"I want to request den Relgan's resignation from the Jockey Club. The better to persuade him, I am of a mind to show him those photographs, which of course he has seen already. I think, however, that I need your permission to do so."

"I've no objection. Please do what you like with them."

He let go of the chair back as if no longer needing it, and walked around me to the door. "I can't exactly thank you," he said. "But I'm in your debt." He gave me a slight nod and went out of the room, dignity intact.

From Marie Millace I learned more. Steve's collarbone had mended and she had come to Newbury to see him ride, though she confessed, as I steered her off for a cup of coffee, that watching one's son race over fences was an agony. We sat at a small table in one of the bars.

"You're looking better," I said.

She nodded. "I feel it." She had been to a hairdresser, I saw, and had bought some more clothes. Still pale, with smudged, grieving eyes. Four weeks away from George's death.

She sipped the hot coffee and said, "You can forget what I told you last week about the Whites and Dana den Relgan. Wendy's very much happier. She says that last Tuesday her husband found out something he didn't like about Dana den Relgan. He didn't tell her what. But he told her his affair with Dana was over, and that he'd been a fool, and would she forgive him."

"And will she?"

"Oh, I expect so. Wendy says his trouble was the common one among men of fifty or so, wanting to prove to themselves they're still young. She understands him, you see."

"So do you," I said.

She smiled. "Goodness, yes. You see it all the time."

When we'd finished the coffee, I gave her a list of agents that she might try, and said I'd give any help I could. After that I told her I'd brought a present for her. I fetched my bag from the changing room and handed her an eight-by-ten-inch envelope.

She opened it. Inside was a photograph I'd taken once of George. George holding his camera, looking towards me, smiling his familiar sardonic smile. George in a typical pose, one leg forward, with his weight on the other, head back, considering the world a bad joke. George as he'd lived.

Marie Millace flung her arms around me and hugged me as if she would never let go.

Chapter 8

Zephyr Farm Stables was fortified like a stockade, surrounded by a seven-foot fence with a gate that would have done credit to Alcatraz. I sat in my car, waiting for it to open. No one went in or out, and after two fruitless hours I booked in to a local hotel.

Inquiries brought a sour response. Yes, the hotel receptionist said, they did sometimes have people staying there who were hoping to persuade their children to come home from Zephyr Farm Stables. Hardly any of them ever managed it; they were never allowed to see their children alone. And the law can't do a thing about it, she said. All over eighteen, they are, see?

I spent the evening drifting around, talking about the Colleagues to a succession of locals propping up the bars.

"Do they ever come out?" I asked. "To go shopping, perhaps?"

Amid a reaction of rueful smiles I was told that yes, indeed, they did emerge, always in groups, and always collecting money.

102

"They'll sell you things," one man said. "Bits o' polished stone and such. Just beggin' really."

"They don't do no harm," someone said. "Always smiling."

"Would they be out collecting in the morning?" I asked. "And if so, where?"

"Sure. Your best bet would be right here in the centre of town."

I thanked them all, and went to bed, and at ten in the morning I parked near the centre of town and wandered about on foot. I had to leave by eleven thirty to get back to Newbury, where I was riding in the third race.

I saw no groups of collecting Colleagues. No chanting people with shaven heads and bells. All that happened was that a smiling girl touched my arm and asked if I would like to buy a pretty paperweight. The polished stone lay in the palm of her hand.

"Yes," I said. "How much?"

"It's for charity. As much as you like." She produced a plain wooden box with a slit in the top.

"What charity?" I asked pleasantly, pushing a pound note through the slit.

"Lots of good causes," she said, and smiled.

"What's your name?" I asked.

She broadened the smile as if that were answer enough, and gave me the stone. "Thank you very much," she said. "Your gift will do so much good."

I watched her move on down the street, pulling another stone from a pocket in her swirling skirt and accosting someone else. She was too old to be Amanda, I thought.

"Would you like to buy a paperweight?" asked another stone seller in my path.

"Yes."

Within half an hour I bought four paperweights. To the fourth girl I said, "Is Amanda out here this morning?"

"Amanda? We haven't got . . ." Her eyes went to a girl across the street.

"Never mind," I said. "Thanks for the stone."

She smiled a bright empty smile and moved on, and I waited a short while before drifting in front of the girl she'd suddenly glanced at. She was young, short, smooth-faced, blank about the eyes, and dressed in an anorak and swirling skirt. Her hair was medium brown, like mine, but straight. There was no resemblance between our faces. She might or might not be my mother's child. "Amanda," I said.

She jumped, looked at me doubtfully. "My name's not Amanda."

"What then?"

"Mandy."

"Mandy what?"

"Mandy North."

I breathed very slowly, and smiled, and asked her how long she had lived at Zephyr Farm Stables.

"All my life," she said limpidly.

"And you're happy?"

"Yes, of course. We do God's work."

"How old are you?"

"Eighteen. . . . But I'm not supposed to talk about myself."

The childlike quality was very marked. She seemed not exactly mentally retarded, but simple. There was no life in her, no fun. Beside the average teenager she was like a sleepwalker. "What was your mother's name, Mandy?"

She looked scared. "You mustn't ask such things."

"When you were little, did you have a pony?"

For an instant her blank eyes lit with an uncrushable memory, and then she glanced over my shoulder at someone, and her simple pleasure turned to red-faced shame. I half turned. A tough-looking man stood there. Very clean, very neatly dressed, and very annoyed.

"No conversations, Mandy," he said to her severely. "Remember the rule. You'll be back on housework after this. Go along; the girls will take you home." He nodded to a group of girls and watched as she walked, leaden-footed, to join them. Poor Mandy. Poor Amanda. Poor little sister.

"What's your game?" the man said to me. "The girls say you've bought stones from all of them. What are you after?"

"Nothing," I said. "They're pretty stones."

He glared at me doubtfully, and he was joined by another man, who had been talking to the now-departing girls.

"This guy was asking the girls their names," the second man said. "Looking for Mandy. He talked to her."

They both looked at me with narrowed eyes, and I decided it was time to leave. I headed off in the general direction of the car park, but they followed along in my wake. There were five more loitering around the car park entrance, and all seven of them encircled me. "What do you want?" I said.

"Why were you asking for Mandy?" one of them said.

"She's my sister."

It confounded the men. They looked at each other. Then one said, "She's got no family. Her mother died years ago. You're lying."

Another one said, "If you ask me, he's a reporter."

The word stung them all into reconciling violence with their strange religion. They backed me up against a brick wall and shoved and kicked a bit, but no one wanted to go too far. They were just delivering a warning, so I pushed against their close bodies and that was that.

I didn't tell them the one thing that would have saved me the drubbing—that if Mandy was indeed my sister, she would inherit a fortune.

HAROLD WATCHED my arrival at the changing room with a scowl of disfavour. "You're late. Why are you limping?"

"Twisted my ankle."

"I hope you're fit to ride. Sharpener's out to win, and you can ride him in your usual way. None of those crazy heroics. Understood?"

I nodded, walked inside, and changed into Victor Briggs's colours, feeling an overall ache. Not enough, I hoped, to make any difference in my riding.

When I went outside I saw Elgin Yaxley and Bart Underfield, who were slapping each other on the shoulder and looking faintly drunk. Yaxley peeled off, and Bart, turning with an extravagant lack of coordination, bumped into me.

"Hullo," he said, giving a spirits-laden cough. "You'll be the first to know. Elgin's getting some more horses. They're coming to my stable, of course. We'll make the whole of racing sit up. Elgin's a man of ideas."

"He is indeed," I said dryly.

Bart took his good news off to other ears. I stood watching him, thinking that I didn't like the sound of it. Elgin Yaxley believed himself undetected . . . and people didn't change. If their minds ran to fraud once, they would again.

The old dilemma remained. If I gave the proof of Elgin Yaxley's fraud to the police, I would have to say how I came by the photograph. From George Millace, who wrote threatening letters. George Millace, husband of Marie, who was climbing back with frail handholds from the wreck of her life. If justice depended on smashing her deeper into soul-wrecking misery, justice would have to wait.

Sharpener's race came third on the card. Not the biggest event of the day, but he was the favourite. With real *joie de vivre* he sailed around Newbury's long oval, and I thought, I could do with the muscle power I'd lost in the car park.

Sharpener won and I was exhausted, which was ridiculous. Harold, beaming, watched me fumble feebly with the girth buckles. The horse, stamping around, almost knocked me over.

"You only went two miles," Harold said. "What's the matter?"

I got the buckles undone and pulled off the saddle, and began to feel a trickle of strength flow again through my arms. I grinned and said, "Nothing. It was a good race."

I went in, and while I was sitting on the bench waiting to get my strength back, I decided what to do about Elgin Yaxley.

I HAD GROWN a habit, over the past two weeks, of taking with me in the car the photographs I might be needing. Lance Kinship's reprints were there, and so were the four concerning Yaxley. I went out and fetched them.

Then I found Yaxley and persuaded him to come with me to the entrance gate, away from the crowd. "You won't want anyone hearing," I said.

"What the devil *is* this?" he said crossly.

"A message from George Millace," I replied.

His sharp features grew rigid, and his small moustache bristled. Complacency vanished in a furious concentration of fear.

"I have some photographs you might like to see," I said, and handed him the cardboard envelope.

Yaxley first went pale, then red. He found the whole story there—the café meeting, George's two letters, the note from the farmer, David Parker. The eyes he raised to me were sick and incredulous.

"Any number of copies," I said, "could go off to the insurance company and the police and so on."

He managed a strangled groan.

"There's another way," I said. "George Millace's way."

I'd never seen anyone look at me with total hatred before, and I found it unnerving. But I wanted to find out just what George had extracted from at least one of his victims, and this was my best chance. I said flatly, "I want the same as George Millace."

"No." It was a wail of horror, empty of hope.

"Yes, indeed," I said.

"I can't afford it. Not ten. I haven't got it."

I stared at him. He mistook my silence and gabbled on, finding his voice in a flood of begging, beseeching, cajoling words.

"I've had expenses. It hasn't been easy. Can't you let me alone? George said once and for all . . . and now *you*. . . . Five, then," he said in the face of my continued silence. "Will five do? That's enough. I haven't got any more. I haven't."

I stared once more, and waited.

"All right, then. All *right*." He was shaking with worry and fury. "Seven and a half. It's all I've got, you blood-sucking leech. . . . You're worse than George Millace."

He fumbled in his pockets and brought out a cheque book and pen. Clumsily supporting the cheque book on the photograph envelope, he wrote the date and a sum of money, and signed his name. Then, with shaking fingers, he tore the slip of paper out of the book and stood holding it. "Not Hong Kong again," he said. "I don't like it."

"Anywhere out of Britain." I stretched out my hand for the cheque. He gave it to me, his hand trembling. "Thank you," I said.

"Rot in hell."

He turned and stumbled away, utterly in pieces. Serves him right, I thought callously. Let him suffer. It wouldn't be for long. I would tear up his cheque after I'd seen how much he'd paid George.

I meant to, but I didn't. When I looked at that cheque, something like a huge burst of sunlight happened in my head, a bright expanding delight of awe and comprehension. Elgin Yaxley's cheque for seven thousand five hundred pounds was made out not to me, or to Bearer, or even to the Estate of George Millace, but to the Injured Jockeys Fund.

I walked around, trying to find the ex-jockey who was now administrator of the fund, and tracked him down in the box of one of the television companies. There was a crowd in there, but I beckoned to him and gave him the cheque.

"Phew," he said, looking at it. "And likewise *wow*."

"Is this the first time Elgin Yaxley's been so generous?"

"No, it isn't. He gave us ten thousand a few months ago, just before he went abroad."

"Have you had any other huge cheques like this?" I inquired.

"Not many."

"Would Ivor den Relgan be a generous supporter?"

"Well, yes, he gave us a thousand at the beginning of the season. Sometime in September." I thanked him and returned to the changing room to get ready for the last race.

In the parade ring, Harold said sharply, "You're looking pleased with yourself."

"Just with life in general."

I *was* pleased with myself. I'd ridden a winner. I'd almost certainly found Amanda. I'd discovered a lot more about George Millace. Sundry kicks and punches on the debit side, but who cared? Overall, not a bad day.

"This hurdler," Harold said severely, "needs a good clear view of what he's got to jump. Understand? Go to the front. I don't want him being jostled in the pack early on."

I nodded. There were twenty-three runners, almost the maximum allowed in this type of race. Harold's hurdler was already sweating with nervous excitement.

"Jockeys, please mount," came the announcement, and when the tapes went up, off we set. Over the first, leading as ordered; good jump, no trouble. Over the second, just out in front; passable jump, no trouble. Over the third—disastrous jump, all four feet seeming to tangle in the hurdle.

We crashed to the turf together, and twenty-two horses came over the hurdle after us.

Horses do their best to avoid a man or a horse on the ground, but with so many, so close, it would have been a miracle if I hadn't been touched. One could never tell how many galloping hoofs connected—it always happened too fast. It felt like being rolled like a rag doll under a stampede. I lay painfully on my side looking at a close bunch of grass, and thought it was a damn silly way to be earning one's living. I almost laughed. I knew I'd thought that before.

A lot of first-aid hands arrived to help me up. Nothing seemed to be broken. I rode back to the stands in an ambulance, demonstrated to the doctor that I was basically in one piece, and winced my slow way into ordinary clothes.

Harold met me outside. "I'll drive you home," he said. "One of the stable lads will take your car."

I didn't argue. We drove in companionable silence towards Lambourn. I felt beaten up and shivery, but it would pass.

Harold stopped at my front door. "Sure you're all right?"

"I'll have a hot bath, get the stiffness out. Thanks."

It was already getting dark. I went around drawing the curtains, switching on lights. Bath, food, aspirin, bed, I thought.

Mrs. Jackson, the woman next door, came to tell me the rating officer had called the day before.

"Hope I did right, letting him in. Mind you, I went right around with him. He didn't touch a thing. Just counted the rooms."

"I'm sure it's fine, Mrs. Jackson."

"And your telephone," she said, as she departed. "It's been

ringing and ringing. I can hear it through the wall, you know."

I called Jeremy Folk. He was out. Would I care to leave a message? Tell him I found what we were looking for, I said.

The instant I put the receiver down the phone rang. I picked it up again and heard a child's breathless voice. "I can tell you where that stable is. Am I the first?"

I regretfully said no. I passed on the same bad news to ten more children within the next two hours. I began asking if they knew how the Colleagues had chanced to buy the stables, and eventually came across a father who did.

"Us and the people who kept the riding school," he said, "were pretty close friends. They wanted to move to Devon and were looking for a buyer for the place, and these fanatics just turned up one day with suitcases full of cash and bought it on the spot."

"How did the fanatics hear of it? Was it advertised?"

"No." He paused, thinking. "Oh, I remember. It was because of one of the children who used to ride the ponies. Sweet little girl. Mandy something. She used to stay with our friends for weeks on end. There was something about her mother being on the point of death, and the religious people looking after her. It was through the mother that they heard the stables were for sale. They were in some ruin of a house at the time, I think, and wanted somewhere better."

"You don't remember the mother's name, I suppose?"

"Sorry, no."

"You've been tremendously helpful," I said. "I'll send your Peter the ten pounds, even though he wasn't first."

After I'd bathed and eaten, I unplugged the telephone from the kitchen and carried it up to the sitting room, where for another hour it interrupted the television. By nine o'clock I was thoroughly tired of it. I took the phone off the hook and went down to the bathroom for a scratch around the teeth; and the front doorbell rang.

Cursing, I went to see who it was. Opened the door.

Ivor den Relgan stood there, holding a gun.

"Back up," he said. "I'm coming in."

I was certain he was going to kill me. For the second time that day I looked into the eyes of hatred, and the power behind den Relgan's paled Elgin Yaxley's into petulance. He jerked the lethal black weapon towards me. I took two or three steps backwards. He stepped through my door and kicked it shut. "You're going to pay," he said, "for what you've done to me. George Millace was bad. You're worse."

I wasn't sure I was actually going to be able to speak, but I did. My voice sounded squeaky. "Did you burn his house?"

His eyes flickered. "Burgled, ransacked, burned," he said furiously. "And you had the stuff all the time."

I had destroyed his power base. Left him metaphorically as naked as on his St. Tropez balcony. George must have used the threat of those photographs to stop den Relgan from angling to be let into the Jockey Club. I'd used them to get him thrown out. He'd had some standing before, in racing men's eyes. Now he had none. Never to be in was one thing. To be in, then out, quite another.

"Get back," he said. "Back there. Go on."

He made a small waving movement with the pistol.

"My neighbours'll hear the shot," I said hopelessly.

He sneered and didn't answer. "Back past that door."

It was the door to the darkroom, solidly shut. No sanctuary there, no lock. I'd have to run, I thought wildly. Had at least to try. I was already turning on the ball of one foot when the kitchen door was smashed open. I thought for a split second that somehow den Relgan had missed me and the bullet had splintered some glass, but then I realized he hadn't fired. People had come into the house from the back. Two burly young men with nylon-stocking masks over their faces.

"Take him," den Relgan said, pointing with his gun.

A flash of Marie's battered face lit in my memory, and her voice: "Like bulls ... stockings over their faces ..."

They were rushing, banging against each other, eager, infinitely destructive. I tried to fight them. God Almighty, I thought. Not three times in one day.

I couldn't see, couldn't yell, could hardly breathe. They wore roughened leather gloves, which tore my skin. The punches to my face knocked me silly. When I fell on the ground they used their boots. I drifted off altogether.

When I came back, it was quiet. I was lying on the white-tiled floor with my cheek in a pool of blood. In a dim way I wondered whose blood it was. Tried to open my eyes. Something wrong with the eyelids. Oh well, I thought, I'm alive.

Did he shoot me? I tried to move, to find out. Bad mistake. My whole body went into a sort of rigid spasm. Locked tight in a monstrous cramp from head to foot, I gasped with the crushing, unexpected agony of it. Worse than fractures, worse than dislocations, worse than anything. . . .

Screaming nerves, I thought. Saying too much was injured, nothing must move. I daresay it was the body's best line of defence, but I could hardly bear it. I won't move, I promised. Just . . . let me go. It lasted too long, and went away slowly.

I lay in relief in a flaccid heap. Too weak to do anything but pray that the cramp wouldn't come back. Too shattered to think much at all. Except of den Relgan returning to finish the job. Thoughts that I was dying. Bleeding to death.

Ages passed.

The lights in the cottage were on, but the heating was off. I grew very cold. Cold stopped things bleeding I thought. I lay quiet for hours, waiting. Sore but alive. Increasingly certain of staying alive. Increasingly certain I'd been lucky. If nothing fatal had ruptured, I could deal with the rest.

I lay on the floor all night and well into the morning. There were splits in my mouth, and I could feel with my tongue the jagged edges of broken teeth. Eventually I lifted my head off the floor. No spasm.

I was lying in the back part of the hall, not far from the bottom of the stairs. The telephone was upstairs. I might get some help if I could get to it. Gingerly I tried to sit up. Couldn't do it. I moved a few inches across the floor, still half lying down. Got as far as the stairs. Hip on the hall floor, shoulder and head on the stairs. In another hour I'd got my haunch up three steps and was again rigid with cramp. Far enough, I thought numbly. I stayed still. For ages.

112

Somebody rang the front doorbell. Whoever it was, I didn't want him. Whoever it was would make me move. I no longer wanted help. Peace would mend me, given time.

The bell rang again. Then someone came in through the broken back door. Don't let it be den Relgan, I thought.

It wasn't, of course. It was Jeremy Folk, standing still with shock when he reached the hall. "*Philip*," he said blankly. He leaned over me. "Your face . . . What happened? Did you have a fall at the races?"

"Yeah," I said. "A fall."

"But the blood. You've got blood everywhere."

"Leave it," I said. "It's dry."

"Can you see? Your eyes are—" He stopped.

"I can see out of one of them," I said. "It's enough."

He wanted to move me, wash the blood off. I wanted to stay just where I was without having to argue. I persuaded him to leave me alone only by confessing to the cramps.

His horror intensified. "I'll get you a doctor."

"I'm all right. Just don't *do* anything."

"Well . . ." He gave in. "Do you want tea or anything?"

"Find some champagne. Kitchen cupboard."

He looked as if he thought I was mad, but champagne was the best tonic I knew for practically all ills. I heard the cork pop and presently he returned with two tumblers. He put mine on the stair by my left hand, near my head. Oh well, I thought. Might as well find out. The cramps would have to stop sometime. I stiffly moved the arm and fastened the hand around the chunky glass, and I got at least three reasonable gulps before everything seized up. But the spasm wasn't so long or so bad that time.

The front doorbell rang yet again, and Jeremy went to answer it. The visitor was Clare, come because I'd invited her.

She knelt beside me and said, "This isn't a fall. Someone's done this to you, haven't they?"

"Have some champagne," I said.

"Yes. All right." She stood up and argued on my behalf with Jeremy. "If he wants to lie on the stairs, let him. He's been injured countless times. He knows what's best."

114

My God, I thought. A girl who understands. Incredible.

She and Jeremy sat in the kitchen, introducing themselves and drinking my booze, and on the stairs things improved. I drank some more champagne. Felt that some time soon I'd sit up.

The front doorbell rang. An epidemic.

Clare went to answer it. I was sure she intended to keep whoever it was at bay, but she found it impossible. The girl who was there wasn't going to be stopped at the door. She pushed past Clare, and I heard her heels clicking speedily towards me. "I must see," she said frantically. "I must know if he's alive."

I knew her voice. I didn't need to see the distraught, beautiful face staring at me, frozen with shock. Dana den Relgan.

Chapter 9

"Oh no!" she said.

"I am," I said in my swollen way, "alive."

"He said it would be a toss-up. He didn't seem to care if they'd killed you. . . . Didn't seem to realize what it would mean."

Clare demanded, "Do you mean you know who did this?"

Dana gave her a distracted look. "I have to talk to him. Alone. Do you mind?"

"But he's—" Clare stopped. "We'll be in the kitchen, Philip."

Dana perched beside me on the stairs. I regarded her through the slit of my vision, seeing her frantic anxiety and not knowing its cause. The gold-flecked hair fell softly forward, almost touching me. The silk of her blouse brushed my hand. The voice was soft . . . and beseeching.

"Please," she said. "*Please*. . . ."

"Please, what?" Even in trouble she had a powerful attraction. I found myself wanting to help her, if I could.

"Please give me what I wrote for George Millace."

I lay without answering. She misread my inaction, which was born of ignorance, and rushed into impassioned begging.

"I know you're thinking, how can I ask you for the slightest favour when Ivor's done this to you? But please, I beg of you, give it back."

115

"Is den Relgan your father?" I said.

"No." A whisper, a sigh. "We have . . . a relationship. Please, please, give me the cigarettes."

The what? I had no idea what she meant. Trying to make my slow tongue lucid, I said, "Tell me about your relationship with den Relgan, and with Lord White."

"If I tell you, will you give it to me? Please, will you?"

She took my silence to mean that at least she could hope. She scurried into explanations, all of them self-excusing, a distinct fiavour of "poor little me, I've been used, it's not my fault".

"I've been with him two years. . . . Not married. . . . Last summer he came up with a brilliant idea. So pleased with himself. If I'd cooperate, he'd see I didn't suffer. I mean, financially." A neat euphemism for hefty bribe.

"He said there was a man at the races wanting to flirt. He said, would I pretend to be his daughter and see if I could get the man to flirt with *me*? Ivor said this man had a reputation like snow, and he wanted to play a joke on him."

"So you did," I said.

She nodded. "He was a sweetie. John White. It was easy. I mean, I liked him. I just smiled and he, well, it was true, he was on the lookout for a pretty girl. And there I was."

Poor Lord White, I thought. Hooked because of his nostalgia for youth.

"Ivor wanted to use John, of course. I didn't see that much harm in it. Everything was going fine until Ivor and I went to St. Tropez for a week. Then that beastly photographer wrote to Ivor saying lay off Lord White, or else he'd show him those pictures of Ivor and me. Ivor was livid."

"Does he know you're here?"

"No!" She looked horrified. "He hates drugs. It's all we have rows about. George Millace made me write that list, said he'd show the pictures to John if I didn't. I *hated* George Millace. But you'll give it back to me, won't you? Please, you must see it would ruin me. I'll pay you if you'll give it to me."

Crunch time, I thought. "What do you expect me to give you?"

"The packet of cigarettes, of course. With the writing on it."

"Yes. Why did you write on a cigarette packet?"

"George Millace said write the list and I said I wouldn't whatever he did, and he said write it then with this red felt-tip pen on the cellophane wrapper of this cigarette packet. He said no one would take seriously a scrawl on cellophane wrapping paper." She stopped suddenly and said with awakening suspicion, "You have got it, haven't you? George Millace gave it to you with the pictures, didn't he?"

"What did you write?"

"You haven't got it! You haven't and I've told you . . . all for nothing." She stood up abruptly, beauty vanishing in fury. "You bastard. Ivor should have killed you." She whisked down the hall and slammed out of the front door.

Clare and Jeremy came out of the kitchen.

"What did she want?" Clare said.

"Something I haven't got."

They began asking what was happening, but I said, "Tell you tomorrow," and they went back to the kitchen and left me alone.

I still ached all over, incessantly, but movement was becoming possible. Movement soon, I thought, would be imperative. I needed increasingly to go to the bathroom. I sat up on the stairs, my back against the wall. Not so bad. No spasms. I could stand up, if I tried.

Clare and Jeremy appeared inquiringly, and I used their offered hands to pull myself upright. Tottery, but upright. Jeremy helped me across the hall to the bathroom, said something about washing the blood off the floor, and left me.

I hung on to a towel rail in the bathroom and looked at my face in the mirror. Unrecognizable. Hair spiky with blood. One eye lost in puffy folds, one showing a slit. Purple mouth. Two chipped front teeth. Give it a week, I thought, sighing. I ran some warm water into the washbasin, sponged off some of the dried blood, and gingerly patted the washed parts dry with a tissue. Leave the rest, I thought.

There was a heavy crash somewhere out in the hall.

I pulled open the bathroom door to find Clare coming from the kitchen. "You're all right?" she said. "You didn't fall?"

"No. Must be Jeremy."

Unhurriedly, we went towards the front of the house to see what he'd dropped, and found Jeremy himself face down on the floor, half in and half out of the darkroom. The bowl of water he'd been carrying was spilled all around him, and there was a strong smell of bad eggs. A smell I knew. Dear God, I thought, and it was a prayer, not a blasphemy. I caught Clare around the waist and dragged her to the front door. Opened it. Pushed her outside. "Stay outside," I said. "It's gas."

I took a deep lungful of the dark wintry night air and turned back. Felt so feeble, so desperate. Bent over Jeremy, grabbed his wrists, and dragged him over the white tiles, feeling the deadly tremors in my weak arms and legs. Out of the darkroom, through the hall, to the front door. Not more than ten feet. My lungs were bursting for air.

Clare took one of Jeremy's arms and between us we dragged him outside. I shut the door, then knelt on the cold road, retching and gasping and feeling utterly useless. Clare was already banging on the house next door.

She returned with the schoolmaster who lived there. "Breathe into him," I said.

"Right." He knelt down beside Jeremy, turned him over, and began mouth-to-mouth resuscitation, knowing the drill. Clare ran back into the schoolmaster's house to call the ambulance.

Jeremy didn't stir. Dear God, I thought, let him live. The gas in my darkroom had been meant for me, not for him. Must have been in there, waiting for me, all the hours I'd spent lying outside in the hall. I thought incoherently, Jeremy, *don't die*. It's my fault. I should have burned George Millace's rubbish . . . not used it . . . not brought us so near to death.

People came out from all the cottages, bringing blankets, looking shocked. The schoolmaster went on with his task, though I saw from his face that he thought it was useless.

Don't die.

Clare felt Jeremy's pulse. "A flutter," she said.

The schoolmaster took heart.

The ambulance arrived, and a police car and Harold and a

doctor. Expert hands took over from the schoolmaster and pumped air in and out of Jeremy's lungs. Jeremy himself lay like a log while he was lifted onto a stretcher and loaded into the ambulance. He had a pulse. That was all they would say. They shut the doors on him, and drove him to the hospital at Swindon. *Don't die*, I prayed. It's my fault.

A fire engine arrived with men in breathing apparatus. They went around to the back of the cottage carrying equipment with dials, and eventually came out through my front door. They told the police that there should be no investigation inside the cottage until the toxic level was within limits.

"What gas is it?" one of the policemen asked them.

"Hydrogen sulphide. Lethal. Paralyses the breathing. There's some source in there still generating gas."

The policeman turned to me. "What is it?" he said.

I shook my head. "I don't know."

He asked about my face.

"Fell in a horse race," I replied.

The whole circus moved up the road to Harold's house, and events became jumbled. Harold got through to Jeremy's father. A police inspector came, asking questions. I told him I didn't know how hydrogen sulphide had got into my darkroom. I didn't know why anyone would want to put gas in my darkroom. I'd tell him, I thought, if Jeremy died. Otherwise not.

The inspector said he didn't believe me. How had I known so quickly that there was gas? he asked. My reaction had been instantaneous, Clare had said. Why was that?

"Because of the smell. Sodium sulphide used to be used in photographic studios. But I didn't have any."

"Is it a gas?" the inspector asked, puzzled.

"No. Comes in crystals. Very poisonous."

"But you knew it *was* a gas."

"Because I breathed it. It felt wrong. You can make hydrogen sulphide gas using sodium sulphide, but I don't know how." Truthfully I didn't.

Now, sir, he said, about your injuries. Are you sure, sir, that these were the result of a fall in a horse race? Because they looked to him, he had to say, more like the result of a severe human attack.

A fall, I said.

The inspector shrugged. When he'd gone, Harold said, "Hope you know what you're doing. Your face was OK when I left you, wasn't it?"

"Tell you one day," I said, mumbling.

Harold's wife gave Clare and me comfort and food and eventually beds. And Jeremy at midnight was still alive.

In the morning Harold came into the little room where I sat in bed, still aching all over. My young lady, he said, had gone off to London to work. The police wanted to see me. And Jeremy was still unconscious.

The whole day continued wretchedly. The police went into my cottage, and the inspector came to Harold's house to tell me the results. "There's a water filter on the tap in your darkroom," he said. "What do you use it for?"

"All water for photographs," I said, "has to be clean."

Some of the worst swelling around my eyes and mouth was subsiding and I could see better, talk better, which was some relief.

"Your water filter," the inspector said, "is a hydrogen sulphide generator."

"It can't be. I use it all the time. It's only a water softener. It couldn't possibly make gas."

He gave me a long considering stare. Then he went away. He returned with a box and a young man in jeans and a sweater.

"Now, sir," the inspector said to me with the studied politeness of the suspicious copper. "Is this your water filter?" He opened the box. One Durst filter. Screwed onto its top was the short rubber attachment that was normally pushed onto the tap.

"It looks like it," I said.

The inspector gestured to the young man, who put on a pair of plastic gloves and picked up the filter. It was a black plastic globe about the size of a grapefruit, with clear sections top and bottom. He unscrewed it around the middle.

"Inside here," he said, "there's usually just a filter cartridge. But inside this particular object there are two containers, one above the other. They're both empty now, but the lower one contained sodium sulphide crystals, and the upper one contained sulphuric acid. There must have been some kind of membrane holding the contents of the two containers apart. But when the tap was turned on, the water pressure broke or dissolved the membrane, and the two chemicals mixed. Sulphuric acid and sodium sulphide, propelled by water. A highly effective sulphide generator."

There was a long, depressing silence.

"So you can see, sir," the inspector said, "it couldn't in any way have been an accident."

"No," I said dully. "But I truthfully don't know who could have put such a thing there. They would have to have known what sort of filter I had, wouldn't they?"

Another silence. They seemed to be waiting for me to tell them who, but I didn't know. It couldn't have been den Relgan. Why should he bother with such a device when one or two more kicks would have finished me? It couldn't have been Elgin Yaxley; he hadn't had time. It couldn't have been any of the other people George Millace had written his letters to. Two of them were old history. One was still current, but I'd done nothing about it, and hadn't told the man concerned that the letters existed.

All of which left one most uncomfortable explanation: that somebody thought I had something I didn't have. Someone who knew I'd inherited George Millace's blackmailing package and that I'd used some of it, and who wanted to stop me from using any more of it. George Millace had definitely had more in that box than I'd inherited. I didn't have, for instance, the cigarette packet on which Dana den Relgan had written her drugs list. And I didn't have . . . What else?

"Well, sir," the inspector said.

"No one's been into my cottage since I was using the darkroom on Wednesday. Only my neighbour, and the rating officer—" I stopped, and they pounced.

"What rating officer?"

Ask Mrs. Jackson, I said, and they replied yes, they would.

"She told me he didn't touch anything."

"But he could have seen the type and size of the filter," the younger man said. "Then he could have come back. It would take about thirty seconds, I'd reckon, to take the filter cartridge out and put the packets of chemicals in. Pretty neat job."

They went away after a while, taking the filter.

I rang the hospital. No change.

Later in the afternoon Harold's wife drove me to the hospital. I didn't see Jeremy. I saw his parents. They were too upset to be angry. Not my fault, they said, though I thought they would change their minds later.

I returned to Harold's house and stayed there until the inspector telephoned to say I could go back to my cottage, but not into the darkroom—the police had sealed it.

I wandered around my home, feeling neckdeep in guilt. There were signs everywhere that the police had searched, but they hadn't found the few prints I still had of George Millace's letters, which were locked in the car. And they had left the box with the blank-looking negatives undisturbed in the kitchen.

I opened it. It still contained the one puzzle I hadn't solved: the black lightproof envelope containing what looked like a piece of clear plastic and two sheets of typing paper.

Perhaps, I thought, it's because I have these that the gas trap was set. But *what* did I have? I needed to find out fast, before whoever it was had another go at killing me, and succeeded.

I begged a bed again from Harold's wife, and in the morning had a call from Jeremy's father. "We want you to know he's awake," he informed me. "He's still on the respirator. But they say he'll recover."

"Thank you," I said, and felt an incredible sense of release. I had been freed. Let off a life sentence of guilt.

Later Clare telephoned.

"He's all right. He's awake," I said.

"I'm so glad."

"Can I ask you a favour? Can I dump myself on Samantha for a night or two?"

122

"As in the old days? Why not? We'll expect you for supper."

Harold wanted to know when I thought I'd be fit to race. I said I would get some physiotherapy and be ready by Saturday.

I still felt distinctly unfit, but I did some packing, collected George's rubbish box from the kitchen, and set off for Samantha's house, where I got a horrified reception when she and Clare saw my black bruises, cuts, and three days' growth of beard.

"But it's *worse*," Clare said, staring closely.

"Looks worse, feels better."

Samantha was troubled. "Clare said someone had punched you, but I never thought . . ."

"Look," I said, "I can go somewhere else."

"Don't be silly. Sit down. Supper's ready."

They didn't talk much or seem to expect me to. With the coffee Samantha said calmly, "If you're tired, go to bed."

They both followed me upstairs. I walked automatically, without thinking, into the small bedroom next to the bathroom.

They laughed. "We wondered if you would remember," Samantha said.

The next morning Clare went to work and I dozed in the swinging basket chair in the kitchen. Thursday I took myself to the Clinic for Injuries for massage and exercises. Between sessions I telephoned four photographers, and found no one who knew how to raise pictures from plastic or typing paper.

When I got back to Samantha's, the winter sun was low, and Samantha was cleaning the French windows in the kitchen. "Sorry if it's cold in here, but I won't be long," she said.

I sat in the basket chair and watched her. She finished the outsides of the doors and came in, pulling them after her, fastening the bolts. A plastic bottle stood on a table beside her. AJAX, it said in big letters.

I frowned at it, trying to remember. Where had I heard the word Ajax? I stood up and walked over for a closer look. WITH AMMONIA, it said in smaller letters. I shook the bottle. Liquid.

"Why would a man ask his wife to buy him some Ajax?" I asked.

"What a question," Samantha said. "I've no idea."

"Nor did she have," I said. "She didn't know why."

Samantha took the bottle out of my hands and continued with her task. I went back to the basket chair and swung in it gently.

She cast me a sideways glance, smiling. "Who punched you?" Her voice sounded casual, but it was a serious question. If I didn't tell her, she wouldn't persist, but we would have gone as far as we ever would in our relationship.

What did I want, I thought, in that house that now increasingly felt like home? I had never wanted a family. No suffocating emotional ties. If I nested comfortably into the lives lived in that house, wouldn't I feel impelled in a short while to break out with freedom-seeking wings?

Samantha read my silence as I expected, and her manner altered subtly, not to one of unfriendliness, but to a cutoff of intimacy. Before she'd finished the window, I'd become her guest, not her . . . what? Her son, brother . . . part of her. She gave me a bright smile and put the kettle on for tea.

Clare returned from work, and she, too, though not asking, was waiting.

So, halfway through supper, I found myself quite naturally telling them about George Millace. "You see," I said at the end, "that it isn't finished yet. There's no going back or wishing I hadn't started. I asked to come here for a few days because I didn't feel safe in the cottage. And I'm not going back there to live until I know who tried to kill me."

Clare said, "You might never know."

"Don't say that," Samantha said. "If he doesn't find out . . ."

I finished it for her. "I'll have no defence."

We passed the rest of the evening more in thoughtfulness than depression, and the news from Swindon hospital was good. Jeremy was still on the respirator, but his lungs were significantly improved.

I SPENT A LONG TIME in the bathroom on Friday morning scraping off beard. The cuts had all healed, and the swelling had gone, although there were still the chipped teeth.

"You need caps," Samantha said, and insisted on telephoning

124

her dentist. And caps I had, late that afternoon. Temporaries, until porcelain jobs could be made.

After another exercise session in the clinic I drove north to Essex, to visit a firm that manufactured photographic printing paper.

I went in person instead of telephoning, because I thought they would find it less easy to say they had no information if I was actually there; and so it proved.

They did not, the front office said politely, know of any photographic materials that looked like plastic or typing paper. Had I brought the specimen with me?

No. I had not. Could I see someone else?

Difficult, they said.

I showed no signs of leaving. Perhaps Mr. Christopher could help me, they suggested at length, if he wasn't too busy.

Mr. Christopher turned out to be about nineteen, with an antisocial haircut and a chronic cough. He listened, however, very attentively.

"This paper and this plastic have got no emulsion on them?"

"No, I don't think so."

He shrugged. "There you are, then. You got no pictures."

I sucked at the still broken teeth and asked what seemed a nonsensical question. "Why would a photographer want ammonia?"

"Well, he wouldn't. Not for photographs. No straight ammonia in any developer or bleach or fix that I know of."

"Would anyone here know?" I asked.

He gave me a pitying stare, implying that if he didn't know, no one else would.

"You could ask," I said persuasively. "Because if there's a process which does use ammonia, you'd like to know, wouldn't you?"

"Yeah. I reckon I would."

He nodded briskly at me and vanished, returning a few minutes later with an elderly man in glasses.

"Ammonia," he said, "is used in the photographic sections of engineering industries. It develops what the public calls blueprints.

More accurately, it's the diazo process. What's the matter with your face?"

"Lost an argument. Please, the diazo process. What is it?"

"You get a line drawing from a designer. Say of a component in a machine. The industry will need several copies of the master drawing. So they make blueprints of it."

"Please, go on."

"From the beginning?" he said. "The master drawing, which is on translucent paper, is pressed tightly by glass over a sheet of diazo paper. Diazo paper is white on the back, and yellow or greenish on the side covered with ammonia-sensitive dye. Bright light is shone onto the master drawing for a measured length of time. This light bleaches out all the dye on the diazo paper except for the parts under the lines on the master drawing. The diazo paper is then developed in hot ammonia fumes, and the lines of dye emerge, turning dark. Is that what you want?"

"Indeed it is. Does diazo paper look like typing paper?"

"Certainly it can if it's cut down to that size."

"And how about a piece of clear-looking plastic?"

"Sounds like diazo film," he said calmly. "You don't need hot ammonia fumes for developing that. Any form of cold liquid ammonia will do. But be careful. If your piece of film looks clear, it means that most of the yellow-looking dye has already been bleached out. If there is a drawing on it, you must be careful not to expose it to too much more light."

"How much more light is too much?" I said anxiously.

"In sunlight, you'd have lost any trace of dye for ever in thirty seconds. In normal room light, five to ten minutes."

"It's in a lightproof envelope."

"Then you might be lucky."

"And the sheets of paper? They look white on both sides."

"The same applies," he said. "They've been exposed to light. You might have a drawing there, or you might not."

"How do I make hot ammonia fumes, to find out?"

"Simple," he said. "Put some ammonia in a saucepan and heat it. Hold the paper over the top and steam it."

"Would you," I said, "like some champagne for lunch?"

I RETURNED to Samantha's house at about six o'clock with a cheap saucepan and two bottles of Ajax. I felt dead tired. Samantha had gone out, and Clare was working at the kitchen table. She scrutinized me and suggested a large brandy. "And pour me some, too, would you?" she added.

I sat at the table with her for a while, sipping my drink. Her dark head was bent over the book she was working on.

"Would you live with me?" I said.

She looked up, abstracted, faintly frowning. "Is that an academic question or a positive invitation?"

"Invitation."

"I couldn't live in Lambourn," she said. "Too far to commute. You couldn't live here. Too far from the horses."

"Somewhere in between."

She looked at me wonderingly. "Well . . ." She took refuge with sips from her glass. I waited for what seemed an age. "I think," she said finally, "why not give it a try?"

I smiled with intense satisfaction.

"Don't look so smug." She bent her head down again but didn't read. "It's no good. How can I work? Let's get supper."

Cooking frozen fish fillets took ages, because she was trying to do it with my arms around her waist and my chin in her hair. I didn't taste the food when we ate it. I felt extraordinarily light-headed. I hadn't deeply hoped she would say yes, and still less had I expected the incredible sense of adventure I felt since she had. To have someone to care about no longer seemed a burden to be avoided, but a positive privilege.

After supper, while she tried again to finish her work, I fetched the black lightproof envelope from George Millace's rubbish box. I borrowed a flat glass dish from a cupboard. Put the plastic film from the envelope into the dish. Poured liquid Ajax over it. Held my breath.

Almost instantly dark, brownish red lines became visible. I sloshed the liquid across the plastic surface, knowing that all of the remaining dye had to be covered with ammonia before the light bleached it away.

It was no engineering drawing, but handwriting. As more and

more developed, I read the revealed words. They had to be what Dana den Relgan had written on the cigarette packet: heroin, cocaine, marijuana. Quantities, dates, prices paid, suppliers. No wonder she had wanted it back.

Clare looked up from her work. "What have you found?"

"What that Dana girl was wanting."

She looked into the dish, reading. "That's pretty damning. But how did it turn up like this?"

"Crafty George Millace. He got her to write on cellophane wrapping with a red felt-tip pen. She felt safer that way, because cigarette wrapping is so fragile, so destructible. But all George wanted was solid lines on transparent material, to make a diazo print. And he got it."

I explained what I'd learned in Essex. "With the list recorded, it didn't matter if the wrapping came to pieces. And the list was safely hidden from angry burglars, like everything else."

"He was an extraordinary man."

I nodded. "Extraordinary. Though, mind you, he didn't mean anyone else to have to solve his puzzles."

"What about all your photographs?" she said in sudden alarm. "All the ones in the filing cabinet. Suppose . . ."

"Calm down. The butcher down the road has all the negatives and transparencies in his freezer room."

"Maybe all photographers," she said, "are obsessed."

It wasn't until much later that I realized I hadn't disputed her classification. I hadn't even thought, I'm a jockey.

She went to wash her hair. I drained the Ajax out of the dish into the saucepan and opened the French windows while it heated, so as not to become asphyxiated. Then I held the sheets of what looked like typing paper over the simmering Ajax, and watched George's words come alive, as if they'd been written in secret ink. Together the sheets constituted one handwritten letter. He must have written it on some transparent material—a plastic bag, tracing paper, a piece of glass, anything. He had then put his letter over diazo paper and exposed it to light, and immediately stored the exposed paper in the lightproof envelope.

And then what? Had he sent his transparent original? Had he

typed a copy? One thing was certain. In some form or other he had dispatched his letter. I knew the results of its arrival.

And I could guess who wanted me dead.

Chapter 10

Harold found me on the veranda at Sandown. "You at least look better. Have you passed the doctor?"

I nodded. "He signed my card." By the doctor's standards, a jockey who took a week off because he'd been kicked was acting self-indulgently.

"Victor's here," Harold said.

"Did you tell him?"

"I did. He says he's coming to see his horses work on the Downs on Monday. He'll talk to you then."

"How about today? Is the horse running straight?"

"Victor hasn't said anything."

"Because if I'm riding it, I'm riding it straight. Whatever he says."

"You've got bloody aggressive all of a sudden."

"Just saving you money. Don't back me to lose, like you did on Daylight."

He said he wouldn't. He also said there was no point in holding the Sunday briefing if I was talking to Victor on Monday. . . . I wondered, after Monday, would there be any need for a briefing?

As I walked towards the parade ring I saw Bart Underfield lecturing a reporter on the subject of unusual nutrients. "It's rubbish giving horses beer and eggs. I never do it."

The reporter refrained from saying—or perhaps he didn't know—that the trainers addicted to eggs and beer were on the whole more successful than Bart.

Bart's face, when he saw me, changed from bossy know-it-all to tight-lipped spite. He took two decisive steps forward to stand in my path, but when he'd stopped me he didn't speak.

"Do you want something, Bart?" Likely he couldn't find words intense enough to convey his hatred.

"You wait," he said with bitter quiet. "I'll get you." If he'd had a dagger and privacy, I wouldn't have turned my back on him, as I did, to walk away.

Victor Briggs was waiting in the parade ring. A heavy, brooding figure—unsmiling, untalkative, gloomy. When I touched my cap to him politely, there was only an expressionless stare.

Coral Key was an oddity among Victor Briggs's horses, a six-year-old novice chaser brought out of the hunting field when he had begun to show promise. Great horses in the past had started that way, and Coral Key, too, had the feel of good things to come. There was no way that I was going to mess up his early career. In my mind, and very likely in my attitude, I was daring Victor Briggs to say he didn't want him to try to win.

Briggs said nothing at all. He simply watched me.

Harold bustled about as if movement itself could dispel the atmosphere existing between his owner and his jockey; and I mounted and rode out to the course feeling as if I'd been in a strong field of undischarged electricity. A spark, an explosion, might lie ahead. Harold had sensed it.

I lined up at the start. Good ground underfoot. Seven other runners, none brilliant. Coral Key should have a good chance. I settled my goggles over my eyes and gathered the reins.

"Come in now, jockeys," the starter said. The horses advanced towards the tapes in a slow line. Thirteen fences, two miles. Important, I thought, to get him to jump well. It was what I was best at.

There were two fences at the start, then the uphill stretch past the stands, then the top bend, then the downhill fence where I'd stepped off Daylight. No problems on Coral Key. He cleared all of them. Then the sweep around to seven fences in quick succession. I lost one length getting Coral Key set right for the first one, but by the seventh I'd stolen ten. Still it was too soon for satisfaction. Around the long bottom curve Coral Key lay second, taking a breather. Three fences to go. Between the last two I caught up with the leader. We jumped the last fence alongside and raced up the hill towards home, stretching, flying. I did everything I could.

The other horse won by two lengths.

In the unsaddling enclosure, Harold said a shade apprehensively, "He ran well," and patted Coral Key. Victor Briggs said nothing. I pulled the saddle off. There was no other way I could think of that I could have won the race. The other horse had been stronger and faster. I hadn't felt weak. I hadn't thrown anything away in jumping mistakes. I just hadn't won. I needed a strong hand for talking to Victor Briggs; and I didn't have it.

I won the other chase, the one that didn't matter much except to the owners, four businessmen. "Bloody good show," they said. Victor Briggs watched from ten paces away, balefully staring.

Clare, who had come to the races with me, said later, "I suppose the wrong one won?"

"Yeah."

I looked at the trim dark coat, the long polished boots, at the large grey eyes and the friendly mouth. Incredible, I thought, to have someone like Clare waiting for me outside the changing room. Like a fire in a cold house. "Would you mind," I said, "if we made a detour for me to call on my grandmother?"

THE OLD WOMAN was markedly worse. No longer propped upright, she sagged back on the pillows. Even her eyes seemed to be losing the struggle, with none of their usual aggressiveness.

"Did you bring her?" she asked. Still no salutation, no preliminaries. Her hatred for me remained immutable.

"No," I said. "I didn't bring her. She's lost."

She gave a feeble cough, the thin chest jerking. Her eyelids closed for a few seconds and opened again. A weak hand twitched at the sheet.

"Leave your money to James," I said.

She shook her head.

"Leave some to charity, then. Medical research?"

"Hasn't done me much good, has it?"

"Well," I said slowly, "how about a religious order?"

"You must be mad. I hate religion. Cause of trouble. Cause of wars. Wouldn't give them a penny."

I sat down, unbidden, in the armchair.

Amanda was lost within her religion. Indoctrinated, cared for,

131

perhaps loved; and fourteen formative years couldn't be undone. Wrenching her out forcibly would inflict incalculable psychological damage. For her own sake one would have to leave her in peace, however strange that peace might seem. If one day she sought change of her own accord, so much the better. Meanwhile, she just had to be provided for.

"Can I do anything for you?" I asked. "Can I fetch anything? Is there anything you want?"

My grandmother sneered. "Don't think you can soft-soap me into leaving any money to you."

"I'd give water to a dying cat. Even if it spat in my face."

Her mouth opened and stiffened with affront. "How dare you?"

"How dare you think I'd shift a speck of dust for your money?"

The mouth closed into a thin line. Then she said, "Go away."

"I will, but I want to suggest something else. In case Amanda ever turns up, why don't you set up a trust for her? Tie up the capital tight with masses of trustees. Make it so that no one who was perhaps after her fortune could get hold of it. Make it impossible for anyone but Amanda herself to benefit, with an income paid out only at the direction of the trustees. Leave it to her with strings like steel hawsers."

She lay quiet. I waited. I had waited all my life for something other than malevolence from my grandmother.

"Go away," she said.

"Very well." I stood up and walked to the door.

"Send me some roses," my grandmother said.

Clare and I found a flower shop still open. All they had were fifteen small pink buds on very long thin stems. We drove back to the nursing home and gave them to a nurse to deliver, with a card enclosed saying I'd get some better ones next week.

"She doesn't deserve it," Clare said.

"Poor old woman."

NEXT AFTERNOON we went to see Jeremy. He was lying in a high bed with a mass of breathing equipment to one side, but breathing for himself. He looked thin and pale, yet the eyes were as intelligent as ever.

I tried to apologize for what he'd suffered. He wouldn't have it. "I was there because I wanted to be," he said. He gave me an inspection. "Your face looks OK. How do you heal so fast?"

"Always do."

He gave a weak laugh. "Funny life you lead. Always healing."

"How long will you be in here?"

"Three or four days. Once there's no danger the nerves will pack up again, I can go. There's nothing else wrong."

We didn't stay very long because talking clearly tired him, but just before we went he said, "You know, that gas was so quick, I'd no time to do anything. It was like breathing a brick wall."

Into a short reflective silence, Clare said, "No one would have lived if they'd been there alone."

After we left, she said, "You didn't tell Jeremy about Amanda."

"Plenty of time."

"He came down last Sunday because he'd got your message that you'd found her. He told me while we were in the kitchen. He said your telephone was out of order, so he came."

"I'd taken it off the hook."

"Odd how things happen."

I drove her to the train, and went on to Lambourn. When I got to my cottage it seemed strangely unfamiliar, no longer the embracing refuge a home should be. I saw for the first time the bareness, the emotional chill which had been so apparent to Jeremy on his first visit. It no longer seemed to fit me. The maturing change had gone too far.

In the morning I spread out on the kitchen table a variety of photographs of different people, and then I asked my neighbour Mrs. Jackson to come in and look at them.

"What am I looking for, Mr. Nore?" she asked.

"Anyone you've seen before."

Obligingly she studied them carefully one by one, and stopped without hesitation at a certain face. "How extraordinary!" she exclaimed. "That's the rating officer. The one I let in here. Ever so sarcastic the police were about that, but you don't *expect* people to say they're rating officers if they aren't."

"You're sure he's the one?"

"Positive. He had that same hat on, and all."

"Then would you write on the back of the photo for me, Mrs. Jackson?" I gave her a felt-tip pen and dictated the words, saying that this man had called at the house of Philip Nore posing as a rating officer on Friday, November 27. "Now sign your name, Mrs. Jackson. And would you mind repeating the message on the back of this other photograph?"

With concentration she did so. "Are you giving these to the police?" she asked. "Will they come back again with their questions?"

"I shouldn't think so," I said.

VICTOR BRIGGS had come in his Mercedes, but he went up to the Downs with Harold in the Land-Rover. I rode up on a horse. The morning's workout got done to everyone's satisfaction, and we all returned to the stable the way we had come.

When I rode into the yard, Victor Briggs was standing by his car, waiting. "Get in the car," he said. No waster of words, ever. He stood there in his usual clothes, gloved as always against the chilly wind darkening the day. If I could see auras, I thought, his would be black.

I sat in the front, and he slid in behind the wheel and drove back out to the Downs. He stopped on a wide piece of grass from where one could see half of Berkshire. He switched off the engine, leaned back in his seat, and said, "Well?"

"Do you know what I'm going to say?" I asked.

"I hear things. I heard that den Relgan set his goons on you."

I looked at him with interest. "Where did you hear that?"

He made a small tight movement of his mouth. "Gambling club."

"Did you hear any reasons?"

He produced the twitch that went for a smothered smile. "I heard that you got den Relgan chucked out of the Jockey Club a great deal faster than he got in."

"Did you hear how?"

He said with faint regret, "No. Just that you'd done it. The goons were talking. Stupid boneheads. Den Relgan's heading

134

for trouble, using them. They never keep their mouths shut."

"They beat up George Millace's wife. Did you hear that, too?"

After a pause he nodded, but offered no comment. A secretive, solid, slow-moving man, with a tap into a world I knew little of. Gambling clubs, hired bullyboys, underworld gossip.

"The goons said they left you for dead," he said. "One of them was scared. Said they'd gone too far with the boots."

There was another pause, then I said, "George Millace sent you a letter."

He seemed almost to relax, breathing out in a long sigh. He'd been waiting to know for sure, I thought.

"How long have you had it?" he said.

"Three weeks."

"You can't use it. You'd be in trouble yourself."

"How did you know I'd got it?"

He said slowly, "I heard you had George Millace's files."

"Ah. Nice anonymous word, files. How did you hear that?"

He thought it over, and then said grudgingly, "Ivor. And Dana. Separately. Ivor was too angry to be discreet. He said you were fifty times worse than George Millace. And Dana, another night, said, did I know you had copies of some blackmailing letters George Millace had sent, and were using them? She asked if I could help her get hers back. I said I couldn't."

"When you talked to them, was it in gambling clubs?"

"It was."

"Are they your gambling clubs?"

He said after a pause, "I have two partners. The clientele in general don't know I'm a proprietor. I move around. I play. I listen. Does that answer your question?"

I nodded. "Yes, thank you. Are those goons yours?"

"I employ them as bouncers. Not to smash up women and jockeys."

"A little moonlighting, was it? On the side?"

He didn't answer directly. "I have been expecting," he said, "that you would demand something from me if you had that letter."

I thought of the letter, which I knew word for word.

Dear Victor Briggs,

I am sure you will be interested to know that I have the following information. You did on five separate occasions during the past months conspire with a bookmaker to defraud the betting public by arranging that your odds-on favourites should not win their races.

I hold a signed affidavit from the bookmaker in question. As you see, all five of these horses were ridden by Philip Nore, who certainly knew what he was doing.

I could send this affidavit to the Jockey Club. I will telephone you soon, however, with an alternative suggestion.

The letter had been sent more than three years earlier. For three years Victor Briggs had run his horses straight. When George Millace died, Victor had gone back to the old game only to find that his vulnerable jockey was no longer reliable.

"I didn't mean to tell you I had the letter," I said.

"Why not? You wanted to ride to win. You could have used it to make me agree."

"I wanted to make you run the horses straight for their own sakes."

He gave me another long, uninformative stare. "I'll tell you," he said finally. "Yesterday I added up all the prize money I'd won since Daylight's race at Sandown. All those seconds and thirds, as well as Sharpener's wins. And it turned out I made more money in the past month with your riding straight than I did with you stepping off Daylight."

He paused, waiting for a reaction, but I simply stared back. "I've seen," he went on, "that you weren't going to ride any more crooked races. You're older. Stronger. If you go on riding for me, I won't ask you to lose a race again. Is that enough? Is that what you want to hear?"

I looked out across the windy landscape. "Yes."

After a bit he said, "George Millace didn't demand money."

"A donation to the Injured Jockeys?"

"You know the lot, don't you?"

"I've learned," I said. "George wasn't interested in extorting money for himself. He extorted"—I searched for the word—

136

"frustration. He enjoyed making people cringe. He did it to everybody in a mild way. To people he could catch out doing wrong, he did it with gusto. He had alternative suggestions for everyone. Disclosure, or do what George wanted. And what George wanted was to stop Ivor den Relgan's power play. To stop Dana taking drugs. To stop other people doing other things."

"To stop me," Victor said, with a hint of dry humour, "from being disqualified. You're right, of course. When George Millace telephoned, he said all I had to do was behave myself. Those were his words. 'As long as you behave, Victor,' he told me, 'nothing will happen.' He called me Victor, as if I were a little pet dog. 'If I suspect anything, Victor,' he said, 'I'll follow Philip Nore around with my motorized telephotos until I catch him, and then, Victor, you'll both be finished.' "

"And was that all? For ever?"

"Besides suggesting that I give a thousand pounds to the Injured Jockeys Fund, he used to wink at me at the races."

I laughed.

"Yes, very funny. Is that the lot?"

"Not really. There's something you could do for me in future. Hearing things, as you do. It's about Dana's drugs."

"Stupid girl. She won't listen."

"She will soon. She's still saveable. And in addition to her . . ."
I told him what I wanted.

He listened acutely. When I'd finished I got the twitch of a smile. "Beside you," he said, "George Millace was a beginner."

VICTOR DROVE OFF, and I walked back to Lambourn over the Downs.

An odd man, I thought. I'd learned more about him in half an hour than I had in seven years, and still knew next to nothing. He had given me what I'd wanted, though. Given it freely—my job without strings for as long as I liked, and help in another matter just as important. It hadn't all been, I thought, because of my having that letter.

Out on the bare hills, I thought of the way things had happened during the past few weeks. Because of Jeremy's persistence I'd looked for Amanda, and because of looking for Amanda I had now met a grandmother, an uncle, a sister. I knew something at least of my father. I had a feeling of origin that I hadn't had before. I had people, like everyone else had. Not necessarily loving or praiseworthy, but *there*. I hadn't wanted them, but now that I had them they sat quietly in the mind like foundation stones.

I reached the point on the hill from where I could see down to my cottage. I could see most of Lambourn, stretched out. Could see Harold's house and the yard. Could see the whole row of cottages, with mine in the centre. I'd belonged in that village, breathed its intrigues for seven years. Been happy, miserable, normal. It was what I'd called home. But now I was leaving that place, in mind and spirit as well as body. I would live somewhere else, with Clare. I would be a photographer. The future lay inside me, waiting, accepted.

I would race until the end of the season. Six more months. Then I'd hang up my boots. I still had the appetite, still had the physique. Better to go, I supposed, before both of them crumbled.

I went on down the hill without any regrets.

Chapter 11

Clare arrived on the train two days later to sort out the photographs she wanted from the filing cabinet. Now that she was my agent, she said, she'd be rustling up business.

I had no races that day. I'd arranged to fetch Jeremy from the hospital and take him home, and to have Clare come with me. I'd also telephoned Lance Kinship to say I had his reprints ready and would he like me to drop them off, as I was practically going past his house. "That would be fine," he said.

"And I'd like to ask you something," I said.

"Oh? All right. Anything you like."

Jeremy looked a great deal better, without the grey clammy skin of Sunday. We helped him into the back of my car and tucked a rug around him, which he plucked off indignantly, saying he was no aged invalid but a perfectly viable solicitor. "And incidentally," he said. "My uncle came down here yesterday. Bad news, I'm afraid. Old Mrs. Nore died on Monday night."

"Oh no," I said.

"Well, you knew. Only a matter of time. My uncle brought two letters for me to give to you. They're in my suitcase somewhere."

I fished them out, and we sat in the hospital car park while I read them. The first was a copy of her will.

Jeremy said, "My uncle told me he was called out urgently to the nursing home on Monday morning. Your grandmother wanted to make her will. Stubborn old woman to the last."

I unfolded the typewritten sheets. "I, Lavinia Nore, being of sound mind, do hereby revoke all previous wills."

There was a good deal of legal guff and some complicated pension arrangements for an old cook and gardener, and then two final paragraphs.

> Half the residue of my estate to my son, James Nore.
> Half the residue of my estate to my grandson, Philip Nore, to be his absolutely, with no strings or steel hawsers attached.

The old witch had defeated me.

I opened the other envelope and found a scribbled note.

> I think you did find Amanda, and didn't tell me because it would have given me no pleasure. Is she a nun?
> You can do what you like with my money. If it makes you vomit, as you once said, then VOMIT.
> Or give it to my genes.
> Rotten roses.

I handed the will and the note to Clare and Jeremy, who read them in silence. "What will you do?" Clare said.

"I don't know. See that Amanda never starves, I suppose. Apart from that . . ."

"Enjoy it," Jeremy said. "The old woman loved you."

I wondered if it was true. Love or hate. Perhaps she'd felt both at once when she'd made that will.

I started the car and we drove towards St. Albans, detouring to Lance Kinship's house. "Sorry," I said. "Won't take long."

They didn't seem to mind. The house was typical Kinship—fake Georgian, grandiose front, pillared gateway. I took the photographs from the boot of the car, and rang the doorbell.

Lance opened the door, dressed in white jeans, espadrilles, and a red-and-white striped T-shirt. Film director gear. All he needed was the megaphone.

"Come inside," he said. "I'll pay you for these."

"OK. Can't be long though, with my friends waiting."

He looked towards my car, where Clare's and Jeremy's interested faces showed in the windows, and then led the way into a large sitting room with expanses of parquet and too much black-lacquered furniture. Chrome-and-glass tables. Art deco lamps.

I gave him the packet of pictures. "You'd better make sure they're all right."

He shrugged. "Why shouldn't they be?" All the same, he opened the envelope and pulled out the top picture. It showed him looking straight at the camera in his country-gent clothes—glasses, trilby hat, air of bossy authority.

"Turn it over," I said.

He did so. And read what Mrs. Jackson had written. "This is the rating officer." The change in him from one instant to the next was like one person leaving and another entering the same skin. I saw the Lance Kinship I'd only suspected existed. Not the faintly ridiculous poseur, but the tangled psychotic who would do anything to preserve the outward show. It was in his very inadequacy, I supposed, that the true danger lay. In his estrangement from reality and in his theatrical turn of mind, which allowed him to see murder as a solution to problems.

"Before you say anything," I said, "you'd better look at the other things in that envelope."

He let the picture of the great film producer fall to the floor. Angrily he sorted out the regular reprints and let them drop too. Then he found the reproduction of Dana den Relgan's drug list. He stood holding it in visible horror. "She swore you didn't know what she was talking about," he said hoarsely.

140

"She was talking about the list of drugs you supplied her with. Complete with dates and prices. As you see, your name appears on it liberally."

"I'll kill you," he said.

"No, you won't. You've missed your chance. If the gas had killed me, you would have been all right, but it didn't."

He didn't say, "What gas?" He said, "It all went wrong. But I thought it wouldn't matter."

"You thought it wouldn't matter because you heard from Dana den Relgan that I didn't have the list. And if I didn't have the list, I didn't have George Millace's letter, and there was no more need to kill me. Well, it's too late to do it now, because there are extra prints of those things all over the place. Another copy of that picture of you, identified by Mrs. Jackson. Bank, solicitors, several friends—all have instructions to take everything to the police if an accidental death befalls me."

The implication of what I was saying slowly sank in. He looked from my face to the drug list and back again several times. "George Millace's letter?"

I nodded. George's letter, handwritten, read:

Dear Lance Kinship,

I have received from Dana den Relgan a most interesting list of drugs supplied to her by you over the past few months. It appears to be well known in certain circles that in return for being invited to places, you will, so to speak, pay for your pleasure with gifts of marijuana, heroin, and cocaine.

I could of course place Dana den Relgan's candid list before the proper authorities. I will telephone you shortly, however, with an alternative suggestion.

"I burned it when I got it," Lance Kinship said dully.

"Did George telephone and tell you to stop supplying drugs and donate to the Injured Jockeys Fund?" His mouth opened and snapped shut viciously. "Or did he tell you his terms when he came here?"

"I'm telling you nothing."

"Did you put something into his whisky?"

"Prove it!" he said, with sick triumph.

One couldn't, of course. George had been cremated, with his blood test only for alcohol, not for tranquillizers, which in sufficient quantity would have put a driver to sleep.

George, I thought regretfully, had stepped on one victim too many. Had stepped on what he'd considered a worm and never recognized the cobra. He must have enjoyed seeing Lance Kinship's fury. Must have driven off laughing. Poor George.

"Didn't you think," I said, "that perhaps George had left a copy of his letter behind him?" From his expression, he hadn't.

"When did you begin thinking I might have your letter?"

He said furiously, "I heard in the clubs that you had some letters. That you'd got den Relgan sacked from the Jockey Club. Did you think that once I knew I'd wait for you to get to *me?*"

"Unfortunately," I said slowly, "I have now come around to you. And like George Millace I'm not asking for money. You see, it's your bad luck that my mother died from addiction to heroin."

He said wildly, "But I didn't know your mother."

"No, of course not. There's no question of your ever having supplied her yourself. It's just that I have a certain long-standing prejudice against drug pushers."

He took a compulsive step towards me. I thought of the brisk karate kick he had delivered to den Relgan at Kempton and wondered if in his rope-soled sandals on parquet he could be as effective. He looked incongruous, not dangerous. A man not young, hair thinning on top, wearing glasses. But a man who would kill if pushed too far.

He never reached me to deliver the blow. He stepped on the fallen photographs, slid, and went down hard on one knee. The indignity of it seemed to break up whatever remained of his confidence, for when he looked up at me, I saw not hatred, but fear.

I said, "I don't want what George did. I don't ask you to stop peddling drugs. I want you to tell me who supplies you with heroin. You must have a regular supplier."

He staggered to his feet, aghast. "I *can't*. It's impossible. I'd be dead."

"He's the one I want," I said mildly. The source, I thought. One source supplying several pushers. The drug business was like some monstrous tentacle creature—cut off one tentacle and another grew in its place. The war against drugs would never be won, but it had to be fought, if only for the sake of silly girls who were sniffing their way to perdition. For the sake of Dana. For Caroline, my lost butterfly mother.

"It will be between the two of us," I said. "No one will ever know you told me, unless you yourself talk, as den Relgan did in the gambling clubs. If you don't tell me, I will tell the police investigating an attempted murder in my house that my neighbour positively identifies you as having posed as a rating officer. This isn't enough to get you charged, but it could certainly get you *investigated*, for access to chemicals, and so on."

He looked sick.

"Then I'll see that it gets known all over the place that people would be unwise to ask you to their parties, despite your little goodies, because they might at any time be raided. I know where you go, to whose houses. I've been told." And would be kept posted in future, I might have added, thanks to Victor Briggs. "A word in the ear of the drugs squad and you'd be the least welcome guest in Britain."

"I . . . I . . ."

"Yes, I know," I said. "Going to these places is what makes your life worth living. I don't ask you not to go or to stop your gifts. Just to tell me where the stuff comes from. What you tell me will go to the drugs squad. But don't worry. By such a roundabout route that no one will every connect it with you. Your present supplier, however, may very likely be put out of business. If that happens, you might have to look around for another. In a year or so, I might ask you for *his* name."

His face was sweating and full of disbelief. "You mean it will go on and on?"

"You killed George Millace. You tried to kill me. You very nearly killed my friend. You think I don't want retribution?"

He stared.

"I ask very little," I said. "A few words written down now and then. Don't worry, you'll be safe, I promise you. Neither my name nor yours will ever be mentioned." Secretive, close-mouthed Victor would see to that.

"You . . . you're *sure?*"

"Sure." I produced a small notebook and a felt-tip pen. "Write now," I said. "Your supplier."

He sat down by one of his glass-and-chrome coffee tables and, looking totally dazed, wrote a name and an address. One tentacle under the axe.

"And sign it," I said casually.

He began to protest, but then wrote, Lance Kinship. And underneath, with a flourish, Film Director.

"That's great," I said without emphasis. I picked up the notebook and stored away in a pocket the small document that would make him sweat next year and the next and the next. The document that I would photograph and keep safe.

He didn't stand up when I left him. Just sat in his T-shirt and white trousers, stunned into silence. He'd recover his bumptiousness, I thought. Phonies always do.

I WENT OUT to where Clare and Jeremy were still waiting, and paused briefly in the winter air before getting into the car.

Most people's lives, I thought, weren't a matter of world affairs, but of the problems right beside them. Not concerned with saving mankind, but with creating local order, in small checks and balances. Neither my life nor George Millace's would ever sway the fate of nations, but our actions could change the lives of individuals; and they had done that.

The dislike I'd felt for George alive was irrelevant to the intimacy I felt with him dead. I knew his mind, his intentions, his beliefs. I'd solved his puzzles. I'd fired his guns.

I got into the car.

"Everything all right?" Clare asked.

"Yes," I said.

144

Dick Francis

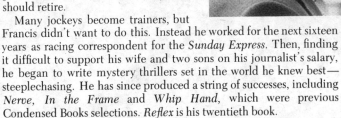

"I wouldn't have been a novelist if I hadn't been a jockey," says Dick Francis. The son and grandson of jockeys, Francis learned to ride when he was five and turned professional in 1948, when he was twenty-eight. Throughout his career he was always ranked among the top half dozen steeplechase jockeys in England, riding for the Queen Mother among others. He suffered his share of broken collarbones, skull fractures, and dislocated shoulders ("You don't count broken ribs"), and in 1957 a particularly bad fall convinced him he should retire.

Many jockeys become trainers, but Francis didn't want to do this. Instead he worked for the next sixteen years as racing correspondent for the *Sunday Express*. Then, finding it difficult to support his wife and two sons on his journalist's salary, he began to write mystery thrillers set in the world he knew best— steeplechasing. He has since produced a string of successes, including *Nerve*, *In the Frame* and *Whip Hand*, which were previous Condensed Books selections. *Reflex* is his twentieth book.

Dick Francis averages a novel a year, starting a new one each January and finishing it by the end of April. He and his wife Mary then spend the rest of the year researching his next book: going to races two or three days a week when they are at home, and travelling all over the world. Mary spent several months studying photography for *Reflex* and is now an accomplished photographer. "She works out a lot of the crimes for the novels. My colleagues say she has a crooked mind," Francis jokes.

Once he has the outline for his next novel firmly in his mind, Dick Francis writes every morning—"after a ride at the stables to get the wind in my eyes."

ONE CHILD

A condensation of the book by

TOREY L. HAYDEN

Illustrated by Ben Wohlberg
Published by Souvenir Press

They were affectionately referred to as the "garbage class": eight physically and emotionally handicapped children who didn't fit in anywhere else. Add to that a cramped classroom and untrained assistants—it was more than Torey Hayden, a gifted young teacher, had bargained for.

Then, to complicate matters, six-year-old Sheila, disruptive, frightened and angry, is placed in the class halfway through the year. Sheila is a tiny child who has known only pain and cruelty in her short life. Abandoned by her mother, brought up in a migrant's shack by her shiftless father, she seems to have everything stacked against her.

How, Torey wondered, could she ever reach this tormented soul?

Using patience and determination, she finds a way, and finds too that hidden within hostile little Sheila is an extraordinarily special child. This moving story of a devoted teacher and her deeply troubled pupil is an unforgettable testimony to the healing power of love.

CHAPTER ONE

I should have known.

The article was a small one, just a few paragraphs stuck under the comics. It told of a six-year-old girl who had abducted a neighborhood child. On that cold November evening, she had taken the three-year-old boy, tied him to a tree in a nearby woodlot and burned him. The boy was currently in a local hospital in critical condition. The girl had been taken into custody.

I read the article in the same casual manner that I read the rest of the newspaper, feeling an offhand what-is-this-world-coming-to revulsion. Then later in the day the story came back to me. I wondered what the police had done with the girl. Could you put a six-year-old in jail? I had visions of the child knocking about in our old, drafty city jail. I thought about it only in a faceless, impersonal manner. But I should have known.

I should have known that no teacher would want a six-year-old with that background. No parent would want a child like that attending school with his or her child. No one would want that kid loose. I should have known she would end up in my program.

I taught what was affectionately referred to in our school district in Iowa as the "garbage class." There were classes for the retarded, classes for the emotionally disturbed, classes for the physically handicapped, classes for the learning disabled—and then there was my class. I had the eight who were left over, the eight that defied classification. I was the last stop before the institution.

The spring before, I had been teaching as a resource person in the same school, supplying help to emotionally disturbed and learning disabled children who attended regular classes for part of the day. I had had a lot of experience working with the severely disturbed, and I liked small children, so I was not surprised when Ed Somers, Director of Special Education in the district, approached me that May and asked if I would be interested in teaching the garbage class in the fall. He knew I liked a challenge, he had said, chuckling self-consciously.

Although I had reservations, I had said yes. I longed for my own classroom again, with my own set of kids. I also wanted to be free of an unintentionally oppressive principal. Mr. Collins was a good-hearted man, but we did not see things in the same way. He objected to my casual dress, to my disorderly classroom, and to my children addressing me by my first name. These were minor issues that had become major sore spots. But I knew that by doing Ed the favor of taking this class, allowances would be made for my jeans and my sloppiness and my familiarity with the kids. So I accepted the job, confident that I could overcome any obstacles it presented.

The first blow came on the first day of school when I saw we were placed in the school's annex which housed only us and the gymnasium. We were totally isolated from the rest of the school. The room was hopelessly crowded, with desks, tables, bookcases, and countless chairs. So out went the teacher's desk, some of the bookshelves, all the extra chairs, and all the students' desks. Moreover, the room was long and narrow, with only one window at the far end. Originally designed as a testing and counseling space, it was wood-paneled and carpeted. I would have gladly traded that grandeur for a room that did not need lights on all day, or for a linoleum floor that was impervious to spills and stains.

Iowa state law required that I have a full-time aide because I was carrying the maximum load of severely disturbed children.

150

I had been hoping for one of the competent aides I had worked with the year before, but no, I received a newly hired one. In our community, which had a state hospital, a state prison and a huge migrant workers' camp, there was a staggering welfare list. Consequently, unskilled jobs were usually reserved for the unemployed listed with Social Services. Although I did not consider my aide position an unskilled one, Welfare did, and the first day of school I was confronted with a tall, gangly Mexican-American. Anton was twenty-nine, had never graduated from high school, and had never worked with children. But you see, he explained, you had to take the job they gave you or you lost benefits. And he had a wife and two small sons to support. He added that if this job worked out, it would be the first time he had ever stayed north all winter instead of following the other migrant workers back to southern California.

So then we were two. A short time later I acquired Whitney, a fourteen-year-old junior high school student who devoted her two hours of study hall each day to working with my class. Thus armed, I met the children.

The first to arrive that morning in August had been Peter. Eight years old and a husky black with a scraggly Afro, Peter's robust body belied the deteriorating neurological condition that caused severe seizures and increasingly violent behavior. He burst into the room in anger, cursing and shouting. He hated school, he hated me, he hated this class. He wasn't going to stay here and I couldn't make him.

Next was Tyler. She slunk in behind her mother, her dark curly head down. Tyler was also eight and had already tried to kill herself twice. The second time, the drain cleaner she had swallowed had eaten away part of her esophagus. Now her throat bore an artificial tube and numerous red-rimmed surgical scars.

Max and Freddie were both hauled in screaming. Freddie was seven and weighed ninety-four pounds. The fat rolled over the edges of his clothing and squeezed out between his shirt buttons. Once allowed to flop on the floor, he ceased crying, ceased everything, in fact, to lie lifelessly in a heap. One report in his file said that he was autistic. One stated that he was profoundly retarded.

151

Peter

Tyler

Freddie

One admitted not knowing. Max, a big, blond six-year-old, carried the label of infantile autism. He also had echolalia, which meant that he repeated what others said over and over. Now he cried and squawked and twirled around the room flapping his hands. His mother looked at me wearily, her relief at being free of him for a few hours showing plainly in her eyes.

I had known Sarah, age seven, for three years. I had worked with her when she was in pre-school. A victim of physical and sexual abuse, she was an angry, defiant child. Sarah had been electively mute throughout the previous year when she had been in a special first-grade class at another school. She had refused to talk to anyone except her mother and sister. We smiled upon seeing each other, both of us thankful for a familiar face.

Next to come were William and Guillermo, both nine. Guillermo was from one of the countless Mexican-American migrant families that came to work in the fields each year. He was an angry boy but not uncontrollable. Unfortunately, he was also blind. I was informed that classes for the blind and partially sighted were not equipped to deal with his aggressive behavior. Well, I thought, that made us even. I was not equipped to deal with his blindness.

William was a lanky, pasty-faced boy haunted by fears of water and darkness and vacuum cleaners and the dust under his bed. To protect himself, he engaged in elaborate rituals, chanting little spells under his breath.

A smartly dressed, middle-aged woman carried in the last child, a beautiful, doll-like little girl. She looked like a model, her soft blond hair carefully styled, her crisp dress spotless. Susannah Joy was six, and already the doctors had told her parents that she

152

would never be normal; she was a childhood schizophrenic. She hallucinated, and spent most of her days weeping and rocking back and forth. She spoke only rarely, and then seldom meaningfully. Yet her mother's eyes implored me to perform the magic necessary to make her fairy child normal. My heart ached. I knew the pain and agony that lay ahead for her parents as they began to see that none of us would ever have the type of magic Susannah Joy needed.

Guillermo

Max

Sarah

So these were the eight leftovers, the eight that had defied classification. With Whitney and Anton, we were eleven in all. When I first surveyed this motley bunch of children and my equally motley staff, I felt a wave of despair. How would we ever be a class? How could I ever get them to learn mathematics or all the other miracles that needed accomplishing in nine months? Three were not toilet trained, two others had accidents. Three could not talk, one wouldn't. Two would not shut up. One could not see. It was more of a challenge than I had bargained for.

William

Susannah Joy

But we managed. My aide Anton learned to change diapers. Whitney learned to get urine stains out of the carpet. I learned braille. The principal, Mr. Collins, learned not to come over to the annex. Ed Somers learned to hide. And so, gradually, we became a class.

153

By the time Christmas vacation came around, we belonged to each other, and I was beginning to look forward to each new day. Sarah had started to talk regularly again; Max was learning his letters; Tyler was smiling occasionally; Peter didn't fly into rages quite so often; William could pass all the light switches in the hallway to the lunchroom and not say one charm to protect himself; Guillermo was begrudgingly learning braille. And Susannah Joy and Freddie? Well, we were still trying with them.

I had all but forgotten the newspaper article that I had read in late November. But I shouldn't have; I should have known that sooner or later we would be twelve.

ED SOMERS APPEARED in my room the first day after Christmas vacation. His kind face was swathed in that apologetic expression that I knew meant trouble. It was the expression attached to things like not getting a special tutor for Guillermo, or yet another hopeless report from the newest doctor Susannah's parents had found. I believed Ed genuinely wanted things to be different; this made it impossible for me to be angry with him.

"There's going to be a new child in your class," he said.

I stared at him a long moment, not comprehending. I already had the state-allowed maximum. "I have eight kids now, Ed."

"I know, Torey. You'll have to pick one to be transferred. Because this is a special case. We don't have any place to put her. Your class is the only option we have."

"What's so special about this kid?" I asked tentatively.

Ed looked pained. He was a big bear of a man, tall and muscular, but padded with middle-aged softness. What was left of his hair was carefully combed across his shiny dome. But, above all, Ed was gentle.

"This is the girl who burned the little boy in November," he said. "The court took her out of school immediately and made arrangements to send her to the state hospital. But there hasn't been an opening in the children's unit yet. So the kid's been at home ever since and getting into all sorts of trouble. Now the social worker is beginning to ask why we aren't doing anything for her."

"Can't they put her on homebound?" I asked, referring to the

154

practice of sending a teacher into the home when for some reason a child could not attend school. Severely disturbed children were often handled in this manner until appropriate placement could be found.

Ed frowned. "No one will work with her."

"They're scared of a six-year-old?" I asked in surprise.

He shrugged, his silence telling more about this child than words could have. "We have to put her in here, Torey. Just until something opens up at the state hospital. This is the only place equipped to handle her."

"You mean I'm the only one idiotic enough to take her. When is she coming?"

"The eighth."

By that point the children were beginning to arrive, and Ed nodded and left. He knew that I would do it. He knew that, for all my bravado, I was a pushover.

After telling Anton the news, I looked over the children, asking myself who should go. Guillermo was the obvious choice, simply because he was blind and I was least equipped to teach him. But what about Freddie or Susannah Joy? Neither was making much progress. Anyone could lug them around and change their pants. Or maybe Tyler. She hardly ever spoke of killing herself anymore. A resource teacher could probably handle her. But as I looked at each of them I knew in my heart that none would survive the rigors of a less-sheltered class. None of them was ready. Nor was I ready to give them up.

"ED?" I CLUTCHED the receiver in my sweating hand. "I don't want to transfer any of my kids. We're doing so well together."

"Torey, I told you we have to put that girl in there."

I stared morosely at the bulletin board beside the phone, with all its proclamations of events my children would never attend. I was feeling used. "Can I have nine?"

"Will you take nine?"

"It's against the law. Do I get another aide?"

"We'll have to see," Ed replied. "Will you need another desk?"

"What I need is another teacher. Or another room."

"Will you settle for another desk?"

"No. There wasn't room for the first eight. We sit at the tables. Just send me the kid."

CHAPTER TWO

She arrived January eighth. Between the time I had agreed to take her and the morning she came in, I had received no files, learned nothing of her background. All I knew was what I had read in the newspaper a month and a half earlier. But I suppose it did not matter. Nothing could have prepared me for what I got.

Ed Somers brought her, holding tightly to her wrist and dragging her behind him. "This is your new teacher," Ed explained.

We looked at one another. Her name was Sheila. She was six and a half, almost; a tiny little mite of a thing with matted hair, hostile eyes, and a very bad smell. Clad in worn denim overalls and a faded T-shirt, she looked like one of those kids in the Save the Children ads.

"Hi, my name's Torey," I said in my friendliest teacher's voice while reaching for her hand. She did not respond. I ended up taking the limp wrist from Ed. "This is Sarah," I went on, "our welcome person. She'll show you around."

Sarah extended a hand, but Sheila remained impassive, her eyes darting from face to face. "Come on, kid." Sarah grabbed her wrist. But Sheila bristled at the familiarity and yanked her hand away, retreating backward. Then she turned and ran, but fortunately Anton was standing in the doorway and captured her. I dragged her back.

"I'll go now," Ed said, that apologetic look creeping across his face. "I left her cumulative folder in the office for you."

Anton slipped the bolt into place after closing the door behind Ed. I pulled Sheila across the room to my chair and sat her on the floor in front of me. The other children cautiously gathered around us.

We always began the day with "discussion." The children all came from such chaotic and disrupted homes that we needed something to reunite us each morning. I also wanted to stimulate verbal communication. The first thing we did was the pledge of allegiance. One child would lead the pledge, which meant he had to learn it, a valuable process because it presented words in an organized way. Next, I'd start discussion with a topic, which usually explored feelings or provided a roundtable for solving problems, such as what would one do if he saw someone else hurt himself. We made sure that everyone had a chance to participate— even Susannah. Then I let each child have a few moments to tell what had happened to him since the end of the previous school day. The kids had a lot to say, and some days I was hard put to terminate the activity. Afterward, I outlined the day's schedule, and finally we closed discussion with a song. I had a repertoire of action songs that I sang with more gusto than tune, pulling one of the kids through the actions like a puppet. The children loved that, and we always ended laughing.

This morning, after the pledge, I said, "Kids, this is Sheila, and she's going to join our class."

"How come?" Peter asked suspiciously. "You never told us we was getting a new girl."

"Yes, I did, Peter. Remember how we rehearsed ways to show Sheila that we're glad she's with us?"

"Well, I'm not glad. I liked us just the way we was." He placed his hands over his ears to shut me out and began rocking.

"It'll take some getting used to, but we will." I patted Sheila's shoulder and she pulled away. "Who's got a topic?"

No one spoke.

"No one has a topic? Well then, I've got one: what do you suppose it feels like when you're new and don't know anyone, or maybe you want to be part of a group and no one wants you? How's that feel inside?"

"Bad," Guillermo said. "That happened to me once."

"Can you tell us about it?" I asked.

Suddenly Peter leaped to his feet. "She stinks, teacher." He backed away from Sheila. "She stinks terrible, and I don't want her sitting with us. She'll stink me up."

Sheila regarded him blackly but did not speak. She folded herself up into a little lump, her arms wrapped around her knees.

Sarah stood up. "She does, Torey. She smells like pee."

Good manners were certainly not our forte. "How do you sup pose that feels, Peter, to have someone say you stink?" I asked.

"Well, she does," Peter retorted.

"That's not what I asked. I asked how you'd feel."

"It'd hurt my feelings," Tyler volunteered, bouncing up on her knees. Any displays of anger or disagreement frightened Tyler and sent her into rounds of appeasement.

"How about you, Sarah?" I asked. "How would you feel?"

Sarah stared at her fingers. "I wouldn't like it too good."

"No, I don't think any of us would. What might be a better way of handling the problem?"

"You could learn her in private that she stinked," William offered. "Then she wouldn't get embarrassed."

"You could learn her not to," Guillermo added.

"We could all plug our noses," Peter said. He wasn't willing to admit yet that his remarks had been inappropriate.

"Then you couldn't breathe," William said.

"You could too. You could breathe through your mouth."

I laughed. "Everybody, try Peter's suggestion. Peter, you too." All the children except Sheila plugged their noses and breathed through their mouths. I urged her to try too, but she refused to unfold. Soon we were all laughing at the funny faces we made. All of us, except Sheila. Fearing that she saw this as a joke at her expense, I explained that it wasn't, that this was the way we solved our problems, I told her. She ignored me.

"How's this make you feel?" I asked her at last. There was a long silence. The other children became impatient.

"Don't she talk?" Guillermo asked.

"I used to not talk either," Sarah offered. "Back when I was mad, I used to never talk, Sheila. So I know how it feels."

"I think we've put Sheila in the hot seat enough for now," I said. "Let's give her some time to get used to us, okay?"

We went on with the morning discussion and finished with a chorus of "You Are My Sunshine." Freddie clapped gleefully; Guillermo directed with his hands, and I manipulated Tyler like a rag doll. Sheila sat, her face stormy, her little body a solid lump.

158

We dispersed for math activities. Anton began orienting the others while I showed Sheila around the room. Actually, I did not show her. I had to pick her up and carry her from place to place because she would not move. Then when I got her where I wanted her, she refused to look, covering her face with her hands. But I was determined that she become part of us. I showed her her cubby and her coat hook. I introduced her to Charles, the iguana, Benny, the boa constrictor, and Onions, the rabbit, who bit if you bothered him too much. I pointed out the books we read before lunch every day and the pots and pans we cooked with on Wednesday afternoons. I showed her our aquarium and our toys. I chattered as if she were very interested in what I had to say. But if she was, she did not let me know. She remained a deadweight, rigid and tense in my arms. And she stank like an outhouse on a muggy July afternoon.

Finally I deposited Sheila on a chair at the table and set a math paper before her. This evoked her first response. She grabbed the paper, wadded it up and threw it at me. I took another. Again she flung it at me. I knew that I would run out of papers before she would run out of energy. So I took her on my lap, wrapping an arm around her wiry body so she could not get her hands free. I set another math paper down with simple addition problems on it and pulled a tray of blocks toward me.

"Okay, now we do math," I stated. "First problem, two plus one." I showed her two blocks and added a third. "How much is that? Let's count them." She averted her head, straining her stiff body against me. "Can you count, Sheila?" No response. "Come on, I'll help. One, two, three. Two plus one is three." I picked up a pencil. "Here, we'll write it down."

I pried her hand free from her body, uncurled her fingers, then placed the pencil in it. Suddenly those tightly clenched fingers relaxed and the pencil slid to the floor. In the moment it took me to pick it up, she had grabbed two blocks with her free hand and flung them across the room. I clutched her hand, shoved the pencil back into it, and tried to recurl her fingers. But I was just not fast enough. She was skilled at this little bit of guerrilla warfare and the pencil fell again. I gave up.

"Evidently you don't want to do math just yet. Okay, you may sit. We're not going to fight about it." I lugged Sheila over to the corner where I put the children when they became overstimulated and needed to regain control, and sat her on the chair. Then I returned to the other children.

In a few moments I looked up. "Sheila, if you're ready to join us, you may come over."

She sat with her face to the wall and did not move. I let her sit. In a few minutes I reissued the invitation. It was obvious that she was not going to do anything I wanted. I went over and pulled the chair away from the corner and into the middle of the room. If she wanted to sit, she could, but I was not going to let her be isolated.

Our morning routine went as usual. Sheila didn't participate. She got up once to use the bathroom but returned to the chair and drew in upon herself, knees up under her chin, her arms enfolded around them. During recess she sat, only this time on the freezing cement outside. I had never seen such a motionless child. But her eyes followed me everywhere I went. Brooding, angry, bitter eyes that never left my face.

At lunchtime Anton helped the children prepare for their trek from the annex to the cafeteria. I waited until the others had left and went over to Sheila. I looked at her and thought for a brief moment that I saw an emotion other than hate flicker through those eyes. Fear? I sat down opposite her.

"You and I have something to get straight."

She glowered at me, her tiny shoulders humping up under the worn shirt.

"There aren't a lot of rules in this room. Generally there are just two. One is that you can't hurt anybody in here. Not anybody else. Or yourself. The second is that you always try to do your best job. That's the rule I don't think you have straight yet."

She lowered her head slightly but kept her eyes on me.

"You see, one of the things you have to do in here is talk. That's part of your best job. I know it's hard, and the first time is always the hardest. Sometimes it kind of makes you cry. Well, that's okay. But sooner or later you will have to talk, and it'll be a lot better if you do it sooner." I looked at her. "Is that clear to you?"

160

Her face blackened with anger. I was fearful of what might happen if all that hate got loose, but I tried not to let my fear show in my eyes. She was a good reader of eyes.

I had always felt strongly about setting expectations for my kids. Some of my colleagues had been skeptical of my directness, pleading the frailty of the children's egos. I disagreed. While certainly all of them had sad, well-trampled little selves, none of them were frail. The fact that they had survived after what most of them had been through was testimony to their strength. But I did not want to add to the chaos in their lives by leaving them to guess what I expected of them.

So Sheila and I sat in icy silence while she digested this bit of information. After a few moments I rose from my chair and went to collect the math papers from the correction basket.

"You can't make me talk," she said suddenly.

I shuffled through the papers. Three-fourths of being a good teacher is timing.

"I said you can't make me talk. There don't be no way you can do that."

I looked over at her. "No, I can't." I smiled. "But you will. That's part of your job in here."

"I don't like you."

"You don't have to."

"I hate you."

I did not respond. That is one of those statements best left unanswered.

"You can't make me do nothing in here."

"Maybe not." I dropped the papers back into the basket and went over to her. "Shall we go to lunch?" I extended a hand. She did not accept it. For a long moment she studied my face. Some of her anger had dissipated, to be replaced by a less readable emotion. Then, without further urging, she got off the chair and came with me, careful not to touch me.

AFTER ESCORTING SHEILA to the lunchroom, I retired to the office to look at her file. I wanted to know what others had done with this perplexing child. Watching her, I had observed that she was not suffering from the kind of crippling, unexplainable disturbances that Max and Susannah displayed. Instead, she was in surprisingly good control of her behavior, more so than most of the children in my class. Behind those hate-filled eyes I saw a perceptive and intelligent little girl. I wanted to know what had been tried before.

The file was thin. Most of my children had thick folders glutted with the erudite discourses of doctors, therapists, judges and social workers. But it was plain that these people never had to work with the child day in and day out. The papers could not tell a desperate teacher or frightened parent how to help, for each child behaved so unpredictably that one day's experience was the only framework for planning the next. There were no textbooks or university courses specializing in Max or William or Peter.

Sheila's file contained only a family history, test results, and a standard data form from Special Services. I read through the social worker's report on the family. It was filled with lurid details.

Sheila's mother had been only fourteen when, two months after a forced wedding, Sheila was born. The father had been thirty. During most of Sheila's early years her father had been in prison on assault-and-battery charges. After his release, he had spent some time in the state hospital for alcoholism and drug dependency. Sheila had been shifted around among relatives, mostly on her mother's side. Then, two years ago, her mother had abandoned her at the edge of a freeway, where she was found clinging to a chain link fence. Taken to a juvenile center, Sheila, then four, was discovered to have numerous abrasions and healed multiple fractures, apparently the results of abuse. Her small size was attributed to malnutrition.

After abandoning Sheila, her mother had taken a younger son with her, and was now living somewhere in California. A court statement indicated that the judge felt it was best to leave the child in her natural home, and she was released to her father's custody. Currently they lived in a one-room shack in the migrant camp. The house had no heat, no plumbing, and no electricity.

There was a memo on Sheila from the county's consulting psychiatrist with the single statement: chronic maladjustment to

One Child

childhood. I smiled in spite of myself. The only normal reaction to a childhood like Sheila's would be chronic maladjustment.

The test results were no help at all. Beside each test was printed: REFUSED. The summary simply stated that Sheila was untestable.

The Special Services questionnaire had been filled out by the father, and since he had been in prison all those crucial years, nothing was known of Sheila's early developmental history. She had attended three schools, not including this one, all the moves resulting from her uncontrollable behavior. At home she reportedly ate and slept normally; but she wet the bed every night, and she sucked her thumb. She had no friends among the children at the migrant camp; nor did she appear to have any solid relationships with adults. Her father indicated that she was a loner, hostile and unfriendly even to him. She spoke at home only when she was angry. She never cried. I stopped and reread that statement. She never cried? I could not conceive of a six-year-old who did not cry. He must have meant she seldom cried.

I continued reading. Her father saw her as a wayward child and disciplined her frequently by spanking or taking away privileges. I wondered what privileges there were in her life that he could take away. In addition to the burning incident, she had been reprimanded for setting fires in the migrant camp. By six-and-a-half, Sheila had encountered the police three times.

I stared at the file. She was not going to be an easy child to love, because she worked at being unlovable. Nor was she going to be easy to teach. But she was not unreachable. Indeed, Sheila was probably more reachable than Susannah Joy or Freddie, because there was no indication that her functioning was garbled with retardation or neurological impairments. That made the battle ahead seem even harder for me. I knew that the outcome rested solely with us on the outside. When we failed with the Sheilas, we had no labels like autism or brain damage to hide behind. This hostile little girl had already learned that life really wasn't much fun for anybody, and that the best way to avoid further rejection was to make herself as objectionable as possible. Then it would never come as a surprise to find herself unloved.

Anton came into the office as I finished leafing through the file. He sat beside me and quietly read Sheila's reports. Despite a clumsy beginning, Anton and I had become a fully functioning team. He was an adroit worker with these children, and having spent his life in the fields and in migrant camps, Anton knew much more intimately than I the world my kids came from. I had the training and the knowledge, but Anton had the instinct and the wisdom. Certain aspects of their lives I would never understand. I had always lived in warm houses, with freedom from violence and hunger and cockroaches. As an adult I had learned that others lived differently, and that this different way of life, to them, was also normal. I could accept that, but I could not understand it. I believe that anyone claiming that extra measure of understanding lies to himself. Anton compensated for my lack, and together we had managed to build a supportive relationship.

"How did she do at lunch?" I asked.

He nodded without looking up from the papers. "Okay. She eats like she never sees food. She probably doesn't. And so bad on the manners. But she sat with the children and did not fuss."

"Do you know her father out at the camp?"

"No. They live on the other side. The junkies are all there. We never go over."

Whitney came in and leaned over the desk. She was a pretty girl in a nondescript way: tall, slender, with hazel eyes and long, straight, dishwater-blond hair. Although Whitney was an honors student and came from one of the community's most prominent families, she was a painfully shy girl. When she had come in the fall, she had carried out her tasks in silence. The only time she did talk was to put herself down or to apologize for doing everything wrong. Unfortunately, in the beginning, Whitney made every mistake in the book. She dropped half a gallon of freshly mixed green tempera paint on the gym floor. She forgot Freddie in the men's room at the fairgrounds. She left the door to our room ajar one afternoon and Benny, our boa constrictor, escaped. And then she was always crying. If I had not been so desperate for help, I might not have had the patience for her.

But like Anton, Whitney had proved to be worth the trouble.

Because she cared so much about the kids, she was hopelessly devoted to us, coming over on her lunch hour or after school to help me. From home she brought the children her own outgrown toys. And always she had that hungry, pleading look to be appreciated. Whitney very seldom talked about her own life. Despite her affluence, I suspected that she was no better off in some ways than the kids in the class. So I tried to make her feel like a valued part of our team. Because she was.

"Did you get your new girl?" Whitney asked.

"Yes, we did." I mentioned briefly what had transpired during the morning. That was when I heard the screaming.

I knew it was one of my children. I glanced at Anton while Whitney went to look out the door of the office. Just then Tyler came careening in, wailing. She motioned out the door, but her explanation was strangled by her sobs. She turned and ran. All three of us sprinted after her toward the annex door. Normally over the lunch hour, aides were in charge of the children. During the cold months the kids played in their rooms after eating, and the aides patrolled the halls keeping order. I kept telling them that my children could not be left unattended at any time, but they hated supervising my room and avoided it by congregating outside the annex door with an ear cocked for disaster.

We stormed into my classroom and found it in chaos. Sheila stood defiantly on a chair by the aquarium, a goldfish clutched tightly in one fist, a pencil in the other. She had apparently caught several fish one by one and poked their eyes out with the pencil. Seven or eight of them were flopping about, leaving little bloody spots on the floor. Now Sheila stood poised, threateningly, while a lunch aide danced nervously near her, too frightened to attempt to disarm her. Sarah was wailing and Max was flying about the room, flapping his arms wildly and screeching.

"Drop that!" I shouted at Sheila. She glared at me and shook the pencil meaningfully. I had no doubt that she would attack if provoked. Her eyes had the glazed wildness of a threatened animal.

Suddenly a piercing shriek knifed the air. Susannah had a psychotic fear of blood, of any red liquid she thought was blood; it would send her into a frenzy. Now, seeing the fish, she bolted across the room. Anton darted after her, and I took that moment to disarm Sheila, hoping to surprise her. But she was not off her guard. She slammed the pencil into my arm with such vehemence that for a moment it stuck before falling to the floor. My mind was filled with too much confusion to feel any pain. Tyler was still wailing; Guillermo was hiding under the table. Whitney was trying to capture Max and Freddie, who were both circling the room, screaming.

"Torey!" came William's cry. "Peter's having a seizure!" I turned to see Peter collapse. Passing Sheila to Whitney, I ran to help him. Sheila gave Whitney an audible kick in the shins and won her freedom. In seconds she was out the door, Whitney in pursuit. I fell onto the floor beside Peter, who was still writhing in his seizure.

It had all happened within minutes. Everyone had lost the tenuous control we fought so hard to gain. All the children except Peter were crying. Sarah, Tyler, and William wailed on the sidelines, their bodies huddled together against catastrophe. Guillermo sobbed from his retreat under the table. Susannah struggled frantically in Anton's arms. Max and Freddie still flew deliriously around the room. Peter lay incoherent in my arms. After months and months of careful effort, everything had fallen apart.

Mr. Collins and the school secretary appeared in the doorway. In all the years the principal and I had worked together, I had always managed my crazy children without a major slip. But now I had failed. My crazies had gotten loose at last.

When Peter's seizure was finally over, the secretary took him to the nurse's office. Mr. Collins helped round up Freddie and Max, and I dragged poor Guillermo out from under the table and hugged him. What must this have sounded like to someone who could not see? Anton was trying to soothe Susannah Joy. Once we had recaptured some semblance of control, Tyler and Sarah were willing to sit down and comfort each other. Only William continued to sob. And Whitney and Sheila were still gone.

Mr. Collins had the decency not to ask what had happened. I thanked him for his help and asked if he could send Mary to me, a very competent aide who had helped me before. I still had one

child on the loose, I explained, and so I could use an extra adult.

When Mary arrived, I went in search of Sheila. After she bolted, she must have been confused by the maze of doors and hallways connecting us to the main building. Whitney had locked the outside doors and Sheila had been forced to go into the gym. I found Whitney standing in the doorway of the cavernous room and Sheila on the far side.

Tears streamed down Whitney's cheeks as she held her post. My heart ached when I saw her. This was too much to expect of a fourteen-year-old. I should never have put her in this spot.

I gave Whitney a pat on the shoulder, entered the gym, and approached Sheila. Her eyes were wild, her face flushed with terror. I spoke softly, my tone gentle and coaxing, but each time I moved closer, she tore off in another direction.

Pausing, I looked around, my mind racing for ideas. Her eyes mirrored her panic. Reacting now from animal instinct alone, she was more dangerous than she had been back in the classroom. I could not think what to do. My head pulsed. My arm was throbbing. If I boxed her in, she would become more terrified. She had to relax and regain some control of herself, because in this condition she posed a real threat, if not to me, then to herself.

I told Whitney to return to the classroom and closed the gym door. Then I came as close to Sheila as I dared and sat down.

We regarded each other. Frantic terror gleamed in her eyes.

"I'm not going to hurt you, Sheila. I'm just going to wait until you're not so scared anymore, and then we'll go back to class. I'm not angry. And I'm not going to hurt you."

More time passed. I scooted forward on my seat. She stared at me. Tremors had taken over her entire body and I could see her scrawny shoulders shake. But she did not budge.

We did not know each other; there was no reason why she should trust me, and she was not going to. Such a courageous little being to face up to all of us who were so much bigger and stronger, without words or tears.

I inched closer. We had been there at least a half hour. I was within ten feet of her now, and she was beginning to view my approach with suspicion. I stopped moving. Reassuring her that I meant no harm, I talked about things the children liked to do in our room, things she would do with us.

Endless minutes passed. I was getting sore from not moving. Her legs were shaking from standing so long without shifting position. This had become a test of endurance.

We waited. The frenzy was fading from her eyes. Tiredness was taking over. Still we waited.

Then the front of her overalls darkened and a puddle formed around her feet. She looked down at it, taking her eyes from me for the first time. She caught her lower lip in her teeth. When she looked up, the horror of what had just happened showed plainly.

"Accidents happen. You haven't had a chance to go to the bathroom, so it really isn't your fault," I said. "I've got some rags back in the room for when this happens. We can clean it up."

She looked down again and then back at me. I remained silent. "You gonna whip me?" she asked hoarsely.

"No. I don't whip kids. I'll help you clean it up. It can be our secret, because I know it was an accident."

"I didn't mean to." Her brow furrowed.

"I know it."

She looked at her overalls. "My pa, he gonna whip me fierce when he sees I do this."

"Don't worry. It'll be dry by the time school is over."

Rubbing her nose, she seemed uncertain for the first time. I slowly rose to my feet. She took a step backward, and I extended my hand. "Come on, we'll go get something to clean it up."

For a long moment she regarded me. Then she cautiously came toward me. She refused my hand but walked back to the classroom at my side.

Things had quieted in the room. Anton and the children were singing songs. Whitney was holding Susannah, and the aide was rocking Max. The dead fish were all gone. Heads turned, but I motioned to Anton to keep them busy. Sheila accepted the rags and a bucket from me and we went back and cleaned the gym floor without speaking. Then she followed me back to the room.

The remainder of the afternoon was quiet. The children were all subdued, fearful of toppling their frail control again. Sheila folded herself up in the chair she had occupied all morning and sucked her thumb. She did not move, yet she continued to watch us. I went around to cuddle and talk to each of the children.

Finally I came to Sheila. Sitting down on the floor beside her chair, I looked up at her. The toll of the afternoon showed on her face. I made no attempt to touch her. I did not want to spook her by being too intimate, but I did want her to know I cared

"It's been kind of a hard afternoon, hasn't it?" Thumb still in her mouth, she did not respond. "Tomorrow will be better; first days are always hard." I tried to read her eyes, to understand what was going on in her head. The open hostility was gone, momentarily at least. But I could see nothing beyond that. "Are your pants dry enough so you won't get in trouble?"

She stood up, inspecting them closely. The damp outline was barely distinguishable from the other filth. She nodded almost imperceptibly.

"I hope so. Everybody has accidents." I wanted her to know that such problems were acceptable in here.

The thumb rotated in her mouth and she turned away from me to watch Anton, who was conducting the closing exercises. I remained near her until dismissal.

After the children were gone, Anton and I cleaned up the room. Neither of us mentioned what had happened, or said much of anything. This certainly had not been one of our better days. When I got home after work, I washed out my pencil wound and put a Band-Aid on it. Then I lay down on my bed and wept.

Whether or not I wanted to acknowledge it, life in my classroom was a constant battle. Not only with the children but with myself. To cope with these youngsters, I locked up my own emotions, because when I didn't I became too discouraged to function effectively. The method worked, but every once in a while a child came along who could really rock my bulwark; then all the frustrations I had so carefully tried to ignore came tumbling out.

Basically, though, I was a dreamer, and my dream—that things could change—died hard. This time was no exception. My tears were short-lived, and later I settled down with a tuna-fish sandwich to watch television. By the time Chad arrived, I had recovered.

Chad and I had been seeing each other regularly for eighteen months. The typical courting relationship—the endless rounds of dinner, movies, dances—was over and we had drifted into a warm and comfortable alliance. Chad was a junior partner in a law firm and spent most of his time as a court-appointed attorney for the drifters and ne'er-do-wells who found themselves in jail. Consequently, he did not win many cases. We would spend our evenings commiserating good-naturedly over my kids and his clients. We had talked about marriage once or twice, but we were both satisfied with the status quo, and that had been the extent of it.

Chad brought with him a quart of chocolate fudge ice cream, and I told him about Sheila as we fixed sundaes. I had met my match, I stated firmly. The kid was a savage, and I did not think I was the one to civilize her. The sooner the opening at the hospital came up, the better.

Chad sympathized and suggested I call her former teacher. After our ice-cream orgy, when I was feeling a little more mellow about things, I looked for Mrs. Barthuly's number in the telephone book.

"Oh, my gosh," Mrs. Barthuly said when I told her who I was and why I had called. "I thought they had put her away for good."

I explained that there had been no openings yet at the state hospital and asked her what she had done while Sheila was in her class during the first three months of the school year. I could hear her making little clucking sounds.

"I've never seen such a destructive child. Every time I took my eyes off her she destroyed something. Her work, the other children's work, bulletin boards, anything. Once, she took all the other kids' coats and stuffed them down the toilets. Flooded the entire basement." She sighed. "Sheila always tore up her work before you could get a look at it. I tried everything to stop her."

Mrs. Barthuly's voice took on a weary note. She had attempted to show affection to this unlovable child, to include her in special activities, to give her extra attention. Sheila had refused to speak to her. She had refused to be touched, to be helped, to be liked.

Next, Mrs. Barthuly tried controlling her outlandish behavior negatively. She took away privileges, confined her to a time-out

171

corner, and at last ended up sending Sheila to the principal for paddling. Still Sheila continued to terrorize the class. Finally Mrs. Barthuly gave up, and Sheila was allowed to do as she pleased. She spent most of the day wandering around the classroom or paging through magazines. Left entirely alone, she was tolerable, and a semblance of peace settled in the room. Then the incident I had read about in the paper occurred, and she was removed immediately from school in response to fears expressed by other children's parents.

The voice on the other end of the phone was sad and pessimistic. Mrs. Barthuly said that despite everything she had liked Sheila. The child had seemed so vulnerable and still so brave, and the teacher regretted that so little had been done. She wished me luck. Then she hung up.

The news filled me with renewed depression. I did not know what I could do that had not already been tried.

THE NEXT MORNING BEFORE SCHOOL, Anton and I sat down to plan our day. Half an hour before class was to start, the social worker came in dragging Sheila. She explained that the only bus they could get to pick Sheila up at home was the high school bus. Therefore, Sheila would be arriving early each day and would not be able to leave until five o'clock, two hours after class was over. I was horrified. First of all, I did not feel Sheila should be riding with high school kids; indeed, I doubted seriously that she could be trusted on any bus. Second, what was I supposed to do with her for two hours after school?

The social worker explained that the school district would not pay for special transportation when existing buses could be used. Transferring Sheila's limp wrist to me, she turned and left.

I looked down at Sheila and felt all my anxiety from the day before flood over me. Her eyes were guarded, the hostility of yesterday hidden. I smiled weakly. "Good morning, Sheila. I'm glad you're with us again today."

I brought her over to one of the tables and pulled out two chairs. She had come with me without protest. "Listen," I said, as we both sat down. "What happened in here yesterday wasn't very much fun for me, and I don't suppose it was for you either."

Her brow wrinkled in a questioning expression. Then she folded herself up into the chair. She was wearing the same worn denim overalls and T-shirt. Neither had been washed, and she smelled very strong.

"Yesterday," I went on, "I think we may have scared you a little bit, because you didn't know any of us, and it might not have been clear what we expected. So I'm going to tell you. I don't hurt kids in here. Neither does Anton or Whitney or anyone else. You don't have to be frightened of us."

The thumb was in her mouth. She seemed so scared and little that it was difficult for me to remember her as she had been yesterday. The bravado was gone, but her gaze remained unflinching as she watched me.

"Would you like to sit in my lap while I talk to you?"

She shook her head slightly.

"Okay. Well, here's the plan. I want you to sit with us when we do things. One of us will explain what is happening until you get used to it." I told her she did not have to participate just yet if she did not want to, but she did have to join us. There was no choice on that.

"And," I concluded, "sometimes when things get out of control, the place I will have you go is over to the quiet corner." I indicated the chair. "You will sit there until you have things under control again. Is that clear?"

If it was, she did not let me know.

The other children began to arrive, so I patted her on the back and went to greet them. She did not pull away from my touch, but then she did not acknowledge it either.

When morning discussion came, Sheila was still sitting in the chair at the table. I pointed to the floor beside me. "Sheila, over here, please, so we can start discussion."

She did not move. I repeated myself, my stomach tightening in anticipation. Still she remained in the chair. I looked to Anton, who was settling Freddie into place. "Anton, would you help Sheila join us?"

When Anton approached her, Sheila came to life, and bolted off

173

the chair. She made a mad dash for the door, falling hard against it when the latch did not respond.

"Torey, make her stop," Peter said worriedly. The other children were watching Anton as he circled to catch her. She had that trapped-animal stare again and was dashing recklessly about, trying to avoid capture. But the room was small, and soon Anton was able to grab hold of her arm.

For the first time she made a sound. She let loose a scream that startled all of us. Susannah began to cry, but the others sat in wary silence while Anton brought the struggling child over to the group. I pointed to the spot I had indicated earlier. Taking her arm from Anton, I pushed her into a sitting position. She continued to scream, a throaty, tearless yell, but she remained seated.

"Okay," I said with fake brightness. "Who has a topic?"

"I do," said William, straining to be heard over Sheila's screams. "Is she always going to be like this?" His dark eyes were fearful.

So the topic that day was Sheila. The other children were watching me anxiously. I tried to explain that Sheila was adjusting and like the rest of us was having a hard time. She needed our patience and understanding.

Sheila was not entirely ignoring our discussion. Her screams diminished to sporadic squawks and grunts, inserted when there was a gap in our conversation, or when one of us looked at her. Otherwise, she was quiet. I let the children ask questions and I attempted to answer them honestly. All had the sensitivity not to be too critical in front of her. All except Peter. The day before, he had complained of her smell. Now he angrily stated that he wanted this girl out of his room. She was ruining everything. I did not protect Sheila from his comments, because I knew he would say them to her later anyway, and I preferred to be present when he talked.

We discussed alternate ways of dealing with the inconveniences put upon us while Sheila adjusted. Tyler suggested sending her to the quiet corner to save our ears. Sarah opted to get free time whenever Sheila started a ruckus. Guillermo thought we all might take turns keeping her company so she wouldn't get lonely.

In the end, we decided that when Sheila yelled or somehow

disrupted the class, the others were to get busy with their own work. I told them that at the end of the week we would have ice cream if everyone cooperated and helped to earn the treat. I looked at Sheila. "Do you like ice cream?"

She narrowed her eyes.

"I expect you'll want some, won't you?"

Cautiously she nodded.

Sheila was more cooperative about moving to a chair while we had math. But she folded herself up and watched me suspiciously as I went from child to child. The rest of the morning passed uneventfully.

At lunchtime I ate with the children. I did not want a replay of the previous afternoon, and besides, the lunch aides had refused to supervise Sheila until she was more predictable.

I sat next to Sheila, who inched away from me on the cafeteria bench. Anton sat down on the other side of her, and she inched back in my direction. She bolted down her food in minutes, cramming it into her mouth as fast as she could chew. After lunch I escorted the children back to the room and graded papers while they played. Sheila resumed her seat, put her thumb in her mouth, and stared at me.

All afternoon she moved as requested. She appeared considerably subdued from the day before, almost depressed, but I made no attempt to question her. I did not want to force myself upon her. The other children seemed disappointed that nothing had happened, and Peter asked if we would still have ice cream if Sheila never misbehaved again. With a grin I assured him that if we went all the way to Friday with no problems, there would certainly be ice cream.

The other children put on their snowsuits and prepared to go home. When they had left, I sat down near Sheila. These two hours were normally my preparation time for the next day, but I thought that today I might use them to get better acquainted with Sheila. "You did a nice job today, scout," I said. "I really liked that."

She averted her face.

I looked at her. Under the dirt and tangles was a handsome child, and I longed to hold her, to take her in my lap and hug away some of the pain that was so obvious in her eyes. But she would not even look at me.

"Have I frightened you, Sheila?" I asked softly. "I didn't mean to. It must be very scary coming to a new school and being with people you don't know. It scares me too."

She put her hand up to the side of her face to block me entirely from view.

"Would you like me to read you a story or something while we wait for your bus?"

She shook her head.

"All right. Well, I'm going to go over to the other table to make plans for tomorrow. If you change your mind, I'll be glad to read to you. Or you can play with the toys, whatever you like."

As soon as I began my work she put her hand down and turned to me, studying me as I wrote. I looked up a few times, but there was no response from that steady gaze.

THE NEXT DAY I decided it was time for Sheila to participate. The bus dropped her off at the high school, two blocks away, so Anton had gone to walk her to our school. When they arrived, Sheila pulled off her jacket and went straight to her chair. I told her that I wanted her to join us as she had the day before, and that I expected her to do some math problems too. Also, on Wednesday afternoons we always cooked. I said I expected her to help us make chocolate bananas.

She watched me as I spoke, her eyes clouding with distrust. I asked if she understood. She did not respond.

During morning discussion Sheila joined us, after I gave her the evil eye. She sat at my feet and did nothing. Math was a different story. I had planned to do some simple arithmetic exercises with her, so I went over to the cupboard by the sink and got out the counting blocks.

"Sheila, come over here, please." I indicated a chair. It was the one she was so fond of. "Come on."

She did not budge. Anton began to move cautiously to catch her in case she bolted when I approached. Instantly, she perceived our plan and panicked. This child was phobic about being chased.

Shrieking wildly, she darted off, knocking children over as she fled. But Anton snagged her at once, and I took her from him.

"Honey, we're not going to do anything to you." I sat down at the table, holding her tightly in my lap as she struggled. Her breathing was raspy with fear. "Take it easy, kitten."

"Hey, everybody be good now," Peter hollered delightedly. Little heads bent eagerly over their work.

Sheila resumed screaming, her face reddening. I spilled out the counting blocks and lined them up. "Here, I want you to count some blocks for me."

She yelled louder.

"Here, count out three for me." She struggled to break my hold. "I'll help you." I manipulated a writhing hand toward the blocks. "One, two, three. There. Now you try."

Unexpectedly she grabbed a counting block and hurled it across the room. It hit Tyler squarely on the forehead. Tyler let out a wail.

I pinned Sheila's arm to her side and lugged her over to the quiet corner. "We don't do that in here. I want you to sit until you calm down and are ready to work." I motioned Anton over. "Help her stay in the chair if she needs it."

I returned to the other children, rubbed Tyler's sore spot, and praised everybody for keeping busy. Then I put a check on the board to indicate how well we were doing in our effort to earn Friday's ice cream. Over in the corner Sheila was still shrieking, kicking the wall with her sneakers. Anton was grimly silent, holding her firmly in place.

Throughout math period Sheila continued the ruckus. When playtime started half an hour later, she was tiring of kicking and fighting. I came over.

"Are you ready to do your math with me?" I asked. She looked up at me and screamed. I went on. "When you are ready for math, you may come over. Until then I want you in the chair." I motioned Anton away, and we turned and left.

Sheila was momentarily startled at being left entirely alone and she stopped yelling. When she became fully aware that neither Anton nor I was standing over her, she stood up.

"Are you ready to do math?" I asked from across the room where I was helping Peter build a highway out of blocks.

Her face blackened at my question. "No! No! No! No!"

"Then sit back down."

She screeched in rage but remained beside the chair.

"I said sit down, Sheila. You may not get up until you're ready to do math."

For an eternal moment she stormed so loudly I felt my head pulse. Then suddenly everything was quiet. She glowered at me with obvious hate and sat down. Then she resumed screaming.

Peter looked at me. "You know, Torey, I think we ought to get two checks this time. She's pretty hard to ignore."

I grinned. "Peter, I think you're right. This is worth two."

Sheila yelled all through playtime. She stomped her feet and rocked the chair. She pulled at her clothes and shook her fists. But she remained seated. By snack time she was hoarse, and all that came from the corner were little strangled croaks.

Anton took the other children outside for recess. This increased Sheila's agitation. She gasped out a few more shouts, but she was tiring. By the end of recess there were no sounds at all coming from the corner, but my head still throbbed.

I did not restate the conditions for leaving the corner. The other children came back in, frosty and red-cheeked, full of tales about playing fox-and-geese in the snow with Anton, who got caught every time. Then, as if the little lump in the corner did not exist, we settled down to read.

Toward the close of the reading period I felt a feather-light touch on my shoulder as I worked with Max. I turned to see Sheila standing behind me, her face puckered with anxiety.

"You ready to do math?" I asked her.

She pursed her lips a moment and then nodded slowly.

"Okay. Let me get Sarah to help Max. You go over and pick up the block you threw and get some more out of the cupboard." I spoke casually, as if it were normal to expect her to comply. She looked at me carefully, then did as I asked.

Together we sat down on the floor and I spilled out the blocks. "Show me three blocks."

178

Cautiously she picked out three.

"Show me ten." Sheila lined up ten cubes on the rug before me. "Good girl. You know your numbers well, don't you?"

She looked up anxiously.

"I'm going to make it harder. Count out twenty-seven." Within seconds twenty-seven blocks appeared.

"Can you add?" She did not respond. "Show me how many blocks are two plus two." Four blocks appeared without hesitation. I studied her a moment. "How about three plus five?" She laid out eight cubes.

I could not tell if she actually knew the answers or was solving the problems as she went along. Yet she clearly understood the mechanics of addition. I decided to switch to subtraction, which would tell me more. "Show me six take away four."

Sheila flipped two blocks out. I smiled. She obviously knew the answer without having to place six blocks out and then remove four.

"Hey, you're pretty smart. But I've got one for you. I'll get you this time. Show me twelve take away seven."

She looked up at me with a hint of a smile in her eyes. She stacked five blocks on top of one another without hesitation. The little devil, I thought. Wherever she had been these past few years and whatever she had been doing, she had also been learning. Her abilities were better than those of the average child her age. My heart leaped at the possibility that under all that protest and grime there might be a bright child.

She did a few more problems before I said she could put the blocks away. It was still reading period, and I rose to check on the other kids. Sheila wandered after me, clutching the box of blocks.

"Honey," I said, turning to her, "you can put those away, if you want. You don't have to carry them around."

Sheila had other ideas. The next time I looked up, she was in her favorite chair at the table with the blocks spilled before her, and she was busily manipulating them.

She was subdued at lunch, and afterward she retreated to her chair and once again hunched up. But when it came time to cook, I coaxed her off quite easily with a banana stuck on a stick.

179

Cooking was an activity that encouraged sharing and conversation. Moreover, it was fun. Once a month we repeated a popular recipe, and this afternoon it was chocolate bananas, a simple but messy affair involving a banana on a stick that we dipped into chocolate sauce, rolled in various toppings, and then froze. All the kids except Freddie and Max could manage this task by themselves. Naturally there was chocolate everywhere, and a good share of the toppings were eaten before they found a banana to adhere to, but we all had a marvelous time.

At first Sheila just clutched her banana tightly and watched from the sidelines as the others babbled gaily. Yet when they had all finished, Whitney was able to lure her over to the chocolate sauce. Once Sheila started, she became fully absorbed, trying to get all four toppings to cling to her banana. It became apparent that she had some definite ideas about how to do it. Voices became hushed, and one by one the other children's curiosity got the better of them. They watched as she redipped the banana in the chocolate after each roll in topping. Finally she lifted up the huge mass carefully. Her eyes rose to meet mine, and slowly a broad smile spread across her face.

THE CLOSING EXERCISES at the end of each day were designed to prepare us for our time apart. One of the activities was the Kobold's Box. I loved to make up stories to tell the children, and I had told them that kobolds were like fairies, and that they lived in people's houses and watched over them to keep things safe. Peter had suggested there might be a kobold in our room who kept our pets, Benny, Charles, and Onions, company during the night. This spawned a number of kobold tales, and one day I brought in a large wooden box and told the kids that this was where the kobold was going to leave messages.

I said that he had watched us at work and had been extremely pleased with how kind and thoughtful everyone was becoming. Therefore, every time he saw a kind deed done, he would leave a note in the Kobold's Box, and during closing exercises each day I would read them. After a while I told them that the kobold was getting writer's cramp and needed a helping hand. I asked the children to be on the lookout for others doing kind things and to put a note in the box, or if they could not write, to come to me and I would do it for them.

Every night there were about thirty notes in the box. This not only encouraged the children to observe positive behavior in others but to show kindness themselves, in hopes that their names would appear in the box. Some notes showed particular insight. Sarah was complimented for not using a favorite vulgar phrase during an argument one day, and Freddie was praised for using a tissue instead of blowing his nose on his shirt. I loved opening that box and seeing what the children had perceived about each other. I seldom contributed to it myself—except to see that each child got at least one note. Admittedly, I also enjoyed finding notes for myself in there.

So closing exercises that Wednesday were particularly enjoyable, because for the first time Sheila's name appeared in handwriting other than my own. Sheila kept her head down when the kids clapped for her. But when I gave her the notes, she readily accepted them.

ANTON WALKED the other children to their buses after school ended, and I settled down at the table to grade papers. Sheila had gone into the bathroom to clean the dregs of the chocolate banana from her face. When she returned, she came over to the table and watched me a moment. I did not look up. Then she came closer, leaning way over on her elbows so that we were only inches apart. I raised my eyes. She examined my face thoughtfully.

"How come them other kids—them big kids—go to the bathroom in their pants and not in the toilet?"

I sat back in surprise. "Well, that's something they just haven't learned yet. But we're working on it. Everyone's trying."

"My pa, he'd whip me fierce bad if I do that."

"Everybody's different, and nobody gets a whipping in here."

She was pensive a long moment. She traced a circle on the table with her finger. "This here be a crazy class, don't it?"

"Not really, Sheila."

"My pa, he say I be crazy and this be a crazy kidses class."

181

"Not really," I repeated.

She frowned. "I don't care much. This here do be as good as anyplace I be before. I don't care if it be a crazy class."

I was at a loss for words, not knowing how to deny the obvious. I had never expected to be involved with one of my children in this sort of discussion. Most were either not this perceptive or not this brash.

Sheila scratched her head and regarded me thoughtfully. "Do you be crazy?"

I laughed. "I hope not."

"How come you do this? How come you be with crazy kids?"

"Because I like boys and girls, and I think teaching is fun. Being crazy isn't bad. It's just different, that's all."

She shook her head. "I think you do be a crazy person too."

CHAPTER THREE

"Sheila, come over here, please," I motioned to a chair next to me. "I have something for you to do."

Thus far, the morning had gone smoothly. I had again used the time before school to tell her what would happen that day. She had been cooperative, joining us for discussion without being reminded, and then for math. Although she still did not speak up in class, she appeared considerably more relaxed.

I beckoned to her. She unfolded from her post hesitantly. I had borrowed a Peabody Picture Vocabulary Test from the school psychologist. It would give a general idea of a child's functioning verbal IQ quickly, and without the child's needing to talk. It is typical for seriously disturbed children to be academically behind. Most of them simply do not have the extra energy available to learn. But yesterday Sheila had evidenced above-normal math skill, and I was excited to think she might have above-average intelligence. I was already beginning to wonder how to keep her out of the state hospital. Of all the things she needed right now, that was not one of them.

"Here, sit down." I had had to get up and bring her over to my table. "Now, I'm going to show you some pictures and say a word.

Then I want you to point to the picture that best shows what that word means. Do you understand that?"

She nodded. I showed her the first set of four pictures and asked her to point to "whip." What a picture to have to start with, I thought ruefully. She studied the four line drawings, looked up at me, then cautiously pointed to one.

I smiled at her. "Good girl. That's just exactly right. Point to 'net.'"

As I read each word, Sheila pointed to a picture, hesitantly at first, then more freely. After a while a small smile slipped across her face and she raised her eyes. "This be easy," she whispered so the others could not hear.

She missed "thermos," a word and an object she had probably not encountered in her short, destitute life. But a child had to miss six out of eight to stop the test, and so we continued. The words got harder. Occasionally she would miss one or two, and I could see the concern in her eyes.

I had suspected she was above average in intelligence, maybe even bright, but she had long since passed my expectations. Now we were moving into a part of the test containing words no normal six-year-old would know—words like "illumination" and "concentric." Sheila was missing words regularly, but never six out of eight. The tension mounted. She was biting her lips and wringing her hands, obviously trying very hard not to make mistakes. I was touched by her concentration.

"Sweetheart, you're doing a nice job," I said.

She looked up nervously. "I ain't getting them all right."

"Oh, that's okay, honey. These are words for great big kids and you aren't supposed to get them all right. This is just to see which ones you do know. I'm proud of you for trying so hard."

She looked on the verge of tears. "These be fierce hard words now. I don't know them all."

Her tiny voice, her slipping hold on her composure, her small shoulders hunched up under the worn shirt all combined to rip at my heart. Such innocence, even in the worst of these kids. They were all simply little children.

I reached an arm out. "Come here, Sheila." I leaned over and

183

pulled her up into my lap. Under my hands her little body was tense. "Kitten, I know you're trying your best. That's all that counts. Why, these are really hard words. I bet there isn't a boy or girl in here who could do better."

I held her, smoothing back the tangled blond hair from her face. While waiting for her to relax, I looked over the test score sheet. Though I suspected she was close to reaching the ceiling of her ability, she had surpassed any other child I had ever tested. "How do you know all these words?" I finally asked, my curiosity getting the better of me.

She shrugged. "My other teacher, she let me have magazines. Sometimes I read the words in there."

I looked down at her. "Can you read, Sheila?"

She nodded.

"Where'd you learn to do that?"

"I dunno. I always read."

I shook my head in amazement. What sort of changeling did we have here? At first I had been titillated by the thought of having a bright child in my class. But clearly Sheila was not simply bright; she was truly gifted. I feared that fact would not ease my job at all. If anything, it would make it much more complicated.

THERE WAS NO SCALE to measure Sheila's score on the Peabody test. For her age group the scale stopped at 99, which translated into an IQ of 170. Sheila had scored 102. I stared at the test sheet. We don't have a concept for that kind of brilliance. Statistics tell us that fewer than one person in ten thousand has that high a level of functioning. But what does it mean? It is a deviant score, an abnormality in a society that worships sameness. It would set her apart as surely as her disturbance could.

After lunch I showed Anton the test and Sheila's score. He shook his head in disbelief. "That can't be right," he muttered. "Where would she learn those words? She just had to guess lucky, Torey."

I could not believe it myself. So I put in a call to Allan, our school psychologist, saying that I had a child I wanted tested.

One thing from the testing situation puzzled me. As Sheila and I spoke, it became increasingly apparent that she used a highly

184

idiosyncratic dialect. I hadn't heard enough to pick out its unusual features precisely, but her grammar was bizarre. Most of the migrant camp children came from Spanish-speaking homes, and often their command of English vocabulary was below age-level but within normal limits grammatically. There was no other major speech variation in the locality. Sheila was not from a Spanish-speaking home; the IQ test substantiated that there was nothing at all wrong with her vocabulary. I could not fathom why she spoke so oddly. To me, she almost sounded like the inner-city black kids I had worked with in Cleveland. Perhaps it was a family speech pattern. I decided I would have to investigate.

THE REMAINDER of the day went uneventfully. I still made minimal demands on Sheila. She moved willingly from one activity to the next, but participated only when coaxed. She would not talk to the other children or to Whitney. Yet, she was peaceful and watched us with guarded interest.

The next major step to be taken with Sheila concerned her hygiene. Every day she arrived in the same denim overalls and T-shirt. Apparently the clothes were never washed, and reeked of urine. I suspected she wet the bed at night and dressed each morning without washing up. Moreover, plain everyday grime was crusted over her face and arms, and her long blond hair was a mass of tangled strands.

I waited until the end of the day to tackle Sheila's hygienic needs. When the other children had gone, I got out the combs and brushes I kept in the cupboard. The night before I had bought a little package of hair clips shaped like bluebirds and ducks.

"Sheila, come here," I said. "I've got something for you."

She came over, her brow furrowed with wary interest. I handed her the bag. For a moment she just held it, looking at me quizzically. I urged her to open it and she did. Taking out the package of clips, she looked at them, still puzzled.

"They're for you, sweetheart. I thought we could comb your hair out nice and put the clips in it."

She fingered the little shapes carefully through the plastic wrapping and frowned. "How come you do this?"

"Do what?"

"Be nice to me?"

I looked at her in disbelief. "Because I like you. Why do you be nice to me?"

"Why? I be a crazy kid; I hurt your fishes."

I smiled. "I just wanted to, Sheila. I thought you might like something nice for your hair."

She continued to feel the clips with her fingertips. "Nobody give me nothing before. Nobody be nice to me on purpose."

"Well, things are different here, kiddo," was all I could reply.

I brushed the tangles out of her hair, careful not to hurt her in any way. She sat very patiently clutching the package of clips, but she would not open it. Her hair was fine and soft, and when brushed out it hung below her shoulders in a thick curtain. She was a pretty girl, with bold, well-formed features. With soap and water she would be even lovelier.

"Here, give me the clips and I'll put them in your hair."

She shook her head and squashed the package to her breast. "Pa, he take them away from me."

"Just tell him I gave them to you."

"He say I steal them. Nobody give me nothing before."

"You can leave them at school until I get hold of your dad and tell him I gave them to you. How's that sound?"

"You fix my hair nice again?"

I nodded. "I'll fix it tomorrow morning when you come."

She looked at the clips a long moment, obviously finding it hard to give them back. Then hesitantly she handed them to me. "Here. You keep them for me."

At that moment Anton came into the room to remind me that it was almost time for Sheila to walk to her bus. We hadn't even washed her up yet and she did smell so terrible.

"Sheila," I asked, "do you get a chance to wash at home?"

She shook her head. "We ain't got no bathtub."

"Can you use the sink?"

"Ain't got no sink either. My pa, he brings water in a bucket from the gas station." She paused, staring at the floor. "It just be to drink. He'd be fierce mad at me if I get it dirty."

186

"Do you have any other clothes?"

She shook her head.

"Well, we'll see what we can do about that tomorrow, okay?"

Nodding, she went to the coat hook for her thin cotton jacket. I sighed as I watched her. So much to do, I thought. So much to change. "Good-by, Sheila. Have a nice evening. I'll see you tomorrow."

Anton took her hand and opened the door to the blowy January darkness. As he was shutting the door behind him, Sheila peered at me from under his arm. She smiled slightly. "By, teacher."

THE NEXT MORNING I came in ready for action, armed with bath towels, soap, shampoo, and a bottle of baby lotion. First I went to check the old-clothes box in the office. Although the school was in an upper-income area, enough needy children were bused in to justify a box of spare clothes that could be given away. Having found a pair of corduroy pants and a T-shirt, I went to my room.

When Sheila arrived, I was running water into the large, kitchen-sized sink in the back of the classroom. The moment she saw me, Sheila yanked off her jacket and came trotting over, her eyes wide with interest. That was the fastest I had ever seen her move toward me. "You gonna put clips in my hair?"

"You bet. But first we're going to give you the full beauty-shop routine. We're going to wash you top to bottom."

"It gonna hurt?"

I laughed. "No, silly."

She had taken the bottle of baby lotion and removed the top. "What do this be for? Do you drink it?"

"No, it's lotion. You put it on your body."

A sudden look of pleasure rippled across her face. "It do smell good, teacher." Her eyes were animated. "Now that kid ain't gonna say I stink no more, huh?"

I smiled at her. "No, I guess he won't. Look here, I found some clothes for you to wear. When Whitney comes this afternoon, she can take your overalls to the Laundromat."

Gingerly Sheila picked up the corduroy pants. "My pa, he ain't gonna let me keep them. We don't take no charity."

"Yes, I understand that. You just wear them until the others are washed. Okay?"

I lifted her up onto the counter beside the sink and took off her clothes. She watched me carefully but made no attempt to help. She was a scrawny little child with all her ribs showing, so a good share of her fitted into the sink. I noticed many scars on her legs and arms. "What happened here?" I asked as I washed her. A scar two inches long ran up the inside of her upper arm.

"That be where I brokeded my arm at."

"How'd you do that?"

"Falling down playing," she said matter-of-factly. "My pa, he says I do be a god-awful clumsy child. I hurt myself a lot."

I formed the dreaded question I had learned to ask of my kids. "Does your pa ever do things that leave scars like these?"

Her eyes clouded over. She regarded me so long in silence that I wished I had not asked such a personal question. "My pa, he wouldn't hurt me bad. He loves me. He just hits me a little bit to make me good. I just be a clumsy child to get so many scars." Her voice was tinged with defiance.

I nodded and lifted her out of the sink to dry her off. Then I dressed her.

"You know what my mama done though?" She lifted up one leg of her pants and pointed to a scar. "My mama, she take me out on the road and leave me there. She push me out of the car, and I fall down so's a rock cutted up my leg. See?" She fingered a white line. "You ain't supposed to do that with little kids."

"No, you're not."

"My mama, she don't love me so good."

In silence I began combing her hair. I did not want to hear any more. It hurt to listen to her.

"My mama, she take Jimmie and go to California. Jimmie, he be my brother, and he be four years old. I ain't seen Jimmie in two whole years." She paused thoughtfully. "I miss Jimmie. I wish I could see him again. He be a real nice boy. He don't yell or be bad or anything. He be a nice boy to have in this here crazy kidses class. 'Cept I don't think he be crazy like me. You'd like Jimmie. My mama, she like Jimmie better'n me. That's why she tooked him

and leaved me behind. You ought to have Jimmie in this here class. He don't do bad things like I do."

I put her in my lap and hugged her to me. "Kitten, you're the one I'd want. Not Jimmie. He'll have his own teacher someday. I don't care what kids do, I just like them. That's all."

A bemused look came across her face. "You do be a funny lady for a teacher. I think you be as crazy as us kidses be."

THAT FIFTH DAY, Friday, Sheila still did not talk to the other kids. After everyone had had their well-earned ice cream and we had finished the closing exercises, we stood around waiting for the buses to arrive. The children were getting hot in their snowsuits, so I suggested a song. Max shouted out that he wanted "If You're Happy and You Know It, Clap Your Hands," a simple action song that required the children to clap, then stomp, then nod their heads. Sheila stood on the edge of the group, not singing but paying close attention. When we had finished all the actions, Tyler suggested a new one. "If you're happy and you know it, jump up and down." So we sang a verse using Tyler's action. I asked for new actions. From her corner Sheila shyly raised her hand. To see this little kid—who thus far had never spoken to the other children, who came in with a history of uncooperativeness—to see her standing there with her hand up was a heart stopper.

"Sheila, do you have an idea?"

"Turn around?" she said diffidently.

And so we sang our song turning around. The first week had ended in the heat of success.

DURING THE NEXT WEEKS Sheila came alive. She began speaking, first with reserve, and then with none. She had thoughts on everything. I was delighted to have a verbal child in the room. The other children enjoyed her company, and I was tickled that she could tell me about so many things.

But Sheila never brought up the burning incident. Most of the kids in my class were aware of the reasons they had been placed there. They knew that their behaviors had frightened or repelled others. They needed to explore the depth of those acts and how they felt when they did them. Mostly I listened, asked a question or two, and mmmm-hmmmed a lot to let them know I heard. And together we set weekly and long-term goals for change.

Sheila, too, knew why she was there. From the third day on, she referred to us affectionately as a "crazy class," and to herself as a crazy kid who did bad things. Yet not once did she mention what she had done, and I never found out what had been going through her mind that cold November afternoon.

ALLAN, THE SCHOOL psychologist, gave Sheila an IQ test. She topped out, earning the highest possible score. Allan was astonished. He had never had a child do that. He vowed to find a test with a higher upper limit that could measure her IQ. Then he gave her a reading test. Though no one had ever taught her to read, Sheila read and comprehended on a fifth-grade level.

Each morning before school Sheila and I worked on hygiene. She was willing to wash herself and brush her teeth if I would fix her hair. She guarded the hair clips like a king's treasure, carefully opening the towel in which they were folded, and deciding which ones she would wear. When she took them out of her hair each evening, she counted them all again to make sure no one had taken any. Her clothes were a bit more of a problem. I kept clean under-pants at school and insisted she change every morning. On Mondays, Whitney trotted her overalls and shirt to the Laundromat. Now at least Sheila did not smell so bad. Cleaned up, she was a handsome child. Her eyes sparkled, and a ready smile showed three gaps on the bottom, awaiting new teeth.

I HAD TRIED relentlessly to get hold of Sheila's father for a con-ference. He had no phone so I sent a note home with Sheila asking him to come to school. No response. I sent a second note. Again no response. Then I sent a third, saying when I was coming to visit him. But when Anton and I went to the house, it was empty. I was getting the distinct impression he did not want to see me. Finally I contacted Sheila's social worker, and we went there together. Only Sheila greeted us; her father was not at home.

I wanted to see him very badly. First I wanted to make some

arrangements for Sheila to get proper outerwear. It was January; the temperature hovered around twenty degrees most days, and Sheila owned only a thin cotton jacket—no gloves, hat, or boots. She would arrive almost blue after her walk from the high school. I gave her more to wear at recess, but the one time I sent things home, they came back the next day. Sheila remarked that she had gotten a spanking for accepting "charity." The social worker explained that she too had tried, even taking the father downtown once to buy clothes for Sheila from his welfare check. But he had returned the clothes later. She did not want to force the issue, she said, because it was a known fact that the man took his anger out on the child.

DURING THE HOURS that school was in session, I tried to provide Sheila with all different kinds of experiences. Every moment of her day was filled with exploring and chattering. The first weeks she constantly followed me around, clutching a book or a box of math cubes. A silly smile would spill over her lips when she caught my eye, and she'd scuttle up ready to share. As she got braver and longed for more physical contact, I would sometimes feel a hand tentatively take hold of my belt from behind. Then, hand locked into the belt, she would go with me as I walked around the room.

Those were weeks of intense devotion, and I was both thankful and dismayed for the two hours we had alone after school. My planning time was shot. Much to Chad's displeasure I had to haul my work home and do it in the evenings. Anton groused about never getting to talk things over anymore unless we both came in at seven thirty in the morning. But for Sheila it was ideal. For six years she had been unwanted, ignored, rejected. Pushed out of cars, pushed out of people's lives. Now there was someone to hold her and talk to her and cuddle her.

The other children were delighted to see Sheila blossom. They were quick to comment that she did not smell so often or so badly now. And they even perceived her budding attempts at kindness.

Sheila had evidently not had much of an opportunity to learn how to be kind. She had been too busy surviving. She was used to

192

having to fight for what she wanted. Consequently, when someone had the toy she wanted, she wrestled it out of the child's hands. I knew that it was not going to be a simple matter to convince her that there was another way to do things. My reprimands did not dent her behavior. But the Kobold's Box did.

Each afternoon Sheila listened carefully as I read the notes and complimented the children who earned them. Greedily she would count hers after each session, and if given the opportunity, she would count other children's also to see if they got more than she did. She wanted to prove that she was the best child in the class, the smartest, the hardest-working, my favorite. When I steadfastly refused to confirm that, she set out to prove it to herself by the number of notes in the Kobold's Box. But that eluded her. She could not figure out how to be kind or polite or considerate enough to earn more of them.

One day after school she asked, "How come Tyler gets so many notes? How come everybody likes her so good?"

I considered the matter for a moment. "Well, for one thing, she's polite. When she wants something she asks, and almost always says please. And thank you too. That makes a person feel more like helping her or being with her."

Sheila frowned, then looked accusingly at me. "How come you never tell me you want me to say please and thank you? I don't know you want that."

I knew she was right. I had never told her, taking it for granted that she would know. The unfairness of my assumption was dawning on me. Sheila might never have heard those words in her environment. Or perhaps they had never been meaningful to her before.

"I'm sorry, Sheil. I thought you knew."

"I don't. I can say them if I know you want me to."

I nodded. "I do. They're good words to use, because they make other people feel good. That's important."

"Will they tell me I'm a nice girl?"

"It'll help them see that you are."

And so, little by little, Sheila began to notice what other children did to be kind and considerate.

UNFORTUNATELY, as in all Gardens of Eden, there were a few snakes. During that first month there were two problems that we did not seem able to lick.

The first was that, despite all her progress, Sheila steadfastly refused to do paperwork—whether in academics or coloring or art projects. She had no objection to oral work, but the instant a piece of paper was put before her, she destroyed it. I tried taping the work to the table. She simply scribbled over it until it tore. If I put it into a plastic folder, she would refuse to pick up her crayon; on one occasion she even ate the crayon. I tried using workbooks, but they were expensive, and I got angry when they were ruined. There was not a method I could think of that she could not foil.

Needless to say, this caused considerable friction between us. I would send her to the quiet corner, but I felt that was not solving the problem. I did not want her to miss too much of the program, and the quiet corner was not intended as punishment, simply as a means of helping the child regain control. So if she was still not willing to do paperwork after twenty minutes of sitting, I let it drop. There was little else that she refused to do. She went to ridiculous heights to please me in other ways, so it did not make sense that she was holding out simply to irk me.

But admittedly the behavior did irk me. I became obsessed with it, and finally one day, in desperation, I dittoed one work sheet off on a whole ream of paper. In class I maneuvered Sheila over to a table, deciding that if we had to sit there until Valentine Day and go through all five hundred copies, we would.

"We're going to do this math work sheet today, Sheila. All I want is this one sheet and it's got easy problems on it."

She looked at me distrustfully. "I don't wanna do that."

"Well, it isn't your choice today." I tapped the paper on the table with one finger. "Come on, let's get started."

She sat staring at me. My stomach was tight and my heart beat rapidly. For a split second I wanted to retreat, but my anger overwhelmed me.

"Do it." My voice was loud and sharp. I grabbed a pencil and shoved it into her hand. "I said, do the paper, Sheila."

She wadded up the first sheet. I carefully straightened it out and taped it down to the table. Sheila gouged it out with the pencil. Grimly we struggled, I putting out new copies, Sheila ripping at them. Math period passed, and the litter of destroyed dittos deepened around our chairs. The other children rose for free time. Sheila glanced around in concern; that was her favorite period, and she noticed Tyler getting out the little toy people she liked to play with.

"Finish this and you can go," I stated, taping down a new paper.

Sheila was losing patience with me, making angry little grunts as we went through another half-dozen copies. Moving my chair close to hers and holding her free hand, I took her other in mine. "I'll help you, Sheila, if you can't do it by yourself," I said doggedly.

Sheila let out an earsplitting yell. I asked her the answer to the first problem. At first she refused to say but then furiously shouted it out. I pushed her hand along the paper, writing a 3. Sheila struggled violently, trying to loosen my hold on her.

We finished the paper with her screaming and me forcing her hand. The second I let go, she scrabbled the paper up and threw it in my face. Running to the other side of the classroom, she turned to glower at me.

"I hate you!" she shrieked. The other children, getting ready for recess, paused to watch us. "I hate you! I hate you!"

Anton took the other kids out. I remained at the table. Expecting her to go off into one of her destructive rages, I was poised to catch her. But after a few moments she regained her composure and stared at me reproachfully from across the room, her mouth turned down, her chin quivering. I was beginning to feel like a first-class heel. Her disappointment in me for behaving so antagonistically was bright in her eyes, and I knew I had done the wrong thing. My teacher's instinct to get work accomplished on paper had overcome my better sense. We had been doing so well in the three weeks since she had come. Had I fouled it all up in one morning?

Her wary, accusing eyes were still on me as she slowly came over to the far side of the table. "You not be very nice," she said, her voice heavy with feeling.

"No, I guess I wasn't, was I? I shouldn't have done that."

195

"You shouldn't oughta be mean to me. I be one of your kids."

"I'm sorry. I just got upset, because you never do papers. It makes me mad, because it is important to me that you do."

She sidled closer. "Do you still like me?"

"Of course I still like you. Sometimes people get mad. Even at people they like a lot. It doesn't mean they stop liking them. They're just mad. After a while the anger goes away. I like you as much as ever."

She pressed her lips together. "I don't really hate you."

"I know that. You were just angry like I was. Look, kitten, for now we won't worry about paperwork. We'll do it some other time when you feel like it."

"I ain't never going to feel like it." She looked at me quizzically. "There gotta be paperwork?"

My shoulders sagged with discouragement. "Not really, I suppose. There are more important things. Besides, maybe someday you will feel like it."

I gave up the paperwork war, or at least the battle.

THE SECOND PROBLEM Sheila presented was more serious. She had a keenly developed sense of revenge that knew no limits. When crossed or taken advantage of, she retaliated with devastating force. Her intelligence made it all the more frightening, because she could quickly perceive what was most valuable to a person and that was what she abused. When Sarah kicked snow on her at recess, Sheila systematically destroyed all of Sarah's artwork. For art-loving Sarah this was crushing. Anton got angry with Sheila for running through the halls to lunch one day, and afterward she throttled all the gerbils Anton had brought to school on loan from his son. Her cold, clear-eyed appraisal of everyone's sensitivities, her long-abiding anger, often at events which were not intentional, left me chilled. Sheila had to be watched every second.

Lunch hour was the most dangerous time of day. Neither Anton nor I wanted to give up our only break. The lunch aides, though still frightened of Sheila, had agreed to supervise her once more. One day, while Anton and I were eating in the teachers' lounge, an aide came in shrieking Sheila's name. Having nightmares of a repeat of the first day, we dashed out after her.

Sheila had gotten into one of the other teachers' rooms, and in only a few minutes she had destroyed it completely. All the students' desks were knocked over, books and personal belongings were strewn about the floor, and the screen of the teaching machine was shattered.

"Sheila!" She whirled around, her eyes dark, a pointer clutched in one hand. "Drop that!"

By now she knew when I meant business. She let the pointer drop. If I could get her to come to me, I could take her out calmly. She already had that wild-animal, frenzied look, and I knew better than to spook her.

By the time I had coaxed Sheila over to the door, Mr. Collins and the teacher, Mrs. Holmes, whose room it was, were behind me. When I finally got hold of Sheila, Mr. Collins began to roar.

I suppose he roared with very good reason, but I knew he was of the old school, where most infractions were punished with the paddle. He took hold of Sheila's arm. I already had her by the overall strap and did not let go. We eyed each other, neither of us speaking, Sheila stretched out between us. We were like two dogs fighting over a bone. I could not let him take her, not after reassuring her that she could never be hurt here. There had been too many spankings in her past already. And too many people who had broken their promises to her.

Finally Mr. Collins spoke, his voice a hoarse whisper. Not only was Sheila going down to his office for a paddling but I was coming along as a witness.

We were hissing back and forth, one- or two-word responses mostly. He was losing patience with me. "So help me, Miss Hayden, you come with me right now or you're not going to have a job when this day is out. Is that clear?"

I stared at him. All sorts of things came into my head then. I had tenure. I belonged to the union. He had no power to fire me. But at gut level I was afraid. Could I ever find another teaching job in town? Who would take care of my class? I had a history of impulsive actions. Was this just one more? And what would everyone think if I lost my job? For that, the worst excuse of all, I let go of the overall strap.

Mr. Collins took Sheila down the hall. I followed at a distance, feeling like Benedict Arnold. Maybe they were right. I had lost control of this kid twice already. Maybe she did need a state hospital. I did not know.

I flopped into a chair in Mr. Collins' office. Sheila was far calmer than I. She stood complacently beside the principal, not looking at me and not making any sound. Mr. Collins shut the door. From his desk drawer he took out a long paddle. Sheila did not flinch as he sized it up next to her.

I was bitter. How could I let him do this? What would Sheila think of me now? Through the chaos in my own head, I was suddenly and deeply touched by Sheila's innocent courage. She looked very much like any other six-year-old just then, with the little duck barrettes in her hair, the worn overalls and T-shirt. I felt like crying. I did not have her kind of strength.

Mr. Collins told her flatly that he had had it. Did she know what she had done? No response. She might even be suspended from school, he said. I knew the lecture was as much for my benefit as for Sheila's. He told her she was getting three whacks with the board. She had sucked her lips between her teeth. She watched him without blinking.

"Lean over and grab your ankles."

She did not move.

"If I have to tell you again, Sheila, I'll add another whack."

"Sheila, please," I said. "Please do as he says."

Still no response. Her eyes flickered toward me a moment.

Mr. Collins yanked her down roughly. With a *whoosh* the board hit her, and she fell on her knees, her face remaining unchanged. Mr. Collins lifted her back to her feet. Again came the whack. Again she fell. On the last two whacks she did not fall. Not a sound came out of her, not a tear came to her eyes. This infuriated Mr. Collins. He had me sign a form saying that I had witnessed the paddling. Then wearily I took Sheila's hand and we went down the hall.

When I got to our room, I peered through the window in the

door. Anton and Whitney had started afternoon activities, and things seemed peaceful enough. I looked down at Sheila. "We need to talk, kiddo."

I knocked on the door and Anton came out. I explained that I wanted to be alone with Sheila for a while. I asked if he thought he and Whitney could manage a little longer without me. He nodded with a smile. So I left them, one uneducated migrant worker and a fourteen-year-old kid, in charge of eight crazy children.

I ended up taking Sheila into a book closet, the only place I could find where we could be alone. I hauled in two teensy chairs, turned on the light and sat down, shutting the door behind me.

"Why on earth do you do those things?" I asked, my discouragement ringing clearly in my voice.

"You ain't gonna make me talk."

"Oh, Sheila, come off it." But inwardly I wanted to apologize to her for letting Mr. Collins paddle her. I wanted to be forgiven.

Finally I shook my head and sighed wearily. "Look, that whole thing didn't turn out so well. I'm sorry."

Still silence. She would not talk to me. Outside the book closet I could hear classes getting ready for recess. Inside it was so quiet no one would ever know we were there.

I looked at her. "Sheila, what *is* it you want out of me?"

"Are you mad at me?"

"You could say that. I'm just a little mad at everybody right now."

"You gonna whip me?"

My shoulders sagged. "No, I'm not. Like I told you a million times now, I don't whip kids."

"Why not?"

"Why should I? It doesn't help any, does it?"

"It helps me."

"Does it really, Sheila? Did Mr. Collins help you?"

"My pa," she said softly, "he says it be the only way to make me decent. He whips me and I must be betterer, 'cause he ain't never left me on no highway like my mama done."

My heart melted. I reached an arm out to her. "Come here, Sheil, let me hold you."

199

Willingly she came, climbing up into my lap clumsily, like a toddler. She wrapped her arms around me, and I pressed her close. I was doing it as much for me as I was for her. I hurt inside.

What were we going to do? She had to stop this destructiveness. I knew that if they suspended her, she wouldn't come back. Sooner or later, it would be off to the state hospital as planned. What then? What chance did a six-year-old have of coming out of a state hospital to live a normal life? We'd lose her, this bright, creative little girl who had never had a chance.

"What're we gonna do, Sheila?" I asked. "You just can't keep doing these things, and I don't know how to stop you."

"I won't do it again."

"I wish you wouldn't. But let's not make any promises we can't keep, okay? I just want you to tell me why you did it."

"I dunno. I do be awful mad at that teacher. She yell at me at lunch and it not be my fault. It be Susannah's fault, but she yell at me." Her voice quivered. "Do they gonna make me go away?"

"I don't know, honey."

"I don't want them to. I won't never ever do that again, I promise. I wanna to stay in this here school." She pressed her face against me.

I stroked her hair, feeling the duck clips under my fingers. "Sheila," I asked, "don't you ever feel like crying?"

"I don't never cry."

"Why not?"

"Ain't nobody can hurt me that ways."

I looked down at her. The cold perception in her statement was fearsome. "What do you mean?"

"They don't know I hurt if I don't cry. Ain't nobody can make me cry neither. Not my pa. Not Mr. Collins. You seen that, didn't you?"

"Yes, I saw it. But don't you want to cry? Didn't it hurt?"

For a long moment she did not respond. She took one of my hands in both of hers. "It sort of hurts. Sometimes I do cry a little at night. My pa, he don't come home till it be real late and I have to be by myself and I get scared. Sometimes it get wet right here on my eyes, but I make it go away. Crying don't do no good, and it makes me think of Jimmie and my mama. It makes me miss them." She fingered my shirt buttons. "Do you ever cry?"

I nodded. "Sometimes. Mostly when I feel bad, I cry. It makes me feel better. It washes out the hurt, if you give it a chance."

She shrugged. "I don't do it."

"Sheil, what're we gonna do to fix up Mrs. Holmes's room?"

A pause ensued. She twisted one of my buttons. "Maybe I could pick it up."

"I think that's a good idea. But what about being sorry? Could you apologize?"

She nodded slowly. "I be sorry this here happened."

"Apologizing is a good thing to learn to do. It makes people feel better about you. Shall we practice saying you're sorry and offering to pick up, so it'll be easier to do?"

Sheila fell against me heavily. "I just want you to hold me for a little bit first. My butt do be fierce sore and I wanna wait till it feels better. I don't wanna think now."

With a smile I clutched her to me, and we sat together in the dim light of the book closet, waiting—she for relief for her bottom and for the courage to do what lay ahead; I for the world to change.

RESOLVING THAT SITUATION did not turn out to be simple. Sheila did apologize to Mrs. Holmes and offered to clean up. As I had hoped, Sheila's innocence, her small size, and her natural beauty all brought out the motherliness in Mrs. Holmes; she was willing to accept Sheila's attempts to make amends.

On the other hand, this had been the last straw for Mr. Collins. Everything came to a head—including things not even related to Sheila's destructiveness. The two of us simply had different value systems, and it all came out in a full-scale war after the incident. Finally Ed Somers had to come and mediate. The three of us sat in Mr. Collins' office late one afternoon. In no uncertain terms Mr. Collins said that he wanted Sheila out of the school. The child was dangerous. She frightened the other children, as well as the staff. She had caused seven hundred dollars' worth of damage in Mrs. Holmes's room alone. There came a point, he said, at which society had the right to protect itself. This child should not be allowed to run loose in a public school. She belonged in the state hospital.

I tried to point out Sheila's progress. I explained that it had only taken three days to get her to work productively. I spoke of her IQ, of her history of abuse and abandonment. I implored Ed to let me keep her. I'd give up my own lunch hour to watch her if I had to. But give me another chance, I asked.

The mood was grim. Ed explained that when word of the incident got out, there would be real pressure from parents. And the court had arranged for Sheila's commitment before I had ever entered the picture. I shouldn't get so involved, he said politely. He added that it was nice that Sheila was making progress, but that was not why she had been placed with me. She was there simply to wait until a space opened at the hospital.

As I listened I could feel the lump in my throat and the stinging in my eyes. I did not want to cry then. I did not want them to know they were getting to me. But I could feel the tears starting. I was a teacher. I wasn't a jailer. Or was that all Ed had wanted when he established my class? I was full of recriminations.

Ed leaned forward on his elbows and tried to reassure me, telling me not to get upset. He was embarrassed that the situation was making me cry, and for a moment I was pleased that he was. I wanted everyone to be as unhappy as I.

I left the room, feeling bitter. I went directly to my car and drove home. My idealism had taken a mighty blow. I had learned that some children were not even worth seven hundred dollars.

As always, Chad proved the calm center in my storm. Listening to me, he shook his head good-naturedly. It would come out in the end, he advised. Everything always does. Not in a mood to be placated, I shut myself in the bathroom and sobbed through a forty-five-minute shower. Chad was still sitting in the living room when I emerged. He smiled. I returned it. I wasn't happy, but I was resigned.

IT DID NOT TURN OUT so badly as I had anticipated. An education had to be provided for every child, and I was at that moment Sheila's only source of education. In compromise, Ed told Mr. Collins that he could have an extra lunch aide solely to supervise my room and that Sheila would never leave my room except under my direct supervision. The matter was at least temporarily settled.

In class Sheila was fitting in, and we were becoming a group again. Academically, Sheila was plunging ahead. I could hardly find enough to keep her agile mind busy. I had dropped the paperwork altogether, and Whitney, Anton, and I tested her orally. She was an avid reader, consuming books as fast as I could find them.

Socially her progress was slower, but it was steady. She and Sarah had become friends and were beginning to share the typical pleasures of small girls' friendships. I also assigned Sheila to help Susannah Joy learn her colors, an activity that gave Sheila responsibility and helped her learn the finer points of an interpersonal relationship. An added benefit was the boost to Sheila's self-confidence. Some days after school she would busily make materials and carry on long, earnest discussions with Anton or me about things she could do to help Susannah learn. Watching her, I wanted to laugh, wondering if I looked like that too. But she took the job with such seriousness that I contained myself.

ONE EVENING early in February, Anton and I finally managed to track down Sheila's father at the migrant camp.

He was a big man, over six feet tall, heavyset, with a huge belly that slopped over his belt. He had only one bottom tooth and very evil-smelling breath. When we arrived he was carrying a can of beer and was already quite drunk.

The tiny tar-paper shack he and Sheila lived in had only one room, divided by a curtain. A lumpy brown couch was at one end and a bed was at the other. The place reeked of urine. Sheila's father motioned us to sit on the couch. Sheila was crouched in a far corner by the bed, her eyes round and wild. She had failed to acknowledge us, but sat folded in upon herself as she had in the first days of school. I mentioned that perhaps it would be best if Sheila were not present since I needed to discuss some things that might be painful for her to hear.

He shook his head and flapped a hand in Sheila's direction. "She's gotta stay in that corner. You can't trust that kid out of your sight for five minutes. She tried to set fire to a place down the road the other night. If I don't keep her in, the police will be here again." He went on to give us the details.

"She ain't really my child," he explained. "That woman who's her mother, that's her bastard. She ain't mine, and you can tell it. Just look at her. That kid don't have a decent bone in her body."

Anton and I listened, mortified that Sheila was in the room. If he told her these things every day, it was no wonder she had such a low opinion of herself. At least, though, it was private. To tell us these things in front of her—I was horrified even to be there. Anton made an effort to refute the man's view, but that only made him angry. We let him talk, fearful of bringing repercussions on Sheila if we upset him.

"Now Jimmie, he was my boy. Better little boy you never seen. And that woman, she just upped and took him right out from under my nose. And what did she do? She leaves this little—" He sighed. "I told her if one more school person came out here—"

"I didn't come to say anything bad," I said quickly. "She's doing a nice job in our room."

He snorted. "With a class full of crazies, she should know how to act. Dammit, woman, I'm at my wit's end with that child."

The conversation never improved. I tried to tell him that Sheila was a gifted child with marvelous intelligence. That was not something he could grasp. What did she need with that? he asked. It'd only give her more of a chance to think up trouble. He went on and on. Finally the conversation turned back to his beloved, lost Jimmie. He began to cry, big tears rolling over his fat cheeks. Where was Jimmie, and why had he been left with this little kid that he did not even believe was his child?

In a detached way I felt sorry for the man. I think he did love the boy, and the loss must have been difficult. In his tangled, immature way he seemed to see Sheila as somehow to blame. If she hadn't been so impossible, perhaps his woman would have stayed. He did not know what to do with Sheila or himself. So he drank, and wept to two strangers about a life thirty years out of control.

As wretched as Sheila's life seemed, I knew we would have a difficult time getting her removed from her father's care. There

were not enough foster homes and welfare checks to go around in this community of losers. Only the most severely abused children were placed outside their homes. Yet I felt compelled to ask her father if he had considered voluntary foster placement.

My question was a mistake. From tears, he exploded into rage. Who was I to suggest he give his child up? He was man enough to solve his own problems without any help from me, thank you. With that he demanded that Anton and I leave his house immediately. Filled with frustration and sorrow, we left, hoping we had not endangered Sheila. I wished we had never gone.

Afterward, we rode across the migrant camp to Anton's. He too lived in little more than a hut—three rooms which he shared with his wife and two young sons. But it was clean and well-kept, the spartan furniture offset by handmade rugs and needlepoint pillows. Anton's wife was cheerful and welcoming. His boys were bright, chattery little fellows who climbed all over me, asking about the classroom where their daddy taught.

The five of us shared soda pop and corn chips while Anton diffidently asked about the possibilities of his going back to school and earning a teaching degree. He had not even graduated from high school, although he told me that he was studying for his general equivalency diploma. He had grown to love the children in our class, and hoped someday to have a class of his own. I was touched by Anton's dreams. Watching his wife beam as her husband talked of his plans, and seeing the boys dance at the thought that their daddy was going to be a real teacher and some-day they might live in a real house, I did not mention the obstacles— the time and money involved in attaining that level of education.

And even while we talked, my mind still wandered across to the other side of the camp, wondering what was happening in the tiny tar-paper shack.

CHAPTER FOUR

I had begun reading to Sheila after school, holding her on my lap as we sat in a corner, surrounded by pillows. Although she was perfectly capable of reading most of the books herself, I wanted to talk with her about them, about some of the passages she did not understand. This was not because she did not know what the words meant, but because, with her deprived background, she had no idea how the words applied to real life.

One day I brought in a copy of *The Little Prince*. "Hey, Sheil," I called to her, "I've got a book to share with you."

She came running across the room, leaping squarely onto my lap and snatching the book from my hands. Carefully she inspected all the pictures before we settled down to read. Once I started, she sat motionless, her fingers gripping my jeans.

This short book is about a little prince who tames a lonely fox and learns the secret of friendship. When we came to the part about the fox, Sheila became very intent.

"Come and play with me," proposed the little prince. "I am so unhappy."

"I cannot play with you," the fox said. "I am not tamed. . . ."

"What does that mean—'tame'? . . ."

"It means to establish ties," said the fox. "To me, you are still nothing more than a little boy who is just like a hundred thousand other little boys. And I have no need of you. And you, on your part, have no need of me. . . . But if you tame me, then we shall need each other. To me, you will be unique in all the world. To you, I shall be unique in all the world . . . Please—tame me!" he said. . . . "If you want a friend, tame me . . ."

"What must I do, to tame you?" asked the little prince.

"You must be very patient," replied the fox. "First you will sit down at a little distance from me—like that—in the grass. I shall look at you out of the corner of my eye, and you will say nothing. Words are the source of misunderstandings. But you will sit a little closer to me, every day . . ."

Sheila twisted around in my lap to look at me and for a long time locked me in her gaze.

"That's what you done with me, huh? Tamed me, remember? I do be so scared, and I run in the gym, and then you come in and you sit on the floor. Remember that? And you come a little closer and a little closer. You was taming me, huh?"

I smiled. "Yeah, I guess maybe I was."

"You tame me. Just like the little prince tames the fox. And now I be special to you, huh?"

"Yeah, you're special all right, Sheil."

She settled into my lap again. "Read the rest of it."

So the little prince tamed the fox. And when the hour of his departure drew near—

"Ah," said the fox, "I shall cry."

"It is your own fault," said the little prince. "You wanted me to tame you . . . But now you are going to cry!"

"Yes, that is so," said the fox.

"Then it has done you no good at all!"

"It has done me good," said the fox. "I will make you a present of a secret . . . a very simple secret: It is only with the heart that one can see rightly; what is essential is invisible to the eye. . . . Men have forgotten this truth. But you must not forget it. You become responsible, forever, for what you have tamed."

Sheila slid off my lap and got on her knees so that she could look directly into my eyes. "You be 'sponsible for me. You tame me so now you be 'sponsible for me?"

For several moments I looked into her fathomless eyes. I was not certain what she was asking me.

"I tame you a little bit too, huh?" she went on.

I nodded. For a moment she was lost in thought, tracing a design on the rug with her finger.

"Why you do this?" she asked. "Why you care? Why you *want* to tame me?"

My mind raced. If only I could say the right thing . . . but they had never told me in my child psychology classes that there would be children like this one. I was unprepared. "Well, kiddo, I guess it just seemed like the thing to do."

"Do it be like the fox? Do I be special 'cause you tame me?"

I smiled. "Yeah, you're my special girl. It's like the fox says, now that I made you my friend, you're unique in all the world. I guess I always wanted you for my special girl. That's why I tamed you."

"Do you love me?"

I nodded.

208

"I love you too. You be my special best person in the whole world."

Sheila scrunched herself down on the carpet with her head resting on my thigh. She fiddled with a piece of lint she had found on the floor. "Torey, you ain't never gonna leave me?"

I smoothed her hair. "Well, someday, when the school year is over and you go on to another class and another teacher—"

She shot up. "I ain't never gonna have another teacher."

"It won't be for a long time yet. When the time comes, you'll be ready."

"No sir. You tame me; you be 'sponsible for me forever. It says so right there."

"Honey." I pulled her into my lap. "Don't worry about it."

"But you gonna leave me," she said accusingly, pulling out of my hold. "Just like my mama done. And Jimmie. You do be just like everybody else."

"It won't be that way, Sheila. When the year is over, things will change, but like it says in the story—the little prince tamed the fox and now he's gone, but really he's always going to be with the fox, because every time the fox thinks of the little prince, he remembers how much the little prince loved him. That's how it'll be with us. We'll always love each other. Going away is easier then, because every time you remember someone who loves you, you feel their love."

"No you don't. You just miss them."

I reached an arm out to her, bringing her close once again.

She wasn't going to be convinced. I held her very tightly. This was too scary for her right now. But the time would come when she would have to leave, either when the state hospital had an opening, or at the end of the school year in June. For a number of reasons I already suspected my class would not exist the next year. So the time was coming, and I did not know if in four short months she would feel much differently from the way she did right now.

"Will you cry when you leave?" Sheila asked.

"Remember what the fox taught us? That every time someone goes away, you cry a little? He's right. Love hurts sometimes."

"I cry about my mama. But she don't love me none. She leaved me on the highway."

"Sheila, I'm never going to leave you that way. When you go somewhere else, we'll still be together, even if we don't see each other. There won't ever be enough miles to make us forget how happy we've been. Nothing can take away your memories."

She pushed her face into me. "I don't want to think about it now."

"No, you're right. This isn't the time. It's a long ways away. In the meantime, we'll think of other things."

ALTHOUGH I HAD ceased to be obsessed with our paperwork war, it was never completely out of my mind. I worried that Sheila would not be acceptable to a regular class teacher with an academic schedule to keep.

I still had no firm idea why she was so negative about paperwork. I suspected that it had something to do with failure. If she never committed anything to paper, it was impossible to prove that she ever made a mistake. Perhaps also she had figured out that reciting her answers to Anton, Whitney, or me, saved her a lot of work and got her the adult attention she craved.

However, there was one thing Sheila seemed to be finding more and more irresistible. I encouraged creative writing in class. The children kept journals in which they scribbled on and off all day, recording things that happened to them and what they felt. Every night I left notes to the children about what they had written. It was a personal communication, and we each valued the opportunity to find out how the other felt. I also gave formal writing assignments almost daily. All of the children—even Susannah—learned to write and to associate words with the feelings they could evoke.

Needless to say, Sheila, with her distaste for paper, did not write. This seemed to bother her a bit, and she would often crane her neck to see what the other kids were writing. Finally a day came in mid-February when her curiosity got the better of her. She came to me and said, "I might write something, if you give me a piece of paper."

It occurred to me that with a little reverse psychology I might be able to swing the whole paperwork issue around to my side. So I shook my head. "No, this is paperwork. You don't do paperwork, remember?"

"I might do this."

"No, I can't risk wasting any more paper on you. You wouldn't like it anyway. You go play. That's more fun."

"I won't waste no paper. I wanna do it, Torey."

I shook my head. "Sheila, you don't like paperwork. You've told me that yourself."

Sheila was getting angry and was trying not to show it. She gave a frustrated stomp with one foot, then changed tactics. "Please? Please? I won't tear it up. Cross my heart and hope to die. Please?"

I regarded her. "Maybe if you do some papers for me tomorrow and I see you don't tear them up, then I'll give you paper during creative writing."

She eyed me carefully, trying to determine a way to make me give in. "If you give me paper now, I'll write something you don't know about me. I'll write you something secret."

"Tomorrow. We're almost out of time today anyhow."

At that she gave a grunt of anger and stalked off across the room. I smiled inwardly. She was cute when she was mad, now that she was learning to handle it appropriately.

After a few moments I wandered over to her. "If you write fast, I could give you a piece of paper today." She looked up expectantly. "Except you can't tear it up."

"I won't. I promise."

"Are you going to do other paperwork if I give you this?"

She nodded emphatically, but said in exasperation. "I ain't gonna have no time left if you keep talking to me all day."

I grinned and handed her a piece of paper. "This better be a good secret."

Clutching the paper in both hands, she scurried over to the table. She had been eyeing the felt-tipped pens for some time, and now she grabbed one and darted off to the far side of the room. Scrambling under the rabbit's cage, she began to write.

211

She *was* fast. Within minutes she was back, the paper folded into a tiny square. She sidled up to me and pressed it into my hand.

"This here be a secret just for you."

"Okay." I began unfolding it.

"No, don't read it now. Save it."

Nodding, I slipped the little square into my pocket.

I forgot about it until that night when I was changing for bed, and the folded square fell out onto the floor. I carefully straightened it out. Inside I found Sheila's very personal note.

A special thing I want you to know but not tell Nobody
You know sometimes the kids make Fun of me and call me names and befor I used not to put on clene Close. But sometimes I dont cos you know what I do but please dont tell I wet the bed. I dont mean to Pa he wips me for it if he knows but He dont mostly. I just dont know why Torey I try real hard to Stop. You wouldnt be mad at me would you. it bothers me alot but it Make me ashamed of myself. Pa he says Im a baby but I be 7 soon. Please dont tell no kids about this ok. Or dont tell Mr. Colinz. Or Anton or Whiteney. I just want you to know.

I was touched by Sheila's openness and amazed by her writing ability. By and large she wrote well. It puzzled me that she used the contraction "I'm," since I had never heard her say it. I smiled to myself and sat down and wrote her a note back.

The first break in the paperwork war had been made. The next day, with help, she managed to do a math paper. Later, she was able to do two or three written assignments without supervision. Occasionally she would slip, destroying a paper that was especially difficult for her. But if I gave her a second sheet, she would try again. I never marked anything wrong. Instead, Anton or I would discuss alternatives with her when she answered questions incorrectly. Otherwise I kept a low profile about her increasing ability to do the tasks. I never wanted her to feel that I was measuring her worth by how many papers she did.

Interestingly enough, Sheila found a great outlet in creative writing. Line after line of her loose, rather sloppy writing would hurry across the page, revealing things that often seemed too personal to say face to face. I could usually count on five or six extra pages in the correction basket each night.

ALLAN, THE SCHOOL PSYCHOLOGIST, returned shortly after Valentine Day with a whole battery of tests for Sheila, including a Stanford-Binet IQ test. I balked a bit when I saw his armload in the office that morning. I knew that Sheila was a gifted child; she proved it daily. What difference did it make if her IQ were 170 or 175 or 180? The numbers were so far beyond normal that they were meaningless. But I relented, because I knew the time was coming when we would have to face the authorities who had committed her to the state hospital. She certainly did not belong there, and I was hoping all the illustrious IQ scores would serve us in the end.

Her extrapolated score on the Stanford-Binet gave her an IQ of 182. One eighty-two was beyond comprehension. Where in Sheila's abused, deprived six years had she learned what words like chattel meant? It seemed to me as if it were some sort of anomaly, like brain damage in reverse. In the back of my head I heard the chant of a TV commercial I had seen once: "A mind is a terrible thing to waste." My gut tightened. There was so much to do with this extraordinary child and so little time. I did not know if it would be nearly enough.

THE LAST WEEK in February I was scheduled to speak at a two-day conference out of state. As the time grew near, I called Ed Somers to make arrangements for a substitute teacher.

The children had been with a substitute before, early in November. It had been for only one day, and I had prepared the kids, so things had gone well. I felt it was important that they have these little tests of independence. Their progress during the year would be meaningless if they performed reliably only while I was there.

Sheila worried me though. She had not been with us long and was still quite dependent. I feared that my absence might frighten her.

On the Monday before I was to leave, I mentioned casually to the children that I would be gone. I mentioned it again on Tuesday.

On neither occasion did Sheila appear to take it in. But on Wednesday after lunch I sat the kids down and explained that I would be gone for the next two days. Anton and Whitney would be there and so would a substitute teacher. We talked about ways of behaving properly around a new teacher, and everyone participated in the discussion. Everyone but Sheila. Then as the reality of what I was saying dawned on her, she regarded me anxiously. Her hand went up.

"You gonna be gone?" she asked.

"Yes, I am. That's what we're talking about. I won't be here tomorrow or Friday, but I'll be back on Monday."

"You ain't gonna be here?"

I nodded. The other kids were looking at her strangely.

"Jeepers, Sheila," Peter said, "you deaf or something?"

Her face clouded over. She rose to her feet and retreated backward to the housekeeping corner. I went on to answer other questions and finally broke up the group when it seemed everyone was satisfied. It was almost time for recess.

Sheila had remained in the corner. When Anton called her to get her coat on, she refused, and I motioned to him to go out with the others. I went over to her.

"You're upset with me, aren't you?"

"You never tell me you go away."

"Yes, I did, Sheil. Both Monday and yesterday."

"It ain't fair you go leave me. I don't want you to."

"I know you don't, and I'm sorry for your sake that I have to. But I am coming back, Sheila. I'll only be gone for two days."

"I ain't never, never gonna like you again. You tame me so's I like you and then you leave."

"Sheila, listen to me . . ."

"I ain't never gonna listen to you." Her voice was almost inaudible now, but pregnant with feeling. "I hate you."

For the first time I saw her bring a finger up to one eye to stop a tear. In panic she pressed her hands tight against her temples, willing the tears back. "Look what you make me do," she muttered accusingly. "You make me cry, and you know I don't like to cry. I hate you. I ain't never gonna be nice in here again. No matter what."

214

For a single moment the tears glistened in her eyes. They never fell. She darted past me, grabbed her jacket, and ran out the door to the playground.

I got my coat and joined the children. Sheila sat on a bench by herself in the very farthest corner, hunched up against the chilly February wind. Her face was hidden in her arms.

"Not taking it so well, eh?" Anton said.

"Nope, she's not taking it so well."

After recess the other children got ready for cooking, but Sheila went back to the housekeeping corner, idly clattering toys around. I let her be. Tyler, ever the class mother, fussed over her, and Peter kept asking why she was not joining us. I explained that Sheila was feeling a little angry just then and was keeping herself in control by not being with us.

I was pleased that Sheila was handling her distress quite well: no tantrums, no destruction, no bolting. She had come a long way in two months.

IT WAS A GOOD CONFERENCE and an even better vacation. It was in a West Coast state with a mild February climate. Chad went with me, and we spent most of the time walking on the beach. It was a marvelous change. When I was working, I seldom realized how tense my involvement with the children left me. Now, on the sunny beach, I felt the weariness drain away. For Chad and me the trip was a spiritual rebirth. Since Sheila had come into my life, forcing me to do my planning work at night, Chad had been slighted. He understood my fascination with the kids, but he still resented the fact that they absorbed every moment. Four days alone together left us happy and relaxed.

ON MONDAY morning I was pleased to be back in school. We had a field trip to a fire station planned in the afternoon, and I had to make last-minute arrangements on the telephone.

Anton met me in the hallway as I was returning from the phone. "We had quite a time in your absence," he said.

"What happened?"

"Sheila went absolutely berserk. She pulled all the stuff off the

215

walls, all the books out of the bookcases. She refused to talk. She gave Peter a bloody nose on Friday. She wouldn't do any work at all. She broke the record player and tried to break the glass out of the door with her shoe. She was worse than she was when she first came."

"Cripes," I muttered. I had honestly believed I could trust her to behave while I was gone, and she had let me down. I had mis-guessed badly.

I planned to discuss the matter with Sheila, but her bus was late. The other kids began to arrive, all bearing tales. "You ought to have seen what Sheila done," Sarah said excitedly. "She wrecked the whole room."

"Yeah!" Guillermo chirped. "That substitute spanked her, and made her sit in the quiet corner, and Whitney had to hold her all afternoon, 'cause she wouldn't stay."

Peter bounced around me, his dark eyes blazing with delight. "And she was real mean to Whitney and Whitney cried and then guess what? Even the teacher cried. All the girls cried. But I didn't. I socked her."

"Her bad," Max confirmed, twirling around me.

My discouragement turned to anger. This incident was far harder for me to accept than even the destruction in Mrs. Holmes's room, for this behavior had been directly aimed at me.

Sheila arrived after we had started morning discussion. She regarded me suspiciously as she sat down. A familiar odor wafted up: she hadn't even bothered to wash since I left.

After discussion I called her over. We sat in chairs away from the others. "I hear you didn't handle yourself very well, Sheila. I'm mad at you, the maddest I've been in a long time. Now I want to hear why you did that."

No response.

"I trusted you for two lousy days, Sheila," I said, my voice soft, the discouragement undisguised. "I trusted you, and do you want to know how it makes me feel to hear that you behaved like that?"

Sheila exploded with fury. "I never told you to trust me! I never said that; you did! Nobody can trust me!" She tore off, careening frantically around the room before scuttling under the table. Her distress was so great that she just sat there emitting little occassional strangled noises.

I sat in the chair without moving. The other children paused to look at us, concern showing in their eyes.

"Well, then you're not going on the field trip with us this afternoon, Sheila," I said at last. "I'm not taking anyone I can't trust. You can stay with Anton."

She crawled out from under the table, looking horror-struck. I knew that the field trip meant a great deal to her. "I can too go," she said.

"No, I'm afraid not. I can't trust you."

She screamed, letting loose high-pitched, earsplitting shrieks. She flung herself on the floor and banged her head violently on the ground. Anton made a flying leap toward her. She had never attempted to hurt herself before.

Anton held her tightly in his arms. She struggled savagely and continued to scream. Then as suddenly as she had started screaming, she stopped, and the room fell into unearthly silence. I dashed over, fearing that she had hurt herself. Anton released her, and she slithered down into a little lump on the carpet. Her arms were over her head, her face pressed into the rug.

"Are you all right, Sheila?" I asked.

She turned her head. "Please let me go," she whispered. "I do be sorry for what I done. Let me go. Please? I'll show you how good I can be."

I looked down at her, beginning to think that all the violent behavior was a con because she had stopped it so fast. That renewed some of my anger. "I don't think so, Sheila. Maybe next time."

She began screaming again, covering her face with her hands. I walked away to work with the other children.

All morning she lay there. She screamed a while longer, then fell silent. By midday my spirits had flagged completely. I was beginning to realize that I had been angry with her for exposing what I perceived as a teaching deficit in myself. I was angry because she had done to me what I had watched her do to so many others: she had taken revenge against me. She had hurt me, and with embarrassment I realized I had done the same thing to her by taking away the field trip, a privilege she didn't even know was in jeopardy. I felt worse than ever.

At lunch I unloaded my guilt on Anton. Why had I ever become a teacher if I had such lousy control over my own feelings? Anton tried to reassure me. Sheila had misbehaved very badly, he reminded me. She had to learn that this was unacceptable.

But I felt like a zero. What Sheila had done was not so unpredictable. She had been right. She had never said I could trust her. The poor kid was upset and was showing it the only way she knew how. That was why she was in my class to begin with. Unhappily I choked down the last of my sandwich.

Back in the classroom, the other kids were getting ready to go on the field trip, but Sheila sat alone in the corner.

I sat down next to her. "Honey, I have to talk to you. I did something wrong this morning. I got mad at you when I was really mad at myself. I told you that you couldn't go on the trip, but I've changed my mind. You can go. I'm sorry I was angry with you."

She did not respond. She did not even look at me, but rose and got her coat.

A STRAINED SILENCE lingered between us throughout the trip. I outdid myself trying to be funny and make everyone laugh. But Sheila remained apart, holding on to Whitney's hand.

After school, when the other children had gone home, I offered to read to Sheila. She declined and busied herself playing with cars. I sat down to grade some papers. The first hour passed. Sheila got up to stand by the window. When next I looked up, she was watching me.

"How come you come back?" she asked softly.

"I just went to give a speech. I never intended to stay away. I like it here."

Slowly she approached me, the hurt clear in her eyes.

"You really didn't think I was coming back, did you?" I asked. She shook her head.

Across a tremendous gulf of silence we looked at each other. I could hear the clock jumping the minutes. I wondered what she was thinking, and I realized sadly that we never do understand what it is like to be someone else. We tend to feel omniscient, especially with children. But we really never know.

Sheila stood twisting an overall strap. "Would you read that book again? The one about the little boy who tamed the fox?"

I smiled. "Yeah, I'll read it."

MARCH CAME IN BREEZY and warm, a welcome relief for the winter-weary North. The snow finally melted, and cool, brown mud rose through the grass. We were all anxious for spring.

March was also peaceful as far as school went; as peaceful as it ever got in a class like mine. There were no disruptions to cause friction, no unexpected changes.

Sheila continued to bloom. Each day she showed more and more improvement. She was always clean now, and she paid close attention to how she looked. She and Sarah had become fast friends—I caught them exchanging notes in class occasionally—and now and then Sheila went home with Sarah after school to play. At the migrant camp, Sheila played with Guillermo. I was pleased.

Academically she sailed. I had her working on third-grade reading material and fourth-grade math; both were considerably below her ability level, but because of her fear of failure I felt it better to cement her knowledge and confidence more solidly.

Most important, Sheila was learning to solve her emotional problems verbally. No longer did she resort to hanging on to me for reassurance; words were enough. And the destructiveness had all but disappeared. Sheila still had a lot of problems, but they were becoming manageable.

Her odd speech patterns still puzzled me, although as time passed she began using more normal ones. The visit with her father had confirmed that her speech patterns did not originate at home. One day I decided to ask her about them. She was surprisingly antagonistic. What did it matter how she talked, she said, if I understood her?

All the speech experts to whom I sent tapes thought it was a family dialect. When I replied that it wasn't, they had no other

219

ideas. Chad suggested that perhaps her frequent use of "be" instead of the past tense was an effort to keep things anchored in the present, where she could control them better. The more I pondered that, the more possible it seemed. In the end, I concluded it was a psychological problem and let it go at that. Perhaps someday she would feel comfortable enough to want to change.

THE ISSUE STILL UPPERMOST in Sheila's mind was abandonment. Often her conversations were punctuated with comments about her mother and her brother, and about how, if she had done this thing or that thing better, maybe her family would still be intact. I felt this was all directly tied to her intense fear of failure.

One day after school Sheila busied herself doing a fifth-grade math exam she had discovered in a trash can at recess. She loved math and excelled in it. She could do basic multiplication and division, but this test was on the division of fractions, an area we had not covered.

"Is it done good?" she asked, handing the exam to me.

All her answers were wrong because she had not inverted the divisor. "Sheil, I want to show you something," I said. On the back of the paper I drew a circle and divided it into four parts. "Now, if I wanted to know how many eighths were in it . . ." She immediately perceived that the way she was solving the problem would not give the correct answer.

"I done them wrong, didn't I?"

"You didn't know, kiddo. No one showed you."

She flopped down beside me and put her face in her hands. "I bet if I could have done math problems good, my mama, she wouldn't leave me on no highway like she done; she'd be proud of me."

"I don't think math problems have anything to do with it, Sheila. We really don't know why your mama left you. She probably had all sorts of troubles of her own."

Slowly her hands slid away from her face. That haunted, hurt expression was in her eyes. "I miss Jimmie."

"I know you do."

220

"His birthday's gonna be next week, on March twelfth. He be five years old then. Could we have a birthday party for him?"

"I don't think so, kitten."

Her face fell. "Why not?"

"Because Jimmie isn't here with us, Sheil."

"It could be just a little birthday party." Her face had puckered, and her voice was pleading.

I shook my head. "Sheila, Jimmie's gone. As much as it hurts to think about, he may not be coming back. I don't think it's a good idea to keep remembering him the way you are, kitten. All it does is hurt you."

She covered her face with her hands again.

"Sheil, come here and let me hold you." She came, and I lifted her into my lap. "I know you feel awful about this."

"I miss him." Her voice broke with a dry sob. "Why did she tooked him and leaved me behind? My pa, he says if I be a gooder girl she'd a never done that."

My heart sank. There was so much to fight and so little to fight with. "Your pa made a mistake on this one, Sheil. He doesn't know what happened either, and he doesn't know what it's like to be a little girl. Believe me, please, because it's true."

We sat in silence. Her pain soaked through my shirt and my skin and bones, to be absorbed into my heart.

At last she looked up. "Sometimes, I'm real lonely. Will it ever stop?"

I nodded slowly. "Yes. Someday I think it will."

Sheila sighed and pulled away from me, standing up. "Someday never really ever comes, does it?"

DESPITE OUR SAD MOMENTS, Sheila had a tremendous capacity for joy. She was never entirely able to escape the emotional devastation she had suffered, but she was never far from happiness either. The smallest thing would ignite a merry sparkle in her eyes and evoke her skitterish laughter. Everything was new to her. She could not get her fill of the many wonders that the world held.

Her greatest discovery in March was the flowers. Crocuses and

221

daffodils waved from every patch of ground. Sheila was fascinated by them. None grew in the migrant camp and, as unbelievable as it seemed to me, she had never seen a daffodil up close. One morning I brought in a huge bouquet from my landlady's garden, and Sheila came over, squealing. Peering at the bouquet she asked, "Them be real flowers?"

"Sure they're real. They're daffodils. Touch them."

She cautiously reached out, touching the edge of one flower with her fingertip. "Oooooh! They do be so soft." She squealed with delight. Jumping up and down, she clutched herself with pleasure. "I feel like hugging them."

I chuckled. "Flowers don't especially like being hugged."

I got out a vase and put the flowers in it. Beside me Sheila bounced in delight, first on one foot and then on the other. Her whole body reflected her joy.

"Sheil, would you like a flower of your own?"

"I can have one? Could it really be mine?"

"Yes, silly, for you. Your own flower."

Her face fell suddenly. "My pa wouldn't let me keep it."

I smiled. "Flowers are different. Your pa wouldn't care about something like a flower. Which one would you like?"

Carefully she chose one, and holding it gently and stroking its golden cup, she smiled. "My heart do be so big," she whispered. "It be so big and I do reckon I be about the happiest kid for it."

THINGS WERE NOT always very funny in our room, but we laughed a lot. At ourselves, at each other, at our sometimes hopeless situation. Laughter normalized our lives. And it was Whitney, more than anyone else, who kept us in touch with normality. I loved her wholeheartedly for that quality, for never letting me or Anton or the kids convince her that our room was different.

Despite her shyness, Whitney had a sense of humor that knew no limits. Her wit could be dry and shockingly adult when with Anton and me, but she was at her best as a practical joker. Her antics consistently took me by surprise. I never failed to be genuinely startled by the spring snakes that jumped out of Susannah's crayon box or by the fake mess sitting on the table while

222

Peter, William, and Guillermo feigned sudden stomach upsets.

One day when we were alone, I said to Whitney, "I love your sense of humor and the way you show the kids how to laugh."

In her shyness she would not look at me. After a long silence she said, "Can I tell you something, Torey?"

"Yeah."

"This class is about the only place in the world I like to be. Everybody teases me about it. All the time. They say: Why do you want to hang around with crazy people all the time? They think I'm crazy too—you know, mental. Otherwise why would I want to be here so much?"

"Well," I replied, "then they must think Anton and I are also crazy."

"Why are you here, Torey?"

I smiled. "I guess because I like very honest relationships. So far the only people I've found to be that honest are either children or crazy. So this place seems to be a natural for me."

"Yes, I guess that's what I like too—the way everybody shows exactly what they feel." She smiled wanly. "The funny thing is, these kids don't seem as crazy to me sometimes as normal people do. I mean . . ." Her voice trailed off.

I nodded. "Yes, I know what you mean."

CHAPTER FIVE

The call that I had been dreading came the third week in March. When the secretary rang my room after school to tell me I had a phone call, I had a premonition this was the one. Then I heard Ed Somers' low, rumbling voice on the phone and I knew, even before he said it.

"Torey, they have an opening at the state hospital."

My pulse began to race. It beat so hard in my ears that I could not hear. "Ed, she doesn't have to go, does she?"

"Tor, the court ordered it. It really is out of our hands."

"But she's changed so much. She's not the same child."

"Listen, it was all settled before either of us got into it. Besides, it'll be in her best interest. Look at her terrible home situation.

She'll never make it. You, of all people, should know when a kid's got too much stacked against her."

"But she hasn't, Ed," I cried. "This kid has so much. She could make it. She can't go into the hospital now."

"Tor, you've done a hell of a good job with those kids. Sometimes I honestly don't know how you do it. But you've gotten too involved with this one. This kid's case was decided long ago."

"Then undecide it."

"It's out of my hands. After that burning incident, the state committed her to placate the boy's parents. That was the only alternative. I'm sorry." He hung up.

I went down to the teachers' lounge, unable to go back to my room where Sheila was playing. I sat and drank coffee, all the while trying to keep the tears back. Ed was right. She mattered too much to me.

When I went back to my room, Anton did not ask what had happened—he knew. He motioned Sheila over to the table where he was setting up a project for the next day and asked her to help him. I stood in the doorway looking around the room. I could have used a teacher's desk right then; something to go and hide behind; something that shouted, "Leave me alone," without my saying it. But there was none. Wearily I went over to the pillows in the corner and sank down onto them.

Within seconds Sheila was standing before me, her hands stuffed into the pockets of her overalls. "You ain't happy," she said quietly. How much she has grown, I thought. There must have been two inches between the overalls and the tops of her sneakers.

"No, I'm not happy."

"How come?"

"Sheila, come over here," Anton called. Sheila remained motionless. I loved the child, and loving her made me " 'sponsible" for her. I could feel the tears in my eyes.

Sheila knelt beside me, worry rippling across her face. "How come you cry?"

Anton came over and lifted Sheila to her feet. "Come on, tiger, you come help me put away papers."

"Uh-uh." Sheila twisted out of his grasp and sat down.

I waved a hand at him. "That's okay, Anton. I'm all right." He nodded and left us.

I could not bring myself to look at Sheila. I was embarrassed to show such shaky composure, and I was worried about frightening her. But touching my hand tentatively, she spoke. "Maybe if I hold your hand, you'll feel better. Sometimes that helps me."

I smiled at her. "You know, kid, I love you. Don't ever forget that. If the times comes and you're alone or scared or anything else bad ever happens, don't forget I love you. Because I do. That's really all one person can do for another."

Her brow wrinkled. She was too young to understand what I was saying, but I had to say it. I had to know, for my own peace of mind, that I had told her I had done my best.

CHAD AND I HAD been watching TV all evening and not talking. I was too preoccupied to concentrate on conversation. At first I had not even told him the particulars of what had happened; but as the evening wore on, my mind began emerging from the first haze of shock.

"Chad," I asked, "is there a legal way to contest what they plan to do with Sheila?"

"What do you mean?"

"Well, could someone like me fight the commitment? Someone who isn't her guardian? The school district might back me."

"I suppose you could try."

I frowned. "But to whom do we appeal?"

"I imagine you'd have to call a hearing with her father and the parents of the boy she injured and the child protection workers."

"Would you take it on, Chad?"

His eyebrows shot up. "Me? You need someone who specializes in that sort of law. My experience is confined to getting drunks out of jail."

I smiled. "Your experience and my bank account are equal."

Chad grinned. "Another charity case, huh? I guess no one ever promised me I'd get rich."

"Oh, someday you will. Just not this year."

WHEN THE SUPERINTENDENT of schools discovered that I had engaged a lawyer, he immediately scheduled a meeting. There I met Mrs. Barthuly, Sheila's former teacher. She was a petite woman in her early forties, with a delicate smile. All five feet nine inches of me in my jeans and tennis shoes towered over her. With her designer scarf and platform shoes, she looked like a model for a perfume ad. She must have found smelly, earthy-minded Sheila hard to contend with.

Ed Somers was also there; as well as Allan, the psychologist; Mr. Collins; Anton; the superintendent, and the resource teacher who had had Sheila in kindergarten.

In the beginning it was not a particularly comfortable meeting for me. Not knowing my relationship with Chad, the superintendent felt that I had overstepped my bounds in consulting a lawyer without going through him. But despite our touchy start, a transformation took place once the meeting got under way. I had brought along examples of Sheila's schoolwork and some videotapes that Anton had made of her in class. Allan reported on his testing results. Sheila's former teachers were impressed and said so. Even Mr. Collins commented on the overall improvement in Sheila's behavior. Unexpectedly, I felt a rush of affection toward him as he spoke.

The superintendent was less enthusiastic. Yet he was encouraged by Sheila's progress and by her unusual IQ. He cautiously agreed to stand behind me in stating that the hospital was not the most appropriate place for Sheila, and that he thought she could be maintained in the public school system without endangering the other students. Despite his attempts to keep the mood of the meeting low-key, I left in jubilant spirits.

The other major person we would need to involve was Sheila's father. Anton went on scouting duty, and the next time he saw the man at home he called me. Chad and I joined Anton immediately.

As before, Sheila's father had been drinking. He had had a bit more this time and was a little jollier.

"Sheila doesn't belong in the state hospital," I explained. "She's doing very nice work in school, and I think she might even be able to go back to a regular class next fall."

226

"Why do you care what they want to do with her?"

The question echoed in my head, a repeat of what Sheila so often asked me. Why *did* I care? "You've got a special daughter," I replied. "Going to the state hospital would be the wrong move for her. I think she can lead a normal life."

"She's crazy as a loon. They told you what she done, didn't they? She damn near burned that little kid to death."

"She's not crazy, but she will be if she goes into the state hospital. You don't want your daughter in there."

He heaved a great sigh. All his life people had been after him. Things had always gone wrong. He'd been in trouble. Sheila had been in trouble. He had learned to trust nobody and so had his daughter. It was safer that way. Now I had come and he did not understand me.

We talked far into the night. Chad and Anton drank beer with him while I made notes. Sheila, who was again keeping vigil from the far corner, fell asleep on the floor. I did not know if she understood what was going on. I had not told her anything specific, because I did not want to frighten her needlessly. But after that night I suspected she would know.

Her father agreed with us eventually. We convinced him that our concern for Sheila was not "charity" or "do-gooding." I had guessed that he did have some paternal instinct under that crust. In his own way he loved Sheila and needed as much compassion as she did.

That was a strange evening. All of us were a little tipsy. Chad, with his experience defending skid-row residents, seemed to get along with Sheila's father better than Anton or I. The two of them would slap each other on the back in boozy camaraderie. Then they'd ply Anton and me with more beer. In a way I was glad the hospital situation had come up. It forced us to recognize each other's place in Sheila's life.

THE HEARING WAS held on the very last day of March. It was a dark, cold, windy day; not a day to boost one's spirits. Anton and I had to take the afternoon off from school, and Mr. Collins went with us. Surprisingly he was very supportive of me, though at first I was suspicious, wondering if he were simply protecting his own interests. Ever since the incident in Mrs. Holmes's room I had nursed a childish one-dimensional picture of him. Now I came to see that he cared as much for the children as I did. Even for Sheila.

It was a closed hearing. With us were Allan, Mrs. Barthuly, Ed, and the superintendent. Across the room from us were the parents of the little boy and their lawyer. Milling about were a multitude of state and county people. Sheila's father arrived late, but he was sober. At the sight of him my heart ached. His face was freshly shaved and he was wearing a suit. The seams were frayed, the jacket stained, the pants torn, but obviously he had tried to look nice.

Sheila sat with a court clerk outside the courtroom. Chad felt it would be best to have Sheila there. He thought he might need her if things did not go smoothly.

It was a very quiet hearing, much different from what I had expected. No one even appeared to be emotionally involved. Each of us presented our material. I had brought along the videotapes to illustrate Sheila's growth in the three months she had been with us. Allan reiterated his findings from the tests. Ed spoke of the programs for her in the public schools, should she continue to need special services after my class.

The parents of the little boy were questioned about the incident in November. Sheila's father was asked how carefully he watched his daughter, and if, in his opinion, she had improved in the last months. Then we were all asked to leave the courtroom while the lawyers and the judge finished up the case.

The boy's parents sat down at the far end of the hallway. The strain showed on their faces. I wondered what they were thinking. Did they have the compassion to forgive Sheila for what she had done, or were their hearts still too burdened with fear and grief over their injured son? Looking at them, I could not tell.

Sheila was sitting on my lap. She had drawn a picture and was telling me about it. "Look, Tor. It be a picture of Susannah Joy. See, she gots on that dress she wears to school so much."

Sheila had long been envious of Susannah Joy and her splendid

228

wardrobe of frilly little frocks. Day after day Sheila would page through catalogues, picking out dresses she would like to own. Recently I had found a creative writing paper on the subject in the correction basket.

> I want to tell you what I do last night Torey. I go down and wait for my father he be at the opptomrix who fistes eye glasses. So I got to walk around and I look in them windows. Some times I wish I could by the things in them windows. I seen a dress that be red and blue and be white too and it gots lace on it and be long and beutiful. I ain't never had a dress like that and it was prety torey. I ask my pa if I could by it but he sad "no". That be too bad cos I could a wored it to school like Susannah Joy do. But I couldnt so we went home and my pa he by me some M&Ms instead and toled me "to go to bed Sheila" so I did.

That little essay seemed one of the saddest things she had ever written.

She prattled on about the drawing she was holding, until at last the doors to the judge's chambers opened. From the minute I saw Chad's face I knew what the ruling had been. He stopped about eight feet from us and grinned. "We won."

Noise erupted in the hallway, and we danced about, hugging one another. "We won! We won!" Sheila shrieked, bouncing amid everyone's legs. We all laughed at her jubilance, although I doubted she knew the impact of what she was saying.

"I think this calls for a celebration, don't you?" Chad asked. "What do you say we go down to Shakey's and order the biggest pizza they have?"

The others were beginning to leave. I glanced down the hallway toward the boy's parents. I wished I had the courage to speak to them, but I found myself unable to. Chad was talking to me about pizza, Sheila was jumping around my legs, school people were yelling good-bys.

I turned back to Chad and nodded.

"What about you?" he said to Sheila. "You want to come with Torey and me to get pizza?" Her eyes widening, she nodded. I bent down and picked her up.

229

Sheila's father stood apart from us, his hands stuffed into the pockets of his ill-fitting suit. He stared at the floor. He seemed lonely and forgotten. It was not to him that Sheila had turned in celebration. I realized with great sadness that even his daughter was not his own. She was one of us.

Chad must have perceived the same loneliness. "Do you want to join us?" he asked.

For a moment I thought I saw a flicker of pleasure on his face. But he shook his head. "No, I have to be going."

"It's all right if Sheila comes with us, isn't it?" Chad asked. "We'll bring her home later."

He agreed, a soft smile on his lips as he regarded his daughter. She was still in my arms, still wiggling with excitement, mindless of her father. For a long moment he and I looked at each other, the universe between us unbridged. Then Chad reached into his pocket, and pulling out a twenty-dollar bill, handed it to him. "Here. Here's your share of the fun."

He hesitated, and I did not think he would accept it, knowing his disdain for charity. But uncertainly he extended his hand and took the bill. He mumbled a thank you, then turned and walked away down the long corridor.

Sheila, Chad, and I all piled into Chad's little foreign car and sped off to the pizza parlor. "Hey, Sheila, what kind of pizza do you like?" Chad asked.

"I don't know. I ain't never had no pizza."

"Never had pizza?" Chad exclaimed. "Well, we might have to do this more often, huh?"

If she had never had pizza before, one would never have known it from her behavior. When the pie arrived, she grabbed for a piece like a pro. Chad had ordered the biggest pizza on the menu, as well as a pitcher of soda pop.

Sheila was alive and animated, talking constantly. She was intrigued by Chad and ended up sitting on his lap. He commented that he had never seen a little kid eat so much food in one sitting. Sheila told him she could eat a hundred pizzas if he had money to buy them, and she burped loudly to prove it. It was clear as they laughed that each thought the other was someone special.

230

Night had fallen, and the evening crowd was beginning to drift into the restaurant. But Chad and Sheila were not yet ready to part company. "What's the thing you'd like best in the world, if you could have it?" Chad asked her.

I flinched, because I feared Sheila would say she wanted her mama and Jimmie back.

Instead, she pondered Chad's question. "Real or pretend?"

"Real."

Still pensive, she answered, "A dress, I think. Like Susannah Joy gots. One that gots lace on it."

"You mean all you'd want in the whole world is just a dress?"

Sheila nodded. "I ain't never had a dress before."

Chad looked at his watch. "It's almost seven o'clock. I don't think the stores in the mall close until nine. What if I told you this is your lucky day?"

Sheila did not understand. "What do you mean?"

"What if I told you that in a few minutes we're going to go to a store and buy you a dress? Any dress you want."

Sheila's mouth dropped open. Then suddenly she was crest-fallen. "My pa, he wouldn't let me keep it."

"I think he would. When we take you home, I'll just tell him that's your share of the fun."

The next hour was a giddy one. Sheila was beside herself. We walked the aisles of a department store with her holding on to our hands and swinging between us. Once we found the little girls' dresses, she turned unexpectedly shy and would not even look at them, shoving her face into my leg. Dreams close up can be hard to handle.

Finally I selected a few, with lace, and dragged Sheila into a fitting room to try them on. Once we were alone she came back to life. Stripping off her overalls and shirt, Sheila lifted the dresses up to inspect them. She became too excited to try one on and danced around in circles. I captured her and shoved her into a dress. What a magic moment! Sheila preened in front of the mirror and then ran out to show Chad. We must have waited half an hour for her to decide among three dresses. At last she chose a red-and-white dress with lace at the neck and the sleeves.

"I'm gonna wear it every day to school," she said enthusiastically.

"You look so pretty," I told her.

She was watching me in the dressing-room mirror. Suddenly her smile faded, and she turned to me. She climbed onto my lap, touching my face softly with one hand. "You know what I wish? I wish you was my mama and Chad was my daddy. It almost seems that way now, don't it?"

I smiled. "We're something better than that, Sheil. We're friends. Friends are better than parents, because it means we love each other because we want to, not because we have to."

She sighed. "I wish we could be both."

"Yes, that would be nice."

Her forehead wrinkled. "Just for tonight, could we pretend?" she asked tentatively. "Pretend that you and Chad was my folks, and you was bringing your little girl out to buy her a dress? Even though she gots lots of dresses, you was buying her another 'cause she wanted it, and you loved her a lot?"

All my training in psychology urged me to say no. But as I saw her eyes, my heart wouldn't let me. "I suppose we could pretend. Just for tonight."

She leaped off my lap and tore out of the dressing room in her underwear. "I'm gonna tell Chad!"

Chad was amused to find out that while we were in the fitting room he had become a father. He played the part to the hilt, and for all three of us it was a night filled with unspoken magic.

Sheila fell asleep in my arms on the way out to the migrant camp, and after Chad parked the car, I woke her.

"Well, Cinderella," Chad said, "it's time to go home."

She smiled at him sleepily.

"Come on. I'll carry you in and tell your daddy what we've been up to."

She hesitated. "I don't wanna go," she said softly.

"It's been a nice night, hasn't it?" I said.

She nodded. A silence fell between us. "Can I kiss you?"

"Yes, I think so." I enveloped her in a tight hug and I kissed her. I felt her soft lips touch my cheek. She kissed Chad as he lifted her out of my lap and carried her into her house.

232

We drove home in silence. In front of my place we sat in the car, still not speaking. Finally Chad turned to me, his eyes shining in the wan glow of a streetlight. "She's a hell of a kid."

I nodded.

"You know," he said, "I pretended right along with her tonight. I wished we were a family too. It seemed so right."

I smiled into the darkness, feeling a comfortable quiet drift down around us.

CHAPTER SIX

April came in with a snowstorm, winter's parting shot. It was one of those big, fluffy snowfalls that are so lovely to look at, but its depth stalled everything, and school was suspended for two days.

When we returned, Sheila announced that her Uncle Jerry had come to live with them. He had been in jail, and now he was out and looking for a job. She seemed excited about this new member of her family, telling us how Uncle Jerry had played with her all day during the snowstorm.

We quickly resumed our routine. There was a trace of euphoria remaining from our victory in court, and both Anton and I stayed in high spirits. And if we were happy, Sheila in her new dress was positively radiant. She wore the prized dress every day.

One morning almost halfway into April, however, she arrived at school wearing her old overalls and T-shirt. She looked subdued and very pale. Sitting down on the outer fringe of the group during discussion, she listened but did not participate. Twice during the half-hour session she got up and went into the bathroom. I worried that she might be ill.

Later, when I was handing out math assignments, I took her aside. "Don't you fell well today, hon?" I asked.

"I'm okay," she replied, going to her place at the table.

I followed and took her on my lap. Her body was surprisingly rigid. I felt her forehead to see if she were feverish. She wasn't, but she was certainly acting oddly. "Is something wrong, Sheil? You're all tense."

"I'm okay," she said again.

I lifted her off my lap. On the leg of my jeans was a widening red spot. I stared at it, not comprehending for a moment what it was. I looked at Sheila. Down the inside of her pant leg a red stain was spreading.

"Sheila, you're bleeding!" Picking her up, I rushed into the bathroom and shut the door behind us. Unbuckling the overalls, I let them fall around her ankles. Blood ran down both legs. Wadded into her underwear were paper towels with which she had evidently been trying to stanch the flow.

"Good God, Sheila, *what* is going on?" I cried, fear rising in me as I pulled away the towels.

Sheila stood unmoving. No emotion showed on her face. Her eyes were blank. She was so pale. I wondered how much blood she had lost. "Sheila, what happened? You have to tell me. What happened to you?"

She blinked like someone coming out of a heavy sleep. She was paying a great price to cut off the pain and the emotion.

"My Unca Jerry, he said he was going to love me. He said he was going to show me how grown-up people loved each other." Her voice sounded far away. "And when I screamed, he said nobody ain't gonna never love me if I can't learn how. He said I was keeping him out, so he cut me there with a table knife."

I went numb. "Oh, Sheila, why didn't you tell me?"

"I's scared to. Unca Jerry said he'd do it again if I told on him. He said worser things would happen if I told."

Fearful that she had already lost too much blood, I wrapped a towel around her and picked her up. Rushing out of the bathroom, carrying her, I told Anton to watch the class. I grabbed my car keys and trotted toward the office. Briefly I explained to the secretary that I was taking Sheila to the hospital, and asked her to have someone find the child's father and get him there. All the time I could feel the warmth of Sheila's blood soaking into my shirt.

Sheila was whiter now, getting sluggish and closing her eyes. I ran for my car. Holding her in my lap, I turned the key in the ignition and jammed the car into gear. "Sheila? Sheila? Stay awake," I whispered, trying to drive and hang on to her at the same time. I should have taken someone with me, I thought.

"I do be awake," Sheila muttered. Her small fingers dug into my skin as she gripped my shirt. "But it hurts."

"Oh, I'm sure it does, baby, but keep talking to me, okay?" The distance to the hospital seemed interminable, the traffic impossible. Maybe I should have waited for an ambulance. I had no idea how much blood she had lost.

She caught her lips in a tearless sob. "Unca Jerry kept saying I had to learn how grown-up people love."

We were nearing the hospital. "Oh, kitten, he just said that so he could do something wrong to you. What he said and what he did were wrong."

Two young orderlies came running down the emergency ramp with a stretcher. Apparently the hospital had been alerted. As I placed Sheila on the stretcher, she registered alarm for the first time. Moaning, she refused to let go of my shirt and struggled fiercely as the men tried to loosen her fingers.

"Don't leave me!" she wailed. "Don't let them take me away!"

"I'm coming with you, Sheil." And in a contorted mass the four of us and the stretcher moved through the door, Sheila retaining her terror-wrought grasp on my shirt. She fought so valiantly that it was finally easier for me to pick her up and hold her than to pry her off.

The emergency-room doctor examined her briefly while I held her on my lap. Her father was still not there, so I signed a form saying that I would be responsible for emergency treatment until he could be found.

Sheila had once again become docile and silent, not even flinching when a nurse came in and gave her a shot. Within a short time I felt her fingers relax, and I laid her on the examining table. Another nurse started an IV in one of her arms while an intern hung a pint of blood above the table. After further examination, the doctor gestured to me to come outside with him. With one last look at Sheila, who lay pale and tiny on the table, her eyes closed, I followed him. I told him what had happened. At that point we saw Sheila's father stumbling down the corridor with the social worker. He was drunk.

The doctor explained to us that Sheila had lost a tremendous amount of blood and that they had to stabilize her blood level. Once that had been done, she would most likely need surgery. From what he had seen, the knife had punctured the vagina wall, a very serious injury because of the likelihood of infection. As the doctor spoke, Sheila's father weaved uncertainly beside us.

There was no more I could do here. It was best that I get back to my class. I looked down at my clothes. I would have to go home and change. Blood had stained the entire front of my shirt. I stared at it, startled by how fragile life really is.

THAT NIGHT I did not go back to the hospital. When I called the doctor after school, he told me that Sheila was not yet out of surgery. Despite the blood transfusions, her condition remained critical. She would go into intensive care after surgery to make sure the hemorrhaging had stopped, and he suggested I wait until the next day to visit. He assured me they would make her as comfortable as they could. I asked about her father. He had been sent home, not sober enough to be coherent. The father's brother, Jerry, had been taken into custody.

After supper Chad came over, and I related what had taken place. Chad was explosive. He paced the room, at first saying nothing and shaking his head in disbelief. Then he raged with hatred against a man who would do such a thing to a little girl.

Although I was heartsick about the incident, a strange feeling nagged at me. Five months earlier, Sheila had been the abuser and someone else the victim. Undoubtedly the boy's parents had felt the same way about Sheila as Chad was feeling about Jerry. It did not by any means excuse the gross inhumanity of Jerry's crime, but it made me aware that the psychological damage I had found in Sheila was probably in Jerry too.

The next day I called the hospital again. The doctor said that Sheila had tolerated surgery well, and had stabilized during the night. This morning she had been alert and coherent, so they had transferred her to the children's ward. I could see her any time I wanted. She was a tough little kid, the doctor said warmly. Yes, I replied, there weren't any that were tougher.

IT WAS VERY DIFFICULT explaining to the other children what had happened to Sheila. Back in October we had talked about abuse, both physical and sexual, in our room. Most of my kids came from a population in which the risk of child abuse was high, and I felt it was important for them to know what to do if they found themselves in such a situation. Nevertheless, sexual abuse was hard to talk about. I had worked up an informal unit in which we simply discussed the appropriate and inappropriate ways of being touched by an adult. It provided a measure of relief for the kids to be able to talk about those things, to express their fears about not knowing what to do when someone touched them and it felt "funny."

Still, I did not know how to handle Sheila's case. Yet I had to say something. The children had seen us leave unexpectedly, and they had seen the blood. So I simply told them that Sheila had been hurt at home, and because of it I had taken her to the hospital.

The children made get-well cards for her the next afternoon, with poignant, brightly crayoned messages. The event, however, affected the kids more than I had perceived. At day's end, as we gathered around the Kobold's Box, William burst into tears.

"What's wrong?" I asked.

"I'm scared about Sheila. I'm scared she's going to die. My grandpa went to the hospital once and he died there."

Unexpectedly, Tyler also began to sob. "I miss her."

"Hey, you guys," I said. "Sheila's doing really well. She won't die or anything."

"But you won't let us talk about it," Sarah complained. "You never even said Sheila's name all day. It's scary."

"Yeah," Guillermo said. "I kept thinking about her, and you kept acting like she never was here. I miss her."

Everyone but Freddie and Susannah was in tears. I doubted that they were all that loyal to Sheila, but what had happened had frightened them. And they knew that I was worried but had said nothing. Children are sensitive creatures who read unverbalized feelings as if they were blatant statements. Moreover, in my classroom we had spent months learning openness and how to put ourselves in other people's places. They had absorbed the lessons

238

too well perhaps, because now I could not disguise my feelings from them.

So the Kobold's Box went unopened while I talked to them, telling them why I had not been as honest as I usually was. "Some things are kind of hard to talk about," I began. "What happened to Sheila is one of those things."

"How come?" Peter asked. "Don't you think we're old enough? That's what my mom says when she don't want to tell me stuff."

I smiled. "Sort of. And sort of because some things scare even big people. And when big people get scared about things, they don't like to talk about them. That's one of the problems with being big."

The kids were watching me—Tyler with her long, ghoulish throat scars; beautiful, black-skinned Peter; Guillermo, whose eyes never really looked anywhere; rocking, finger-twiddling Max; Sarah, William, Freddie. And my fairy child, Susannah.

"Remember I told you that Sheila got hurt at home? And remember back when we were talking about the ways people can touch you? And the places they have no right to touch?"

"Yeah, like where it's private on you, huh?" said William.

I nodded. "Well, someone in Sheila's family touched her where he shouldn't have, and when Sheila got unhappy about it, he hurt her."

Foreheads wrinkled. Their eyes were intent.

"What did he do to her?" William asked.

"Cut her." As I listened to myself talk, I wondered if I was doing the right thing. Instinctively I felt I was. Our relationship was grounded in the truth, however bad it might be. Moreover, I could not believe that knowing could be worse for them than not knowing, nor worse than the many things these children had seen already. The fact that nothing in their lives was so bad that it could not be talked about had been a cornerstone of our class.

"Who done it to her?" asked Guillermo. "Was it her father?"

"No. Her uncle."

"Her Uncle Jerry?" Tyler asked.

I nodded.

For a minute there was silence. Then Sarah shrugged. "Well,

at least it wasn't her father. Before I came to school, my father . . . sometimes he'd come in my room when my mother was at work and . . ." She paused, looking from Tyler to me and then down at the rug. "It's worse when it's your father, I think."

"Let's not talk about this anymore, okay?" William said. Fear had creased his brow.

"I wanna," Sarah said. "I want to know how Sheila is."

"No," William said again. Tears returned to his eyes.

I reached a hand out. "Why don't you sit with me."

He rose from the floor and came over. I put an arm around him. "This is a scary thing to talk about, isn't it?"

He nodded. "There's dust under my bed sometimes. That dust scares me. Sometimes I think maybe that used to be people. It says right in the Bible that you came from dust and you turn to dust after you die. Maybe it's dead people under my bed. Maybe it's my grandpa or Sheila."

"I don't think that's what the Bible means, William," I said. "And Sheila isn't dead. She's going to get better."

"Torey," Tyler asked, "how come Sheila's uncle did that to her? She just told us the other day that he was nice and played with her."

I did not have an answer. "I don't know, Ty."

"Did he have problems?" Sarah asked. "Like my father? They put him in the ward at the state hospital 'cause he had problems. That's what my mother told me. He never came back."

"Yes, I guess you could say he had problems. He didn't understand the right way to touch little girls."

"When's Sheila coming back?" Peter asked.

"As soon as she's better."

We talked for a long time. The bell to go home rang, the buses came and went, and still we talked. About sexual abuse. About Sheila. About ourselves.

Afterward, I loaded all eight of them into my car and drove them home. Even in the car, the questions kept coming at me. No one ever kidded or made a joke. The need to talk about these things surpassed all other needs that afternoon. And all our differences.

240

AFTER I HAD DROPPED the children off, I headed for the hospital with the get-well cards and a few books Sheila especially liked. I found her alone in a large glassed-in observation room near the nurses' station. She was lying in a crib with high metal sides. An IV and a unit of blood dangled above her. The arm with the needles in it was tied to the side of the crib with a restraint. She looked so young and small.

Tears spilled over my cheeks before I could stop them. Why had they put her in a crib? She would be embarrassed to have me see her in it.

Sheila turned her head toward me as I entered.

"Don't cry, Torey," she said softly. "It don't hurt much. Really it don't." She smiled softly, as if I were the one to be comforted, and reached up to touch my face.

Humble in the presence of such courage, I stared at her. "It makes me feel better to cry a little bit. You scared me so much, and I was so worried about you, Sheil. I can't help it."

"It don't hurt bad." Her eyes had lost some of their expression. Perhaps medication was causing the glassy effect. "But I do get sort of scared sometimes. Like last night, I didn't know where I was at. But I didn't cry none. And pretty soon the nurse comed over and talked to me. She be right nice. But I still be a little scared. I wanted my pa."

"I know, honey. And he'll be here when he can."

"No sir. He don't like hospitals none."

"Well, we'll see."

"I want you to stay with me."

"I will as much as I can. And Anton and Chad will come sometimes too."

She glanced up at the IV, and suddenly the hurt and the fear were alive in her eyes. "I want you to hold me," she whimpered. "My arm hurts fierce bad, and I do be so lonely. I want you to hold me."

I smoothed back her hair. "Oh, I know you do, sweetheart, and I want to. But we can't. It'd mess up all that stuff they have hooked up to you."

Her eyes glazed over again. She took a deep, shuddery breath

241

and that was all. Once again she was passive, locking up one more thing she could not bear to feel.

"I brought some books. Maybe you'd like me to read to you. It might take your mind off things."

She nodded. "Read me about the fox and the little prince."

SHEILA REMAINED in the hospital through the rest of April. During that time her uncle was arraigned and tried; he was found guilty and returned to prison. Her father did not visit Sheila the entire time, pleading a phobia about hospitals. I went to see her every night, and Chad came most evenings and played checkers with her. Anton visited regularly, and Whitney was allowed a couple of brief stops, though she was underage. Even Mr. Collins showed up one Saturday afternoon. Sheila turned out to be one of the most popular children on the unit, with a whole entourage of well-wishers coming and going constantly. Best of all, she was getting three balanced meals each day and was beginning to put on much needed weight.

But her emotional problems seemed to have been totally eclipsed by recent events. For as severely disturbed a child as she had been, there was no evidence of her acting up in the hospital. In fact, the nurses commented on her outstanding behavior. This concerned me. I feared that, as with her absurd ability to keep from crying, she had sublimated her misery, making it seem as if the vastly traumatic incidents had never happened. That to me was an indicator of the seriousness of her disturbance.

DURING THIS TIME I learned that my class would be disbanded permanently for a number of reasons. The district now felt that placement of many disturbed children could be accomplished without maintaining a separate class. Moreover, several of my kids had made enough progress to go into a less restrictive placement. Perhaps most important were rumblings of a new bill in Congress that would mandate the mainstreaming of handicapped children—putting them back into normal classes. In anticipation of this, rooms like mine were being eliminated, so that specially trained personnel would be free for consultation to regular teachers. Last,

242

money was running tight, and maintaining children in special classes was very expensive.

While the news saddened me, it was not unexpected. In fact, I had my own plans. I had applied to graduate school and had been accepted. I already held a master's degree in special education and a regular teaching certificate, but I did not have full certification for teaching special children. While the state did not yet require the full certificate, I could see it on the horizon. I did not want to be caught short of credits, and now seemed as good a time as any to return to school.

While I loved teaching, the months just past had been filled with soul-searching about my future. In addition, Chad was eager to marry and settle down. The evening that followed Sheila's court hearing had affected him, and now he openly acknowledged that he wanted a family. Yet I was getting restless. When the acceptance from the university came in April, I decided to go. After school let out in June, I would be moving half a continent away from Chad and Sheila, and from a place that had given me several of the best years of my life.

SHEILA RETURNED to school early in May with the same extroverted gusto she had displayed in the hospital. During the first few days she gave no indication of any problems. But one cannot stifle that much pain and get away with it, and by Thursday the veneer was beginning to wear thin. I started demanding more of her, and she found herself making mistakes. This put her in a sulk. The other kids were not giving her the attention to which she had grown accustomed. This provoked a bit of angry fussing. But, importantly, she began to talk to me again. At first she spoke only about safe things, but now and again a statement would creep in that mirrored what was below the carefree surface.

She had come back to class wearing the old overalls and T-shirt. But she had gained weight in the hospital and was too large for them. I wondered what had become of the red-and-white dress, and on Friday after school, I asked. Sheila was helping me cut out figures for the bulletin board, so we sat together at one table, the work spread between us.

She pondered my question for a moment. "I ain't gonna wear it no more."

"How come?"

"That day . . ." She paused, concentrating on her cutting. "That day my Unca Jerry . . . Well, he says it be a right pretty dress. He could feel under it. So I ain't wearing it no more. Besides, it got all blooded up. My pa, he throwed it away when I was gone."

"Oh." I did not know what to say next, so I just continued to work on the cutouts.

Sheila looked up. "Torey, I liked Unca Jerry. He played games with me. Why did he want to hurt me?"

Putting down the paper and scissors, I pushed back my hair. "You're asking me an awfully hard question, sweetheart. And I don't really know the answer. Sometimes people just lose control. It's something that happens."

Sheila stopped her cutting, and sat motionless for a long moment. Her chin quivered. "Things never are the way you really want them to be, are they?" She put her face down on the table in a gesture of defeat. "I don't wanna be me anymore. I wanna be somebody like Susannah Joy and have lots of nice dresses to wear. I don't wanna be here. I wanna be a regular kid and go to a regular kid's school. I just don't wanna be me anymore. I'm sick of it. But I can't figure out how to do it."

I watched her. Somehow I always think I've seen the worst; the next time it isn't going to hurt me as badly. And I always find it does.

I DECIDED THAT as a last major activity of the school year our class would put on a Mother's Day program. Children in special education programs almost never get to participate in the traditional holiday fun that children in regular classes do. For them, just getting through from day to day seems to be enough of an achievement. But I tried to create some of the more popular activities of the regular school program in our room. With the help of my parents' group we put together a few songs, a poem or two, and a skit full of the flowers and mushrooms that always seem to bloom in small children's plays.

The kids were all excited about the event, except that they wanted to do a more ambitious skit. Most of the children had just seen "The Wizard of Oz" for the umpteenth time on television and were determined we should do that. I explained that that might be a bit difficult, especially since no one but Sheila could read much. Peter in particular was adamant. He would not be any woodland flower; he wanted to be the Tin Woodman. I finally gave in. If Peter, with Sarah as his helper, could develop a rough skit that included parts for the others, I would let them do it.

So we began practicing. I was grateful for Sheila's agile memory, and I padded the program with her and with Max, whose disturbance had equipped him with the ability to repeat vast quantities of material, although not necessarily on demand.

Many fathers and mothers would be coming to the show. I asked Sheila if she wanted her father to attend. She screwed up her face in consideration. "He wouldn't."

"I bet he'd be proud to see you in the play," I said. "You know, Sheil, you've come a long way since January. You're like a different girl. Your pa will be proud of you when he realizes what an important girl you are in this class."

Sheila ruminated awhile. "Maybe he would come."

I nodded. "Maybe he would."

THE MORNING OF the program Chad arrived in the classroom, carrying a big box for Sheila. "I understand you're going to be in a play," he said to her.

"Yeah!" she cried, bouncing around him in excitement. "I'm gonna be Dorothy. Torey's gonna braid my hair up in pigtails an' I'm gonna sing a song and say a poem, and my pa's gonna be here and *watch* me!" She went on breathlessly. "Are you gonna come?"

"Nope. But I brought you a good-luck present."

"Me?" In glee she hugged his knees with such gusto that Chad wobbled unsteadily.

I knew what was inside the box—a beautiful long dress, red, white and blue, with lace on the front. I had told Chad about Sheila's feeling that dresses made her vulnerable, and so he had bought a long dress instead of a short one. The night he had come over to show it to me, his eyes sparkled like a little boy's. Chad had been confident that he had found something that would erase the horror of the past month and recapture at least a little of the magic we had found the night of the court hearing.

Sheila lifted the lid of the box. Momentarily she hesitated. Very, very slowly she took the dress out, her eyes huge and round. She looked at Chad who knelt on the floor next to her. Then she let it drop back into the box and lowered her head. "I ain't wearing dresses no more," she whispered hoarsely.

Chad turned to me, disappointment clear in his face.

"Don't you think it might be okay this once?" I said to her.

She shook her head.

I looked at Chad. "I think we need a minute alone, if you'll excuse us." I took Sheila to the far side of the room. I knew she must have been in torment. She loved pretty things so much. Yet what had happened to her was too fresh, the hurt too raw.

Her face contorted into a teary-eyed grimace. She pressed with her fingers, trying to keep the tears back. But for the first time she was unable to, and she dissolved into sobs.

The time had finally come, the time I had been waiting for. I gathered her into my arms, hugging her tightly. I picked her up. The other kids would be arriving soon so I needed to find some place where we would not be disturbed. The only place I could think of was the book closet.

Chad's face was distorted with concern. "I didn't mean . . ."

I shook my head. "Don't worry. I'll get back to you later, okay?" I asked Anton to watch the kids. Then dragging a chair along with me, I carried Sheila into the closet. She cried and cried and cried. I simply held her in my lap and rocked her back and forth. Ultimately the tears stopped. Exhausted, Sheila had been reduced to a quivery, soggy lump. I smoothed her damp hair back from her face and wondered what had happened in her head to make Chad's gift the final snapping point.

"Do you feel a little better?" I asked gently.

She did not reply but lay against me, her body convulsed with the hiccupy gasps and shudders that are the aftermath of hard crying. We sat for a while, saying nothing.

246

"I can hear your heart beat," she said at last.

I touched her head gently. "Do you think we ought to go back to class? It must be the middle of math period by now."

"No."

Again silence drifted around us. Finally she said, "Tor, why did he buy me that dress?"

Across my mind trickled the horrible thought that perhaps Sheila believed that safe, kind, lovable Chad had got her the dress for the same reason that Uncle Jerry had told her he liked the other one. I knew I must not reply that Chad had done it for love.

"Because I told him your other one was ruined. He thought you might like something pretty to wear in the play." When she did not respond, I continued, "You know, don't you, that Chad would never hurt you."

"I know it. I didn't mean to cry."

"Oh, sweetie, no one minds that you cry. Sometimes that's the only way to make things better."

"I wanted the dress," she said softly, pausing. "I wanted it. I just got scared, that's all. And I couldn't stop."

"That's okay. It really is."

"Do you suppose I could still have it?" she asked.

I nodded and smiled. "Yeah. Chad will leave it for you."

BOTH L. FRANK BAUM and Judy Garland probably turned over in their graves that May afternoon. Except for bearing the same title and characters as Baum's famed story, the children's production had little in common with the book or the movie.

Peter, who seemed to have authority over the casting, had selected Sheila as Dorothy. She managed the role mostly by virtue of her ability to think fast and make up dialogue quickly. Tyler was given the ignominious task of portraying the Wicked Witches. Sarah was transformed into the Scarecrow, William played the Cowardly Lion, and Guillermo was the Wizard. Peter selected Susannah to play the good Witch Glinda. She was so delicately pretty that she made a very realistic fairy even without a costume. Freddie was the sole Munchkin and Max, a lone Winged Monkey. Peter, of course, was the Tin Woodman.

247

Only parents, teachers or folks with an uncanny love of unintentionally funny children would have properly appreciated our "Wizard of Oz." Sheila had fully recovered from her troubles of the morning and had donned the dress Chad brought, refusing to wear the costume Whitney had made for her. She bounced all over the stage as she spoke, knocking over scenery and props. Freddie, on the other hand, would not move. He simply sat in his place, a ridiculous Munchkin hat stuck on his head, and waved at his mother in the audience. When his part was over, Anton had to drag him off. The Cowardly Lion was typecasting for William; knowing so well the feeling of fear, he gave the truest performance of all, quivering and quaking about. Susannah Joy, as Glinda, drifted onto the stage and floated around, as out of touch with reality as always, muttering to herself in a high-pitched little squeak. It looked astonishingly natural. Sheila often felt the need to explain parts of the play to the audience; her lengthy monologues left the other kids standing around dumbly. Finally Peter walked onto the stage and told her to get off.

Afterward, we had cookies and punch while the children showed their parents things they had done in school. Sheila's father had come, dressed once again in the tattered suit. For the first time I saw him smile at his daughter when she came bounding over to him after the performance. He had had the kindness to show up sober, and he appeared to enjoy being with us. He didn't comment on Sheila's new dress until, toward the end of the party, I told him that Chad had bought it for her. He regarded his daughter carefully and then turned to me, pulling a worn wallet from his pocket.

"I ain't got much here," he said quietly. "But would you take Sheila to buy everyday clothes? I know she needs some things and well, you need a woman for . . ." His voice trailed off, and he averted his eyes. "If I keep hold of the money . . . Well, I got a little problem, you know." He handed me a ten-dollar bill.

I nodded. "Yes, I will. I'll take her out next week."

He smiled faintly, and then before I knew it he was gone. I stared at the bill. That wouldn't buy much clothing, but he had tried to make sure that the money went where it was supposed to before it went for a bottle. I liked the man in spite of myself, and I was flooded with pity. Sheila was not the only victim; her father undoubtedly needed as much care as she did. Once he had been a little boy whose pain and suffering were never relieved.

If only there could be enough people to care, enough people to love without reservations.

CHAPTER SEVEN

Suddenly only three weeks remained until school was over. I had not told the children yet that the class was to be disbanded. Some of them already knew that they would be in less restrictive placements the next year. For the past three months William had been going to a fourth-grade class in the main building for reading and math, and he would move to a regular fifth-grade class with resource help. Tyler would be placed in a new program. She would still be in a special classroom most of the time, but she would be closer to the life of a regular student. We hadn't decided what to do with Sarah yet. Although she coped nicely in our room, she still withdrew when in a larger group. I suspected she would need at least another year in a special class. Peter would never leave a special setting, I feared. His behavior continued to deteriorate as a result of increasing neurological destruction, and he was too disruptive for anything but a tightly structured environment. Guillermo's family was planning to move. Freddie was being placed in a room for the severely retarded. The teacher who had been over to observe him hoped he would not be too much of a behavior problem. Max was doing beautifully. He was using much more normal speech and less echolalia. Both he and Susannah would go into a program for autistic children.

And Sheila? Sheila had come a long way from that frightened little lump that was dragged into our room in January; far from the dependent belt-hanger of February. Her little brother, Jimmie, had been forgotten, and she almost never referred to being put on the highway anymore. I did not think she would need a special class any longer. But she was still fragile. What she needed was simply someone who cared. I was thinking of suggesting to Ed

Somers that she be advanced to third grade so that she would be closer academically and socially to the other children. Besides, I had a friend, Sandy, who taught third grade in a school on the other side of town. It was close to the migrant camp, and Sandy would take care of Sheila for me. That assurance I needed for myself.

In an attempt to ease Sheila into regular classroom life, I decided to mainstream her for math into a second-grade class in our school. I wanted her out of my room for a period during the day so that she could become adjusted to the change. Since math was her most secure subject, that seemed the best place to start. I spoke to one of the second-grade teachers, Nancy Ginsberg. A pleasant, dedicated woman, she agreed to take Sheila.

"Guess what?" I said to Sheila as we were putting away toys.

"What?"

"You're going to do something neat from now on. You're going to go into a regular class for part of the day."

She looked up sharply. "Huh?"

"I talked to Mrs. Ginsberg, and she said you could come have math in her room each day."

She bent back over the pieces of an Erector set she was putting away. "I don't wanna."

"Sheila, remember once you told me that you wished you were in a regular class? Now you will be."

"I ain't going."

"Why not?"

"This here be my class," she replied, using the word "be" which had become almost extinct. "I ain't going in nobody else's."

"It's just for math."

Her nose wrinkled. "But that's my favorite in here. It ain't fair you make me leave my favorite time in here."

"You can have math in here too, if you want. But you'll have math in Mrs. Ginsberg's room too, starting on Monday."

"No, I ain't."

The rest of the day Sheila alternately sulked and stormed and clattered about. By afternoon I had had enough. I gave her the two alternatives: she either got her act together or she'd have to

250

sit in the quiet corner. Sheila marched defiantly off to the corner, and banging the chair around, she sat.

She stayed there the remainder of the afternoon. Since she was obviously interested in making me feel bad, I ignored her. After school I left her with Anton and went down to the teachers' lounge to make lesson plans. When I returned just before five, she was lounging on a pillow reading a book.

"You done being mad?" I asked.

She nodded casually, not looking up from the book. "You're going to be sorry you made me go."

"And what is that supposed to mean?"

"I ain't going to be good if I have to go. I'm gonna be bad and she'll send me back here. Then you can't make me leave."

"Sheila," I said in exasperation, "think about that one a while. That's not what you want to do."

"Yes, it is," she replied, still not looking up.

Going over to where she was sitting, I dropped on my knees beside her. "I thought you'd like being in a regular class."

She shrugged.

"Sheil, I want your thoughts. I can't believe you want to cause trouble."

"I do."

"Sheil . . ."

She finally looked directly at me. "How come you don't want me in here no more?"

"I do want you in here. But I want you to learn what's happening in a real class too, so you can go back to one."

"I already know what a real class is like. That's where I was before I came here. I wanna be in this crazy class."

It was almost five o'clock. "Sheil, listen, we're out of time. I'll talk to you more about it tomorrow."

But Sheila would not discuss it the next day. On Monday morning I sent her off for thirty-five minutes in Mrs. Ginsberg's class. Within fifteen, Anton had to retrieve her. She had ripped up papers, thrown pencils and tripped some poor unsuspecting second grader twice her size. Anton came dragging her in kicking and screaming. The moment the door shut behind them, Sheila stopped. A pleased smile touched her lips. I sank into a chair and covered my eyes. I was angry and did not trust myself to confront her about her behavior immediately.

After school I walked out to the buses with the other children. When I returned to the room, Sheila stood against the far wall by the animal cages, her eyes wide and fearful. I jerked my head in the direction of one of the tables. "Come over here, kiddo. I think it's time we talked."

Hesitantly she approached, sitting in a chair across the table from me. "You mad at me?" she asked warily.

"I sure was this morning, but I'm not now. No, I just want to find out why you don't want to go. You usually have good reasons for what you do, but last week you refused to talk to me about it."

She studied me. "This here be my class."

"Yes, it is. I'm not trying to kick you out of it. That's just thirty-five minutes out of a whole day." I regarded her a long moment. "Sheil, it's May. The school year will be over in a few weeks. I think it's time to think about next year."

"I'm going to be in here next year."

My heart was sinking. "No," I replied softly.

Her eyes flashed. "I am too! I'll be the baddest kid in the whole world. I'll do terrible things, and then they'll make you keep me. They won't let you make me go away."

"Oh Sheil, it isn't like that. Kitten," I said softly, "this class isn't going to be here next year."

Like a wave, the expression on her face changed. The anger drained away, leaving her pale. "What do you mean? Where's it going?"

"This class won't be here. The school district decided they don't need it. Everybody can go to other classes."

"Don't need it?" she shouted. "Of course they need it! I need it! So does Peter. And Max. I'm still crazy. We're all still crazy."

"No, Sheil, you're not. I'm not sure you ever were. But you're not now. It's time to stop thinking that."

"Then I will be, 'cause I ain't going nowhere."

"Sheil, I'm not going to be here either."

Her face froze.

"I'm moving in June. After school is over, I'm going away. It's really hard for me to say that to you, because I know we've gotten to be such good friends. I don't love you any less, and I'm not leaving because of anything you did or didn't do. It's a separate decision I made. A grown-up decision."

She stared at me. With elbows on the table, her hands were clasped together, and she rested her cheek against her fist. She studied my face without seeing.

"All things end, Sheil. We've had terrific times together, and I wouldn't have changed that for anything. You've changed so much. And so have I, really. We've grown together and now it's time to see how good the growing was. I think we're ready. I think you're ready to try it on your own. You're strong enough."

Tears suddenly filled her eyes and spilled over, making paths down her cheeks and onto her chin. Slowly she lowered her head. Then she rose and turned away from me, going over to the far side of the room and sitting down amid the pillows on the floor. Once there she covered her face with her hands.

I could feel her pain, which I suppose was my own pain too. Had I gotten too involved? Would it have been better to have simply taught her, rather than let her get accustomed to the trials of loving someone? I belonged to the better-to-have-loved-and-lost school, which was not a popular notion in education. I could not teach effectively without getting involved with each child, but when the end came I could leave. It always hurt, but I could do it because I took with me the priceless memories of what we had had. Even if I worked with Sheila the rest of her school career, I couldn't ensure happiness for her. Only she could do that.

Yet, watching her, I worried that there had not been sufficient time to heal her hurts, that she might not be strong enough to tolerate my painful way of teaching. I rose and went over to where she sat snuffling. "Go away," she stated quietly.

"Why? Because you're crying?"

The hands came down, and she looked at me briefly. "No." She paused. "Because I don't know what to do."

I sat down. For the first time I did not feel like putting my arms around her to soothe away the hurt. Dignity was as tangible as a cloak about her. We were equals then. I was no longer the wiser one, the stronger one. We were equal in our humanity.

"How come you ain't staying to make me good?" she asked.

"Because it isn't me that makes you good. It's you. I'm only here to let you know that someone cares if you are good or not. That someone cares what happens to you. It won't matter where I am, I will always care."

"You're just like my mama," she said.

"Maybe leaving you was just as hard for your mama as it will be for me. Maybe it hurt her that much too."

"She never loved me. She loved my brother. She left me on the highway like I didn't even belong to her."

"I don't know why she did that. And you don't either. All you know is how it felt. Your mama and I are different. I'm not your mother. No matter how much you want it to be that way, I'm not."

The tears renewed in intensity. "I know that."

"Yes, but I know you dreamed. In the same way, I guess I did too at times. But it never was any more than a dream. I'm your teacher, and when the school year ends, I'll just be your friend. And I will be your friend for as long as you want me."

She looked up. "What I can't figure out is why the good things always end."

"Everything ends."

"Not some things. Not the bad things. They never go away."

"Yes, they do. If you let them, they go away. Not as fast as we'd like sometimes, but they end too. What doesn't end is the way we feel about each other. Even when you're all grown up and somewhere else, you can remember what a good time we had together. Even when you're in the middle of bad things and they never seem to change, you can remember me. And I'll remember you."

She smiled sadly. "That's 'cause we tamed each other. Remember that book? Remember how the fox was crying 'cause he had to leave?" She smiled in memory. Her tears had stopped. "We tamed each other, didn't we?"

I nodded. "We sure did."

"It makes you cry to tame someone, doesn't it?"

Again I nodded. "That seems to be part of being tamed."

Sheila pressed her lips together and wiped away the last traces of tears. "It still hurts a lot though, don't it?"

"Yeah, it sure does."

SHEILA WENT BACK to Mrs. Ginsberg's room the next morning and made it through the thirty-five minutes without too much trouble. But our problems were by no means resolved. Sheila could not understand that our parting was different from what had happened between her and her mother. Time and again we had to discuss the issue. She clung to *The Little Prince* as literary proof that people did part and it did hurt and they did cry, but they all still loved each other. The book was never far from her hands and she could quote parts of it from memory.

She certainly had learned to cry. Like a leaky faucet, tears streamed from her eyes even when she was smiling or playing. She often did not know why she was crying. But if it helped her to prepare for what lay ahead, so much the better. Slowly the tears began to disappear.

Underneath it all, her marvelous core of joy and courage gleamed. She struggled to take control of herself, and as I watched her coping with her tears, hugging the copy of *The Little Prince*, and relentlessly plaguing me with questions about what was happening and why, I knew she would make it. She was strong.

In the midst of all the flurry over the ending of the school year, my birthday came. We made a big thing about the children's birthdays, and it seemed only reasonable that the kids should get to celebrate mine or Anton's as well. So on my birthday I brought in a big yellow elephant-shaped cake and chocolate ice cream.

The day did not go well. Peter had gotten in a fight on the bus and arrived with a bloody nose. During recess Sarah got mad at Sheila, who in turn got mad at Tyler, who cried. The quiet corner did a booming business all day long. However, it wasn't until afternoon that I lost my patience. When Whitney went down to the teachers' lounge for the ice cream, she found that one of the fifth-grade classes had thought it was theirs and had taken it. I set the cake out anyway. Peter and William were horsing around while we were getting ready for the party. Then *crash*. William had thrown a block to Peter, who bumped into Sheila sitting on the floor. He fell on her, and they both came up swinging. Before I knew it Sheila had one of the blocks to throw at Peter. He picked up a chair and flung it toward her. The chair hit the table, then the cake. My yellow elephant splattered onto the floor.

"Okay, you guys, that is it!" I shouted. "Every single one of you in your chairs with your heads down."

"But it wasn't my fault," Guillermo protested.

"Everybody."

All the kids, even Max and Freddie, found chairs and sat down.

I looked at them. What a ragtag lot. Whitney and Anton were picking cake out of the carpet. Anton rolled his eyes when I came over. I smiled wearily. I had wanted a special day and had gotten an ordinary one.

I looked at the clock. "Okay, you guys, if you can act like human beings, you can get up. There's about ten minutes left. Help pick up the rest of the cake and then find something quiet to do."

Sheila remained at the table with her head down.

"Sheil, you can get up. I'm not mad anymore."

"Uh-uh," she said. "This here's my birthday present for you. I ain't gonna be no trouble for the rest of the day."

After school Anton and I went to the teachers' lounge. I sat in the one comfortable chair, my head back, my arm over my eyes.

"What a hell of a day," I said. When Anton did not respond I looked up. He was standing over my chair.

"Happy birthday." He handed me a fat envelope.

"Hey, you shouldn't have done anything."

Inside was a crazy cartoon card with a green snake on it. Out fell a piece of folded paper.

"My present to you," Anton said.

I opened the paper. It was a letter.

Dear Mr. Antonio Ramirez:

With great pleasure Cherokee County Community College announces that you have been chosen as one of the recipients of the Dalton E. Fellows Scholarship.

Congratulations. We look forward to seeing you in our program this fall.

I looked up at him. His grin spread from ear to ear. I wanted to congratulate him, to tell him how pleased I was. I said nothing. We just stared at each other. And smiled.

I HAD CALLED ED about Sheila's future placement, and we held a meeting. I wanted Sheila placed with my friend, Sandy McGuire, but Ed did not favor the plan. He disliked advancing children ahead of their age groups. We did a lot of soul-searching. In Sheila's case there were no perfect solutions. In the end, he agreed to try Sheila in Sandy's room. She would also get two hours a day in a resource room to help meet her emotional needs and her advanced academic status.

The second to the last week of school I told Sheila that she would be at Jefferson Elementary the following year and that I knew her teacher very well. I asked if she would like to visit Sandy in her classroom some day after school. Sheila vehemently announced that she would not now nor would she ever want to meet Sandy. But later, after the other kids had heard of Sheila's placement and had got excited because she was skipping a grade, Sheila decided that she might not mind meeting Sandy after all.

Wednesday afternoon Sheila and I climbed into my little car and started off for Jefferson. Because we had almost half an hour before Sandy's class was finished, I stopped at Baskin-Robbins for ice-cream cones. Sheila selected a double scoop of licorice. It was a mistake. By the time we arrived at Jefferson, she had black ice cream all over her cheeks and chin, in her hair and down the front of her shirt. I wiped off what I could, and with Sheila clutching my hand, we went into the school.

Sandy laughed when she saw Sheila with all that ice cream on her. "Boy, you look like you had something good," Sandy said, smiling. "What was it?"

Sheila stared at her wide-eyed and pressed close to my leg. "Ice cream," she whispered. I wondered what Sandy must have been thinking. I had enticed her into accepting Sheila mostly by elaborating on the child's giftedness and verbal ability. Right then Sheila sounded like anything but the epitome of intelligence.

I should have trusted Sandy more. Bringing over chairs, she sat down with us and proceeded to get all the details of Sheila's ice-cream passions. Then she took us on a tour of the room. It was huge, easily accommodating twenty-seven desks and a variety of learning centers around the perimeter. I had never been known for my neatness, but Sandy's clutter surpassed even mine. Stacks of workbooks defied gravity on the corner of a table, and bits of construction paper were strewn everywhere. The children must have had half a dozen projects going in all states of completion. In the back of the room was a well-stocked bookcase.

Slowly Sheila came to life. She began to wander around on her own, inspecting the premises. Sandy flashed me a knowing smile as we watched Sheila. She'd make it.

The workbooks interested her, and standing on tiptoe Sheila took one from the top of the stack and paged through it. She came over to me. "This here's different than them you got, Torey." She turned to Sandy. "I don't like doing workbooks so well."

Sandy pursed her lips and nodded slowly. "I've heard other kids say that too. They aren't a lot of fun, are they?"

Sheila eyed her a moment. "I do 'em though. Torey makes me. This here one don't look too bad." She examined a page carefully. "This here kid made a mistake. Look, it gots a red mark by it."

"Sometimes people make mistakes," Sandy said. I made a mental note to tell her of Sheila's allergy to correction. Reducing Sheila's anxiety about her errors would be one of next year's tasks.

"What d'you do to them?" Sheila asked.

"When they make a mistake?" Sandy said. "Oh, if they don't understand, I just help them. It's no big deal."

"Do you whip kids?"

With a grin Sandy shook her head. "Nope. I sure don't."

Sheila nodded toward me. "Torey, she don't either."

We stayed with Sandy for almost forty-five minutes, Sheila becoming bolder with her questions. Finally, when it was time to leave, Sandy mentioned that perhaps Sheila would like to come over for part of a day before school let out to see how it was when the children were there. I thanked her, and we walked out to the car.

Sheila was quiet through most of the ride back to our school. In the parking lot, she turned to me. "She ain't so bad, I guess."

258

"Good, I'm glad you liked her."

"Tor, do you suppose I could go over to Miss McGuire's class sometime? I wouldn't really mind."

I nodded. "Yeah, Sheil, I reckon we could arrange that."

MONDAY OF THE FINAL WEEK Anton drove Sheila over to Sandy's class. Sheila had elected to remain the entire day. She wanted to eat in the cafeteria, selecting her own lunch and paying for it like the other children did. At our school my class had lunch trays fixed for them and laid out on the table. Sheila wanted to see how it felt to be a regular kid.

She was wearing the red, white and blue dress Chad had bought her rather than the jeans and shirt that we had gotten with the money her father had given me. She asked me to put her hair in a ponytail and had found a piece of yarn to tie around it. My heart lurched a little, watching her leave with Anton. She looked so tiny and so vulnerable.

Sheila returned that afternoon a satisfied veteran. The day had gone smoothly, and she smiled with pride as she related how she had carried her own lunch tray clear across the cafeteria without spilling anything, and how a girl named Maria, who had the longest, shiniest, prettiest black hair she'd ever seen, had saved a place for her. There had been hitches. She had lost her way coming back from the rest room but had finally made it. At recess she had tripped while running and skinned her knees. Sandy had seen it happen and had given Sheila comfort. Beaming, Sheila told me how Sandy had held her close and blown on her knees until they felt better. All in all, it had been a successful day. Sheila affirmed that it would be an okay class to be in. For the first time she did not get that stricken look about leaving my class. Instead, her conversation was punctuated with "Next year, Miss McGuire says I can . . ." or "When I'm in her room next year . . ." It was a sweet-sad moment for me because I knew I had been outgrown.

ON THE LAST DAY of school we had a picnic. I contacted everybody's parents, and a number of them met us in the park a few blocks from school. We brought packed lunches and ice cream

259

from the cafeteria, while the parents brought cookies and other goodies. The park had a small zoo, a large duck pond, and gardens filled with flowers all gleaming in the June sunshine. Children scattered in every direction with a parent in tow.

Sheila's father did not come; we had not really expected him. But when Sheila showed up in the morning, she was dressed in a bright orange-and-white sunsuit her father had bought for her the previous night. It was the first new thing she could ever remember him getting her. Anton raved about the beautiful color and teased her about stealing it if he got the chance. She went into a fit of giggles. Mirth bubbled up in her so brightly that she could not stay still. All the way to the park she pirouetted down the sidewalk, her blond hair swirling in the air.

Once at the park Anton and Whitney and I sat in the sun by the duck pond watching her. She was apart from us, listening to some inner music and gliding around in harmony on the walk that circled the pond. A skip, now a twirl, then a few rhythmic bends; it was eerie watching her dance alone in the sunlight. Oblivious to everyone, she satisfied a dream to dance. Anton watched without speaking. Whitney cocked her head as if trying to catch the music none of us could hear.

Anton turned to me. "She looks like a spirit, doesn't she? Like if you blinked too hard, she'd be gone."

I nodded.

"She's free," Whitney said softly. And indeed she was.

THE END OF THE DAY came all too quickly. We returned to the classroom to pass around the last of the papers and say our final good-bys. The narrow, wood-paneled room was almost bare. Pictures and stories were down from the walls, and the animals had all gone to my apartment. The finality of what was happening dawned on Sheila and she lost her merry spirit, retreating to the corner now empty of its pillows. The other children were all chattering excitedly about summer vacation and their changes for next year. While Anton led them in a song, I went to Sheila.

The tears coursed silently over her cheeks. "I don't want this to be over. I wanna come back, Torey."

"Of course you do, honey. But that's just how it feels now. In a little while you'll be in third grade, a regular kid."

"I don't wanna go, Torey. And I don't want you to go."

I smoothed her hair. "Remember, I told you I'd write you letters. We'll still know what's happening to each other. It won't be like we're really apart. You'll see."

"No, I won't. I'm not gonna be nice at all in Miss McGuire's class. I'm gonna be bad and then you'll have to come back."

"Hey, that's the old Sheila talking."

"I won't be good. I won't. And you can't make me."

"No, Sheil, I can't. But you know it won't change things any. It won't make this year come back or this class. Or me."

She was staring at the floor, her bottom lip pushed out.

I smiled. "Remember, you tamed me. You're responsible for me. That means we'll never forget we love each other. We'll cry a little right now, but pretty soon we'll only remember how happy we were together."

She shook her head. "I won't ever be happy."

Just then the bell rang and the room was alive with shouts. I rose and went to the other children. Hesitantly Sheila trailed over too. The good-bys came. Tyler and William were teary-eyed. Peter whooped with joy. We all exchanged hugs and kisses, and then they were gone, running out into the June warmth.

This last day Sheila's bus was to leave early. After saying good-by to Anton and Whitney and collecting her things, she would have enough time to walk the two blocks to the high school.

Parting from Anton was hard for her. At first she covered her face and refused to even look at him. He kept coaxing her to smile, saying that they'd still see each other at the migrant camp and that he'd bring her over to play with his two little boys. Finally I delivered an ultimatum: I'd walk her to her bus, but she had to leave right away. With this she hugged Anton, her tiny arms locking him in a wrestler's hold. She kissed his cheek and trotted back to me. Then she waved to Whitney and picked up her things, a few papers and the worn copy of *The Little Prince*, a tangible memory of what had been. She took my hand.

We did not speak on the way to the high school. We had gone

beyond needing words. The bus was waiting in the drive, and Sheila ran in to put her things on a seat. Then she came back out to where I stood and looked up at me. "By," she said very softly.

I sank to my knees and embraced her. My heart was roaring in my ears, my throat too tight to speak. Then I rose, and she ran to the steps of the bus. But as she started up them she stopped. She looked over at me and suddenly came running back.

"I didn't mean it," she said. "I didn't mean it when I said I would be bad. I'll be a good girl." She looked up solemnly. "For you."

I shook my head. "No, not for me. You be good for you."

She smiled slightly. Then she scurried up the steps of the bus and disappeared. In a moment I saw her face at the rear window. The driver shut the door. "By," she was mouthing, her nose squashed flat against the glass. The bus pulled down the drive. A small hand waved, frantically at first, then more gently. I raised my hand and smiled as the bus turned onto the street and disappeared from sight.

"By-by," I said, the words squeezing themselves almost inaudibly from my stricken throat. Then I turned to go back.

Epilogue

In the mail a year ago, came a crumpled, water-stained piece of notebook paper inscribed in blue felt-tipped marker. No letter accompanied it.

> To Torey with much
> "Love"
>
> All the rest came
> They tried to make me laugh
> They played their games with me
> Some games for fun and some for keeps
> And then they went away
> Leaving me in the ruins of games
> Not knowing which were for keeps and
> Which were for fun and
> Leaving me alone with the echoes of
> Laughter that was not mine.
>
> Then you came
> With your funny way of being
> Not quite human
> And you made me cry
> And you didn't seem to care if I did
> You just said the games are over
> And waited
> Until all my tears turned into
> Joy.

Torey L. Hayden

One Child is Torey Hayden's first venture into the world of publishing, but she has been writing, she says, "ever since I first figured out that I could capture the tremendous world in my head and make it last forever on paper. When exactly that was, I don't recall. Although I do remember that when I was eight I made a blood pact with my best friend, George. We cut our little fingers, mixed our blood, then smeared it on pieces of paper that supposedly held the secrets of our futures. George wanted to be a cowboy. On my paper I wrote that I wanted to be an author."

An only child, born in the mountains of southern Montana, Torey carefully nurtured her dream, writing her first book the same year she made her pact. The book, intended to be a collection of short stories, consisted of "one story of three pages, and nineteen titles of future works. I never did come up with nineteen more stories, and the book still sits in a box in my closet." At thirteen, she began recording the discoveries of her adolescence in a journal that is now her most prized possession. Her grandfather encouraged her creative efforts. "He showed me how to plane a piece of wood and to catch a fish," she recalls. "And to do my best even when nobody else cared. He conveyed to me that I could become anything I wanted to in life, if I only wanted it badly enough and was willing to pay the price."

Torey adopted his philosophy as her own. Today, at twenty-nine, she is a candidate for her doctorate in special education and child psychology, and is an established psychologist. Her interest in severely disturbed children was triggered during her college years when she worked as a teacher's aide in a pre-school programme. Since then, she has taught at the University of Minnesota and briefly at London University, and in places ranging from state schools to locked psychiatric wards.

It was during this time that she met Sheila—an experience she remembers with awe: "Hardly a day goes by in my work that I am not influenced by something that occurred in the six months I spent with

Sheila. Her courage, her strength, and her inadvertent ability to express that great gaping need to be loved that we all have, had a profound effect on me. I wrote *One Child* because I wanted to capture the magnificent essence of this youngster who gave me so much. And I wrote the book because of Sheila's poem, which sits in a frame on my desk. I am asked repeatedly about it. It seems only fair that those who ask about the poem should know the child who wrote it."

Torey recently moved to Wales, where she divides her time between writing and teaching at the University College of North Wales. She speaks Welsh fluently and is enthusiastic about her move: "The pace here is slower than in the States," she explains. "And the whole country is one big neighbourhood."

Although she now lives far from Sheila, Torey communicates with her former pupil regularly. Sheila is doing well in school, though she admits that because she finds it so difficult to be trusting, she has a hard time making friends. She is planning to visit Torey this summer in Wales.

RANDOM WINDS

A CONDENSATION OF THE BOOK BY
Belva Plain

ILLUSTRATED BY MICHAEL DUDASH
PUBLISHED BY COLLINS

This is the unforgettable saga of a proud
family, united by love and loyalty, tormented
by conflicting emotions, dedicated to
medicine. There is Enoch Farrell, a stubborn
New England country doctor who believes the
old ways are best; Martin, his son, a brilliant
surgeon whose enduring passion for a woman
he can't have almost destroys him. And Claire,
Martin's daughter, who turns her back on
romance only to find that some sacrifices are too
painful. Inextricably linked with the Farrells
are the two Meig sisters: beautiful Mary Fern,
whose marriage to an aristocratic Englishman
is not as idyllic as it seems; and high-spirited
Jessie, whose physical affliction places her
in cruel contrast to her lovely sister. As these
lives intertwine and diverge, the reader is
swept into a rich tale of family life, of ties
that bind and the many kinds of love.

Prologue: Day of Wrath

ON ADIRONDACK lakes ice boomed and cracked. Grainy snow, melting at last, slid into the ditches along mired roads. Dr. Enoch Farrell drew his watch out of his vest pocket; he had made good time. Once past the Atkins' farm the road flattened and there were only three easy miles to home. He drew the buggy's curtains tighter against the sweeping rain that threatened his fine, polished bag. The best black calf it was, with brass fittings, the parting gift, along with a well-bound Gray's *Anatomy*, of Dr. Hugh Mac-Donald, his preceptor in Edinburgh. He never went anywhere without the *Anatomy*. He never went out without his current reading either, for this hour trotting home at the end of the day was his only truly private time. And rummaging, he searched for *Bleak House*. To think that Dickens was dead thirty years or more and now, in this first year of a new century, his work was as alive as if it had been written yesterday!

Things were heaped in the bag. Jean was always straightening it, but it never stayed that way. Laudanum, hop bitters, stethoscope, but no Dickens. He must have left it home. He was always forgetting things. If it weren't for Jean . . . Well-matched they were: she so practical and precise, while he—could he dare

269

think of himself as a leaven, bringing brightness and humor to the household?

So his thoughts ran.

Left now, and across the bridge, where the river, which had been iced over only last week, was running fast. The mare began to speed, and there was home with its twin chimneys and front porch. Very nice! Nicer still when the mortgage should be paid off. But these days a man could count himself lucky to keep abreast of daily expenses: four children with another on the way.

Enoch climbed down in the barn, unhitched Dora and led her to the stall. When he entered the house, the children were halfway through supper. Alice, the baby, clattered on the high-chair tray when she saw him.

"I thought you'd be even later in this weather," Jean said. "Heavens, your knickers are soaked! Sit down, while I get the stew. I've kept it hot, and there are biscuits, too."

Jean's hands rested on the apron beneath which lay her growing baby, in its seventh month. Her pink, anxious face was flushed from the kitchen's heat. Four child faces turned toward Enoch, mixed of his flesh and hers: her almond eyes in Enoch Junior and the baby, Alice; his laughter in May; her quickness in Susan.

He washed his hands at the sink, then took his place at the table. "Well, anything new happen around here today?"

"Nothing much. Oh, yes, Mrs. Baines came. Sounds like Walter has the quinsy sore throat again."

"I suppose I'd better hitch up and go over there."

"Indeed you'll not, after the day you've had. Besides," she added mischievously, "I told her what to do."

"You did what?"

"I told her what to do. I've heard you tell it often enough. Red flannel around the throat, goose grease on the chest, soak the feet in a tub of hot water with powdered mustard. Right?"

"Dad! I did elevens in multiplication today and—"

"Enoch Junior," Jean rebuked him, "you're interrupting. And anyway, this is grown-ups' time. You're not supposed to talk at the table."

"Let him talk, Jean. What'd you want to tell me, son?"

"I wanted you to hear my multiplication."

"Tell you what. You go start your homework, and after I finish my supper I'll join you. May and Susan, you're excused, too."

The room grew quiet. Alice sucked on her bottle and Jean dished out the pudding. "You look so tired," she said softly.

"I didn't know how much till I sat down, I guess."

She peered through the window into the dismal murk. "This weather's enough to exhaust a person. Seems as if spring'll never come and it'll never stop raining."

When they went to bed, the rain was still beating mournfully upon the roof. By morning it had not slackened. All through that second day it never varied in its determined fall, neither speeding up nor slowing down, just marching evenly, like soldiers' stern and solemn feet.

On the third day the north wind came. It struck with fury, and the night was loud with complaint. Water poured through the gutters; the house shuddered. From his bedroom window Enoch peered into the yard and saw that the chicken coop was holding. But he went to bed with uneasy thoughts.

The next morning the sun came out at last. Water stood two inches deep in the yard. Under the porch roof, soaked sparrows clustered, chirping through the daily family prayers. After Enoch closed the great Bible in the parlor, the children asked whether there would be school that day.

"Of course there will," Jean told them, "but the road will be a mess. You'll need your high galoshes."

She packed the lunch boxes and tied May's scarf, fastening it down with a large safety pin on the chest. May, like her father, always lost things.

"Now, Enoch Junior, mind you don't run ahead. I want you to help your sisters through the muddy spots."

"Aw," said Enoch, "why do I always have to?"

"Because you're a big eight-year-old boy, and your sisters are small."

The parents watched their three march down the road, the boy obediently between his sisters. There marched the future! Yes, and the sum of the parents' pasts; such love, such hope encompassed in those chattering three, so carelessly kicking pebbles on their way to school. They watched until the children were out of sight, then smiled at each other. Jean went back into the kitchen, and Enoch went to the barn and hitched the horse. The storm had set him three days behind with his house calls and he would have to cover a lot of ground.

At noon it began to rain again. But it was a light rain this time. No need to send the children home early, the young teacher thought as she glanced out the window, especially since they had already missed a couple of days this week. By two o'clock the drizzle had stopped.

And at two o'clock, a mile and a half upstream, in one incredible instant an old earthen dam collapsed. Rumbling and crumbling, with a thunderous roar and a colossal surge, it fell apart. A blinding spray rose into the air, splashed and crashed. The lake behind the dam, swollen by tons of melted ice, poured into the river. And the river slid over its banks, plunging through the valley. It gathered strength and speed. Like a merciless army come to pillage, it advanced.

At two thirty the children were dismissed from school to walk home. A quarter of a mile behind them the mighty wall of water rushed, flooding the whole valley now, wrecking and smashing. It gained on the little flock of children as they meandered. They heard its distant rumble before they saw it. Towering doom rose high at their backs. They began to run. Horrified and screaming, they raced. But the water raced faster.

LATE in the afternoon, Enoch came down from the hills and beheld catastrophe. He pulled on the reins and stared. Water lay where farms had been that morning. Stagnant at the edges, it was torrential in the middle, speeding in a brown froth.

My God, the schoolhouse! That was the schoolhouse's red roof! A dreadful faintness almost toppled him. He saw treetops poking up from the swirling current, strewn with debris: here a dead cow, there drowned chickens in a coop.

Enoch trembled and went cold. Then panic came. He thought he heard himself screaming at the mare. He whipped her, which he had never done before, and the mare sped toward home.

His own house lay beyond the place where the river curved, and he saw as he approached that the water had risen over the front steps. A maple that fronted the road had been ripped up.

He jumped down, waded thigh-deep to the porch, and banged the front door open. "Jean! Jean!"

Water had seeped into the parlor, soaking the carpet. He ran upstairs. "Jean, for God's sake, where are you?"

He went back to the porch and looked wildly around. It was so quiet! The yard was always noisy with the cackle of chickens and the dog's bark. Then he realized the chickens and the dog had been drowned. He climbed back into the buggy, lashing the mare toward the village center, which lay well beyond the curve of the river and the flooding.

At the church there was a crowd of buggies and wagons. He pulled into the yard and jumped down.

"Where . . . Do you know where—" he began, addressing a man whose face he knew. But the man looked blank and hurried past.

People filled the narrow stairway that led to the church basement. Enoch pushed his way down. Against the back wall, on the floor, the bodies lay in a long double row covered with sheets. Beginning at the left, Enoch lifted the covers from the faces. Nettie Rogers. Jim Fox's boy, Tom. He moved faster.

"Doc! No!" Someone caught his sleeve, pulling hard at him. "Doc! No! Sit down!"

"Damn you, leave me!" Enoch cried, wrenching his arm free. And then— Oh, God! Almighty God! His children! Enoch, Susan and May lay side by side in a row. Stiff as dolls they lay, May in the pink scarf, the cotton-candy pink that Jean had knitted, still wound about her chest and secured with a safety pin.

My girls. My little boy. He sank to the floor, rocking on his knees. "Oh, my God, my girls, my little boy!"

Strong arms came at last and drew him away.

THEY had taken Jean and Alice to a house near the church. Reverend Dexter led Enoch there. "Have they told you about Jean?" he asked.

"What?"

"The shock, you know. But the women took care of her."

"The shock?" Of course. Jean was in her seventh month. He hadn't thought— He quickened his steps.

In the kitchen of a strange house Alice was sitting in a high chair while a stout woman spooned cereal into her mouth. "She's in there, sleeping," the stout woman said.

Enoch walked to the bedroom door and stood looking at his wife. Her face lay in the crook of her arm. He moved to the bed, drew the blanket softly over her shoulder, and she opened her eyes. "I'm not asleep," she whispered.

Enoch knelt on the floor, laying his face against hers.

"God's will," she whispered. "He wanted them home with Him."

God's will that their babies should drown? Reared on the Bible he was, but he couldn't believe that. Yet it gave her comfort.

He leaned over to kiss her. "Jean, Jean, my girl, we'll start again. We'll have to love each other so— And I'll take care of you and Alice and me. We're all that's left."

"You're not forgetting him, the new one?"

"Him?"

"The baby, the boy. You haven't seen him?"

"But I thought—"

Mrs. Fairbanks, the lady of the house, coming in with a cup of tea, overheard. "You thought it was a stillbirth? No, Doc. Look here." She raised the window shade. A sad lavender light slid into the room. On a table near the window lay a box, and in it one of the smallest babies Enoch had ever seen.

Jean called out, "I want his name to be Martin Thomas."

"All right," Enoch said. He looked at the child. Four pounds, if that.

"Poor Jean, poor lamb," Mrs. Fairbanks whispered.

The baby fluttered. Its toy hands moved, its legs jerked weakly. Mrs. Fairbanks shook her head. "No, he can't live."

Something welled up in Enoch, and he shook a furious fist at the universe. "No!" he cried fiercely. "Look at those eyes! Look at the life in those eyes! He will live, and he'll be strong, too. So help me God, he will."

The Ascent

CHAPTER ONE

AT THE top of the long rise, Pa guided the horse into the shade, then pulled off his jacket. "Professional dignity be darned!" he said. "The next patient will have to look at me in my shirt sleeves."

The sun was ahead of the season, Ma had remarked that morning. Shadbush was still in bloom, and barn swallows were barely back from the south in time for Decoration Day.

"We'll let the mare rest a minute," Pa said. "Something's bothering her." The sweating animal slapped her tail. She had been making a strange, plaintive sound for the last half hour.

"Black flies, do you think?" Martin said.

"Don't see any." Pa climbed down to examine her. "Look at this!" The flesh along the horse's back was rubbed bloody raw. "Laid open with a whip," Pa said, "and left to suppurate."

Martin nodded, feeling a twinge at sight of the wound, feeling also a certain pride at being the only boy in the fourth grade who knew the meaning of words like "suppurate."

"Poor little livery stable hack!" Pa cried. "Reach in my bag for the salve and a wad of gauze, will you?"

The little mare quivered, and when Pa was finished, Martin gave her an apple. Then the two stood watching, pleased with themselves, while the mare chewed.

"Wish I had the money to buy her and give her a decent home," Pa said. Then he sighed. "Well, might as well start. One more call at the Bechtolds' and then home in time for the parade."

They moved on again. "Martin, look up at that mountain! You can gauge the height by the kind of trees. At the bottom there's oak, but oak won't grow more than thirteen hundred feet up. After that, you get balsam. Way up top there's spruce." He leaned forward, pointing. "Those are the oldest mountains in the United States, you know that? See how the tops are rounded? Worn away. And I'll tell you something else." He pointed to the left. "Down there all that land was once underwater."

"You mean the ocean was here once?"

"Yes, sir, that's just what I do mean."

At the foot of the hill, making a wide S-curve, lay the river. "Pa, is that the river that drowned Enoch Junior and Susan and May?" Martin knew it was, yet he always asked.

His father answered patiently, "That's it."

"Then I was born, and you had me instead of Enoch Junior as your boy. Do I look like him?" To that, too, he knew the answer.

"No, he was small and sandy, like me. You're going to be tall, and you're darker, like your mother's family."

"Do you like me more than you liked him?"

"The same. A man's children are the same to him." They drew into the Bechtolds' yard. "Wait out here, Martin," Pa said. "I have to change a dressing."

"Can't I come in and watch?"

"It might make you feel bad to see the cut."

"No it won't, Pa. Honestly, it won't."

"All right then, come in."

A scythe had sliced Jake Bechtold's leg to the bone. Pa pulled the nightshirt up. Carefully he unwound the bandage, revealing a long gash, black and crisscrossed with stitches. "It's doing well," Pa said. "No infection, thanks be."

"We're grateful to you, Doc." Mrs. Bechtold wrung her clasped hands. "You always seen us through."

"Not every time, Mrs. Bechtold," Pa said seriously.

"Oh, that! That was in God's hands, Doc."

When they got back in the buggy, Martin asked what he'd meant. Pa sat in silence for a while. Then he said, "It was an awful thing that happened in my second year here. Jake Bechtold had the flu. While I was in the bedroom examining him, their little girl, just three years old, pulled a washtub full of boiling water off the stove while her mother's back was turned. We laid her on the kitchen table. I can still hear how she screamed. Once in my life I'd ordered a lobster. A lobster is bright red when it's boiled, you know. The child looked like that. I thought, I don't know what to do. I'm supposed to know and I don't. Finally I got a scissors and began to cut her clothes off.

"Her body was one terrible blister. When I pulled off the

276

stockings, the skin came with them in long strips, like tissue paper. I took some salve out of my bag. It had melted from the sun, and I dribbled it over the child's body. Everybody was looking at me as if there were some magic in that jar of melted salve.

"The child lay moaning on the table all afternoon, but her pulse was so faint, I don't think she felt anything. We waited. Nobody talked. Shortly before dusk she died."

Martin shivered. Pa's tales always made him feel he had been there when they happened.

"I shouldn't be telling you this," Pa said. "Your mother would say you're too young to know how hard life can be."

"I'm not too young. I'm nine."

"You're older than nine in many ways." His father's arm slipped to Martin's shoulders.

"Pa," he said, "I want to be a doctor."

Pa looked at him carefully. "Are you saying so because you think I'd like to hear it? Is that it?"

"No. I really mean it."

Pa had a little twist at the corner of his mouth, the way he looked when he was pleased about something. "Well, you're smart enough," was all he said.

The buggy rumbled across the bridge and circled through Cyprus. Men were putting red, white and blue bunting around the bandstand, and all the stores were closed, except for the soda fountain. They trotted down Washington Avenue, from which the side streets led to open country. These were shady streets; iron deer stood on lawns, and porches held stone urns filled with red geraniums. You wondered what lay inside the lofty houses where maids in striped aprons swept the steps.

A woman in a white dress and a flowered hat was coming out of a house. Two little girls, all white and lacy, walked beside her. They were younger than Martin. One of them looked very queer. There was something wrong with her shoulders.

Pa halted the buggy. "How are you, Mrs. Meig?"

"Very well, Doctor, thank you. Is this your boy?"

"Yes, this is my son, Martin."

"He's going to be a handsome man."

"Handsome is as handsome does."

The lady laughed. Even her laugh was pretty. Narrow silver bracelets flashed on her wrists, and Martin could smell her perfume. He stared at her, then at the daughter who was just like her. The girl had a gold locket lying in the hollow of her throat. He looked at the other girl and quickly looked away; you weren't supposed to stare at a cripple.

Pa tipped his hat and clucked to the mare.

"Who was that?" Martin asked.

"Mrs. Meig. That's her house."

Martin looked back. The house was strong and dark, built of stone. It had a curlicued iron fence and starry flowers scattered in the grass. "Have you ever been inside, Pa?"

"Yes, once. The parlormaid was sick and they couldn't get Dr. Pierce. That's how Mrs. Meig came to recognize me."

"What's a maid for, Pa?"

"Why, to take care of a big place like that. The Meigs own the Websterware factory where they make pots and pans. I guess half the men in Cyprus work there."

But Martin was thinking of something else. "What was wrong with that other little girl?"

"She has a curvature of the spine."

Martin shuddered. It would be terrible to be like that. The kids would make fun of you in school.

Ma and Alice were waiting on the porch when they drove into the yard. They had summer dresses on and white shoes.

"Don't they look pretty, standing there?" Pa asked.

"That lady was prettier than Ma. And the little girl was a whole lot prettier than Alice."

Pa rebuked him. "Don't you ever say that, Martin."

"I only meant Ma and Alice haven't got big white hats like those." It was not what he had meant, however.

His mother was in the mood of the holiday. She ruffled Martin's hair, grazing his cheek with the harsh skin of her fingertips. "Hurry up and change, you two!" she cried gaily.

Passing his mother and sister as he went into the house, Martin could not have explained what he saw in them just then. He only felt the dim confusion of contrast: that startling glimpse of a house, of a fragrant, slender woman and a flowery girl child; then this house and these two whom he knew so dearly. Something stirred in his heart; a kind of longing, a kind of pain.

Some days are marked for recollection, days which on the surface are not very different from all the others. But seeds have been sown which will lie hidden until a shaft of light breaks through; then all the concentrated life in the seeds will stir and rise. Perhaps it was unusual for a boy of nine to make a resolution and have a revelation all in one day; perhaps more unusual still for him to know that he would remember them.

CHAPTER TWO

MARTIN awoke with instant awareness that this morning was different. He was leaving home. The college years close by at Hamilton had been little more than an extension of home, but this, he knew, would be a final departure. After four years at Cornell University Medical College, in New York City, he would be changed for all time.

The suitcases stood near the door, black shapes in the graying dawn. Pa came in just as he was getting out of bed.

"You realize I haven't been in the city since I arrived on the boat from Ulster? And I wouldn't be going now if I weren't riding down with you." He yawned. "Excuse me. Didn't sleep well last night. I was up most of Wednesday watching old Schumann die. It's sad that after eighty-seven years a human being can't go out without a struggle. Even morphine didn't help much."

Martin, pulling on his sharply creased new trousers, thought, How will it be for me when I witness my first death?

"Hurry down for breakfast, Martin. Your mother's got pancakes and sausage." At the door he turned back. "Just one thing more I want to say. Martin, I envy you; born in a time when you'll learn things I couldn't dream of! The answers to dark secrets will come as clear as day. Maybe even cancer in your lifetime! Well, I'll see you downstairs."

Martin stood still in the center of the room. Point of departure.

Yes, he wanted to be a doctor. Yet, what if he didn't do well? Suppose he were to discover that he wasn't fitted for it! How would he face his father and face himself?

In a copybook, between thick cardboard covers, Martin kept a diary. He liked to believe that when he was older, in more leisured hours, these pages would keep time from consuming him without a trace.

Turning his pages then, flipping and skipping at random, the searching eye perceives the intimations and the forecasts.

My first week in New York is over. Pa stayed long enough to see me settled in. We had a good dinner at Luchow's. I watched him counting out the bills. These years will be hard for him. Later I took him to Grand Central to catch his train. I shall miss him with his ragtag quotations, his stars and rocks. Tender, feisty, absent-minded little man!

I am on my own.

This was my first day in the dissecting room. I thought I would vomit. Then I looked at my partner, Fernbach—we were assigned alphabetically to share a cadaver—and he looked sick, too. So we both began to laugh, a stupid, embarrassed laugh.

My best friends are going to be Tom Horvath and Perry Gault. Tom is six feet tall, with what they call a leonine head and a big homely face. He's a little opinionated, but I admire his honesty and gentleness. His gentleness makes me think of Pa.

Perry Gault is the brain. He's got a photographic memory for everything from anatomy to baseball scores. He's small and quick, with a hot temper and a soft heart.

They think I'm superstitious because I have "feelings" about the future. I feel that Perry and Tom and I are going to be involved in life together, perhaps even in great struggles. Ridiculous? Maybe!

Six months already fled. I've been trying in my free time to learn something about this enormous city. There's so much out there! Went down to the Fulton Fish Market. Shoving crowds and red faces. Piles of iridescent fish. Thought of that Flemish artist Brueghel I saw at the museum one Sunday.

I heard Edna St. Vincent Millay read poetry in the Village. I went to the opera—standing room, of course, but it was worth it. How splendid it is! New York is a feast and I am so greedy.

My second year! I've been watching some surgery and it's very, very sobering. Saw a radical mastectomy on a woman about my mother's age. Quiet, resigned face. Knows she will not beat this illness. Watched Alben Riker remove a tuberculous kidney yesterday. A master, with golden hands.

Wouldn't it be marvelous to be a surgeon? But how to get the training? Who can afford it? I do believe, though, that the day will come when there will be more specialists than general men. Tom Horvath disagrees. Anyway, he can't wait to be finished, to open an office and marry his girl, Florence. He says I'm lucky to have my father's practice to step into. He's right about that, I know.

My time is racing so. I'm three quarters of the way toward writing "Doctor" in front of my name. Sometimes I'm in a panic because I'm already twenty-four and I'll never do or see everything I want. I didn't know there was so much; how could you know, living in a little place like Cyprus, New York?

I wish I didn't have this itch. I feel that if I don't discover something or develop some stupendous skill, I will have failed. They say that most beginners are romantic about themselves, that it's only naïveté and youth. I wonder.

Home on vacation. A curious thing happened today. I went with Pa to one of those fussy Cyprus houses that I used to think so grand. The man of the house had the grippe. I waited in the library while Pa went upstairs. It was a dreadful room, with too much heavy oak furniture and an awful picture of a barefoot running nymph. I was staring at it when someone spoke.

"Horrible, isn't it?"

I jumped. Then I saw who it was: a small girl barely five feet tall. She was about twenty years old, with a sweet face, a fine head of dark curly hair, and a curvature of the spine.

"Sorry I scared you," she said. "I'm Jessie Meig."

I told her I was the doctor's son.

"I thought you were calling on my sister," she said. "If you want to see her, she's in her studio across the hall."

281

I told her I didn't know her sister.

Then she said, "Well, when you do know her you'll probably fall in love with her. Men always do."

I was so dumbfounded by all this that I didn't know how to answer. She just went on. "But Fern's not interested in men right now. She wants to be a great painter. Besides, she's timid to start with. If I looked like her, I wouldn't be timid."

"I would hardly call you timid," I said.

She laughed. "I'm not. For a person like me it would be fatal. Now take you—you're not timid, but you are a worrier."

Perhaps she felt she had to be startling, to entertain? I don't really know. But I was beginning to be amused.

"I guess I am," I said. "It runs in the family. My father worries about the progress of mankind and my mother worries about the roof over our heads."

"I suppose you're poor," she said.

By this time nothing surprised me, so I said yes, we were.

"Too bad. Country doctors work so hard for so little."

I was beginning to like the bite in her speech! Most people talk and don't say anything real. This girl was honest and intelligent. What a foul trick nature played, attaching that bright head to such a body! Suddenly something flashed into my mind.

"Why, I remember you. We were in the buggy, passing this house, and you came out with your mother and sister. I can see you clearly." What a bumbling idiot I was! Because what I meant was, *I remember the crippled girl.* So I tried to cover up. "I especially remember your mother."

"She died seven years ago."

Then I tried to cover up some more and moved to the bookshelves. I started mumbling about Sandburg's *Lincoln* and how I was going to buy it when I could afford it.

We talked some more about books until Pa came downstairs. I'm still feeling red in the face. A strange encounter.

A week later Pa found a package on the front porch. It was for me, Sandburg's *Lincoln*, with a card from Jessie Meig! "Anybody who wants anything as reasonable as a book shouldn't have to wait for it. So please accept this and enjoy it."

I decided to stop by with my thanks. I went in and asked the maid for Miss Meig, but instead of seeing Jessie, I was taken to the sister. She was at work before an easel and I could see she didn't want to be disturbed, so I said I was sorry about the mistake and backed right out.

It's queer, though, how much I remember of those few seconds! The most startling face looked up at me: dark, almost olive, with extraordinary, pure blue eyes. She wore a white smock. There was a drop of paint on her sandal. And that's all. I don't understand why the picture stays so sharp in my mind.

That nonsense Jessie spoke about people falling in love with Fern? No need to worry! I shall probably never even see her again.

SENIOR year was flying by faster than any of the years before it. Martin really began to feel like a doctor. He was reaching with curiosity into far corners, to the Academy of Medicine to hear a lecture on hypnotism, to listen to new theories about cancer and new procedures in the operating rooms.

One neurosurgeon attracted him especially. He was a Spaniard, Jorge Maria Albeniz, a frail, elderly man. The medical staff thought him talented but odd. He could have made a fortune. But most of his time was spent in his basement laboratory or at the clinic, where he treated the sick and taught. He liked to operate only when the case was so difficult that other men were reluctant to take it. Martin watched one day while he tried to remove a pituitary tumor from a young woman. The tumor was too far gone for complete removal.

Albeniz spoke as he worked. "With X-ray treatments, she may have a few more years. We're buying time, that's all." He looked up at the silent young men surrounding him. "As you see, there is a terrible lot we still do not know how to cope with."

This simple honesty touched Martin. Brain work, he thought, must be the most challenging field of all. He began to feel a new and unfamiliar restlessness.

It followed him home on winter vacation. Suddenly he noticed that his father had some absurd and ignorant opinions.

One afternoon Martin went with him on a house call. The family had a fat four-year-old boy of whom the mother was proud.

"He's a bruiser, ain't he, Doc?"

"Yes," Pa said, "a fine, fat boy. Anyone can see he gets plenty of your good rich cream and butter."

"Only thing, all last winter he complained that his arms and legs hurt. Not real bad. They just ached him, you know."

Pa waved his hands. "Nothing. Just growing pains."

Outside, Martin observed, "Don't you think you ought to consider rheumatic fever? And the child's too fat besides."

"No, I don't and he isn't," Pa said shortly.

The next day at the noon meal his mother inquired about someone's baby. "A lot better," Pa told her. "Dover's powder and an enema. That does it."

Again Martin couldn't resist. "Pa, we don't use Dover's powder anymore."

"What do you mean 'we don't'? Why, I've been using that stuff since before you were born!"

Martin opened his mouth to retort. Then he thought, If I'm to show him anything new, I must do it carefully and in private. We'll need to work well together, and we will— Still, the same restlessness came over him. The meal seemed endless.

"How about my borrowing the flivver this afternoon?" he asked finally. "Thought I'd do a couple of errands in Cyprus."

When he had finished at the drugstore and the hardware store, he got back in the car to go home. There was, after all, no place else to go. That being his intention, it was never quite clear to him how it happened that on Washington Street he suddenly swung the car around and found himself, three minutes later, parked at the curb facing two iron deer in front of a dark stone house.

THERE was the same shocked disturbance of equilibrium as the first time.

"Why are you staring at me?" she asked.

"Because I've never seen a face like yours."

"It can't possibly be that unusual!"

"You must know it is. Blue eyes don't belong in such a Spanish face, such a Greek face."

"There's no Spanish in me, or Greek either."

He supposed she was not beautiful in the accepted sense; she

284

was tall, almost as tall as he, and her coloring was too strange. But there was something so *dreaming* in her soft expression, as if she were seeing things he couldn't see!

In one hand she held a palette. Choosing a brush, she bent to an easel and laid a stroke of red on a bird's wing: three scarlet birds sat on a wire fence against a background of snow.

He knew almost nothing about art. But this picture was vivid and it appealed to him. So he said, "That's a pretty piece."

She frowned slightly. "I can't tell. So far, I've only imitated, you see. Look at this, for instance."

This was a small canvas covered in tones of pink, whirling from fuchsia to pearl. Looking closely, he saw these were trees in blossom. "I was trying to be Monet. The water lilies, you know."

"'MFM,'" he read in the corner. "What's the M for?"

"Mary. My name is Mary Fern. They call me Fern at home because Mother's name was Mary. But I prefer Mary."

"Then I'll call you Mary. I saw you once when I was about nine years old," he said irrelevantly.

"I know. Jessie told me. She says you'll be a wonderful doctor. You weren't embarrassed, the way most people are when they meet her. They never seem to know how to talk to her."

"How hard it must be for her, having to live so close to you!"

Instantly Martin regretted the exclamation. But Mary answered simply, "I know. We don't get along very well."

"She can't be much older than you?"

"Younger. We're thirteen months apart."

There was a stillness in the airy and white room. This studio had no relation at all to the rest of the cluttered house.

"I like this room," he said. "I feel peace here."

"There is peace here. Except when I'm in one of my rebellious moods." Mary laughed. "I'll bring coffee. Just clear those paintpots off the table, will you."

The sun struck glitter from the ring on her finger, moving around and around as she stirred her coffee. The ring was a topaz set in twisted gold. Her nails had sharply marked half-moons. There was a small mole in the center of her cheek. He had never felt such tremendous, intense awareness of another human being.

"What did you mean by your 'rebellious moods'?" he asked.

For a moment she didn't answer. Then she said, "You see— maybe it's entirely foolish, this thought of greatness in art—but how can I know unless I'm taken seriously?"

"And no one does?"

"My mother did. But Father thinks it's all nonsense. If I had any money of my own—"

"You'd go away?"

"Oh, yes! I do want to see somewhere else!" And she gestured with her arm. "Haven't you ever wanted to get beyond?"

"All my life, as far back as I can remember."

"And have you done it?"

"In a way. My beyond is my work. Medicine."

"Ah, then you're lucky! I don't even know whether my work is good! I've done nothing yet. And I'm already twenty." Then, embarrassed, she said, "I'm sorry. You can't be interested."

"You're wrong."

"Well. You did ask about my rebellion, didn't you? Though sometimes I'm ashamed of it."

"Why should you be?"

"Because of Jessie. I have so much. She has so little."

He nodded. What conflict must be within these walls!

His eye fell on a watercolor hung on the wall between the windows: a girl in a swing, her curved back half hidden by a fall of leaves. "That's Jessie?"

"Yes. She didn't like it."

"People don't always want to see the truth."

"Oh, Jessie sees it well enough! It's Father who doesn't, or won't. She needs so much to talk to somebody about her life! What's to become of her?"

"Won't she just stay here as she is?"

"Father won't live forever. And I'll do what I can for my sister, but I probably won't stay here, either."

He felt absurd alarm. "Suppose you were to be married?"

"I doubt I shall marry anyone from Cyprus."

He wanted to ask, Why? Is there anyone? Do you— But that, too, would have been absurd.

When they went to the door, he told her he'd be back in the summer, after graduation, and asked if he might come again.

"Come. But come and see Jessie, too."

"Do you always think of Jessie?" he asked curiously.

"Wouldn't you, if she were your sister?"

"Yes," he admitted. "I probably would."

HE THOUGHT of all the clichés in the language. Head over heels. First sight. Chemistry. All were expressions which he had once found unbelievable. But now joy pierced him through: his own, and the joy of the eyes in that dark, poetic face.

Summer came and he hurried back to her. But he hardly ever saw her alone and the summer days were vanishing. Twice Martin took her to the movies. The third time, at the father's suggestion, Jessie went along. In the evenings the family sat together in the library, Jessie and the father playing chess.

Mr. Donald Meig was a prim snob, faintly supercilious. Clearly Martin's presence was tolerated only because he was the doctor's son. "Fancies himself an aristocrat," Pa said.

One afternoon Martin walked with Mary in warm rain. Outside someone's open window they hid behind a wet syringa, listening to an aria from *Rigoletto* coming over the radio. "I remember," Martin said, "the first time I knew that music could make you laugh or cry. There are so many different kinds! The organ in church, all waves and thunder, or the band in the town square that makes your feet dance."

"My mother played the piano," Mary said. "We used to get out of bed to listen. The house was different then."

"You really want to get away, don't you?" he asked gently.

"I think I do, Martin. And then I think, It's home, I'd miss it. I'm confused. What I really want is to paint! Put everything down that I feel in my heart. The meaning of life!"

How young! he thought, with tenderness.

"I HOPE you don't have any ideas about that girl," Pa said at supper one night. "They're not our kind, Martin."

"What kind are we, Pa?" Martin asked mildly.

"Why, it's self-evident. Can you see that girl washing dishes in this kitchen? The worlds don't mix."

Worlds. Are we destined to stay in the one world for which we were made? Yet, look about you; it is often so.

"I wonder how long the Meigs will go on living like that," his father said. "They say the plant's going downhill."

Martin was surprised. "Websterware—backbone of the town?"

"I've some patients who work there, and they tell me the business has been running on its own momentum for years. Meig isn't the man his father and grandfather were, you know. He's in over his head and too proud to acknowledge it."

Martin's sister, Alice, remarked, "Rena works at Webster's. She says Mr. Meig keeps Fern shut away here until he finds the right marriage for her. Disgusting, isn't it? As if a woman were a prize racehorse to be mated with a prize stallion."

"Alice!" the mother cried.

Alice tittered. Ever since she had been going with Fred Partridge, she had become bolder. Soon she would be a married woman. Fred, who taught gym at the consolidated school, was a decent fellow, as neutral as his own eyes and hair. Once Alice had had yearnings. Now she was settling for Fred Partridge.

Ma was saying, "I hear the crippled one is smart."

"Her name is Jessie," Martin corrected stiffly.

"And is the other one really so good-looking?"

Alice answered, "She's thin, Ma, and much too dark, and—"

Martin stood up, murmuring something, and fled.

In the motionless air the candles made stiff tips of yellow light. Conversation, on this last night before Martin's departure for the city and his internship, moved around the table among Jessie, Donald Meig, and an aunt and uncle from New York. Mary and Martin were silent. He was ill at ease and his feet hurt. He had bought white shoes, an extravagance, but he couldn't have come to dinner here without them.

Jessie was laughing, such a hearty, appealing laugh. It was really a pleasure to watch her! Martin had become accustomed to her, sitting with her summer shawl gathered in stiff, concealing folds, her bright eyes observing everything. And recalling suddenly what she had said about her sister at that first meeting, he wondered what she might be guessing, what she knew. . . .

A sharp ache shot through Jessie for the young man in the cheap suit and the stiff, new shoes; the earnest young man who looked so hungrily at—someone else!

Oh, if I had Fern's body what I would do! she thought. I would make sure of that young man. He's worth a dozen of any others I've seen. Oh, if I had her body!

Long ago I heard the maids talking, two of them standing in the bathroom. "Poor child," they said.

I looked around for the child before I knew the child was I.

In the mirror I saw myself, naked. There were Fern and Fern's friend, come to stay overnight. And I saw they were alike, and I the different one. How old was I? Four?

Aunt Milly wants Fern and me to go to Europe with her and Uncle Drew this winter. They'll stay at the Carlton in Nice. Me at the Carlton! Tea-dancing. Steps leading down. You stand at the top, waiting to be seated. Eyes turn to see who you are. And I shall be standing next to Fern. No, thank you!

Across the table, Mary stirred uncomfortably. That look on Jessie's face! A moment ago she was laughing and now she seems thunder-dark. Will I never grow used to her?

I remember the day I first noticed her back. "What is that? Does it hurt?"

"No," Mother said, "it hurts only in her mind."

Yet Jessie was tougher than I. It was always she who did the hitting. "You must never hit her back," people said. "Never. You're so much stronger! Suppose you were to hurt her?"

But once I did hit Jessie back. She struck the table edge and a great reddening lump rose on her forehead. I was stiff with fright. She wailed and Mother and Father picked her up. Father whipped me. "Don't you ever hit her again! Do you hear?"

Now she doesn't want to go to Europe this winter. If she doesn't go, Father will want me to stay home too. But I'm going. No matter what, I'm going.

I shall be sorry to leave Martin. I might fall in love with him if

I could know him a little longer. And yet it seems I've always known him. Is it possible that he loves me already? But he's going away tomorrow. Maybe, when he comes back . . .

I think Jessie has fallen in love with him, though. I'm sorry if she has. Life is very, very harsh.

"It will be such joy having you with us, Fern," Aunt Milly was saying, and then, addressing Jessie, "I do wish you would change your mind and come along, too. It would do you the world of good, you know. You really need—"

"I really need a new spine," Jessie said, and laughed.

Aunt Milly blushed. "Oh, Jessie, I only meant—"

"I know what you meant. You meant well."

Aunt Milly said to Fern, "You'll be seeing the great art of the world. It'll help immensely in your career."

"Career!" The father was irritated. "Please, it's a pretty hobby and that's all it is."

"Excuse me, but you're hardly a judge," Mary said.

"Was that thunder I heard, by any chance?" Uncle Drew asked, changing the subject.

Martin smiled at him and received a knowing, answering smile. A kindly soul! Worlds removed from the petty tyrant at the head of the table!

"Mary, let's go for a walk," he proposed when they had finished the meal.

Mr. Meig frowned. "It's going to rain any minute."

"We'll not go far," Martin said.

The town was closed for the night. They circled through dwindling streets from pavement to dirt, and where the fields began, turned back, talking of nothing in particular.

"So you'll be going away," Martin said. "I'll miss you." The words were unforgivably banal. He wanted to say such beautiful, extravagant things: I'm enchanted, I think of you all day. Why was he so tongue-tied? Perhaps in a more private setting, or if he were farther along and had something definite to give . . .

The smell of rain was in the air when they came to the gate. Eastward, the clouds were darkening, but in the west the afterglow still streaked the sky in lines of copper and rose and yellow.

"Oh, look!" Mary cried. "It sparkles! Martin, look!"

But he was not looking at the sky. He was looking at her, standing there with wonder on her face.

They stood at the front door, cramped between overgrown laurel. And quite suddenly the rain came.

"Well," he said. "I guess I'd better start."

"I'll think of you. We all will."

He had meant only to kiss her good-by. But when he had caught her to him, he was unable to let her go. How long he would have held her there he didn't know. But someone stirred in the vestibule. So she turned quickly into the house and he went down the steps into the rain.

THIS was the way of it: He was Dr. Farrell, intern, responsible for lives. Agitated relatives waylaid him and the squawk box pursued him. His irrevocable signature went on every record. Pray it wasn't witness to a mistake! Best not to think about that, though; just step forward and begin, the way a child learns to walk.

The emergency room stayed in motion all night. He lived on black coffee. He slept on a cot until a nurse shook him awake again. The doors would swing open, and another stretcher come rolling through. Unbearable pain was unbearable to watch. At times he felt the weight of the building lying on his shoulders.

If only the work were all he had to think about! But there was Mary. She sent a card from Lake Champlain. "Visiting here for a few days. Love." He read it over and over, studying the shape of the words. She wrote in backhand. He wondered what that meant about her personality. Then a card came from Cherbourg. He imagined her walking in the rain on a cobbled street. He ached for her, a definite physical ache.

One night a young girl in a pink sweater was on the stretcher. A necklace of cheap beads spelled out her name: Donna. She had been run over in the rain. Her face was gashed and her arms, which she must have flung out to save herself, had been crushed.

Standard procedure, Martin thought. Neurosurgery later to save the ulnar nerves. Useless hands, otherwise. Patch the face while waiting. Sedation, of course. Local anesthesia. He called out orders. Black silk. Fine needle.

"This won't hurt," he said.

Never did this before. Trick is very, very small stitches. Careful. Suture. Tie. Knot. Cut. Again. When he was finished, the pathetic face was crisscrossed with black silk and he was sweating. He leaned down. "Donna? I'm through."

She was half asleep. "Will my face be all right?"

"Yes," he said confidently.

The mouth quivered. "Do you promise I won't be scarred?"

"I promise."

The neurosurgeon who operated on the girl was Dr. Albeniz. Martin arrived when it was all over and the doctors were back in the locker room.

"It was very close," Albeniz said, replying to Martin's question. "But I'm fairly sure she'll be all right. Do you know the girl?"

"No. I was on duty when she came in. I sutured her face."

"You did?" There was strong emphasis on the "you."

Martin felt quick dread in the pit of the stomach. "I'm afraid I'm the culprit."

"Culprit?" Albeniz, who was tying his shoes, glanced up. "On the contrary. It's a superb job. She'll have scarcely a scar."

Martin swallowed. "I guess I was lucky." Then, because it seemed necessary to say something polite in return, he added, "But after what you did, my suturing seems unimportant."

"Not so. It's not very good for one's mental health to have scarred cheeks, you know."

"That's true. But your work is vital. I've seen you operate and I've been—I guess you could say I've been thrilled each time."

Albeniz smiled. "Well then, I give you a standing invitation to come and watch whenever you're free."

THE excitement in the operating room was unlike anything Martin had ever felt before. Bare and exposed lay a human brain. Dr. Albeniz looked up from it to the X ray, hanging directly in his line of vision. There lay the clump of tumor. Martin's heart pounded. He tried to remember what he had learned about the brain, and could only think, Somewhere in that corrugated mass ran the electricity of thought and reason.

"Clamp," said Albeniz. His gloved hands moved inside the patient's brain, moved among those billions of neurons.

"Cautery," he said. "Suction."

Five hours later it was over. Albeniz looked up. His eyes, above the mask, were weary. "I think I got it all out."

Martin knew he probably had, but no surgeon would ever say, "I know I have."

He was awestruck. A fine surgeon is an artist, he thought. He may be a simple, modest man like Albeniz or a bully like some others. But either way he is respected; he has a great gift. I wish I could be like Dr. Albeniz.

In the limited free time Martin had, he continued to observe Dr. Albeniz. He went to his laboratory and to his clinic. He followed some cases through surgery and rehabilitation—or to postmortem. He asked questions, but not too many.

One afternoon he was about to go off duty when he was summoned to Dr. Albeniz's laboratory.

"I was wondering whether you like Italian food," Albeniz said when he got there. "There's a place just a few blocks away."

"I've never had any," Martin said.

"Good! It'll be a new experience."

Fifteen minutes later they were seated in the restaurant, with a clean, darned cloth and a basket of bread between them. "Would you like me to order?" Albeniz asked.

"Please do."

"All right then. Clams *oreganata* to begin. Pasta, of course. Salad. Veal *pizzaiola*. Isn't it ridiculous to eat like this without wine? You Americans and your Prohibition." He sighed, rubbing his hands to warm them, and was silent a moment.

"You know, I've been watching you watch me these last months. Tell me, why did you want to be a doctor?"

Martin said slowly, "It always seemed, as far back as I can remember, the most exciting thing I could imagine. It's like solving puzzles. You want to go to the next one."

Albeniz smiled. "I'm glad you didn't say 'to help humanity,' or

294

some such rubbish. I hear young men say that and I don't believe them. Of course you rejoice when you've done something good for another human being! And of course you feel pity when things go wrong! But too much pity and you break your heart." He waved an admonishing finger. "You have to be disciplined. Then, when the mind is clear, you can do some good. Sometimes."

The clams were brought. Albeniz took a mouthful, then laid the fork down. "We know so little," he continued. "Take my field. Neurosurgery is a new discipline, and most of what we know we've learned since the war." He paused, picked up the fork and put it down again. "Did you know we're going to have a separate department starting in September? At last we'll be removed from general surgery."

"I didn't know."

"Well, it's just been decided. Of course, that will be only a start. What we ought to have is an institute where neurosurgery and neurology could be combined. Then we could truly study the whole brain: its function, pathology, even the tie-in with what is called mental illness." He sighed. "But that's only my dream. I haven't the money or the influence to make it come true." He made a small pyramid with his fingertips. "Tell me, what are you planning to do when you finish in June?"

"Work with my father. He's got a general practice upstate."

Dr. Albeniz studied Martin. "Are you happy about it?"

No one had ever put the question like that. He waited a moment and then, for the first time, expressed the truth. "No, sir, I don't think I am," and he turned away.

"I've upset you with my questions, haven't I?"

"A little, maybe."

"More than a little. Do you know that I've been observing you? Ever since you sewed up the girl's face. I knew that the hands which could do that could do much more. You're aware, of course, that you've earned a reputation this year?"

"Well, I—"

"Come, come! Dr. Fields tells me you're the best intern he's had in his service in ten years. So, hear me. I'm coming to the point. In this new service that I'm to have, I can train two young men for three years. I already have one coming from Philadelphia in the fall. I'm asking you to be the other."

Martin looked at him dumbly.

"You understand what I'm driving at. I want a man who will grasp the whole concept of the brain, someone who has curiosity. That's the key word, curiosity. What do you say?"

"Forgive me. I'm stunned."

"Of course. This is another world from the one you've been planning on—sore throats, measles and cut fingers. Not that we don't need good men to do that. Men like your father. What do you think he will say to this?"

"He'll be terribly disappointed, I'm afraid."

"Yes, I can imagine. Still," Albeniz said quietly, "there are always some who have to break family ties no matter how it hurts. I was forty before I got married. In Europe, men marry later; it gives them time to develop. Do you have a girl?"

Martin flushed. "There's nothing official, but—"

Albeniz smiled. "Well, you'll work that out." He stood up. "You will get twenty dollars a month and your keep. You will live penuriously. There are worse things." He shook Martin's hand. "The next time we come you'll try the spaghetti *carbonara*."

Martin was halfway back to his room before he realized that Albeniz hadn't even waited for his acceptance. He had simply taken for granted that no young man could do anything other than accept. And of course he had been right!

He thought of Mary. How foolish of him not to have told her how he felt before she left! Well, she would be home soon and he would put everything into words then; he'd buy her a ring; three years wouldn't be that long to wait.

He sat down at his desk and began a letter. He thought of asking her then and there to marry him, but the words looked too stark and he decided he'd wait to speak them aloud. For the present he would only describe the marvel that had occurred.

By two o'clock the following day everybody knew about Martin. It was something to be talked about, to be impressed by. But Tom Horvath puzzled over it.

"Oh, it's a stupendous opportunity," he admitted. "Still, I don't

296

know, Martin. It's a depressing specialty. Most of the patients die; you know they do."

"But if we take that attitude, they always will."

"Well, I can't wait to get out on my own." Tom and Florence were to be married in July and he was to set up practice in Teaneck, New Jersey. The early marriage Martin could understand, but not the haste to leave the hospital.

I love it here, he thought. For me it's the heart of the world. And Perry Gault would still be around. He was going to stay on at the hospital, to do his residency in anesthesiology.

Then one day he decided to tell Tom and Perry about Mary. Their goodwill, their good wishes for him brought tears to his eyes—and their jokes about those foolish tears.

He'd had only a postcard from her since he had written his news. They had been moving about all over England; she would write a real letter soon. In the meantime she wanted him to know that his news was wonderful.

At last there came a thick envelope, postmarked London. Cutting his lunch hour short, Martin went to his room, locked the door, and sat down. His eyes sped over the pages.

> Alex's mother has been a friend of Aunt Milly's and Uncle Drew's for years. He's a wonderful person. You would really like him! His wife died when their baby was born, a beautiful little boy, Neddie. . . . Jessie and Father will come over for the wedding, and we shall have the ceremony at Alex's house, not far from London. I know you will be surprised at the suddenness of all this. I am myself! But I am so very, very happy.

He thought at first that she was talking about a friend who was going to be married. He read it again. Then he sat on the edge of the bed. He put his head in his hands and felt ill.

"You would like him," she dared to write! Like him! Martin groaned. Didn't she know what *he* felt for her?

He pounded his knees with his fists. Timid fool that I am! To assume that she would be there, waiting. Instead of saying, that last night on the front steps— He went into the bathroom and was violently sick. Then he came back and sat for a while, staring at the wall. After a time he picked the letter up, ripped it over and over and flung the shreds on the floor.

It seemed hours later that someone pounded at the door. Martin opened his eyes to weak, departing sunlight.

"Are you in there? Open the door." It was Tom Horvath.

Martin got up and went to the door. "Where've you been?" Tom cried. "Didn't you hear the squawk box? They've been calling you for an hour!"

"I didn't hear. I don't seem to be feeling well."

"What's the matter? Are you sick?"

"Yes. No. I've had a kind of blow, that's all." He looked at the floor. "Mary's being married in England."

"I'm sorry! Oh, Martin, I'm so sorry!"

A fire engine clanged in the street below. When it had passed, the silence was absolute. After a minute Tom spoke. "I have to hit you again, Martin."

Martin looked up. "What do you mean?"

"Your sister telephoned. When you didn't answer, they called me instead. Your father's had a stroke."

CHAPTER THREE

MARTIN slid the rattletrap car into the shed. Dean, their old brown horse, thrust his head out of the stall. He'd outlived his usefulness and Pa was simply saving him from the glue factory. Martin walked to the animal and laid his head against the rippling shoulder. He felt such loneliness! With Alice married and gone to Maine, with his mother herself in need of strengthening, there was no one to talk to. And what was there to talk about?

Should he talk about Mary? No use in that. It was over and done with. Talk about his father, the withered flesh, the tottering walk? What is there to say about a life that's running out?

Anybody coming in would think he'd lost his wits, standing here like this. And abruptly, repelled by his own sadness, Martin straightened and went into the house.

"Pa gone up to bed this early?" he asked.

"No, he had his supper and went to his desk in the office." Jean

298

lowered her voice. "Martin, I didn't know he'd taken a new mortgage on the house, did you?"

"No. He's never talked business affairs with me."

"Well. The original mortgage had been paid off before you went to high school. I don't understand." Her lips trembled. "How could he have worked so hard and we still have nothing?"

He didn't answer, there being nothing to say. She set his plate on the table, poured coffee and sighed.

"Did you see Ken Thompkins today?" she inquired.

"Yes. He won't last the night. He's been vomiting from a strangulated hernia since last Wednesday and they didn't call till today. His wife thought it was colic." Martin could hear the exasperation in his voice. "My God, what ignorance!" He threw out his hand in a gesture of hopelessness, tipping the coffee cup.

His mother rose to wipe the spill and handed him two letters. "I forgot. Here's mail for you."

Martin propped the letters against his water glass, reading over a lifted fork. Tom wrote that he had opened his office. He had gotten privileges at a good hospital. Florence was keeping her job, and they were gradually furnishing the house. Martin must somehow get down to see them.

The second letter was from Dr. Albeniz. He was holding Martin's place open. He understood the circumstances, but hoped Martin would be able to set things in order at home soon.

"Something wrong, Martin?"

"No. Tired, that's all."

"I don't know what we'd do without you," his mother said. "Isn't it the hand of Providence that if this had to happen to your father, it waited until you were ready to take his place?" She stood, frowning a little, wiping and wiping the spot, now dry, where the coffee spill had been.

"Pa's doing better, you know," Martin said gently.

"Martin, you mean well, but I'd rather have the truth. I see him going downhill. What's going to happen?"

"Ma, I don't know. I'd tell you if I did. I'd be surprised if he improved any, but he could go on no worse than this for years. Or he could have another stroke tonight."

There were shuffling steps in the hall. His father appeared in the doorway and greeted Martin without interest.

"How are you feeling, Pa?" Martin asked.

"I'm bored," the old man said petulantly. "There's nothing to do here all day."

"You'll just have to learn to kill time," Jean told him, "until you get to be yourself again."

Enoch stared at her. "Kill time! That's the worst thing you could have said. It's time that's killing me. Well, I'm going up to bed. Good night, folks."

So Martin and his mother sat, not speaking, stirring their coffee. The dog barked and Martin got up to look. Someone had put a basket of apples on the front porch.

"Martin, what is it?" his mother asked.

"Somebody's left greenings on the porch. That's odd."

"Not odd. People do that lots of times when they can't pay. They give whatever they can." She went back to the kitchen.

He sat down on the porch step next to the apples. A fox barked from across the road. Low on the horizon, just above the trees, Orion shone. You couldn't be Pa's son, he thought, without having learned the constellations. After a little while Jean came to the doorway.

"I'm going to bed. You coming up?"

Martin and the dog went in. "Soon. I thought maybe I'd go over some things in Pa's desk."

"Oh, I wish you would! I know the bankbooks are there someplace. I guess you can find them. Only don't stay up too late."

The old rolltop desk overflowed with paper. Under a pile of prescription blanks, old postcards, letters and calendars, Martin found three savings books. He opened them and added the sum. Four thousand four hundred eighty-three dollars and seventy-six cents. He rummaged incredulously for another book. But there was none. This was all Pa had, after a lifetime of labor.

He sat in stunned despair. The pity of it! Four thousand dollars, this modest house and a basket of apples left by a grateful patient. Who would take care of them now, except their son? For a long time he sat, then he reached for a piece of paper.

Dear Dr. Albeniz,
    Thank you for waiting until I could reach a final decision. I appreciate your patience and your understanding . . . grateful and honored by your offer . . . impossible because of my family situation . . . regret. Very good wishes.

Short and sweet. He put his hands over his face. His sadness was so vast it emptied him. Everything that had been so bright had just quietly slipped away, fallen from his outstretched hands. Gone. All gone.

THE year hurried toward its close. The lakes froze; a thin film of dimpled ice hardened and thickened. Christmas morning brought a sugary fall of snow. In the afternoon Martin was called out. When he got back, it was almost time for dinner.

Pa looked up. "Anything important today?"

"Well, I persuaded Mary Deitz to have the goiter operated on."

"She's had that goiter fifteen years! Cut, cut, that's all you young fellows know how to do."

"I'm not the one who's going to do it, more's the pity."

"Hmph. I daresay there's good in a lot of this new stuff. But those fellows don't know everything, Martin. Don't let them fool you."

"No, Pa. I won't let them fool me." He looked so small and old, standing there.

"What'll happen when you fellows have divided up the whole human body among yourselves, hey? One'll study the left ear, the other will study the right knee. Why, there won't be a doctor among the lot of you fit to treat a whole patient!"

Pa used to say, "You will see such marvels in your lifetime, Martin!" But now illness and the hidden envy that can corrupt old age had changed him into someone else.

The Christmas table was set in the dining room.

"Martin," Jean said, "you carve the turkey."

That had been his father's job. It would be Martin's now, so he guessed he'd better learn. Strip the leg off first, then cut the wing. Slice neatly from the breast.

301

"My, that's expert," his mother said, too heartily.

The platters passed among the three of them. Pa's plate was mounded with creamed onions, turkey, mashed turnip, mashed potatoes and cranberry sauce. He had not lost his enormous appetite. Silently, voraciously, he ate. Martin tried to think of something to say to break the silence.

"I do wish Alice were here," Jean remarked.

He understood that his mother was attempting a conversation. He tried to cooperate. "Do you suppose she'll have a chance to visit before spring?"

"I shouldn't think so. The roads are awfully bad and the train connections are dreadful. Though I know she wants to see her father. Anybody like to try my mincemeat? I brought two jars up from the cellar. It's so good the next day with cold turkey. Enoch! Enoch! What is it?"

Pa's hands clutched at his chest. "I don't feel well." He pushed his chair violently away from the table. "I have a terrible pain. Terrible!" he cried, very loud.

And while in an instant of dumb shock they stared at him, he stood up, stretched tall and, reaching, stiffened, buckled at the knees, and toppled. His face struck the edge of the table with a dreadful, tearing sound. Then the chair broke, splintering as Enoch crashed to the floor.

"Oh, God!" Jean screamed. "Oh, God! Enoch, get up!"

ENOCH was laid out in the parlor between the two front windows. When Martin looked down at his father, it was not the face that moved him most, it was his father's hands folded on his chest, where the undertaker had arranged them.

My father, you've gone so far away. It terrifies me, this death of yours. I've seen death so often by now, but not your death. There are things I would like to have talked to you about when you were yourself and well. In so many ways Ma has been the head of the household, for somebody had to try to manage things. But you were always the heart. You were the heart.

In the pile of letters that arrived during the next week, there came a note from Jessie Meig.

302

Father and I were so sorry to learn of your father's death. He was a kind, old-fashioned man. He will be missed. If you ever have time, would you come to visit us? Would the Sunday after next for tea at four be all right?

He whipped the letter against the table's edge. Be damned if he would walk into that house again! What did they think of him? Then he felt foolish. Very likely they weren't thinking anything.

A few weeks later his mother reported, "Jessie Meig telephoned today. She wondered whether you had gotten her note."

He was ashamed of his rudeness. He thought of Jessie, seated in the enormous wing chair as though she felt protected by the wings. And he thought, Out of pure decency I ought to go.

So, on the following Sunday afternoon he strode up the walk between the iron deer, stood under thawing icicles on the porch, and entered the house he had never expected to enter again.

Jessie put the remainder of the lunch into a bag and capped the thermos. "Do you want to drive, Martin, or shall I?"

"It's your car. You drive."

Ever since winter's end, Jessie had been going with Martin on his far-country house calls. He wasn't sure how the habit had formed; her father may have suggested it. At any rate, that inhibiting person had been surprisingly cordial these past months.

"It'll do you good to get out more," he had said to Jessie.

Certainly that was true. Jessie's need for companionship was visible enough. The same need was in Martin. His boyhood friends had all dispersed; and after five close years, he felt the loss of men like Tom Horvath and Perry Gault. In all of Cyprus it seemed the one person to whom he could really talk was Jessie Meig.

"You're worried about something," she said now.

"It's that call I made before lunch. That woman has lost sixteen pounds in the last two months. I know it's a malignancy." Martin shook his head in recollection of the young woman with the delicate face. "I told them she needs to go to the hospital for tests. But the husband kept saying, 'She's just weak after birthing.'"

Jessie shook her head. "I would never want to be a doctor."

303

"And if I couldn't have been a doctor, there's nothing else in the world I would have wanted to be."

Around a bend, they were slowed by a wagon with an enormous load of hay. A woman called cheerfully, "Hi, Doc!"

"That's good fodder you've got there," Martin called back.

"Yes, and we'll be needing it before you know it."

"Just don't throw that back out again unloading!"

"They like you, Martin," Jessie said when they drove on.

"I like them." In his few short months of practice he had been touched a dozen times with powerful emotion. In their houses, in their beds, the people turned to him in trust and gratitude. And yet he knew that what he did was often not enough.

"Most illnesses are self-limiting," he mused aloud. "Fluids, bed rest and warmth will cure them in a matter of days. But what bothers me, Jessie, is the other kind. This morning's case, for instance. I'm stymied, battling lack of facilities and ignorance. The patients' ignorance and my own. Mostly my own. What I do could be done so much better!"

"I'm sure it could," Jessie said.

They passed a field where cattle chewed dreamily in pasture shade. In Gregory's Pond, the confluence of three streams, a few small boys were swimming. "Why don't we bring our suits sometime?" he proposed. "Oh, I forgot, you don't like to swim."

"That's not true. I really do like to. I only said so because I didn't want you to see me in a bathing suit. Now all of a sudden, I wouldn't be ashamed."

"Jessie, there's nothing to be ashamed of!"

"Well, not ashamed exactly. I'm afraid people will find it . . . disgusting," she said, so low he barely caught the word.

"*Nihil humanum mihi alienum est.*"

"Nothing human is alien to me," she said quietly, and after a moment, "Thank you."

"You ought to put a higher valuation on yourself."

"I suppose I should. But then, so should you. You ought to be doing something more important than what you're doing."

"But what I'm doing *is* important."

"Of course! But you're one of the movers, the advance guard."

"Maybe you overestimate me."

"Oh, I despise false modesty! What's that magazine sticking out of your bag? You've had it there since last week."

"This?" He drew out a copy of *Brain*. In a moment of high hopes he had subscribed to it. "Oh. There's a fascinating article here about an operation to remove the frontal lobe."

"Incredible! Delving inside the brain!"

"Yes. I used to watch Dr. Albeniz operate. It seemed almost magical to me." He would have to stop thinking about that.

"I'm sorry I brought all this up," Jessie said. "It's like taunting you with your impossible dream, and that's cruel."

"It's all right. I'm not the most deprived person in the world."

"No, but you are depressed more than you should be. Oh, you don't show it. But I can sense hidden things in people."

Astonishing girl! For it was true. Melancholy, sticky and gray as cobwebs, had been clinging to him.

The little car spun along. Jessie's keen face frowned at the road. Then she turned back to Martin. "There's something I've been wanting to ask you, Martin. Were you terribly in love with Fern?"

Ah, but this was too much! "In love with her?" he answered curtly. "I scarcely knew her."

"There's no reason to be angry."

"I'm not angry!"

"Offended, then. I'm sorry. I went too far."

"But what made you think—"

"What made me? Because Fern is—Fern. If I hadn't had my own problems, I would have loved her myself." Jessie sighed and shifted gears to climb a hill. Then she said, "Fern's the total sentimentalist, you know. Mother used to say Fern would rather *suffer* than destroy her idea of perfection. For instance, she would never get a divorce if she made a bad marriage. That would be an admission of defeat. Did I tell you she's pregnant?"

"No."

"They didn't lose any time, did they? But I'm glad for her. I really am. Alex is awfully nice, and he's giving her the encouragement she needs with her art. It should be a very good life for her at last, not having me to keep her from going places."

"Don't dwell on that, Jessie. Things probably weren't nearly as bad as you're making them."

"Yes, they were. But I swear to you, Martin, that I really want everything to be good for Fern. Do you believe me?"

"I believe you and I think you're wonderful," he said gently. "You're perceptive and honest. I'm glad I know you."

She answered with untypical shyness, "Are you? Then I'm glad, because it's the same for me."

ONE evening, during Martin's second winter of practice, Donald Meig telephoned. "Martin, could you run over tonight? There's something I'd like to talk to you about."

"Surely, I'll be right over," Martin said, surprised. Half an hour later he was in the familiar library.

"Excuse us, Jessie, will you?" Meig said. "I've a medical matter to discuss with Martin." He closed the double doors. "Have a brandy. It'll warm you. You're wondering why I called."

Meig took a seat and sighed, and Martin waited. "You have problems. I have problems," the older man began. "I'd like to talk about yours first. I know you're not satisfied with your life here."

Jessie must have talked, making him look like a malcontent. So Martin defended himself. "I feel I've been doing a fairly good job, learning practical things I need to know."

Meig waved him aside. "Nonsense! You're not a country doctor, and we both know it. So let's get to the heart of the matter. Jessie tells me you once had the opportunity of a lifetime and had to pass it up for want of a few dollars!"

"A great many dollars, I'm afraid."

"All relative. Anyway, you've heard of Hugh Braidburn in London, the neurosurgeon?"

That was almost like asking whether one had heard of Darwin or Einstein! "Of course. He's coauthor of the textbook. Cox-Braidburn."

"Well, I'm acquainted with him. His father-in-law was the head of our plant in Birmingham. We sold the plant, but the contacts are still there." Meig sipped his brandy thoughtfully. "I could get any favor I asked him for."

On a table behind the sofa stood a photograph that Martin had never seen before. Framed in silver, Mary held an armful of calla lilies, a lace veil swirling to her feet. He tried to decipher her expression but could see only the calm, reflective smile of the traditional bridal picture.

"I said," Meig demanded, "what do you think of the idea?"

"Excuse me. I wasn't—I didn't quite understand."

"Good grief, man, pay attention! I asked you how you'd like to spend a couple of years in London, studying with Braidburn."

What sort of a charade was this? "Like it, Mr. Meig? It would be paradise! But it's impossible!"

Meig laughed. "It's not impossible at all." He leaned forward, lowering his voice. "Of course, I must give you the whole story. So now let's go to my problem. I have angina. I go to a doctor in Albany, because I don't want anyone around here to find out. Especially not Jessie."

"If you'll excuse me, do you think that's wise? If anything were to happen to you, it would be harder for her not to have been prepared, and Jessie is nothing if not a realist."

"You know her rather well, then."

"We've had a lot of talks this past summer and fall. I can tell you I think she can cope with things very well."

"She's a bright girl. Both my girls are. They're like their mother. Curious about everything. Music. Pictures. Books." He looked away from Martin. "Damned injustice! My wife never drew a happy breath after Jessie was born."

Martin moved restlessly. What did all this have to do with neurosurgery in London?

"Now let me tie all this together. I have angina, I have a daughter who will be alone when I die. That is my problem. If I could only see her well and wisely married before I die . . ."

Martin was silent. Was it possible Meig was going to say what Martin thought he might say?

"Well. I've turned this over and over in my mind and I want to make a proposition." Meig took a deep breath. "Marry Jessie."

Martin felt his mouth drop open.

"I'll see that you get the best medical training in the world. I'll

307

subsidize you, and your mother, until you can support a family. Marry Jessie, and make a life for yourself."

Martin was stunned. But one couldn't just tell a man he was out of his mind.

"You don't have to give me your answer now. Think it over. Take plenty of time."

"I appreciate that, Mr. Meig. But I have to tell you that I hadn't thought of marriage for years yet. As you say, I am—at least I hope I am—a responsible man, and marriage isn't—"

"Martin, let's do without diplomacy, shall we? This is a time for plain talk. I know Jessie isn't precisely what you had in mind for a wife. But I also know, and you do, too, that burning love affairs usually go up in smoke anyway. Now, Jessie is intelligent and she's good company. She'd be a trusted companion all your life." He paused. "And she'd be grateful to you."

Martin winced and Meig saw it. "Yes, I did say grateful! But you'd be grateful to her, too. Because without her you'd spend the rest of your life here, going to waste."

Martin stood up to get his coat. "I understand what you've said, Mr. Meig, but—"

Meig waved him aside. "You think if you accept, you'll be selling yourself. That's sentimentality, Martin, sentimentality!"

Martin had one foot out the door.

"Of course, she doesn't have the remotest idea of what I've been saying and must never find out, whatever you decide."

Martin was horrified. "No need to worry about that!"

"Very well, then. Just give it some thought."

It was a cold night, but Martin sweated. The shame of it! He looked back at the house, wondering which of the lights came from Jessie's room. And he thought how it would be for her if she knew what had just passed between her father and himself.

The proposition had been well-intentioned, born of desperation. But the thing was impossible. And now a fine friendship had been spoiled for good.

For two weeks he stayed away. Then it occurred to him that such an abrupt disappearance would be a cruel hurt to Jessie. And when he did call on her at last, he found that it had been.

"I thought maybe my father had antagonized you the last time you were here," she said, looking anxious.

"Well, he didn't. Anyway, I don't antagonize so easily."

"That's not true. The truth is exactly the opposite."

"You're right, as usual," he admitted, and she laughed.

She was seated, as always, in the great wing chair. Her cheeks were pink from the fire, and there were pinpoint sparks of gold in her ears. She could have been so lovely! If only— And he wondered whether anyone would ever love her. Respect, admiration, companionship—these would come easily in all the virtuous ways through which human beings relate to one another. But love?

"I have something for you, Martin." She jumped up and went over to the bookshelves. "Here. It's Rolland's *Jean-Christophe,* a beautiful story of a musician in Paris. Especially good for you."

"Why for me?"

"Because it's a story of a struggle. He always knew he was going to be a great composer. He faced everything—loneliness, poverty, rivalry; but he never gave up."

"And did he win in the end?"

"Read it." She forced his eyes to meet her own. "You're tenacious. You'll get what you want. I feel it in you." A sudden brightness came into the little face, a fervor so glowing that it seemed he was seeing deep into her. She loved him.

Good Lord! He hadn't intended that! How had this come to be? Well, it would have to be stopped, that was all. And swiftly, with such grace as he could summon, he escaped from the house.

During the next weeks Martin's office was crowded with coughs, sore throats and several rampant cases of measles that should have stayed home instead of polluting the waiting room. At the end of one such day he closed the office and went to the car.

Ordinarily he would not have answered a summons fifteen miles into the mountains, especially in snowy weather, but these were old patients. And Pa would have gone, he told himself grimly.

Sliding and struggling up the hills, the flimsy car shook through fierce crosswinds. The windshield wipers clacked. After two miserable hours he pulled up before a ramshackle house with no light poles. If anybody needed cutting, he would shine the car headlights into the room. Rural poverty like this in the twentieth century!

In the kitchen stood five runny-nosed children and their terrified mother. The man had pneumonia. Martin left medicines and a sheet of instructions. "Take his temperature regularly," he told the woman. "And try to get to a phone to call me tomorrow."

She was concerned about his bill. "I can't give you anything now, Doctor, but I'll be at my sister's right near your place in a couple of weeks. I'll bring it then."

"Don't worry about it," he said gently, knowing quite well that he would never be paid.

He left to slide, downhill this time, the fifteen miles homeward. The man should be taken care of in the hospital, and this frustration, along with so many others, nagged Martin as he drove.

I don't know anything. I'm not an expert obstetrician, cardiologist or orthopedic surgeon. I'm not an expert anything. That arm I set last week wasn't done right, I know it wasn't.

My father's kind hands lay folded over his black vest in the coffin. He gave the best care he could. He tried. My God, he did! And that's better than no care at all! A man has to be satisfied with it. My father was satisfied.

The road curved around the lip of a plateau from which he could see white fields and hills, folding back to the mountains. Grand. Eternal. Majestic. A man might well stand in awe of it. But everybody wasn't meant for it, and Martin hated it, hated the loneliness, the monotony, the awful cold. He could have wept.

When he crept into the yard an hour later, the house was dark and he remembered that his mother had gone to a church supper. She had left his meal on the stove. It was stone cold. Then he noticed that the house smelled dank and musty. He ran down to the cellar. There was no fire in the furnace.

Blasted boy! His mother had arranged with Artie Grant to tend the fires today while she was gone, but obviously he hadn't come. Martin went upstairs to the porch for kindling. Then down to the cellar again. But first the ashes must be cleaned out. His head pounded as dust from the ashes set off a fit of coughing.

Finished in the cellar, he went back up to the kitchen. His

mother had just come home. She wore her old black "good" coat; the black feather on her hat was turning green. Humble. That's how she looks, he thought. Mean word. Humble.

"Goodness, you're all over ashes!" she cried.

"Yes. Where in blazes was Artie Grant?"

"I guess the weather was too bad for him to get here."

"It was, was it? Wasn't too bad for me! I only traveled thirty miles round trip to Danielsville and back!"

"Martin," his mother said mildly, "you're tired and hungry."

"Of course I am. Why not?"

When his supper was reheated, Ma sat down in the rocker near the table. "That shutter keeps banging. The hinge is loose. If I get a new hinge, will you put it on sometime?" And without waiting for him to answer, "Your father never cared about things like that. The world of ideas, that's what he lived in." She sighed. "Sometimes he'd read aloud about places far away. Places like Afghanistan or the Amazon. And I'd ask him, 'Don't you wish we could go there?' 'I am there in my mind,' he'd answer."

"I'm not like him," Martin said.

"That's true. I've never known anyone like him."

In the hall the old clock struck with a tinny bong. His mother coughed, a thick phlegmy cough that she hadn't been able to get rid of. And he had a sudden projection of himself on long winter nights like this one, sitting in a shabby room like this one. The future was an endless dull road stretching through an unchanging landscape. Life would go by without sparkle or aim.

But all the time, in other places, some men would be doing what they wanted to do! They learned, they lived, they moved ahead! And there came again that old sense of rushing time which had haunted him since adolescence. He was already twenty-eight! He smashed a fist into his palm and sprang up.

His mother looked at him. "Where're you going?"

"I don't know. Just out."

"Oh, I forgot to tell you. Jessie Meig telephoned. Not very clever for a girl to telephone a young man, if you ask me. For the life of me I can't understand what you can see in her."

"I've told you, Ma. She's a friend. There are so many things she understands about me!" He went on vehemently, "Because she has a few misshapen bones, is she any less a woman? Is she to be put away as damaged goods because of that?"

His mother was silent.

"What did she want?"

"Just to know why you'd been staying away and whether you might want to come over this evening."

Twenty minutes later Martin stood in the Meigs' library. It went very quickly. His mind had simply made itself up. The father grasped Martin's hands in both of his. "It's probably the wisest decision you'll ever make."

Jessie was surprisingly calm. "Are you sure?"

"I'm sure."

"Because I don't want to be an albatross around your neck."

"You will never be that, I promise!"

She had a pretty mouth and when she smiled, two charming dimples appeared at the corners. Taking her face between his hands, he kissed her gently. "I'll make life good for you," he said. He meant it, with all his heart.

The Web

CHAPTER FOUR

FERN always teased Alex that she had married him because she loved his house. "Well, naturally," he would answer, "how could anyone help but fall in love with Lamb House?"

Among its oaks and orchards it lay as though, like them, it had been planted there, so farsighted had they been, those Elizabethans with a sense of home and long generations. Through diamond-paned casements one looked south toward the village of Great Barrow. On the slope above the valley, pear trees flowered and the hills rolled back into a haze.

Fern stood on the lawn and raised her eyes to the living picture beyond her easel. In the upper left-hand corner lay a green square dotted with tiny spots of white. They were sheep on the Ballister farm. Everything was small and perfect.

"Now that I know you well, I'll confess," Alex's mother had told her a few weeks before. "I wasn't very happy about having an American daughter-in-law. So many American girls are simply not ladies. But you are, and so very charming, Fern!"

They had been in the upstairs hall, which was blazoned with family portraits: squires in breeches, clerics in black, and over one fireplace the original Elizabethan to whom this manor had been given for favors to the Crown. They were all Lambs.

"I had this photo of Susannah put here in the hall while you and Alex were on your wedding trip. It used to be in the drawing room, but I think that not fitting now."

Fern had murmured that she wouldn't have minded, which was true. She felt no jealousy. The girl was dead, after all. Here she sat in her patrician simplicity, with hands on lap and a pearl rope looped around her finger. Her one memorable feature was a timid expression in the prominent eyes. Did she have some foreboding that she was going to die and leave her newborn boy?

"It's a good thing Neddie has no idea about his mother," Alex's mother said.

"He'll have to be told I'm not his mother."

"Why, yes, sometime. But he does love you, Fern."

"And I adore him." She knew it was said she was marvelous with Neddie, making no difference between him and her own infant girl. They didn't understand. Neddie *was* her own.

"He's not been jealous of the new baby at all! Usually they carry on dreadfully, or so I hear. Unfortunately, I had only one child. You're sure you're not rushing things?" This last had been spoken with a glance toward Fern's midsection, where the new swelling was just visible. "After all, Emmy's not a year yet."

"The doctor says I'm quite healthy. If this one's a boy, we shall name him Alex, of course."

"He will be the sixth Alexander Lamb. Of course, it's Neddie who should have borne the name. I think it's disgraceful that Susannah insisted on naming him for her father."

"Well, anyway, he looks like Alex," Fern had assured her, although it was not true. Neddie would be narrower and darker than Alex. But it was what the older woman wanted to hear.

Pregnancy, like love, she thought, can be calming. The doctor said some women became euphoric. This contentment with her own body and the people who surrounded her must be euphoria. Taking up the brush, she corrected some greens.

A little group came around the corner of the house: Neddie, running ahead of the nanny who was pushing Emmy in the perambulator. Fern held out her arms and the little boy ran into them. She put her face down on his hair, which smelled of pine shampoo.

He wiggled free. "Shall we have music again, Mummy?"

"Later, darling. We'll put a record on."

"The singing man?"

She laughed. "Yes, yes, the singing man."

A few weeks ago Neddie had come into the room when Alex had a Caruso recording on the phonograph. Without making a sound, the little boy had sat down to listen, and then had waited while Alex wound the phonograph again to repeat it.

"And can I have yellow cake, too?"

"If you promise to eat your supper," Nanny said.

The baby, Emmy, was asleep. She was blond, and would be large-boned, as if she belonged entirely to Alex. Fern touched the pink hand that lay curled on the blanket. I don't know her yet, she thought. Everything is closed up, a gift in a glossy box.

"If you don't mind my saying so, ma'am, you ought to put up your work," Nanny said. "You've been at it since noon. And it's fearful hot today."

Funny what the English called fearful heat! It couldn't be more than eighty. Still, she obeyed, as Nanny drew the wicker lounge chair into the shade.

"There you are! A nice nap will do you good. I'm to take Neddie down to his pony and he'll go for a ride with Mr. Lamb."

Fern closed her eyes. She was so catered to, so loved! How many women with two children had leisure to go all deliciously relaxed and limp?

Old Carfax, stirring in the perennial border, struck a stone with his hoe. Fern opened her eyes and watched him move on through the rose beds. Behind them stood a solid wall of yews.

315

"The yews are as old as the house," Alex had told her the first time he had brought her here. They had been sitting on the stone bench, the one where Carfax had just now set a flat of asters. They'd sat there talking for an hour, then quite suddenly Alex had asked her to marry him and as suddenly she had accepted.

Yet they had been leading up to that moment from the time they had been introduced in the winter. Aunt Milly had pursued her purpose with utmost tact. Ordinarily Fern would have been outraged by any such scheme, but because she herself was so strongly drawn to Alex, she hadn't objected.

He was delightful. It was, quite simply, good to be with him. There was a kind of crinkling good nature in his face even when he was being earnest, and she had told him so. He had a fine curiosity about everything. At dinner he could listen to Uncle Drew's talk of securities and German reparations. With a cricketer he talked scores. One felt he could manage anything.

And he also had a certain reserve; Fern was comfortable with that. Traveling through Europe, she had had to fend off too many young men on hotel terraces. But Alex had been satisfied to go slowly, sensing her wish to feel the way, to move as a river flows, deepening to the place where all the streams gather in a final rush, which would be the more marvelous for having come gradually.

So she had read, and so she believed.

All during the late winter and early spring she and Alex saw London together. They dined at Claridge's, they walked in the parks and on streets which Fern had visited with Thackeray and Galsworthy. She fell in love with the grand old mellow city.

In a mews near Curzon Street Alex had a flat, furnished with discerning taste. She told him he ought to be in some business having to do with the arts: antiques or a picture gallery. He had been pleased, but content to continue running his substantial maritime insurance business.

"Insurance is more lucrative," he explained. "I can always buy art. Someday I'll be buying a Meig."

They had been having dinner at the flat, so he was a host being courteous and that was all. Yet she remembered everything

316

that had been said. She had sighed. "I'm so confused. I wish I knew whether I had potential."

"It's a shame you haven't had more encouragement."

"More? I've had none at all."

Except for Martin Farrell's. And she thought of the letter which had arrived from Martin that morning.

It had been written in a state of joyous excitement. A door had been flung open, and she was very, very glad for him.

But there had also been a faint sense of shame. She had thought, all that hot, lovely summer in Cyprus and especially on the last night, that something was growing, that perhaps when she came home ... She had obviously been mistaken. Three years of further study! Very likely he wouldn't marry until long after that.

"London suits you," Alex had remarked abruptly.

"I'm also a country person," she reminded him.

"What you need," he'd said, "is to have a home in a quiet country place where you can paint, yet be near enough to the city for classes." And he had reached across the table for her hand.

Not long afterward they had driven to his village. It had a cobbled High Street, a chemist's and tobacconist's, and an ancient church. "There's where the Lambs are christened, married and buried," Alex explained. "And that's the lych-gate. We trim it with white flowers for brides."

They had rounded the corner of the lane and come upon the house, drowsing in hazy, filtered light. There it lay, sturdy and secure. It seemed like a place Fern had always known. And suddenly it seemed there could be no deeper joy than to stay here with this gentle, loving man, in this golden peace.

Promptly then, cablegrams went out to Father and Jessie. Letters went back and forth across the ocean. Lists were written and arrangements made. Aunt Milly rejoiced.

The wedding was at Lamb House. Neddie wore a powder-blue velvet suit and had his picture taken with the bride and groom. Everyone in the village had been invited. There was champagne, and dancing under the enormous chandeliers. The dining hall was illuminated by silver candelabra, and the vermeil dinner service glittered between bowls of Carfax's prize roses.

317

"Positively medieval," Jessie remarked. "I didn't think they still did this sort of thing."

The honeymoon was a voyage to India. Unfortunately Alex had been seasick most of the time. Fern felt sorry for him, not only on account of his physical misery but because she saw that he was humiliated.

Then at the end of the sixth week she, too, became a victim of nausea, but for a different reason: she was pregnant. It must have happened almost immediately, on the night they spent ashore at Gibraltar. That, and the few other nights they had slept on land, had been the only normal ones on the trip. So it had been rather a strange honeymoon. Poor Alex!

Now, with Emmy not yet old enough to walk, she was pregnant again, and because of her latest spells of nausea she had to disappoint him on many nights. But he was considerate and patient.

He was considerate in other ways as well. True to his promise, he had arranged for her to attend the best art classes in the city, particularly an outstanding class in oils. For the first time she felt she was learning.

"Well, how are you doing?" Alex came around the house and laid a hand on her shoulder.

"Stomach's queasy. How was the ride?"

"Marvelous. After this baby we'll go every morning. We'll take Neddie, too. You should have seen him on his pony."

"He wasn't scared? He's only four, Alex!"

"That's the time to start. And he loves it."

A bicycle bell tinkled up the drive. In a moment Mrs. MacHugh from the village would appear, bringing the afternoon mail.

"I'll get it," Alex said.

It was past time for a letter from home. Fern stood up and followed Alex to the front of the house. "Letter from America!" he said. "Two of them! Looks like one from your father and one from Jessie."

She sat down on the step to read. The note from Jessie filled just one page.

"I shall be in England a week after you receive this." In England? But how? "Read Father's letter. He will explain it all."

318

Prick of pin, quiver of apprehension as she opened her father's letter and read it quickly through.

"Oh, no!" she cried.

"What is it?" Alex asked.

She gave him the letter, then leaned back against the doorpost, fighting a sudden heaving of nausea.

"Well," he said, "this is news, isn't it?"

"I think it's— I think it's disgusting!"

"Why? I suppose one wouldn't exactly *expect* Jessie to marry, but it's not that strange. Do you know the man?"

"Yes, he's a doctor. A country doctor."

"Well, if he and Jessie love one another, I don't see why you call that disgusting."

"She may be in love with *him*. I've no doubt she is. But as for him, well, could you be in love with Jessie?"

"I'm not, so I can't answer for myself. That doesn't mean some other man couldn't be."

"Did you read the whole thing? They're taking a flat in London. He'll be working here for the next three years."

"So then he won't be a country doctor after all, will he? They'll have a whole other life."

"Yes, a whole other life."

Alex got up and drew Fern to her feet. "Let's go in," he said. "I need to bath and change. Then I want tea."

MARTIN Farrell stepped outside into a fragrant morning. Here in England June still had the feel of spring. It was a long walk to St. Bartholomew's, but he enjoyed starting his day at the hospital with the vigor and well-being that came after exercise.

It had been, beyond expectation, a good year. He smiled, still warmed by the hour he had spent since he had gotten up in the pleasant flat. Jessie and he had breakfasted at the bow window that overlooked the square of chestnut trees and sycamores. His last sight before leaving was of her puttering in the little room which had been readied for the baby, who was due any time, perhaps even today!

He hadn't really planned to have a child this soon. But apparently Jessie had. She would be an excellent mother, he reflected, with all that energy. Well organized, too; everything was planned out beforehand so that the actual doing seemed always to be easy. He marveled at this ability of Jessie's to manage things in her capable, cheerful way.

Suddenly he recalled the day they had moved into the flat; it was a furnished sublet, drably decorated. But what wonders Jessie had done with those rooms! She'd filled them with flowers, inexpensive daisies in bright blue bowls. She'd hung travel posters on the walls, delightful scenes of golden places: the fountains of Vaucluse and Venice and Segovia. She'd become a devotee of the flea markets; one day she'd come home lugging a tarnished, wretched old pot that turned out to be a splendid silver teakettle. She'd been so pleased with herself! She knew how to enjoy the hours, Jessie did, and knew how to stretch her mind.

Yes, it had been a remarkable year. Not that he hadn't had some trepidation before coming to England. Once having passed the shock and splendor of the opportunity to work with Braidburn, he had realized that he would see Mary again; the thought had plagued him all the way across the Atlantic Ocean.

When they arrived, he and Jessie had been driven straight to Lamb House. It was one of those gray-green English afternoons, halfway between rain and heavy mist. Mary had been standing in the doorway when they drove up, the boy, Neddie, on one side of her and a tiny girl on the other. And he had wondered whether she was aware of the picture she made, blooming with her two children and her pregnancy.

He remembered that day so well. They had gone walking about the grounds. Jessie had described Lamb House to him, but no description could have done it justice. Intending nothing by the remark, he had said, "This is a long way from Cyprus, isn't it?"

And with anger, Mary had repeated, "Yes, isn't it?"

Surely she couldn't have been jealous of Jessie? After all, she hadn't wanted him for herself! So he thought she must be resentful over the marriage because she thought him a fortune hunter. This idea had stung him, for, after all, he intended to repay Jessie's father for everything.

320

Despite the initial strains, the relationship between the two couples became cordial, although not close. Now and then they met in town for dinner or theater. But the Lambs' world was different. They ran an expensive establishment; Alex had countless business obligations. Their lives were complicated. The Farrells' life was simple. And they were satisfied with its simplicity.

Martin quickened his walk. He was due in the operating room at eight. This was Mr. Braidburn's day. "Mr."—funny English mode of address to a doctor! And now Martin's mind turned away from his own concerns to the hospital.

BRAIDBURN talked as he worked, his steady voice instructing and explaining. This was the third hour and he was tiring. "Look here. The size of an orange."

Martin blotted seeping blood with gauze. He remembered his fear a year ago when a brain was first exposed beneath his hands, when he was first permitted, under supervision, to take the knife.

"Sponge," Braidburn ordered.

The patient was young. Martin had seen him at the clinic, waiting with his wife and children. He had a clerk's face, respectful and scared. Relating his symptoms, his mouth had twisted.

"I can't seem to stand up straight. I feel like vomiting. The headache's splitting and my eyesight's queer."

Through the ophthalmoscope Martin had observed the hemorrhaging retina and the enlarged head of the optic nerve.

"See anything, Doctor?"

"Well," he'd answered evasively, "we'll need to take X rays. Then we'll see about straightening you out."

He had known then what the pictures would show: a tumor in the left lobe. But now, as the growth lay before him, a little thrill went through him as he saw that it was benign and encapsulated.

"The rest is up to the gods," Braidburn said. "We've done all we can. Close the flap, Farrell, please."

A little while later Martin was about to leave for lunch when the telephone rang. He spoke a moment and hung up.

"My wife's at the hospital in labor," he told one of the doctors, and raced outside to the taxi stand.

At the hospital they told him Jessie was already in the delivery room. "Make yourself comfortable. We'll call you as soon as we know anything."

The waiting room was vacant except for a woman reading a book. When Martin entered, she put it down and he saw that the woman was Mary Fern. She smiled.

"You were operating, so Jessie called me when the pains came very suddenly. I've been with her until just now."

"Thanks very much. Is she all right?"

"Very excited. Very happy, between pains."

Martin sat down, took a magazine, and couldn't read it.

"You're reading the same words ten times over and you don't know what they mean," Mary observed.

"I know."

"She'll be all right. She really will."

"Thanks again."

"I'm glad I happened to be in our flat here in town."

It occurred to Martin that he hadn't been alone in a room with Mary since—since Cyprus, and seldom enough even then. She turned a page and he heard the faint jingle of an ornament on her gold bracelet. For some reason the sound was irritating. He wished she would go. Almost as if she'd caught his thought, she looked at her watch and stood up. "I'm supposed to meet Alex's mother and bring her home for dinner. Will you think it awful of me if I leave you?"

"No, no, go ahead. And give my best to Alex."

"Please call me the minute you hear."

He stood at the window and watched her go down the street. She still had that slight sway in her walk. Her skirt swung gracefully. And he saw a man turn to look after her as she passed; struck, maybe, by the blue eyes in the dark face.

But what should all that matter to him? He felt abruptly angry. His life was filled. He had his work, his home and now a child. And the child would be normal! By the law of averages it would!

Think of bright things, good things, of the years to come. I'll come back to Europe one day, he promised himself. I must see Epidaurus and the temple of Asclepius. I'll bring my son with me! Yes, my son! I'll show him things I never saw. He'll be tall and easy, not tall and rigid like me. I can hear his voice, its first deepening when he starts to become a man. My son and I.

A doctor was walking toward him. "Mr. Farrell?"

Martin stood up.

"A healthy child, and your wife is all right, too. Just coming out of anesthesia. You may see her now."

They entered the elevator. "We had to do a cesarean section," the other man said. "There wasn't enough room. The spine, of course." Martin followed him down the corridor. "I would not recommend having any more, Mr. Farrell."

"I understand. Certainly not."

He went in to Jessie. Her face was white, but her eyes were triumphant. He stooped and kissed her forehead, and stroked her damp, curly hair. Murmuring, she closed her eyes.

"She'll sleep now," the nurse said. "Would you like to see the baby?"

At the nursery door he was shown a bundle wrapped in a pink blanket, and he felt a draining disappointment.

"A lovely girl," the nurse said.

He stared at the baby. He knew he was supposed to respond with the usual awkward pride of the new father, but there was only a sinking in his chest. His son! And this was the last chance.

The baby opened her eyes. She seemed to be staring straight back at Martin. For a few moments they regarded one another. Then she yawned, the pink mouth making a perfect O, raised her hand and dropped it in exquisite relaxation.

Martin put his finger into that miniature palm. At once the fingers curled around his thick one. How strong she was! Already reaching out to life and grasping! He felt a lump in his throat. She was perfect, without a flaw. A rush of gratitude went through him; he felt the warning tingle of rising tears. At the same time he wanted to laugh. Perfect! His girl.

"What will you name her?" the nurse asked.

He had to think a moment of the name they had selected for a girl. "Claire," he said finally. "Her name is Claire."

That night he sat down and wrote a letter.

Darling Claire,

On this the day of your birth I want to tell you how I feel before any of my thoughts can slip away. We don't know each other yet, but already you are part of me, like my hand or my eyes. I wouldn't have believed it possible. I love you so.

SOMETIMES Fern thought of the bed as a kind of throne, raised as it was on a shallow platform. Everyone came to her here, where she leaned against fresh white linen pillows under a canopy upheld by mahogany posts. Neddie and Emmy climbed up to be read to; the new baby, Isabel, was placed here in her arms to be fed.

Waking early, she would open her eyes in the familiar haven of the lovely room. She would lie quite still, feeling that fine brightness of the spirit which is called well-being.

But all this was of the past. For months now she had lain alone in the bed. Alex slept on a narrow cot in the dressing room next door. He had begun to sleep there during the winter, when he'd had the flu. Then, in order not to wake Fern after late meetings in town, he had kept on using the cot.

She found it impossible to talk about. That was puzzling, because Alex and she had once talked about everything. Now she ought to be able to say, "What's wrong?" Yet she could not. Instead, humiliation knotted in her chest; she felt a prickling sense of shame.

There was another woman; there had to be. Who, then? Perhaps that Irish girl, Delia somebody, who won the jumping trophy at the horse show? She couldn't be more than eighteen. She had an absurd way of stretching her eyes, slanting them up at a man. Alex had danced with her five times at the Elliots'.

Her mind sped. He'd gone riding with Delia last Thursday. They were out two hours, at least.

"We went all the way to Blackdale. It was marvelous!" Delia cried. Her hair falls like black silk. . . . It's not possible. Things like this happen to other people.

One Sunday afternoon, in dark and threatening autumn weather, Alex stood up suddenly and stretched. "I've a yen for exercise. I think I'll take a canter up to Blackdale. Not far."

"Not far! An hour and a half there and back. And it's going to rain." She knew she sounded critical and cross.

"I'll be home before the rain comes, I think."

He had been gone half an hour when her decision was made. What sort of fool did he take her for? A canter in this weather?

She pulled on a mackintosh and rain hat, for the rain had begun. She would be waiting for them at the stable. She would smile, and then see what Alex would have to say.

She walked swiftly to the stable yard. No one was about. From the little office next to the tack room where Kevin, the head groom, had a desk, came an oil lamp's glow. It wouldn't do any harm to wait inside with Kevin. She would still be able to hear them trotting up the path. Let Kevin think what he might.

The window was next to the door, so that, standing with one hand on the knob, one's eyes were drawn into the room. Something caught Fern's attention before her hand had turned the knob.

A cot, covered with a plaid blanket, stood opposite the desk, along the far wall. Someone was lying on it. She leaned forward. Blinked. Frowning, she flattened her nose on the wet glass. It was like looking into an aquarium. The shape on the cot—no, there were two shapes . . . For several minutes she stood there, failing to understand. She saw, yet did not grasp the meaning of what she saw.

Then a face came into view. It moved into the path of the lamplight. It was a face and a bright head that she knew. Alex spoke. Then Kevin sat up. And she understood.

She gave a harsh cry and clapped her palm to her mouth and fled. She heard Alex crying, in a voice of terrible alarm, "Who's there? Who's there?" And she ran. Crouched and stumbling, she ran. A bramble ripped her leg. She fell.

"Oh, my God!" she gasped. She got up and ran to the house. She banged the door open and raced to her room. She threw the mackintosh and hat on the floor and sank down on the bed. It was unreal! Untrue! She could not possibly have seen it!

Downstairs, a door opened and closed. Footsteps sounded: Alex's familiar tread. He came in and stood beside the bed.

"So it was you," he said softly.

Fern's dry, scared eyes stared up at him. He looked the same. The strong shoulders, the humorous tilt to the eyes, were the same.

He shook his head. "Well, now you know. I'm sorry. Oh, God, I'm sorry."

New terror passed over her. She was alone. Alex was not Alex anymore. Then who was there? "I thought it was Delia," she whispered. How much better if it had been Delia!

"You thought it was Delia? That fool?" He laughed.

There was no mirth in the laugh; it was only bitter, nervous, agitated. But the sound of it was too much for Fern. Everything that had been held back for months burst open in one long, wild, frenzied scream.

"Stop it! Stop it, Fern, stop it!" Alex cried.

She wasn't able to. Her mind was working clearly; she understood that this was hysteria. What she had read of it was true. You slid down and down, hearing from some far distance your own appalling screams. Over the edge you went, over the edge.

"Quiet! Quiet! Fern, people can hear you." A decanter and small green glass for his nightcap stood on a tray. He filled the glass. "Take some," he commanded.

She twisted away. "Don't put your hands on me!"

"All right. But please talk to me, Fern. Let's talk together."

She thought, I can't stay here. For one mad instant she saw herself walking out, leaving everything behind—the children, her pictures, and most of all this loathsome man.

Alex was speaking softly. "At least, though, you must see that Kevin's no threat to the marriage, as Delia would have been."

"The marriage? What marriage? If I could walk out tonight, if there were a train leaving, I'd go. I'd go this minute."

"You're forgetting your children."

"They'll go with me wherever I go."

Alex shook his head. "No," he said. In the straight-backed chair beside the bed he sat erect, with a look of determination.

"What do you mean? Do you think you're a fit father to rear a family? Why, any court would—"

Alex held up his hand. "Wait. Even if you were able to prove it—you couldn't, but for the sake of argument, let's say you

could—then, of course, I would lose my business. How do you think we should all live then? If you have any idea that inherited wealth supports us, you're terribly mistaken. You know what's happened to investments here since the crash in America. I *need* to work, Fern."

"Then I'll simply take the children and go, that's all."

He raised his eyebrows. "Where? Your father's been almost wiped out in the market. He'd hardly welcome a returning daughter and a brood of children, would he?"

She wiped her eyes roughly. "Alex, tell me, if you can, why? Why did you marry me?"

"I thought it would work. I wanted it to! From that first time at your aunt's— Fern, you were the loveliest thing I'd ever looked at. Everything about you, your voice, all the life . . ." His face twisted as if he were going to weep. "My heart aches for you; I wish I could love you as you ought to be loved."

"In the name of decency, then, give me a divorce." He shook his head. "Alex, please, why not?"

He wept. "Because I would never see my children again."

"I would let you see them. I swear I would."

"I want to live with them."

"You have no right! You've forfeited the right."

Alex brought himself under control. "I'm a good father. You know I am. This other thing—this has nothing to do with it."

"You disgust me," she said. "I want a divorce."

"No, Fern. Freedom, yes. But the household stays as it is. When you're more calm in the morning, I'll explain to you—"

A shudder rippled down Fern's back. "I don't want explanations," she cried. "Just leave, Alex! Get out where I don't have to look at you!"

When she was alone, Fern got off the bed and walked into the bathroom. And on the icy tiles she knelt down, something she had not done since adolescence. "God help me, please," she murmured. "Help me, please." But nothing moved inside.

Then she realized that Alex had come into the room and was standing there watching her. She struggled to her feet.

"You find this theatrical, I suppose?"

"No, I've done it myself on occasion."

"And did it help?"

"No."

She picked up the bathroom glass and threw it at him. Falling short, it smashed on the floor. "Get out!" she cried. "Get out of my sight!"

When he had gone, Fern got down again on her knees in the splintered glass and cried and longed to be dead. There had to be someone she could talk to. But who?

And she knew even as she put the question that the answer was Martin Farrell.

A COAL fire burned in the grate. The walls were covered with books bound in leather. Martin had explained that the office belonged to Mr. Braidburn, but he sometimes saw patients here.

Fern kept looking around the room, aware that Martin also was considerately looking elsewhere. She had told him about Alex and now he was giving her time to calm herself. She was conscious of every sound, every creak of a chair.

She said abruptly, "People don't know anything about each other when they marry. It's absurd."

"Yet you must have loved him."

"I didn't know anything about him, as you see."

"The part you knew, you loved. You wouldn't have married him otherwise. Would you have?"

She passed her hand wearily across her forehead. "I don't know. Feelings rush over us. It's just—tricks."

"You shouldn't be bitter. Shouldn't deny the feelings you had. That is, if they were true ones."

She saw that he was looking at her closely for the first time since she had come into the room. "Were they?" he asked.

"Yes, I suppose so. Oh, I don't know." These last weeks she had grown thinner, and her rings were loose. She twisted them. "If you had asked me before all this, I would have said, 'Yes, I loved him.' Now I don't understand anything. I don't know where I'm going. I have no patience with the children, can't work, can't paint, can't bear to look at Alex."

"But the goodness that was in Alex—isn't it there still?"

"I don't know."

"You do know. He's not *wicked*, Mary! And let me tell you, he suffers. It's obvious he can neither change himself nor accept himself. Can't you see how hard this is for him?"

"I haven't thought about it."

"Well, think about it. Maybe you'll come to understand."

"When I found out about Alex," she said slowly, "it was as if a trapdoor had opened up and I'd been dropped. Violently. I'd been living all my life in a cocoon. Tell me. What am I to do?"

"No, you tell me. What is the most important thing you have to do from now on?"

For an instant she wasn't sure of his meaning. Then it came to her. "To take care of my children. Is that what you mean?"

"Of course."

She smiled warily. "That isn't all one gets married for."

"People marry for many reasons. Because they're lonely, or need a companionable mind. Many reasons."

Neither spoke for a moment. Then Martin said, "Work. Work is always the salvation, Mary. You have a gift. Use it."

"No," she said. "I've no gift. Father was right. It's only a very little talent that I have."

"You can't be sure yet. Give it time."

"Time! I'll have plenty of that."

He added thoughtfully, "A very good thing is your home. There's great comfort to be had from 'place.' It's not like that for me, but for some people it's—as they say—the essence. It's true for you, isn't it? And Lamb House is the place?"

"Yes," she said. "I walk around sometimes just *touching* things. There are certain trees, an old sycamore where I sit and feel the world breathe. One can feel such peace among trees." Suddenly she was very, very tired. They had said everything there was to be said. She rose to leave.

Martin stood up, too, but did not offer to shake her hand. It crossed her mind that he really disliked her, after all.

"Mary," he said, "I wanted to help you. Perhaps I haven't succeeded, but I did try."

"It's helped me to talk to you. Yes, it has."

"I'm glad." He might have been expected to say, Come back anytime, but he did not, and so she thanked him with a correctness to match his own, and went out.

THE rattling suburban train swayed around the last curve before her station. Martin had been right; there was comfort in "place." The High Street gave cheerful assurance. The butcher came out on the step to remark, as always, upon the weather. The seed store had hung out its little packets of nasturtiums, delightful scraps of orange and yellow.

As she reached the house, Neddie came around a corner. "Guess what?" he cried. "We had ice cream at Rob's. Chocolate!" He pranced, jiggling the pompom on his woolen cap.

Oh, my heart, my darling! How could I ever leave you? "Chocolate!" she repeated brightly before, remembering some other errand, he sped away.

The house enfolded her. She went slowly up the stairs, sliding her hand on the smooth old banister. Alex, coming upstairs a moment later, knocked on the open door. "May I?"

"Yes, come in."

They faced each other. Then, astoundingly, he said, "You've seen Martin."

"What? What makes you say that?"

"You know I sense things. You told him, didn't you?"

"Yes. Are you angry?"

"No. What did he say?"

"I don't know exactly." She stammered. "I suppose—he tried to explain, to help me understand."

"I'm very grateful to him. I've known for a long time that he's in love with you. He's the man you should have married."

"Don't be absurd!"

"Haven't you seen how he always manages to leave a room the minute you enter it?"

"No, I haven't," Fern said tightly. She turned away. A small pain flashed through her temples. She touched them lightly. He oughtn't to have said that about Martin! There were enough ter-

331

rible things for her to think about already without adding more.

"Are you all right?" Alex said.

She sat down on the bed. "It's been a hard day."

Alex knelt on the floor and took her hand. "Fern, I'll be the best friend you could have." He rested his cheek on her hand, and she could feel his tears. "I've been through hell," he said.

"I believe you."

"Hell for you, too. I don't ever want you to think that what I am has anything to do with you. It's just me. It didn't work with Susannah. But then, she was a sharp-tongued shrew, and I thought it might have been partly her fault. I hoped it would be different with you. And I tried, Fern, you know I did."

In these few minutes night had come, and an iridescent afterglow poured through the window. It fell upon the man's bowed head. He looked up. "Fern, everything I have belongs to you and the children. I don't mean just things, I mean caring. My devotion. I can't help what I am. But I'll never ask what you do with private portions of your life. So we could live here, couldn't we, with our children, and be happy in other ways?"

Fern had not wanted to be so moved. She had wanted to keep the hard anger. But at last pity came, and she bent down to rest his head against her shoulder, rocking and swaying as if he were a child and she his mother. Or as if he and she, survivors of some awful cataclysm, must cling together out of need and then, because of common humanity and trust, must stay.

Passages

CHAPTER FIVE

No SELF-RESPECTING institution at home would have put up with so ancient a building, Martin reflected, as he prepared to leave the hospital for the afternoon. These steps on which he stood had been laid down in the eighteenth century, while the wings of the central structure were Victorian.

"Making your plans for the day?" One of his colleagues, Mr. Meredith, tucked his umbrella under one arm.

"Great plans. I'm going to the park with Claire."

"Taking a bus?"

"Later. I want to walk a little before I catch it."

"Fine. I'll go partway with you."

As they fell into step, Martin said, "I can't believe I've been here three years."

"Does it seem longer to you or shorter?"

"That depends on mood. Longer or shorter, it's been wonderful. It's opened worlds for me."

"I must say you've taken good advantage of it. Your cytology paper is impressive, Mr. Braidburn tells me. You're going to the conference in Paris next week, of course?"

"I wouldn't miss it. Dr. Eastman's coming over from New York and I'll have a chance to see him again."

"Have I congratulated you on your association with him? Great fortune for you."

"I'm indebted to Mr. Braidburn forever. When Eastman wrote that he was looking for a new man to join his practice, Mr. Braidburn could have recommended half a dozen others."

"You must come for a weekend in the country with us before you leave. Well, I turn off here. Enjoy your afternoon."

Glancing after him, Martin thought, Funny, in the beginning the formal manners, the bowler hats, put me off. He smiled, recalling some of those first impressions.

They had taught him much, those men: Meredith, Braidburn and the rest. All those dark winter afternoons in the pathology lab. Those early mornings watching Braidburn in the OR. And the lunchtime discussions on clinical neurology; the diagrams drawn on the backs of menus; the questions; the arguments! Yes, he would take good memories back with him.

From the top of the double-deck bus, he enjoyed the city. This was the first real warmth of the season, and people were already stretched out wherever there was a plot of grass. At Kensington High Street he got off the bus and began to hurry home.

Claire was waiting for him. They started for the park, she riding ahead on her tricycle. Her dark curls just touched the velvet collar of her yellow coat. He couldn't take his eyes from her. And he wondered whether she would ever know what she meant to him. There was such a softness in him! That nothing, nothing, should ever happen to this child!

Once in the park, Martin led the way to the statue of Peter Pan. (He had read the story to Claire; Jessie said it was too advanced for her, yet he was sure she had understood it.) And, finding a bench, he settled down to watch Claire ride.

He breathed deeply. A tart fragrance blew from behind him. Primeval, burgeoning spring! New life, bursting, reaching, wanting. Wanting so! Until it—it hurt! And suddenly the old, familiar melancholy seeped into Martin. The shade was drawn down on the day which had been so charming till a moment ago. And he remembered that this melancholy had been lying upon him for many months.

There had been such cheer when Claire was born! So much joy! What had happened to them? And when? But it was impossible to say, "There, that's the moment we began to be unhappy."

There had been scenes. He hated them. And Jessie was always miserable afterward. Yet they happened, again and again.

A few weeks before, they had gone to see *Giselle*. A new ballerina had been dancing. A dream of a girl. Her dark red hair, caught in a ponytail, fell to her shoulders. She rose *en pointe,* her arms reaching in a perfect curve, her mauve skirt drifting. And all the while Jessie had been watching, not the dance, but him.

Coming into the bedroom that night, he had caught her standing naked in front of the mirror. She had turned on him furiously. "Why don't you knock? Did you come in here to stare at me?"

"I wasn't staring at you! But, for heaven's sake, I'll look away if you want me to."

"Yes, do! It's a lot more pleasant for you to look at ballerinas, waitresses—almost anyone but me."

"Jessie, can't you try not to think about yourself? Other people don't pay that much attention to your—"

"To my what?"

"Your—disability."

"You can't say it, can you? Well, I can! Hump. H-U-M-P. Go on. Say it!"

334

He sat down wearily, covering his eyes with his hands, and let her exhaust her anger. In the end, when she had said everything she could say, she had apologized, in shame.

"Oh, you are patient with me, Martin. It's just that when we're out together, I feel the thoughts in the air, the messages passed from one to the other. And I know what they'll say after we're gone, how the women will talk the next morning."

For a week or two after that they had gone nowhere, except on Sunday to a country inn, where they had sat on a high-backed settle and watched the locals play shove-halfpenny. For those few hours it had been as it was when they rode around Cyprus on house calls, talking about medicine and everything else under the sun. He understood now that these things had interested Jessie because she could hide behind them: they were not about *her*. But she couldn't hide in anonymous places forever.

He looked for Claire. She was pedaling down the walk, her short legs working like pistons. He looked at his watch, last year's Christmas gift from Jessie. She was always buying things for him. Next year at Christmas they would be in New York and he would be earning money. He would buy a splendid present for her. A ring? She had slender fingers.

His memory made one of its senseless associations. Mary wore rings. She still wore that curiously fashioned topaz ring. Only a few weeks ago, coming home earlier than usual, he found that she had dropped in for tea. Every nerve in him had been aware of her. And he had seen that she still wore the topaz ring. Her eyes avoided him, and he concluded that she was embarrassed. He had seen her perhaps six times since that day, more than a year ago, when she had sat before him and told the story of wreckage.

There had been no way to find out how she was faring. From the outside everything looked handsome enough. But he wondered about many things: whether Alex had any idea how much Martin knew; whether Mary had someone else by now.

Claire climbed up on the bench. "Read to me," she commanded.

He opened a little book which he had thrust into his pocket before leaving home, and she explained earnestly, "It's about dinosaurs. This one is Allosaurus. He eats vegetables."

335

"Shall I read about him, or about this one?"

"This one. He's Tyrannosaurus rex. He eats people."

"Oh, he's fierce all right," Martin agreed. "We'll read about him."

By the time he had finished, the sky was clouding over toward a sudden shower. Holding Claire's hand, he guided the tricycle across the street.

He had had the best years of his life here in London. "Why don't you stay?" people often asked. For it was a civilized place. New York, on the other hand, was aggressive. One was battered by the noise of traffic and hammering rivets. A restless, unsettling place!

Yet he had felt its lure and power from the very first, and it was time to go back. But the true reason? The answer struck Martin like a slap across the cheek. Because it will put an ocean between *her* and me.

"IT's *Otello* tonight, isn't it?" he called from the bathroom. Jessie didn't answer. When he came into the bedroom, she was sitting at the window, looking out.

"Why, you're not dressing!"

"I'm not going to the opera," she said. "I've nothing to wear and I refuse to go out anymore in makeshift clothes."

"You always look fine," Martin said.

"I'm tired of having you ashamed of me."

"I have never been ashamed of you, Jessie!" He was so weary of having to cope with this again!

"You know, Martin, you don't fool me. You never say, 'I love you.' Do you realize that?"

"I'm not much for words. Maybe that's a fault. But how do I treat you? You should ask yourself that."

"You've been exemplary. You made a bargain and you've stuck with it. You couldn't get my sister, so you took me."

"Jessie, you're making trouble where there is none."

"Don't fence with me. Father warned me not to marry you. He knew it was Fern you wanted and he was right."

"He warned you?" Martin was totally confused.

Jessie began to cry. "Yes, yes. He only wanted this for me after I convinced him. After all, you were a solution for me."

He was stunned. Anger surged in him and quickly died. What difference did it make now who had conceived the marriage?

"I loved you, Martin. We were alike in a way. We were prisoners. Your prison was poverty and mine was my body. I knew you didn't love me, but still you liked me tremendously, and I believed we could manage with that." She looked up half timidly, half in defiance.

"Jessie," he said softly, "you're wrong. You think I don't love you, but I do." And that, in its way, was true. "We have so much— a home, a beautiful child. We can't allow this sort of thing to go on, for her sake, if for no other reason."

"I know." She stood up and laid her head on his shoulder. "I'm drifting. I'm floating with nothing to hold to."

He put his arms around her and held her gently. "You have me to hold to. You'll climb out of this slump, Jessie. I'll pull you out of it. Now let's hurry. How fast can you dress?"

"I don't want to go tonight, Martin. Truly. You can go without me. I won't mind."

"All right then. I'll go," he said. "Have a good sleep."

THE singers had taken their final bows, and the departing crowd was moving through the lobby when Alex Lamb touched Martin on the shoulder. "Hello there! Where's Jessie?"

"Didn't feel up to par tonight. She went to bed early."

"Come back to our flat for a spot of supper. It's my birthday and some friends are coming."

"Well, I really ought—"

"Come on. You can spare an hour or two for your brother-in-law. Jessie must be asleep by now, anyway."

The Lambs' table was bright with iris and narcissus, flowery porcelain, laughter and wine. The women were so lovely! Even the older ones had a pearl glow, not from the candlelight but from something within. A subtle warmth began to stir in Martin.

"Fern hasn't been able to shake the cough," he heard Alex say. "So I'm insisting she take a week on the Riviera to get over it."

"You're not going?"

"I can't. Too much on the fire at the office."

337

A woman said, "That's a splendid necklace, Fern!"

Everyone turned to look. The necklace, a filigree of gold and garnets, rested as in a velvet case on Fern's naked shoulders. "Her present for my birthday," Alex explained, with the smile of a fond husband.

Martin, observing that smile, felt a current of compassion. He was surely the only one of the guests who knew their truth. How capricious, how reckless was life! Once he had seen it as a steady journey, as something that one *controlled*. He had, of course, been very young when he had thought so.

For nothing he had willed had brought him to where he was now. And where was he? Quite simply, he was a man in love, a man obsessed with loving, driven by it. Never, in spite of all his self-denials, had he ceased to love this woman.

Someone was addressing him. "So you'll be leaving us, going back to America, I hear?"

"Yes, soon," he replied.

Someone remarked to Fern, "You'll miss your sister."

She made some acknowledgment. Glancing up, he caught her gaze. And a strange thing happened: she did not turn away. Her eyes fastened on Martin's and held there.

Talk bubbled around the table; still the eyes held to each other. Unmistakably her look said, If you want me, I shall not refuse. Wild, reckless joy surged in him.

The talk kept on swirling. He did not hear it. At last people pushed their chairs back and left the table. Someone put music on the record player and dancing began in the hall.

From the bay window in the drawing room a balcony projected, a little space affording room for no more than two or three to stand and look down on the square. Mary stood there, leaning against the railing. When he stepped behind her she did not move.

"Who stole my heart away? Who—" The little tune floated with a poignant sweetness from the room at their backs.

Their shoulders touched. Still neither of them moved. Someone inside turned a lamp on; the beam of its light fell over a blossoming azalea in a tub, turning the white buds rosy.

"My God," Martin said at last. "What are we going to do?"

"I don't know."

"We have to do something. Don't you know that?"

"Don't," she whispered. "I'm starting to cry."

He understood that tenderness would bring more tears. So he waited a minute or two and then spoke. "I'll be in Paris at a conference next week. I can leave after the second day. Will you—"

"Yes . . . yes."

"Darling," he said. "My darling Mary."

THEY had six days. Eastward through the Provençal spring they drove until they came to a white town, to a house with tall, blue-shuttered windows, where the air smelled of lemons.

"We're here," Mary said. "Menton."

"Do you remember enough French to ask for a good room?"

"We already have one."

"Then shall we go upstairs right away?"

"Do you want to?"

"You know I do."

In the evening they sat and talked. They went back to the beginning.

"Didn't you *know* I wanted you? Why did you marry Alex?"

"Oh," she said, "what had I seen or known? I had never been touched by anyone. Yes, you touched me. I thought when I came back from Europe, we'd see each other again. But your letter! You were so glad about Dr. Albeniz—"

"You remember the name!"

"I remember everything. I understood then that your work would always come first. I thought perhaps I had imagined the other—about me. And I felt ashamed. That same week I met Alex."

Martin was silent. Yes, she would have welcomed Alex then, with all his cheer and strength. "I understand," he said.

"Would you have asked me to wait three years, Martin?"

"I don't know. I've asked myself whether you would have waited for me, whether I would have given up the offer if you wouldn't. What a tangle it was—and is!"

"And I," Mary spoke quietly. "I wanted to get away from that dim house. Would I have waited three years more? I don't know."

She clasped her hands under her chin. "How easily one throws oneself away! I would do differently now."

But what's to become of us? he thought. We have begun something that can't go on and also can't end. He roused himself. "Come. We'll go down and walk on the beach. It's too beautiful to waste a minute of it."

One day they drove to Nice, where they walked on the Promenade des Anglais while a stream of smart Renaults went by. From a terrace they observed a nineteenth-century panorama: a gauzy sky, sailboats, white dresses, pillars and balustrades. Sprightly music played and no one, Martin saw, noticed that the musicians had threadbare cuffs.

"Let's go back to Menton," Martin said abruptly.

"You're a funny duck! We just got here!"

"Do you mind? If you really do, I'll stay."

"No. We can have a country lunch if you'd rather."

They bought food at a market in a walled village: cheese, fruit, bread and black olives. On the side of the road they stopped to eat. "This is better than all that splendor," Martin remarked. "That sort of thing's a snare. A doctor must never forget ordinary people. It's too easy."

"For you, do you mean, or for anyone?"

"I'm no different from anyone else. Or maybe I am. I want beauty terribly, and beauty can be expensive."

"I think you're too hard on yourself."

"That's what Jessie always says."

Mary looked away. "I'd managed for at least two hours not to think of her."

He closed his eyes. "We couldn't have helped it—the whole thing, from the beginning."

"I'm so sorry for us all!"

"For Alex, too?"

"No, he's as happy as possible, in his circumstances."

"Mary . . . tell me, is it terribly hard for you now, the way things are?"

She was silent for a while. Then she said, "It's as if I were a widow, living with a kind brother. Not the worst fate in the world,

340

I suppose. Thank goodness I have my children and my art, such as it is." She stood up. "No more talk! Let's go back to the beach and pretend we have all the time in the world."

Three more days. For long hours they lay in a hidden hollow of the beach, under the escarpment of hills out of whose rocks these ancient villages had been carved. He took her hand, and he thought that ultimate joy would be to lie forever in this sun, with this woman next to him.

And then it was the last day. Late in the afternoon Martin came out to the terrace. Mary sat with bowed head. She had changed into traveling clothes; their neutral tan was sober in the pastel afternoon. "The bags are downstairs," he said. She nodded. He sat down and took her hand, wishing, wishing they were just beginning.

"What is to become of us?" she whispered.

"I don't know. . . . I'll think. There must be something."

"Oh, Martin!" she cried. "Do we just get on the train and go back? Nothing more? I'm twenty-eight," and he understood that she meant, I'm too young to settle for "nothing more."

All through the long trip home to England, his mind went around and around, like a poor blinded mule at the threshing floor. There must be a way. . . . There is no way. . . . There must be a way. . . . There is no way. . . .

They were astonished to be met at the station in London by Alex Lamb.

"Nothing wrong with the children, it's all right!" he said at once. "But you have both made a mess of things!"

"What? What are you saying?" Mary cried.

"Good grief, Fern. If only you had told me! Then I would have known what to say." And on the platform, surrounded by luggage and hurrying feet, they heard the story.

"What happened is Jessie decided to call the hotel in Paris and let Claire talk to her father. And the concierge told her—" Alex turned to Martin. "He told her you had left. Or rather, he said that Monsieur and Madame had left, that he had got them a reservation on the Blue Train for Nice.

"So then Jessie, having thought that over, telephoned my house

and asked for Fern. And I said, quite naturally, that you'd gone to Nice for a week's rest. How could I have known?"

"Oh, Lord!" Martin cried. "How is Jessie now?"

"Now? I really couldn't say. She and the child left Monday for New York."

THE double doors of the familiar library had been slammed. Donald Meig's angry words beat the walls like fists.

"You scum! To shame the family that took you in and— No, let me talk! If it weren't for me, you'd still be driving thirty miles in the middle of the night for two dollars."

Martin trembled. It had been a hard voyage through ferocious seas. After disembarking, he had rushed at once to the train. Now, tense with humiliation and foreboding, he stood before a man who appeared to have gone mad with rage.

"All right, Mr. Meig. It was terribly wrong. I have no excuse. Still, I ask you again: I want to go upstairs and see Jessie."

"Jessie doesn't want to see you. Jessie wants a divorce. And you are going to give it to her! Do you understand?"

"That's between Jessie and me. We have a child."

"A child? Yes! And my English society daughter might have remembered that she's got a houseful of children. Oh, a wonderful pair, the two of you!"

Above, Martin heard running feet, a child's feet, cross the floor. "At least I want to see Claire," he said.

"No. I've consulted lawyers, and it is in my legal power to keep you away from that child forever on grounds of moral turpitude. You've seen the last you'll ever see of her."

Martin's stomach churned. "You're an unforgiving man, Mr. Meig. Haven't you ever heard of a second chance?"

"An axe murderer doesn't get a second chance, and that's what you are, an axe murderer. You've axed my family. You've driven two sisters apart and robbed me of Fern and her children. And when I think that you owe me everything you are!"

"As far as that goes, you needn't worry. You'll get back every cent with interest."

"Oh, interest, is it? All right then, make it five percent. That's the going rate. You can go to New York and pay me what you owe. After that, we want no more to do with you."

On the train back to the city, Martin closed his eyes. His child. His Claire. He would lose his mind if he couldn't see her.

Her curls, finger-wound, lie on the collar of her tiny coat. "Allosaurus eats vegetables," she informs him.

Surely, if he wrote to Jessie, she would feel some compassion!

"You couldn't get my sister," Jessie says, "so you took me."

She would be most unlikely to feel compassion.

Mary Fern. She comes through a door at noon with an armful of marguerites; she drops them on a table. She laughs—

The train jolted toward the city and Martin dozed.

IN THE end it was work that saved him. He went to New York, joined Dr. Eastman's thriving practice, and purposely exhausted himself in the office. Eastman was a tall man, with the long, handsome face that seemed indigenous to old American wealth. He had welcomed Martin graciously into his practice. Soon, thanks to Martin's long hours, they were seeing far more than the doubled number of patients that would have been expected by the addition of one other man. Eastman remarked that Martin worked like a demon.

As the months passed, inevitably and mercifully the memories blurred. Now and then Martin had an unexpected vision of Lamb House in soft fog; and sometimes still, a woman with a swaying walk would pass on the street; foolishly he would turn around and stare.

Sometimes a child passed, a girl who would be about the age of Claire. And he would wonder how tall Claire was and whether she remembered him at all.

CHAPTER SIX

THE picnic had been cleared away, the remains of watermelon and potato salad stowed in the kitchen, and the last of the children put to bed. Now they sat on Tom Horvath's narrow porch, watching the slow approach of summer night.

Perry Gault spoke out of the darkness in the corner. "If I didn't know New York was just across the George Washington Bridge, I'd think I was back in Kansas."

"I've come to love small-town life," Flo said. "I never thought I would. Martin, I wish you'd stay for the rest of the weekend. You'll miss the fireworks tomorrow."

"Can't. Eastman's leaving tonight to join his family in Maine and I'm on call."

"You surely don't have many emergencies!" She meant, It can't be like Tom's life; people call him out any old time.

"You'd be surprised. We get gunshot wounds, car accidents. Tell her, Perry."

"It's a fact," Perry said. "I was thinking," he mused, "we go back a long time, don't we? Ten years since med school! It doesn't seem possible."

"Say, Martin," Tom added, "do you ever see anything of your first hero—what was his name? Albeniz?"

"Not much. He's still at Grantham Memorial and I'm at Fisk. My first hero, you say? My only one, this side of the Atlantic."

"Why? What's the matter with Eastman? Not a hero?"

"No. He's a great surgeon, I admit that, but— I don't know. Maybe it takes the edge off heroism to be so rich!"

"I read about him in a society column," Flo said. "His wife comes from the Harmon Motors family."

"A lot of us were invited to their place over Decoration Day," Martin said. "It looked like a movie set—butlers serving drinks around the pool. Didn't seem like a doctor's house at all." And he added somewhat sheepishly, "I had a good time, though."

"That's a long way from emergency relief!" Tom said. "We only get a dollar a call, but at least you're sure of the fee."

"Speaking of Albeniz," Martin went on. "It bothers me that outside of his own hospital you don't hear much of him. He doesn't get his just due at all. I don't know why."

"Yes, you do!" Perry said. "It's simple; he doesn't write enough or travel to meetings to blow his own horn. He doesn't play the social game, either. There's an awful lot of that in a big medical center, you know." He spoke earnestly, explaining to Tom. "I

345

never realized how much! Hospital committees, racket and tennis clubs, golf— That's how you build a practice."

"Sounds like a bunch of stockbrokers, not doctors!" Tom's old indignation flared.

"You can't crusade against the world, Tom," Perry said. "You'll only bang your head on a stone wall." He stood up. "Listen. I've got to pick up my girl. Do you mind if I run?"

They watched Perry stride across the grass to his car and drive away. "Salt of the earth," Martin said.

"Always was, and one of the best anesthesiologists around," Tom answered.

When Martin entered his apartment that night, the telephone was ringing. Over the wire came the familiar command.

"Dr. Farrell? You're wanted in Emergency."

When he reached the hospital, the resident reported, "An auto accident out on Long Island. It was a wedding party. The girl injured was a bridesmaid. The ambulance ought to be here soon."

"You tried Dr. Eastman? He mightn't have left yet."

"Yes, he had. We called you next."

The ambulance siren wailed, and a stretcher rushed in carrying a young girl in a blue silk summer dress made for rejoicing. The contrast of this with the bloodied young blond head of its wearer was obscene.

Martin made a swift examination, ordered X rays, and stepped out into the corridor. A man wearing striped trousers and a dark coat with a carnation in the lapel came up to him.

"I'm Robert Moser. My daughter—" he began, and stopped.

Martin took his arm and led him to a bench. "I'm Dr. Farrell, Mr. Moser. You want to know what we found."

"The truth, Doctor. No soft soap."

"Well, we're doing X rays now, but your daughter's skull is fractured in several places. There's almost certainly pressure on the brain. How much damage, we can't tell until we look."

"Then you'll have to operate?"

"Yes. Right away."

"I see." Mr. Moser stared at the floor. His lip was twitching. He looked up. "Dr. Eastman should be here any minute, then?"

"No, sir. Dr. Eastman's out of town. I'll be in charge."

The twitching ceased and the lips firmed. "You're very young. How long have you been with Dr. Eastman?"

"Four years. I'm perfectly qualified, I assure you."

"Excuse me, but your assurance won't be enough. This is my daughter's life. You're positive you can't reach Dr. Eastman?"

"Positive. He's gone to Maine for two weeks."

Mr. Moser stood up. They were almost toe to toe, as in a confrontation. "I'm a trustee of this hospital, do you know that?"

"I didn't know it."

"I want an experienced man. I've no wish to insult you, Doctor, but I've no time to waste. I want a list of neurosurgeons on a par with Dr. Eastman."

"We don't have yardsticks to measure doctors," Martin said heatedly. "But I can name some competent surgeons. There's Dr. Florio on the staff, and Dr. Harold Samson."

"I'll call them."

Martin waited until Moser came back from the telephone. "Neither one is home. But there must be other neurosurgeons!"

"You said you wanted the best."

"Well, give me second best, then."

"You're looking at one right now."

"You're pretty damned impertinent, you know that? Dr. Eastman ought to be told about you."

Martin controlled his anger and said nothing. Then, all at once, Moser sank onto the bench. He looked as though he had used his last strength. He put his head in his hands and his shoulders were shaking.

"Go ahead," he said at last. "Go ahead with whatever has to be done and God help you."

Martin wasn't sure if that was a prayer or a threat.

It was nearing midnight when he entered the operating room. Perry Gault looked up, his eyebrows rising like parentheses above the mask. He had been fetched out of a movie theater where he had been with his girl. Martin was thankful they had found him. The assistants waited. A fine calm came to Martin: I can do it.

On the girl's naked skull, brown coagulated blood clumped in

347

dark beads. Martin selected a knife. His eyes narrowed, his lips pressed shut. And he brought the knife down, into a spurt of fresh blood, which was at once sucked up and sponged away. Down through the scalp the knife sliced.

He asks Perry, "Everything all right?"

"Everything okay," comes the answer.

Electric drill. He draws a small circle on the skull. Careful not to penetrate the brain beneath the bone! Complete the circle. He is aware of voices, the swish of rubber-soled shoes. "Steel blade," he commands. He flicks out the disk of bone and calls for his magnifying glasses. Then he peers in, holding his breath.

From the force of the blow, the smash of metal on bone, a splinter of that bone, needle-sharp, has pierced the dura mater. He perceives a leakage of the spinal fluid and sighs. Dietz, the senior resident, is peering in, too. His eyes convey to Martin that he has seen and understood.

Carefully—oh, every movement is so tense—he pries the needle point of bone, retrieving it securely in the forceps. Now there is nothing to do but wait. The leakage will cease of its own accord, or it will not. The meninges will heal without infection, or they will not. So he sutures the scalp. It is all over and he is terribly, terribly tired.

Both parents were waiting in the hall. "We've done what we could," Martin said, knowing it was not enough to tell them. The mother began to weep, and Moser led her away. Martin did not know what he could have answered if they had pressed him.

After he had changed his clothes, he went to look at the girl again. The family had taken a suite, and she lay in the center of a large white room, like a carved stone queen on a tomb, a long white ridge under white covers.

"Can I get anything for you, Doctor?"

He hadn't noticed the nurse sitting in the corner. He strained through the weak light to see her. What he saw was the full body of a Venus and a mild young face, too round for beauty.

"Have we met before?" he asked.

"I don't think so. I only started here two weeks ago." She stood beside Martin as he looked down at the unconscious girl. "I've got her bridesmaid dress hanging in the closet. Her mother said to throw it out. But I couldn't do that. Doctor, what's going to happen to her?"

"You know better than to ask that."

"Well, I do, of course. But this has really gotten to me."

He saw brimming tears, and he said gently, "You mustn't let a case do this to you."

"I know. I'm not at my professional best." She gave him a rueful smile. "Sometimes I think I wasn't meant to be a nurse! Though I'm not always like this. I just haven't much resistance right now. You know the way you are after the flu, for instance?"

The nurse for the next shift came in, and Martin and the young nurse walked down the corridor together.

"And have you just gotten over the flu?" he asked.

"Not the flu. A broken engagement. That's why I transferred, to change my luck. Would you like some coffee?"

"I don't need another cup, but I'll take one, anyway."

There was no use going home now. It was past three and he had office hours at nine. A few hours of sleep would be as bad as none at all. He followed her into a cubicle where a coffeepot stood on a table.

A chill came through the window. The girl drew a sweater from a hook. The sweater had a name tag: Hazel Janos.

"That's me. Hungarian."

"My best friend is Hungarian. Tom Horvath. He taught me to eat *palacsinta*."

"I make good *palacsinta*, with cherries and sour cream."

He sat back and observed her. She had very white skin, and brown hair that was too fine and soft. Resting her chin on her hand, she looked out into the night sky and sighed.

"You're all knotted up, aren't you?" Martin asked.

"Yes."

"Want to tell me about it?"

"There's not much to tell. It was only a case of a girl who wanted to get married and a man who didn't. One day I gave him an ultimatum and I lost. That's it."

"Perhaps he'll think it over," Martin suggested.

"No. He's gone to Kansas City. He needed to get away. I can't blame him, really. The juice seems to go out of things when you have to wait too long for them."

Her candor touched Martin. "That's true."

"Oh, why am I telling you all this? Because you're a doctor and people think they can say anything to a doctor?"

Good Lord, not again, he thought, and answered, "I think people feel that way." He sensed that she wanted to be comforted, so he said, "Time heals everything, they say."

"Do you believe that, honestly?"

"No."

She laughed, and the laugh changed her face. Comely, he thought. That's the word. Comely.

"I'm not laughing because anything's funny. I think it's because I feel better for having told you."

He reflected, "I never do remember why laughter and tears are related. One of my philosophy professors spent a week on the subject, but for the life of me I can't remember what he said." He bent forward, clasping his hands around his knees. "I have a little girl," he said suddenly, surprising himself. "I haven't seen her since she was three years old, and she's seven now. Her mother and I are divorced and she has custody." He wondered why *he* should be talking like this to *her*. But he went on, and heard himself saying aloud the names of people and places which he had scarcely used since they had passed out of his life. Menton. Mary. Jessie. Lamb House. Claire.

Hazel's eyes never left his face. "And it's over between Mary and you?" she asked when he had finished.

"Yes," he said harshly. He was angry with himself. Why had he spilled everything out to a stranger? He stood up. It was five o'clock. "I'd better go shave and change before I go to work."

She rose and touched his arm. "You're probably sorry you told me so much. You're worried I'll talk about it. But I never will. You can trust me."

He looked down into a face so gentle that it pained him. One saw such faces on lonesome children, and sometimes on women of radiant goodness. "Yes," he said, "I trust you."

350

EASTMAN MOVED BACK FROM the respirator. Vicky Moser lay unmoving, except for the slight rise and fall of her chest. He beckoned to Martin and they went out to the corridor.

"For the sake of my blood pressure, I had to wait a whole day before I could talk to you, Farrell," he began.

"I don't understand."

"You had no right to take the knife to Vicky Moser! You had no authority. What made you think you had?"

Martin was dumbfounded. "But you were out of town! I tried Dr. Florio and Dr. Samson and they couldn't be reached."

"What about Shirer, then? These are prominent people, Farrell. Moser's a trustee."

Anger began to boil up in Martin. "In the first place, sir, I don't care about prominence. In the second, I didn't recommend Dr. Shirer because I consider myself a better surgeon."

"Oh, I suppose you consider yourself better than I am, too?"

"Of course I don't. But there are some procedures I *can* do as well as you can, and this was one of them."

Eastman's cheeks reddened. "I'll want to talk about this again, Farrell. I'm not sure you and I can get along in the future unless certain things are clarified."

In Martin the anger now boiled over. He had done a thorough job! If it didn't work out, if the girl should die, or should live and merely vegetate, why, then, it would have happened anyway! I truly and honestly know my limitations, he thought.

With a calmness that surprised himself he said, "I don't think we will get along, Dr. Eastman, unless you give me the respect and freedom I deserve."

For a second Eastman stared at him; then, without replying, he turned and walked down the hall.

For three days they poured glucose and oxygen into Vicky Moser. She was now Eastman's patient; Martin had been removed from the case. But he continued to look in on her and found no change. The pupils were still enlarged and made no move under the shaft of his pencil light. On the fourth day came momentary hope when normal breathing resumed, and she was taken out of the respirator. But still she lay inert and unresponsive.

351

At the office Martin continued to hold regular hours. Eastman did not come in. Obviously he had interrupted his vacation only for the Moser girl. Then one afternoon as Martin was about to go into Vicky's room, he met Eastman coming out. "Anything you want?" the other man asked bluntly.

"Just to know how the patient is doing."

"My patient," Eastman said, "is doing badly. I plan to operate again in the morning."

Martin was appalled. "Operate again? But why?"

"There are splinters in there, and I'm going back for them."

"Doctor," Martin said earnestly, "I give you my word there are none. There was only one and I removed it."

"Damn it! There must be more!"

No stranger would believe this man had ever been genial. His eyes were hostile; his lips made a gash across the chin. "I'm having X rays in the morning, but I can tell you now what they will show." He swung around and strode to the elevator.

That night Martin scarcely slept. At five o'clock he got up and walked to the hospital. He half hoped Hazel Janos would be there, but a middle-aged nurse sat in the chair beside Vicky's bed.

"Any change?" he whispered, and the woman answered, "None."

Gently Martin raised one eyelid, then the other, and turned his pencil light on. There was no contraction of the pupils. Then he lifted the blanket, reached for a limp arm and stroked it. Was there a very faint reaction to his touch? He pressed harder. Was there a movement?

"Did you see that, Nurse?"

She turned up the light and leaned over the bed.

"Here. I'll show you." Again Martin pressed the arm, and now he was sure he saw a slight withdrawal. "Did you see it?"

"Yes, I did. Oh, Doctor, do you think—"

"I don't dare hope," Martin said. It may be only a reflex, he told himself. Yet he hoped.

At eight o'clock orderlies arrived to wheel the girl downstairs for X rays. At eight fifteen Mr. Moser entered the room, and frowned when he saw Martin. "I thought you were off the case."

"I am. This is purely unofficial."

Mr. Moser sat down, and Martin walked to the window, looking down at the aimless scurry on the street below. When Dr. Eastman came in, he did not turn around.

"We shall have to operate," he heard Eastman say to Moser. "There's undoubtedly a splinter in there. We'll know as soon as the X rays come up."

At eight fifty a technician came in with the X rays. Now Martin turned around as Eastman held the films to the light and studied them. At last Moser spoke. "Well, Doctor?"

Eastman pursed his lips. "Perplexing. There's nothing. No splinters—that I can see."

So I was right, Martin thought.

When the door opened and the patient was brought back, the little group re-formed around the bed. "What do you suggest now, Doctor?" Moser said.

"I've been thinking—another set of X rays. I'm still—"

"Look at this," Martin said. He turned his pencil light on. "The pupil. She reacts. And this morning I thought I saw—"

"What?" Moser asked. "What did you see?"

"I'm not sure. I don't want to give you false hopes." He pinched the girl's arm. He thought her lips moved. A little sound, the faintest groan came into the silence around the bed. Martin bent over her.

"Are you Vicky?" he whispered. She groaned again and her eyes flew open. Her dry lips moved, but no sound came out.

"Are you Vicky?"

The girl nodded.

"Have you been sick?"

She nodded.

"There's someone here to see you," Martin said softly. "Look," and he motioned to Moser.

Moser leaned over the other side of the bed.

"Is this your father?" Martin asked.

It was a long minute. The girl's eyes struggled to focus. There was no sound in the room as the three men waited. And finally, into that agonizing silence came a word.

"Daddy," she said.

BOB MOSER GRASPED MARTIN's hands. "I was half out of my mind, Dr. Farrell! You can understand that, can't you? Try to forgive me. I'll never forget you till my dying day. I—we—all of our family—we'll never forget you."

So much emotion, so much gratitude was oppressive. As quickly as he decently could, Martin fled.

Eastman caught up with him outside the solarium. "I don't mind telling you, Martin, this has been one of the worst experiences of my professional life. I just went off the deep end. It looked so bad there."

"I understand," Martin said.

"I'm sorry if I was unjust to you. I sincerely am."

Martin fidgeted. "That's all right. It's turned out well."

"Turned out well? The girl's going to come out of this and what can you add to that?" Eastman beamed. "So let's forget the whole business and take up where we left off."

Martin said quietly, "I've been doing some thinking."

"Yes?"

"And the sum of it is that I really want to go it alone from now on. It's been a fine opportunity, working with you, but—perhaps it's a matter of temperament—I'd rather work alone."

"Martin, you can have all the freedom you want."

"Thank you, Doctor, but I've made up my mind. I can wait a few weeks until you find another man, of course."

"Don't be foolish, Martin. There's a depression out there, in case you haven't noticed."

"Oh, I've noticed! But my wants aren't very many." He put out his hand. "Thank you for everything, all the same."

He walked on past the solarium, past stretchers in the corridors and visitors waiting in the lobby. The loudspeaker called with urgency: "Dr. Simmons—stat, Dr. Feinstein—stat." My world, he thought.

Hazel Janos, powder-white from cap to shoes, was coming up the steps. Her eyes brightened when she saw Martin.

"I think our girl's going to make it," he told her jubilantly. "She spoke this morning, recognized her father."

"Oh," Hazel cried, "I'm so glad! I prayed for her."

"Say a little prayer for me, too, will you? I've left Eastman and I'm on my own."

"I will, but I don't think you'll need prayers. You've got success written all over you."

"Have I? Strange, I don't especially want it, if it means being another Eastman."

"You'd never be like that. You're soft inside." For a moment she looked frankly into his eyes. Then, flushing, turned away as though she had been too intimate, and went inside.

Martin ran down the steps. He felt more free than he had in a very long time.

CHAPTER SEVEN

THE child knew her mother was different from other mothers, from other people. She knew also that her father had gone away and that there was something wrong about that. She remembered great height, someone bending down and picking her up and hugging her. There had been a statue in a wide green place, and they two had stood in front of it. She asked her mother about this memory, but her mother had forgotten. Her mother had forgotten everything, it seemed.

In a cabinet in the library, Claire found a black photograph album with a broken spine. The pages were loose, and some of the pictures had slid out. This was Grandpa, when his hair was dark; and Mother as a little girl, twisted even then. Here she was again, standing next to a laughing girl, much taller than Mother and not twisted. Claire carried the album to Grandpa.

"Who's the pretty girl with Mother?" she asked.

"That's your aunt, Mary Fern. We don't talk about her."

"Why? Is she dead like Grandma?"

"No, she's not dead, but she might as well be. She did bad things."

"What bad things?"

"Stealing, for one. Taking things that weren't hers."

When Mother came in, she was very angry. "I will not have you talking to the child like that, Father," she said.

"Why not? She might as well know the truth."

"At her age?"

"She can start getting used to the idea. When she's older, she'll have been prepared for it."

"Never! Never, do you hear? It's my business, my trouble! Don't let me hear you say one word about it again, Father. I mean it."

Mostly, though, Mother was nice to Grandpa. She said she was sorry for him because he was old and sick. Maybe she could be sorry for sick people because she wasn't made right and knew how it felt. When you walked behind her you could see how one shoulder stuck up higher than the other. Why didn't she look like other mothers? Why did a person have to have a mother like her?

Yet she could do things the other mothers couldn't do. She could make anything with her hands. She made a patchwork quilt for Claire's bed and silk flowers for the bowl on the hall table. She sewed a Tinker Bell costume for Claire to wear in *Peter Pan*. It was all feathery white, with hidden, tinkling bells. Miss Donohue, the teacher, kept talking about Claire's costume. It was the best one in the class.

Today was the final dress rehearsal. Claire felt so beautiful and so clever, tinkling her bells. And suddenly, when they were about to take the costumes off, something came into her head.

"I really saw Peter Pan once," she said. "There's a statue of him in the park in London. I was there with my father."

Jimmy Crater scoffed. "You did not! There isn't any such statue!"

"There is, too, and I saw it."

"You're a liar."

"I am not. Go ask Miss Donohue."

"Why, yes," Miss Donohue said. "Peter Pan in Kensington Gardens. It's famous."

"There," Claire said, "I told you so."

"Ah, you're full of baloney. You never were in London."

Now a little circle of allies and enemies gathered around Claire and Jimmy Crater. "I was born in London!" Claire cried triumphantly. "I lived there with my father and mother."

"You haven't even got a father," Andy Chapman said.

"I have so. Everybody has a father."

"Oh, yeah? Where is he, then?"

"None of your business."

"Hasn't got a father, hasn't got a father!"

Claire stuck out her tongue. "You're mad, Jimmy Crater, because I can knock you down."

Jimmy's fists went up. "Come on! Fight, then!"

"I don't want to fight, but I can if I have to!"

"Ah, you're scared! You haven't got a father, and your mother's funny-looking, and you're scared!"

Claire's fist struck Jimmy's nose. When he fell, chairs clattered. Andy Chapman shoved Claire. They all fell, ripping the Tinker Bell dress down the back.

Miss Donohue came running. "Boys! Boys! What's happening?"

Claire got up. "Look what they did," she said.

Miss Donohue turned her around. "Oh, Claire, I'm so sorry. I'll sew it for you, dear. It won't show onstage, I promise. Claire, where're you going? School's not out yet!"

But Claire had already gone.

She took the long way, past the yellow house that belonged to her best friend, Charlotte. Charlotte's house was much nicer than home. Sometimes Claire was invited there for Sunday dinner. After dinner Charlotte's father and mother would dance to the Victrola. They called it doing the tango.

As she neared her own house, Claire saw her mother on the front porch with Aunt Milly. Claire liked it when Aunt Milly came to visit. She had a nice laugh and always brought good presents.

"Claire!" her mother cried. "What are you doing home? And your Tinker Bell costume is all torn! What happened?"

"I had a fight with two boys."

"Oh, my," Aunt Milly said. "Oh, my, I'm surprised!"

"Do you want to tell me what it was about?" Mother said.

"No," Claire said. *It was about you, stupid.*

"Well, girls mustn't get into punching fights."

"Why not? Why can boys do everything?"

"But you don't want to be a boy, do you?"

"No. But I want to do the things boys do."

"It doesn't work that way."

357

"Why?"

"I don't know. But when you grow up you'll be very pretty. And a wonderful man will come along to take care of you." Mother stroked Claire's hair. "Come, I'll put peroxide on that scratch."

She followed the lopsided back upstairs. No man was taking care of Mother except Grandpa, and he didn't count. No man like Charlotte's father danced with her. Because she was funny-looking, just as Jimmy Crater said. Claire's eyes filled with tears.

"Ouch! That peroxide makes my eyes sting!"

"It's not this little bit of peroxide you're crying about."

"I am not crying!"

"Yes, you are. Is it because the costume's torn? It's too bad, but I can fix it by morning."

"I'm not going to school in the morning. I don't want to be in the play."

Mother shook her head. "I don't believe that," she said gently. She looked away, and in that same quiet voice she said, "I won't be coming to the play tomorrow, either. I've too many things to do at home."

But that's not true, Claire thought. She wanted to come! She's been talking and talking about it. Then why?

Her mother seemed to be thinking of something, making up her mind. She was quiet for a long time. At last she spoke. "Oh, you've had a bad time, haven't you? I know! It's awful for you because I look so queer next to the other mothers. And your father isn't here." She grasped Claire's shoulders. "But I'll make it up to you. I owe it to you and I will. I don't know how, but I swear I will."

The words were almost angry, but Claire knew her mother wasn't angry. "Come to the play tomorrow," she whispered. "I want you to come, Mama."

"Do you really? You don't have to say so if you don't mean it."

"I want you to," Claire repeated.

A GLOW came through the slatted blinds. The city sky was never truly dark; the city never truly slept. Martin looked at the clock. It was five a.m. This early waking had been happening to him of late. Slowly he got out of bed and went to the window.

Light was turning mother-of-pearl at the edge of darkness.
Martin stood there thinking of Hazel Janos. He'd been seeing her
for some time now and he still didn't know how to describe her.
A simple person? She found such pleasure in small things: a row
on the lake in Central Park, a movie and ice cream afterward.
She took the complications out of living. She was restful.

And yet—she was not happy. Her tears disturbed him, and he
would question her, although he knew the reason quite well.

"It's nothing," she would say, denying because she was afraid
of driving him away. She wanted him to marry her. She loved him.

Why hadn't he married her, then? Waiting for that old longing,
the sweet obsession? But perhaps the obsession was something
one did better without.

He felt such tenderness for Hazel and believed he saw her
clearly. She was a woman afraid she would never be married. She
was afraid of growing fat, like her immigrant mother. Afraid of
being overdressed or underdressed, of not possessing the virtues
of the refined middle class.

Certainly Martin was doing well enough to support a family.
He was acquiring a bit of a name. The younger general men referred patients to him because they respected his work. Also, his
fees were surely more reasonable than Eastman's!

He put on his new record player. Mr. and Mrs. Moser had given
it to him on the anniversary of their daughter's operation, along
with the happy news that she was playing tennis again. He laid
his head back and listened as the Bach *Magnificat* sang.

My life is half over, he thought. I'm thirty-seven.

On the bookshelf stood a framed snapshot of Hazel, taken one
spring afternoon when he had brought her to the Horvaths' house.
She was holding Tom and Flo's newest baby.

"That becomes you, Hazel," Tom had said. Martin recalled
the dowdy, cheerful house, the scuffed woodwork, the noise.
Why did it ache in him, in him who loved order and serenity?

In the park where he sometimes walked with Hazel, a father
and a little boy came to sail a toy boat. He stopped to watch them.
Machismo, was it? A man wanting a son? Yes, yes! But a daughter
was—and he thought of Claire again. Not an hour passed without

359

some glancing thought of her. Forever lost and gone, like Mary

The music stopped. Carefully he slid the record back into it cardboard case. I am overwhelmed with loneliness, he thought Overwhelmed with it. And then something swept through him, a fine resolution, a purity of hope.

He picked up the telephone. "Hazel," he said, when she answered sleepily. "Hazel, I want to ask you something."

NINETEEN thirty-seven was the darkest year. Jessie sat before the desk where bank statements, tax bills and accountants' report were spread. Oh, the darkest year, in which Father's heart had finally given out and the Websterware plant, after three quarter of a century, had closed its doors!

She raised her eyes from the papers. A monotonous rain poured from the somber sky. This was the fifth month of winter.

Place where I was born, you have grown cold to me. Once I belonged here and was intimately known. The workmen in my father's factory would tip their caps. Now they are unemployed and don't tip their caps, certainly not to me. My taxes are in arrears There is really no excuse, Depression or no, for the mess Claire and I are in. How many times I told Father to cheapen the line Who buys copper pots in times like these? Better if he had given more thought to business instead of ranting these last years about Martin and my sister!

I feel so sorry for Martin and Fern. Isn't that strange? But I knew about them from the very first. When they stood together in this house, I knew. When they walked in the orchard at Lamb House, I knew again. Those eyes of hers! Lapis lazuli, someone said. Still, it would have been no good for Martin and me even if Fern had not existed. Oh, we would have stayed on, but what good would it have been? I'm too proud for that.

So, I don't hate, but I don't love anymore, either. Let them live and prosper, far from me. But the child—the child is mine.

Across the hall Aunt Milly had been fiddling with the radio. Whatever did she do with her time before the thing was invented? Kate Smith's hearty voice cheered her; the tribulations of King Edward and Mrs. Simpson enthralled her. Now, though, she switched it off and came to the door. "Jessie, are you through yet?"

"I have to go over these figures before the tax people come."

"Jessie, I wish you'd let me help out. That's why your uncle sent me up this week, to see what we could do."

"No. Thank you, but no. I've got to stand on my own feet."

A car door slammed and Jessie peered out the window. "They're here. Two of them. Donovan's from the tax office and the bald one's Jim Reeve, the new mayor."

"Would you like me to stay for moral support?"

Jessie shook her head. "No, dear. You go read in the parlor. This won't take very long."

"After all, you're now two years in arrears," Donovan said. He had the placid manner of the overfed, but his voice was not as mild as it had been half an hour earlier.

"I suppose I'm the only one in town who is!"

"No. But that's got nothing to do with this case."

Sweat gathered under Jessie's arms and on the palms of her hands. Four generations of Meigs had lived in this house, and no men such as these had ever sat down in the parlor. Yet now they had come to tell her they had the means to confiscate the house itself. "I will not let you sell my house for taxes," she said. "I'll burn it down before I let you take it away." She caught her breath. "Don't look so amused. I know I'd be arrested for arson. But that wouldn't help you, would it?" She turned to Reeve. "I happen to know you'd like to live in this house."

Reeve had a nervous twitch and now his eye jumped. "Where did you get that idea? I never—"

"Come on, come on. Let's not waste each other's time. I know your wife wants this house. Very well, then. Give me a fair price, and she can have it."

There was silence. Donovan lit a cigar, and Reeve stared down at the floor. Then he asked, "What's a fair price?"

"Twenty-eight thousand dollars. That's what the Critchleys got down the street. Their house is a twin to this one."

"That was a year ago. Prices have fallen since."

"Twenty-eight thousand," Jessie repeated. "Less the back taxes."

Then Donovan said, "You're forgetting. We can take the house for taxes and put it up for public sale."

"Public sale!" she said with scorn. "You don't expect me to believe that? You think you'll get the house for half nothing, don't you?" She lowered her voice. "Listen here, you either give me a fair price, or I tell the newspapers you've got a private deal to take it for taxes and buy it cheap yourself. Then you'd have to put it up for public sale, and I'd get a decent price after the tax lien had been paid. And you'd have a lot of explaining to do."

Donovan looked at Reeve with a silent question. Jessie stared out the window. Maybe it won't be so bad to get out of here, she thought. Except that I don't know where I'll go.

Presently Reeve said, "I'll bargain with you. I'll give you twenty-five, less the taxes."

"Twenty-eight, Mr. Reeve. Take it or leave it."

"Twenty-six and that's overpaying."

"It's not and you know it. Twenty-eight, Mr. Reeve."

Reeve stood up. "Twenty-seven and not a cent more."

She saw that he had gone as far as he would go and thought quickly, I didn't expect to get what I asked, anyway. She held her hand out. "We'll shake on it. And good luck to us both."

Aunt Milly trembled. "Jessie, you're marvelous! I couldn't help but hear. I don't know how you did it. But where will you go?"

"Believe it or not, I haven't the faintest idea."

"Oh, dear heaven!" Aunt Milly's chubby hands clasped and unclasped. "Don't you think you really ought to ask for help now? For Claire's sake?"

"If you mean I should go to Martin, you can save your breath. We made a bargain: a painless divorce in return for his not coming near us ever again." Her voice quavered, and she thought, It's been a terrible day; I could just lay my head down and cry.

"You know he's married again? I heard by accident from a woman who lives in the same apartment house."

Jessie made no answer. A soreness which had been absent a long time spread in her chest. Aunt Milly lit another lamp, throwing a sickly yellow light on the floor.

"How I hate this room!" Jessie cried suddenly. "To think we spent most of our lives in it!"

"You're upset, and no wonder. Come out on the sun porch and unwind a bit." The clear little voice chirped kindly, "Goodness, what you've done with this porch! It's like sunshine even on a day like this."

The old wicker furniture and the floor had been painted. An indigo rug with a scalloped ruby border lay in the center of the floor. Ferns flowed out of hanging baskets, and a brass Indian jug held knitting needles and wool. The room had the boldness and cheerful confidence that is unconcerned with fashion. Because everything in it was of purest taste, it looked like a rich man's country retreat.

"That rug you hooked is handsome, Jessie. It's really different. Original and bright." Aunt Milly looked thoughtful. "You know what? You ought to come to New York."

"And what would I do in New York, tell me that?"

"For one thing, Uncle Drew and I would be there, so you wouldn't be entirely alone. And you know what else? I think you should go into the decorating business. You have marvelous taste."

"I've had no training! I couldn't possibly—"

"You could take courses toward a degree while you were working. It's been done."

"And where would I find customers?"

"I could start you off. I know a Mrs. Beech who has a place in the Berkshires. A room like this one would appeal to her. And there's a friend of mine whose daughter's being married. They're pretty strapped financially, but you could fix an apartment for her without spending too much. That's two. And those women would recommend you to their friends; that's how it would grow."

For the moment Jessie had nothing to say. The idea was so foolish, so daring, that no sensible answer could weigh against it.

"You'd have the money from the house to start with," Aunt Milly urged.

True. Perhaps it would work. No. No. It was crazy! "The world isn't waiting for me," she said.

"The world isn't waiting for anybody."

That was true, too. To be one's own mistress! Never to have to ask anybody for anything! Imagine it!

"It would be a whole other environment for you, Jessie. Cosmopolitan people are so much more tolerant."

Indeed. And there would be such fine schools for Claire. She stared at the floor, then looked up. A kind of daring excitement raced through her. "Aunt Milly, you may be right! And after all, I don't have a wealth of other choices, do I?"

ON THE final morning, Jessie rose early and threaded her way through cartons to the kitchen. For the last time she put the coffee on, and in a kind of mental fog waited while the water purred. "I'm a teary mess," she said aloud, "and I don't want to be. I can't afford it. I've got to make sense and order."

She walked into the living room and stood in the bay window where the minister had married her to Martin, she knowing all the time that it was wrong.

So, he had married again. A beauty this time, like Fern? A woman whose body he could adore, not pity? Damn it, enough of this! You'll get nowhere, Jessie!

Six o'clock. She went softly up the stairs. Outside Claire's door stood a carton of books with ice skates on top. She pushed the door open and went in.

The small hand gripped the pillowcase. She shall have everything, Jessie thought: dresses, dances, young men and trips to the stars. And they will all come from me.

She leaned over and touched the child on the shoulder. "Come, darling. Time to get up. Time to go."

CHAPTER EIGHT

FROM her place at the breakfast table, Claire couldn't see the backyard, but she knew that the skimpy forsythia had stretched weak yellow strands over all the board fences between Park and Lexington avenues. In their own yard a few scattered hyacinths had poked through the hard earth. Sparrows chittered and fought. They always grew more strident as spring approached.

Jessie mused over the toast and cereal. "Someday I want to build a terrace and plant trees. Oh, what treasures these old brownstones are! Just look at those tiles around the fireplace. You'll never see work like that again."

Every day she walked around admiring things: the ten-foot ceilings, the pineapple newel-posts, the pegged floors. "This house was built with love," she would say.

Claire was bored by such preoccupation with the house. The only thing she really admired was the dumbwaiter on which the meals were hauled up from the kitchen. They ate on the second floor because the dining room was occupied by the business.

Jessie reflected now, "Funny, I had to pay about as much for this little place as we got for the big house and one and a half acres back home. You know, I've been thinking. I may rent a proper shop over near Madison Avenue. I saw one that's fairly cheap. And the business really needs more space." She sighed. "Things haven't gone too badly for us, have they, Claire?" And, without waiting for an answer, Jessie picked up *The New York Times*. "It's not polite to read at the table, but breakfast is different," she said.

Claire had expected her to say it, since she did so every morning. She waited for her mother to hand over one section.

"Here, you read, too. You ought to know what's going on in the world, now that you're in fifth grade. Yes, look, the ad for that store is in again. Maybe I'll just go ahead and take it. These bad times can't last forever, can they? Anyway, the people who have been coming to me don't seem to be suffering from the bad times, I must say."

The paper crackled as the pages were turned. "You know, Claire, sometimes I think I've just been dreaming about these last three years."

Claire didn't hear the rest. Out of all the thousands of black letters on the spread page, her eye had fastened on a handful that spelled a name: *Dr. Martin Farrell*. There was something about speeches at the Academy of Medicine, then a short list of participants. *Dr. Martin Farrell* stood out from the rest. She had not thought about this name for a long time.

365

"It's eight fifteen," Jessie said suddenly, "and you haven't finished your breakfast."

Claire picked up the spoon and began swallowing cereal. Something had fixed itself in her head. She drank the milk and then got her coat. Jessie kissed her forehead.

"Be careful at the crossing," she admonished, as she did every morning.

Claire went downstairs. From the front hall you could look into the shop. Along one wall were dark shelves with shining objects on them: a marble head of Shakespeare, a gilded clock, a porcelain tureen with blue roses. There were old, carved chests, lamps and pictures and a crimson velvet sofa. All of these things were for sale except her mother's desk with its tidy, stacked papers. Aunt Milly and Uncle Drew said Mother was very clever, and it was astonishing what she had managed to do in only three years. Yes, her mother was very smart. But she was not thinking of her mother.

She hurried down the front steps. Under the bay window was a neat, small sign: JESSIE MEIG, INTERIORS. It bothered Claire that her mother's name was different from her own. Her mother said that here in the city divorce wasn't anything to be shocked about. Claire knew that was true. Still, for some reason, it bothered her this morning.

Claire walked quickly down Sixty-seventh Street. When she arrived at school, she sat at her desk, and at noon went to lunch as on any ordinary day. But a curious excitement stirred in her all that time.

THE apartment building looked like the ones where many of her friends lived: white stone with a green awning that reached from the door to the curb. She had copied the address out of the phone book. Now a doorman with brass buttons directed her.

The waiting room was vacant. Claire marched up to the receptionist's desk. "I want to see Dr. Farrell," she said.

"Have you an appointment?"

"No. I only just decided to come."

"Well!" the woman said. "Well—what is it about?"

"A personal matter," Claire answered.

"I'm sorry, but I can't take up the doctor's time unless you will state what—"

She felt a sudden strengthening of nerve. "Just tell him that Claire is here. He'll know who I am."

HE HADN'T cried out or jumped up and squeezed her, which was a relief. He had started to get up and come around to the front of the desk, but then he had sat down again, as though he hadn't been able to stand. His face had gone very pale.

From the opposite side of the desk she regarded him furtively. She didn't want to seem to be staring. He was medium, neither very young, nor bald and tired. He had nice hair, brown and thick. He didn't wear glasses and he looked, she thought, like a doctor. Yes, he looked like a doctor and he was her father.

A cry came out of her. "I feel scared!"

He answered softly, "Yes. Yes, you must be. Does your mother know you're here?"

"No. I came from school by myself."

"From school? You go to school here in New York?"

"Yes, since second grade. I go to Brearley."

"You live in New York?"

"Yes. We didn't have any money in Cyprus and we came here so Mother could earn some. She went to school and she has a degree now."

Her father took out a handkerchief and wiped his forehead. She could see he was very upset. "Tell me about it," he said.

"Well, you see, Grandpa lost all his money and then he died and the factory closed and we couldn't afford to stay in our house anymore. So Mother learned to be a decorator and now she has a lot of customers."

"Your mother ought to have come to me. I would have given you money."

"She wouldn't have taken it. She doesn't like you, does she?"

"No, I suppose she doesn't. I'm sorry about that, because I like her. And you I love, Claire. I've never stopped loving and thinking of you." And he looked at her, straight into her eyes.

367

She looked straight back. "Why don't we live together, then? Why did you go away?"

Her father shifted his eyes. "People sometimes change, Claire. They expect to be happy together. Then they find they've made a mistake, and it's better for each to go his own way."

"That's not the whole story," Claire said.

Her father sighed. "You're right. But perhaps you aren't quite ready to understand it."

"I think I know why. It's because Mother looks funny, so you didn't want to live with her anymore."

Her father got up from his chair. "Oh, no! You can't be allowed to think that of me. Never, Claire. Never."

"Then it's because you wanted to be a famous doctor. That's why you went away."

"That isn't true, either. Besides, I'm not famous."

"Aunt Milly says you will be someday."

"Your aunt Milly talks about me?"

"Only sometimes, when Mother's not there. She said it was wrong to never talk about you, as if I had no father. She says it's wrong to keep so much hatred."

Her father turned around and faced the window. Claire realized that he was crying. Then he came and laid his cheek on her head. She sat very still.

"I hope you haven't been too sad about all this," he said.

"Oh, no. Only sometimes, well, I get in a thoughtful mood. Then things go around in my head and I feel bad for a while."

"Tell me, can you remember anything about England?"

"Not very much. Just odd things. I remember Christmas in a house, not our own, because it had stairs. There were children there, bigger than I. One was a boy. The dining room was down a long hall, and the Christmas tree was in the hall."

"Yes. I'm amazed that you can remember all that."

"Whose house was it?"

"It belonged to your aunt, Mary Fern."

"I thought it might have! And why is she a secret, too? Why will Mother never answer a question about her own sister?"

"I can't help you, Claire. I'm sorry."

"I wish I had a sister. I hate being an only child."

Her father said quietly, "You have a brother."

Astonished, she cried, "I have?" And, following his glance to a photograph on a bookshelf, she saw a woman holding a little boy on her lap.

"Yes. His name is Enoch, after my father. Your grandfather."

"Is that your wife in the picture?"

"Yes. Her name is Hazel."

"What shall I call her when I visit?"

"Let's ask her what she'd like, shall we? But then, your mother may not allow you to visit, you know."

"I'm going to, anyway. Besides, you have a right to say what I may do, haven't you?"

"Not really, Claire."

"Why not?"

"Well, because—well, I haven't ever done anything for you up till now, have I?"

"You can start, then."

"Oh, I want to. Is there anything you need? Tell me."

"I don't need any *things*. Mother's making a lot of money. Every time she fixes up somebody's house, they tell their friends, and then the friends call her."

"Remarkable. A remarkable woman. And are you interested in decorating, too?"

"No. I like leaves and bugs and all that. Science is my best subject. I'm going to be a doctor."

"You are? And when did you decide that?"

Proudly Claire affected carelessness. "Oh, about a year ago."

"But you'll marry and have children when you grow up."

"Not if it interferes with being a doctor."

Her father was silent, and then he said, "You're only ten."

"Ten and a half."

"Yes, yes. Ten and a half. Enthralling Claire! You always were. Enthralling." And he kept looking at her.

When the desk clock rang six chimes, he jumped up. "Your mother will be worried sick about you! Come, I'll walk to your street with you and watch until you're inside the house."

JESSIE STARED INTO THE darkness past the window. Claire waited. After the furious preliminary scolding for frightening her mother, they had sat down in the living room and Claire had told the whole story. Now, scared, she waited for punishment.

Jessie laughed. "Good grief!" she said. "It's just the kind of thing I would have done." Claire's heartbeat slowed.

"So, then, how is he, your father?"

"I thought he would be older."

"He looks—he looks well?"

"I guess so."

"What did you talk about?"

"A lot of things. He has a little boy."

"I see. And you'll be going back to visit, I suppose."

Something forlorn had come into her mother's voice. "Don't you want me to?" Claire asked.

"You can imagine I'm not happy about it. But you'll do what you want, anyway."

"I wish you wouldn't mind too much, though."

Jessie didn't answer that. Instead she said, "Well, next time let me know where you are, that's all." She stood up. "It's time for your bath, and you haven't done any homework."

At the door, Claire turned around. "Mother, don't worry. Things will be the same. This won't make any difference."

"Of course, dear. I know it won't."

But of course she didn't know it. And Claire didn't know it either. For it could never be the same again. It wasn't just the two of them, anymore.

MARTIN moved his chair back from the table. "This was a great dinner. Had enough?" he asked Claire.

The devastated Sunday roast stood on the sideboard with the peas, the sweet potatoes, the homemade rolls and the apple pudding. "I'm stuffed," Claire said. "You're a better cook than our maid, Aunt Hazel."

Hazel smiled. "If you still want to take Enoch to the park, Claire, you'd better start. It gets dark early."

"I'm ready," Claire said.

371

"All right, then. I'll get his snowsuit on. Be sure to hold his hand very tightly; he can slip loose before you know it."

"You can trust me," Claire assured her.

"She likes coming here," Hazel observed when they had gone. "I guess it's fun for her to be with Enoch. Her own house must be very quiet, I suppose."

"I suppose," Martin answered.

"Well, I'll clean up the kitchen. You going to work?"

"Just for an hour before the Philharmonic comes on."

He had fixed up a room for himself and his personal treasures: his desk, his books, records and the radio on which he listened to the Sunday broadcast of the Philharmonic. The rest of the house was Hazel's. She had made it cozy; somewhat tasteless, but inoffensively so. There was a clutter of pillows and fringe in cloudy colors which tended to cloud Martin's mood. Old rose, and tans that reminded him of tea stains.

The afternoon was murky and still. He looked down to the street. Claire, holding Enoch by the hand, had just crossed Seventy-third Street and headed toward the park. Tenderness filled his chest. That they might know grace and mercy all their lives! How extraordinary that after all his own fruitless efforts, his daughter, without any act of his, should have been returned to him. His entrancing daughter!

He went over to his desk. A reminder had been propped against a bookend: "The Mosers have invited us for dinner next Friday. Are you free? Shall I accept?"

As it happened he was free, yet he knew if he had not been he would have made an effort to become so. The Mosers were amiable and decent people. They were all gratitude. Vicky was in fine health; and now Moser believed in Martin's special genius, a belief as ill-founded as his first refusal to believe in Martin at all.

Martin sighed. It would be a long drive out to the Mosers' Long Island place. Still, Hazel liked to go there. It was no average experience. You turned in at the great iron gates, traveled half a mile up a driveway between immense walls of shrubbery, and were greeted by a servant at the top of a flight of steps.

Ah, well! He started on the pile of reports, but his mind wandered. Why was it that, on days when he was with Claire, he thought more of—of *her*? Were she and Claire alike? Not the eyes, for Claire's were dark. But there was something, some joyous movement of the head, something in the child of eleven that reminded him they were of the same flesh, after all.

In the kitchen, Hazel was singing, and the sound was sweetly, faintly mournful, like herself. She wanted to make everything between them perfect. She made herself read whatever he had just read. She was not especially fond of music, but she had bought a book to learn about it. What she really liked was domesticity.

She came into the study. "The concert will be coming on in five minutes. If you want me to listen to it with you, I'll stay."

He said fondly, "Only if you want to."

"I want to try to like music, Martin, so we can share it together."

Try to like it! Mozart and Bach, their celestial mathematics! The glory and the peace, like stroking fingers, like quiet hands. "All right," he said, and turned the dial.

There was static. A voice rumbled. Then it came clearly. "At seven fifty-five this morning, a large force of Japanese planes attacked the United States naval facilities at Pearl Harbor, inflicting great damage on Ford Island, as well as at the army air base, Hickam Field. Casualties are mounting—"

"My God!" Martin cried.

Hazel's hand went to her mouth. She always covered her mouth when she was frightened. "Does it mean—" she began. They stared at each other, her broken question hanging in the air.

THE last thing Martin saw before he turned the bedside lamp out was his uniform hanging in the closet. For half a year uniforms had been his daily garb.

"Martin," Hazel whispered into the darkness, "how long will you be at Fort Dix?"

"Dear, I haven't the least idea."

"I know you're not supposed to tell anything, and I understand why, but—" She clung to him. "I'm trying not to cry. I'm so ashamed of myself."

"It's all right. I don't want to leave you and Enoch, either."

"Martin? You won't be angry if I ask you something?"

"Of course I won't. Ask me."

"It's something we've never talked about. Well, if you should go to England—I'm not asking whether you are, but it does seem possible—well, would you want to see her again? Mary?"

It was the first time in years that anyone had spoken the name aloud to him. "You know that's over," he said softly. "Long before I met you. And now we're married."

"Yes, we are truly, aren't we?"

She picked up his hand and kissed the palm. So soft! Why did women make a man feel as if he held their lives in his hand? He'd better be worthy of this trust! He would cause no pain and no tears, ever. No, never, never.

CHAPTER NINE

FIRST he put the lamp out, then pulled the blackout curtains aside. The outline of the main building was inked against the sky. Set in woods a half mile outside of London, it had once been a sanatorium for the nervous diseases of wealthy Englishmen, casualties of the peace. Now it had been turned over to casualties of the war.

How many years, Martin wondered, might this go on? He had confused emotions when the wounded were brought in: thankfulness that he was not lying on a stretcher, and shame that he was not.

He spent long hours with his patients. Some of them touched him especially.

A boy from North Carolina told him, "I was sure I was going to be killed in this war. I never thought about anything like this."

"This" was a shattered arm and a ruined face. Martin had been more successful with the arm than the plastic surgeons had been with the face. On the left side the patched cheek was tight and immovable, while out of a raw socket glared a glass eye.

"Tell me, Doc, I mean, do you think that girls will—"

Girls will shudder and pretend and be very, very tactful; at least most of them will, I hope.

"Sure, why not? You're a kind of hero, son."

Could he tell these young men the truth of what he felt, that their wounds were a personal affront to him? An outrage? We are outraged when vandals destroy a painting, but *this?*

By the end of his first year in the army Martin was a full colonel. His life had evolved into a routine, as if he were a bank clerk, except that his work was to mend the wreckage of the war. When the working day was over, he would wash his hands and go to dinner or, now and then, up to London. It was absurd, surrealistic. The only remedy was not to think about it much.

Long afterward, Martin couldn't recall where he had been going, only that he had been hurrying down a London street when he saw in a gallery window a watercolor: three red birds sat on a wire fence. He stood quite still.

It's not the same, he thought. That other had a background of snow, and this picture was dark green, full summer. Yet the resemblance was unmistakable.

He went inside. An elderly lady came forward and he asked about the picture.

"It's a nice piece, isn't it? It's part of an amateur exhibit the gallery is sponsoring. The proceeds go to needy children."

"Is the artist perhaps—"

"Her name is Mrs. Lamb. She's given us quite a few things."

"I'd like to buy it," Martin said.

"How very nice. The lady will be so pleased. She brought it in from the country just last week."

When he got back to his room, Martin took the picture out of its wrapping. In the lower left-hand corner she had placed her initials: MFL. Slowly he traced the letters with his fingernail.

So she was still living at Lamb House with Alex! But of course, he had expected nothing else. And he wondered whether by now any other man had come into her life, and if so, who and how.

Some three weeks later, on a Saturday afternoon, Martin stepped out of a train and walked down the village's High Street. The church, he recalled, was on the left. There one turned into a country lane that led to Lamb House.

He had taken no more than a few steps up the lane when he saw

375

Mary. Her back was toward him. She was hoeing the cabbage that had been planted on the front lawn. He felt a powerful urge to go away. Afterward, he wondered whether he might have done so if she had not looked up at that moment.

She stood still as he approached. She wore a white shirt and a brown skirt. There was a smudge of earth on her cheek.

"I bought your red birds in London," he said.

She looked at him, not understanding. "What are you doing here?"

"Here? Or in England, do you mean?"

"You've just come to England?"

"No. Since last fall."

They stood looking at each other for a minute.

"You've not grown any older," she said.

"Eleven years older."

The years had told on Mary. There were some lines on her forehead, and a thinning of her cheeks so that the enormous eyes were deeper.

"Is Alex here?" he asked.

"With Montgomery in North Africa. He volunteered."

There seemed then nothing to say.

"You're well?" she asked. "Your family's well?"

"My family?"

"Your wife. Your boy. Aunt Milly writes to me sometimes. That's how I know."

The word "wife" flustered him. "Oh, yes, yes, everyone is well," he answered awkwardly.

"I was glad to hear you're seeing Claire again."

He thought, How correct she is! The sun, glittering in his eyes, gave him an excuse for looking away. He felt he hardly knew this woman.

"Will you come inside, Martin? We have five children now and I have to help with the supper."

He was astonished. "Five?"

For the first time she smiled. "No, no, mine are away. Ned's in the RAF and Emmy and Isabel are at boarding school. These are evacuees from the bombing."

He followed her into the house and sat down stiffly with his cap on his knees while she laid the places at the carved oak table. He shouldn't have come.

"Have you arrived by car?" she asked abruptly.

"No, I took the train."

"Then you'll have to stay the night. The last train's already left."

"I'm sorry. I never thought—"

"It's all right. We've plenty of room."

He tried desperately to think of something to say. "All these children. They're quite an undertaking."

"Not really. They keep me company. But I'm afraid you'll find it bedlam here until they're asleep."

"I shan't mind," he answered politely. It seemed to him they were behaving like relatives who no longer liked each other very much.

A FIRE was snapping on the hearth when Mary came into the room. "I'm sorry I took so long. Hermine—she's the youngest—still cries sometimes for her mother." Kneeling, she stretched her hands out to the fire. A tall clock ticked, making a lonely sound in the stillness. At the supper table the children had created distraction. Now again there was nothing to say.

Mary stared somberly into the fire. Presently she looked up. "Are you happy, Martin?"

The question startled him, and he evaded it.

"Can anyone be happy in 1943?"

"Tell me about your children. First, Claire."

"Oh," he answered, "Claire's going to be *somebody!* Whatever she does will be on a large scale. She'll have a great deal of joy or a great deal of pain. Probably both."

"That's rather like you, isn't it?"

"Perhaps. But she's like her mother, too."

"I think of Jessie all the time. I suppose it's conscience nagging."

"Eleven years," Martin said softly, "and it still nags?"

"Why? Don't you ever feel it?"

"Yes," he said. "But talk about something else."

"All right. Tell me about your little boy."

"Enoch was three when I last saw him, a quiet, sweet baby. Very different from Claire."

Mary rose from her knees to sit near the fire, resting her hands on the arms of the chair.

"So—Alex volunteered?" Martin asked.

"Yes. He had strong convictions about the Nazis long before most people did, and he wanted desperately to go."

"He's a man of spirit."

"If he weren't, I don't think I could have stood it all these years."

"Has it been terribly hard, even so?"

She clasped her hands. He had forgotten that passionate young gesture of hers. "I don't know. Maybe I wouldn't have been as close to my children if things had been different."

"You've been very strong, Mary."

"You do what you have to do," she said quietly. And then she smiled, and with that courageous, lovely smile, time contracted. Eleven years was yesterday.

"Blue eyes don't belong in such a dark Spanish face. Or is it Greek?" he said.

"There's no Spanish in me, or Greek either, Martin."

He stood up. She was so close that he could see the pulse in her throat, could even see a glistening of tears.

"I didn't come here to begin it all again."

"Oh, my dear, I know that."

Enormous happiness surged in him. He could have shouted to the skies. He could have sung.

How COULD he ever have convinced himself it was over? He had wanted to believe that those few days on the coast of France so long ago had been simply an interlude, one of those delights, mingled with a piquant grief, that life occasionally bestows. Now he knew those days had been not an end, but a beginning.

They met in Mary's flat in London or at Lamb House or at an inn near the hospital. The less one has of money or time, the more skillfully one learns to use them. An hour for a supper, one night in the flat—these were the equal of weeks in an ordinary life.

In stormy weather they took shelter in museums or stopped to watch Lady Cavendish—Adele Astaire—dancing with GIs. They wandered the streets. One day Mary took Martin to the place where Alex's mother had been killed in the 1940 blitz. "She was on her way to a shelter and was hit not six feet from the entrance." The very earth was mutilated, an open wound filled with a rubble of blasted stone and tumbled brick.

"Come," Martin said. "Come now."

Back in the flat they sat down to their plain supper, boiled potatoes and eggs, eaten by candlelight. Her hands, which had once worn polished nails, looked rough. The naturalness of these things made him feel married to her. "You look tired," he said. "With that house and those children, aren't you doing too much?"

"There are only two left. The others have gone back to their families. Anyway, you do too much also."

"I have no choice. Besides, I'm used to it."

"And I'm not. I've been spoiled all my life."

"That's not a word I would ever use about you."

"But it's true, Martin! All that life we had before the war, that's over. I only hope we'll be able to hold on to Lamb House."

"I hope so. I know what it means to you."

"Oh, not for me! For Alex and the children. It's their heritage."

"Not for you?"

"When the war's over," she said quietly, "I'll leave Alex. The girls will be grown then, and it won't matter anymore. We've lived under the same roof so long, he and I. But it's time."

He wanted to say, Then you and I? But a packet of unopened letters lay in his pocket, like a warning hand. They had arrived that morning from home. Home. So long ago! So far away!

He shook his head. Not now. She hasn't left Alex yet. Just let pure sweetness flow tonight. Imagine flowers on the table. Think of Mary wearing velvet again. Remember night birds, lemons, the sigh and crash of the sea.

HE DOZED. He had been on his feet in the OR for eighteen hours straight. Mary stroked his forehead. Her fingers soothed and soothed. A pity to waste our little time together in sleep, he thought, and struggled to keep awake, but lost.

He woke abruptly. Mary was sitting near the telephone, her head in her hands. He saw that she had been crying.

"You didn't hear the phone," she said.

"No. What is it?"

"They called from home. My friend Nora did. She didn't want me to walk in alone and find the telegram. It's Alex. He's dead. Oh, Martin, Alex is dead!"

Kneeling on the floor, he put his arms about her waist. "I'm sorry. I'm so sorry. He was gentle, he was kind." For a long time he held her with her head resting on his. At last she spoke.

"How am I going to tell Ned and the girls? I won't be able to think of any words."

"You'll think of them."

"Emmy's been homesick. I've spent hours on the telephone with her and Isabel. They've been so afraid for their father."

"You'll know what to say. Tell me, isn't Ned stationed near me?"

"About an hour's drive, I should think. Oh, could you?"

"There's a fellow in transport who'll get me a car. You remember, he's dropped me off a few times at Lamb House?"

"I remember," she said. She put down her head and began to cry again.

WINTER fog hung in the trees. The car was an open one, and the cold beat about their heads as Martin drove. The boy stared straight ahead, his first tears shed and swallowed. They sped through villages, deserted, as afternoon neared evening.

"You know he's to get a medal for heroism?" Ned spoke unexpectedly. "He saved four lives. Crazy, isn't it?"

"Crazy? I don't understand what you mean."

"He didn't have to go to fight, that's what I mean. They wouldn't even have taken him if they'd known."

"Known what?"

The boy turned toward Martin. His Adam's apple bobbed. "Why—what you know. Don't make me say it when you already know."

"I see." Martin was appalled. "Who told you?"

"I heard it around the village years ago."

"I see," Martin said again.

"People are rotten about it. Some boy said he couldn't fight his way out of a paper bag. They won't be able to say that now." They rode on silently until Ned spoke again. "My father said you were the only person who'd really understood."

"You spoke of this with him?"

"Yes. After I'd first heard talk, I went and asked him. And he told me. I guess it's one of the hardest things a man might ever have to tell his son. But he did it."

"And how did you feel?"

"Sick about it. I ran out of the room and cried. I couldn't even look at him for days. But then, after a while, I realized that he was a better father than most of my friends had."

A boy like this one could make a lot of people ashamed of themselves, Martin thought.

"I felt sorry for Mother, though," Ned went on. "She stayed because of the girls and me. I knew that."

"She loved her children. You were worth it to her."

At Lamb House, the driveway was full of cars. With his arm around Ned's shoulders, they walked together, Martin with Mary's boy, into the house.

A WEEK or more before the sixth of June in 1944, Martin had gone south on medical affairs and stood where one could look across Southampton water to the Isle of Wight. From Weymouth Bay across to Portland Bill lay a thousand ships or more, destroyers, landing craft and minesweepers. So in his bones he had known, and was therefore not surprised to be awakened toward morning on the sixth of June by the sweep and drone of hundreds of airplanes flying overhead. It had begun.

The first announcements, oddly enough, came via German radio: "The Allies have attempted a small landing on the coast of France."

Later in the morning a short statement came over the BBC: "Allied naval forces, under the command of General Eisenhower, began landing Allied armies on the coast of France."

By noon the churches are filled. Old men and women with sons, and young women with husbands, bow their heads to pray. Through summer and autumn the momentum quickens. Paris is liberated; de Gaulle strides down the Champs Elysées. Then, in dark December, the Germans gather strength for their last stupendous effort in the Ardennes. At first the radio brings bleak reports. But in the end, the stupendous effort fails and, late in the winter, the Germans are driven back. The Allies cross the Rhine at Remagen Bridge. The war in Europe is as good as over.

One day, Mary speaks what for many weeks has been unspoken between them. "They'll be sending you home soon," she says.

HAZEL wrote, "Lorraine Mays tells me your unit is to be home by summer. She was surprised you hadn't told me, but I understand, darling. You didn't want to raise my hopes until you could be absolutely sure."

There were only three weeks left before departure.

One day in London, Martin saw in a toy shop a wooden horse like one that Enoch had played with. Later he had an errand that took him past the Brompton Oratory, where he had pushed the newborn Claire in her perambulator. He was trembling when he arrived back at the hospital. He sat down at his desk before a sheaf of records that had been left for his signature. The words made no sense.

Was there any way he could request postponement? He needed time! Time to think! But of course that was nonsense. He put his head down on the desk.

Write to Hazel? Take courage and put it all on paper? For one sharp moment, he saw her sitting at the desk where she used to read the mail; he saw her eyes crinkling in a smile as she opened his letter. He shivered.

Go home and tell her then. Give her, as gently as you can, the truth. But what of Enoch? What of Claire? *Carpe diem*, it is said; seize the day, seize life. I'm forty-four years old.

That night he knelt beside the chair where Mary sat knitting. He took the wool away and kissed her wrists. Had he been asked what he was feeling, he could have said it was not worship, it was not comfort, it was not joy or desire. It was all of these and it

was beyond them. It was beyond the farthest reach of longing.
"I can't go away," he said.

After a few days another letter came.

Enoch will be in the second grade next fall, imagine! He wanted
to have a picture of you in his room, so I had a duplicate made
of the one on my night table. It's the last thing I see at night and
the first thing I see in the morning. I think sometimes that if you
were to stop loving me, I couldn't bear it. But then I know that
couldn't happen any more than I could stop loving you.

Martin reread the letter as he sat in the London flat. If only
there were some meanness in her, some selfish streak which could
assure her survival while it gave him an excuse!

He went down to the street. Mary wouldn't be in from the country until later, and he needed to move. In the middle of London
Bridge he lit a cigarette, then threw it into the iridescent, oily
water of the river below.

Some soldiers passed. Hearing their muttered, "Had too many,
that one!" he realized that they had heard him groan. Did he look
as wretched as he felt?

Mary was asleep on the sofa when he let himself in. Dismayed,
he remembered that he had left Hazel's pages scattered. She had
picked them up and placed them on the table.

She opened her eyes. "I didn't read it," she said. "It's from home,
isn't it?"

"Yes." And kneeling down, he laid his head on her lap.

"You're going home to stay?"

"Yes," he murmured.

She got up and, going to the window, pressed her cheek against
the glass. At last she said, "A commitment. I understand."

He couldn't answer. What words could he have found?

"Our timing is always wrong."

"That's certainly true."

"Bitterness is ugly, Martin. And I am so damn bitter."

When she came out of the bedroom in the morning, he had already collected his things.

"Just your clothes, Martin? Not the Churchill mug or the Rowlandson prints I gave you or anything?"

"Only your *Three Red Birds*. I don't want anything else."

They stood in the little hall. "Do you think we'll ever be in the same place at the same time again?" Mary asked.

"I don't think so."

"If we ever are, I'll walk quickly away, and you do the same. Will you promise me, Martin?"

"I promise." Was he absolutely mad to be doing what he was doing, or was it the only way to keep from going mad?

They went downstairs and out to her car. She got in, then looked up at him. "Are you all right?" he asked. "Can you drive?"

She nodded. He wanted to say, Oh, my dear, my love, forgive me. And he said nothing.

She put out her hand and touched his. Her little car began to move. Martin turned and rapidly, blindly, walked away.

Visions

CHAPTER TEN

MARTIN was propelled by events. He needed only to stand still and be swiftly moved as if on a conveyor belt, from that first moment of hearing Hazel's glad shaking cry, then of catching the cheerful little boy up in his arms.

Claire came, quieter now, wearing a feminine blue dress. He talked with her about college. Should it be Smith or Wellesley? Where were the better science programs? The telephone kept ringing, and friends arrived. One evening the door was opened to Perry Gault, back from the Aleutians; a week later, Tom Horvath telephoned from California that he was on his way home.

On the first Sunday they could borrow a car, Hazel and Martin went to visit the Horvaths. The men hid great gulps of emotion, then sat down to eat one of Flo's enormous dinners.

"You've still got your appetite," Flo observed.

And Martin answered that, yes, there hadn't been much good eating in England. So he filled himself, while Hazel watched, not able to take her eyes away. He was grateful for Enoch, who demanded his attention and made a kind of natural barrier between himself and Hazel's intensity.

He was in a hurry to be busy again. Work would be his salvation. The first thing he had to do was open an office. He had been prepared to borrow the considerable money needed. But when Hazel showed him how much she had saved from his allotment checks, he saw there was more than enough. He was much moved.

They needed a new apartment, for without doubt they would soon have another child. Not a day went by without mention of it from Hazel. Martin had no real objection. No desire, either.

As with their first home, Hazel had free reign with the new one. Only his study was to remain as always, a refuge for books and music and plants. He considered hanging Mary's *Three Red Birds* above the bookshelves. But then he realized it would be an affliction to him every day, and he laid it away at the top of a closet.

He began to fit back into the routines of home: the sounds of Enoch roller-skating down the hall; Claire's dropping in after school; Hazel's resumption of needlework classes and PTA.

"It's almost as if you hadn't been away, isn't it?" she remarked during the third month. "I was afraid we'd never make up for our lost time, but it's not been like that at all."

The following spring Hazel gave birth to another boy, whom they named Peter. He gave promise of being placid, like Enoch.

They made plans to rent a house in Westchester for the summer, near the beach yet close enough to the city so that Martin could commute. On busy days, he would stay in the apartment.

So they were on their way, he in the hospital, Hazel at home, both of them in a bustle of work and children and meals, of coming and going and living.

AT THE far end of the apartment's hall was a dank room used for storage. Inevitably Enoch was drawn to it. His mother objected that he messed it up. But since the room was only a jumble, Claire didn't see what additional harm the child could do.

There were cartons of dusty books, two old microscopes, his grandfather's medical kit, phonograph records of Caruso. Now to all these had been added some possessions of Grandmother Farrell's, sent on after her funeral. Claire sat down on a broken chair. She was minding Enoch, Peter and the newest baby, Marjorie, until their parents came home.

"Look," Enoch said, "the hinge broke off."

"That's Dad's old trunk. Don't go prying in it, Enoch."

He had already pulled out a uniform. "Gee, look at the hat!" It came down over his little head, while the visor grazed his eyebrows. "Why didn't Dad ever show me this before?"

"I guess he'd just as soon forget about the war."

"Look at this! 'Washington High School, Martin T. Farrell.'"

"That's a diploma. You'll have one someday."

"Will you?"

"I'd better, if I want to get into Smith and then med school. What have you got there?"

"It's pictures."

"Here. Put them back in the envelope. You're tearing it!"

A packet of snapshots fell to the floor. The faces were clear: her father's and an unknown woman's. They had been taken during the war; her father was in uniform. The woman was slender; her hair was short and curly. In one photograph they were holding hands. On the back was written: "You are everything to me and always will be." The signature read: "Mary Fern."

Heat rose into Claire's face. Mother's sister, Mary Fern! This must be the reason one was forbidden to ask about her! Mary Fern and my father! He had intentionally hidden these pictures, he so meticulous, who never left things lying around! He wouldn't have kept them if they hadn't meant "everything" to him, too!

"Come," she said to Enoch. "We're putting this stuff away." She slipped the snapshots into her purse, replaced the uniform in the trunk, and led Enoch out into the kitchen to feed him cookies. Then she wandered into Martin's den, trying to fit the part of her father she knew—analytical and serious—with the man in the snapshots. That there could be such—such taint in one's own family!

The door opened, and Hazel came in with Martin. "We hurried back as fast as we could," Hazel said. "You're a dear to baby-sit, Claire. Was Enoch a good boy?"

"Oh, yes. And the babies are still napping."

"I'll get them up," Hazel said.

For a moment Claire stared at her father. It crossed her mind that in the flash of a few seconds her concept of him had changed. It was the angle of view that mattered. The woman who had written "You are everything to me" must have seen him one way. Hazel had another view. And Jessie? Her view was well hidden.

Hazel came back with the newest baby, Marjorie, drooped over her shoulder. The mother and the child wore the same expression of innocent, domestic tranquillity.

"You'll stay for supper, Claire?" Martin asked.

"Thank you," she said coldly, "I'm going home."

They had talked till past eleven. Then Jessie parted the curtains and stood thoughtfully looking out into the night. "You shouldn't have taken the pictures," she said.

"I stuck them into my purse and then I didn't know what to do with them." The snapshots lay spread out on the coffee table. Claire picked one up, then slapped it down. "How I would hate her if I were you!"

"Oh, I've had my fill of hatred, make no mistake about that!"

"She spoiled your one chance. She could have had dozens, couldn't she? And she took your only one."

"Yes, she did." The love seat at the fireplace held small silk pillows, round as jewels. Jessie fussed with them now, patting and rearranging. "Yet I always knew I'd been foolish to marry Martin. And after all that—happened—it would have been more foolish to hold him. Fern ought to have married him in the first place. I knew it the first time I saw them together."

"What? Love at first sight?"

"Don't scoff! It happens."

"It's just not real."

Jessie smiled. "You're sure you know what's real and what isn't? You're sixteen and you already know that?"

"Well, I read, don't I? I see things, don't I?"

"But you haven't lived them."

Jessie played with the gold chains at her neck. She wore too many and they were too valuable. Why were they so important? Claire wondered. "So you're saying they couldn't help it? That sounds almost noble."

"Noble! I? No, it's just that I've had to come to terms with things or go crazy." She looked at the photographs. "You can keep these or destroy them."

"Not return them?"

Jessie shook her head. "They'd wreck that family."

"You care if they do?"

"There are children. How can one wish that on children? And besides, that woman—Hazel—never did anything to me." Jessie got up and stroked her daughter's hair. "Now come to bed. You've had a hard time. You've done a great deal of growing up today."

Alone in her room, Claire stood brushing her hair. Suddenly it came to her, so suddenly that she stopped the brush in mid-stroke, that she pitied her father. He who was able to solve everything—she pitied him! And in this pity there was something new, another kind of love. Wasn't that strange?

THE day the new office opened, Martin had been terrified lest he had undertaken too much and wouldn't be able to afford it. But he need not have worried. Very quickly the appointment book began to fill. His old friends in the profession kept the referrals coming, and it became clear that, for the first time in his life, he would not be short of money, would even have it to spare.

One afternoon he sat at his desk before the office had begun to fill. "You're early," his secretary said. "There's no one booked till one thirty."

"I know, Jenny. I finished early at the hospital." The truth was he hadn't finished in any way he wanted to finish. The patient, a young father, had died. Thrusting aside the sandwich and coffee on the desk, he went over the morning's agony.

Even before the hemorrhage started, he had known. Disaster had a certain feel and smell. From the growth attached to the carotid artery, the blood had just come gushing. Bearing down on the gauze packing, he'd used his whole strength in an attempt to stop the flow, but it had kept coming.

"The cardiograph is flat," Perry Gault had finally said. The words were mournful, final. "There's no heartbeat."

Martin had drawn off his gloves and slapped them furiously to the floor. Then he had gone down to the waiting room to tell the family that the son, the husband, the father was dead.

Later he had talked to Perry, protesting. "It need never have been, if I'd gotten to him a year ago."

"I know," Perry said softly. He had always been a foil when Martin was in trouble, offering some cheerful comment or remark to offset a stillness in Martin, offering as now his listening silence when events exploded.

"Idiots!" Martin cried. "Treating him for a neurosis when he complained of headache! Pressure of the job, they said. It's shameful. Talk of the unity of the neurological specialties!"

Now Martin's secretary opened the door. "Thought you might want a second cup of coffee, but you haven't touched a thing," she said reproachfully.

"I know. I've been thinking."

"You've only got another fifteen minutes."

Obediently he unwrapped the sandwich and leaned back in his chair. On top of his desk lay a letter from Mr. Braidburn, asking whether Martin had any suggestions for a most excellent young man who wanted to go to America. He had done some fine research in neuropathology and would like to combine that with surgical training. Could Martin find a place for him?

Research! A kind of angry shame crept over Martin. What had he to offer such a man? Very little, except what Eastman had offered him: a chance to do important surgery and make money. There was nothing wrong in that. But it wasn't what he had had in mind at the beginning, was it?

Jenny knocked at the door. "There's a man outside who says you operated on his son-in-law this morning."

"Let him in."

Martin stood up and put out his hand. "I'm so sorry, Mr.—"

"Ambrose." The man was slight, tired and apologetic. "I just took my daughter home."

"Oh," Martin said again, "I'm so sorry!"

389

"You did your best, Doctor. It was too late. I knew that."

"You knew? How could you?"

"No reason." The man held his fedora on his knees and kept smoothing the crown with his hand. "It was just a feeling. So my daughter and I talked about it. We thought, If Michael dies, we want to know why."

Because, Martin said silently, the diagnosis was delayed. And there's not enough cooperation between the fields.

"We want to help so it won't happen again. I've read about all this research in brain diseases, so I've written you a check. We want you to use it wherever you think best."

"It's five hundred dollars," Martin said. "I don't want to take it. There are children."

Mr. Ambrose stood up. "Dr. Farrell, it's the way we want it."

They stood there looking at each other, with the presence of the dead boy between them. Then Mr. Ambrose shook Martin's hand. "Thanks, Doctor," he said, and went out.

Martin got up and walked around the room, picked up a book, put it back, and sat down again. He looked at the snapshots: his children with Hazel; himself with Claire at Smith College; his father, standing on the running board of his first car.

"You will learn things I couldn't dream of," Pa had said.

Braidburn's letter still lay on Martin's desk. Oh, if he had a place to take in that young man, he knew exactly what it would be like! He'd planned it, outlined it on many a sleepless night.

The whole problem of circulation in the brain—there was so much he wanted to find out! And it would have to be combined with surgery. Psychiatrists would be welcome, too; they'd be needed in problem-solving.

He thrust a fist into his palm. There'd be room then for Braidburn's protégé, and many more. Perry Gault, of course, to head anesthesiology; good, dependable Perry at one's side.

As soon as Martin reached home that evening, he called Robert Moser. "Hello, Bob? This is Martin Farrell."

"Everything all right with you?" The voice held surprise. Martin had never called Moser at his home before.

"Yes, but I want to talk to you about something. You may re-

390

member years ago I mentioned my—well, pipe dream of a neurological institute here at the hospital?"

"I remember."

"Well, something happened this morning that has galvanized me into action. And since you're a trustee, it seemed logical to begin with you."

"Money's not plentiful, Martin. You're talking millions. And besides, there's no lack of neurological centers."

"True. Although they're not exactly what I have in mind. But aside from that, don't you think our hospital, one of the finest in the country, deserves this honor, this crown on its head?"

Moser smiled. Martin could hear the smile in his voice. "You put it well. You'd like to run it, naturally."

"I'd like, Bob, to teach and do the research I've been missing. That's what I'd like."

"I'd never get the trustees to go along."

"Once the building's up and the work is being done, they'll be the first to applaud, I promise you. And, Bob, I'm going to do it, even if you won't help me. I already got my first contribution this afternoon."

"How much?"

"Five hundred dollars."

There was a silence. "You're not serious, Martin? Just what do you think you can do with five hundred dollars?"

"The Chinese have a saying, 'Every journey begins with the first step.'" Suddenly inspired, he cried, "Bob, if there hadn't been this kind of drive all through the history of medicine, your daughter wouldn't be playing tennis now."

Again there was a silence, much longer this time. At last Moser sighed. "Okay, Martin, you've got me. Get some figures together so I'll have some idea of what we're talking about."

"All right. Give me three weeks. I'll call you."

"Fine, Martin. You do that." And Moser hung up.

ARRIVALS and departures made a modest bustle in the Connaught Hotel as Fern waited for Simon Durant in the lobby. He hadn't wanted her to go upstairs with him to meet the customer.

He'd be able to get a better price for her work if she wasn't present, he said.

The money would be very welcome, she reflected. Alex had told her there wasn't sufficient inherited wealth to live on, and there certainly wasn't.

She opened the newspaper to the critic's column which had delighted Simon. "Not to be missed," she read again, "is the exhibit by M. F. Lamb at the Durant Gallery. Once past the earlier works, all seemingly in mourning in a gray-black world, and influenced, it is rumored, by depression after the loss of her husband in the war, one will be enchanted by a lyricism which recalls the young Matisse. Her paintings display a balanced organization and taut harmony." And so on.

Well, it was all wonderful. It would never have happened if she hadn't met Simon a few summers before. He'd given her a tremendous push, and, she saw clearly, he had forced her to grow. Recognition was tonic. She *was* doing better work.

The elevator opened and Simon came out. By his smile she knew that negotiations had gone well. "Sorry to keep you," he said.

"I haven't minded. It went all right, then?"

"Splendidly. We got our price. Shall we have lunch?"

"But I've got the car in town, and I wanted to drive home this afternoon."

"Can't we at least have a quick salad or a sandwich someplace? I never get to see you."

"You do. We had dinner only last Sunday."

"Well, but this is Friday, isn't it?"

She smiled. "All right, then."

They sat at a table in a bay window. Simon gazed out to the street, his lively face gone still. Ordinarily he had so much to say. He talked with a great deal of sophistication and yet very little skepticism—an unusual combination. He was an attentive listener, too. Sometimes he looked at her as if he were seeing far inside, as if she could hide nothing from him.

She glanced over at him. A few gray strands had come into his sandy hair. He would stay young for a long time, being of the thin, supple type that at eighty remembers how to dance.

Presently he asked, "Everyone all right at home?"

"Oh, yes. I heard from Emmy yesterday. She still adores Paris. I don't suppose she'll ever come back."

"You never know. She may marry a sturdy British businessman."

"Maybe," she agreed.

Silence. Why was it especially awkward today?

"Strange how different my daughters are. Emmy knows four languages, so she's perfect in the European business world. I can't see her satisfied living Isabel's life, having babies."

"I didn't know Isabel was—"

"No, not yet, but I'm sure she will be. She and her husband both want lots of children."

"The way it looks," Simon said, "you'll be rattling around alone in Lamb House, won't you?"

"Well, I don't know. It was left to Ned, naturally, although I have the right to live there as long as I want. When Ned marries, of course, I'll move out. Although he doesn't show any signs of settling down. He's due back from Egypt soon, but someone's put a bee in his bonnet about America. I really think it's just change he wants. He ought to do splendidly in advertising."

"Of course, New York's the base for that."

"So, very likely he'll be flying off again. I miss him," she said simply.

"From what I see, children are ungrateful wretches. You put everything you've got into them, and all they do is forget you."

"They have to live their own lives, Simon."

"I suppose." He took a cigarette from the pack, choosing it carefully, lighting it, blowing the curled smoke toward the ceiling. Then he ground it roughly out and reached across the table for her hand. His own was trembling.

"Marry me," he said. "I've been on the verge of asking you so often. I've all but said it a dozen times."

"I know." His gaze was so strong that it frightened her. I am not ready for this, she thought.

"With a little encouragement from you, I would have said it long ago. Well, now I am saying it. Marry me, Mary."

"You just called me Mary," she said. "No one ever does."

"You told me once you liked it better. I try to remember that. I try to remember everything you like."

"You're so good," she said. "There's no other word," and tears sprang into her eyes.

"I know I'd take second place to Alex." She didn't reply.

"I would be good for you."

She looked up. "Oh, I wish I could," she cried. "Oh, Simon, you deserve so much better!" Tears rolled down her cheeks.

"Don't cry," he said gently. "We'll go now. I'll take you to your car."

The top of the little automobile was down and the rushing wind calmed her. That Simon's proposal should have been so painful! Dear trusted friend! What was wrong?

That ache. That other. Still she saw him as on that last morning, walking down the street, walking out of her life. She had not been on that street since. The flat had been given up, the excuse being, and it was true, that it was too expensive to keep.

Her thoughts ran in tangents. Even Lamb House could only be maintained by opening it to the public two days a week. But the house speaks to me, she thought. Martin saw that. "You love each tree," he told her once. It always came back to Martin. Everything always came back to him.

The car moved off the highway and slowed around the curve of the road. It crept up the drive and into the garage at Lamb House.

The maid, Elvira, had seen her from the window and come running. "There's a young lady in the hall. She's been waiting. An American, I think."

In THE summer before their final year at Columbia University's College of Physicians and Surgeons, five young women were traveling through Europe. They followed the route trod by generations of students; through Italy's museums, cathedrals and ruins and up over the Alps, northward to the château country, and at last across the Channel to London, with its Tower and its palaces. The group was then to spend a week in Scotland before going home. On the morning they were to depart, Claire had made a decision. Now she stood in the high, square hall of the very old house.

Someone asked, "You wanted to see me?" A thin, dark woman stood in the doorway. She could have been a young woman aging too soon, or an older one who had stayed young.

"You don't know who I am," Claire said. "But—"

"But I can guess. You're Jessie's daughter. You look like her."

"I've startled you most awfully, haven't I?"

"You've startled me, yes. Why have you come?"

"No reason except curiosity."

"Well, that's a good enough reason, I suppose."

The eyes, Claire thought; those strange, startling eyes, at once dreamlike and perceptive, they—they struck you!

And she said softly, "All that secrecy for all those years! Do you ever think how sad it's been?"

The fantastic eyes swept Claire from head to foot. "Oh, yes, I think!" The eyes looked away for a moment and then returned. "Won't you have a cup of tea with me?"

Claire followed into the kitchen. The maid had disappeared. Fern poured water into the teapot. "Come and sit down," she said.

Her long hands were clasped tightly and nervously in her lap. She loosened them and put them on the table, as if commanding herself. "I used to wear my hair like that when I was your age."

"I've seen pictures of you," Claire said. "They didn't do you justice. You're beautiful."

"Thank you."

"What shall I call you? My mother calls you Fern; once, a long time ago, my father spoke of you as Mary."

"I didn't know I was spoken of at all."

"Well, you aren't very often. But you still haven't told me what I should call you."

"Whatever you choose. I don't mind."

"Well, Mary then. Although it doesn't make much difference, does it, since I shall probably never see you again?"

Mary poured the tea. A huge white cat slept on a chair and the old clock chattered on the wall. A stranger entering the kitchen would think these two women were carrying out a daily ritual.

Mary said abruptly, "I wish I could see Jessie again. I wrote to her. I tried to explain. But she never answered."

"What could she have said?" Claire defended. "'It's all right, forget it.' She couldn't have done that, could she?"

"That's true." And the two plain syllables touched Claire.

There was a little silence until Claire spoke again. "My mother has no ill will toward you anymore."

"And you?"

"I? Well, I would hope to have some understanding of people, since I'm a doctor, or will be next year."

"Yes, I know you are."

"Aunt Milly, I suppose?"

"Of course. The town crier. That was what we called her when we were children. How is she, by the way?"

"Failing, since Uncle Drew died. She's long past eighty." Silence again. When ought she to leave? Claire squeezed more lemon into the cup, fussing to occupy her hands. "This is an enchanting house," she said finally.

"If you've finished your tea, I'll take you around."

They walked into the dining hall, Mary explaining, "It hasn't been used in years."

"But I remember it!" Claire cried.

"Yes, you were here a few times. Can you remember Emmy and Isabel, too? And Ned?"

"Only vaguely."

"Would you like to see the grounds?"

They went outside. It was late afternoon, when the sun slants at so acute an angle that the grass is gilded and trees are washed in silver light. Mary walked on the path ahead of Claire and opened the door of a small brick structure. "Here's where I work," she said.

A glass wall faced the northern sky. The other walls were covered with paintings. Even at first look, Claire saw that they were of important quality. She was stunned.

"Surely not all yours?"

"All mine."

Claire walked slowly around the room, past the fair head of a genial girl; past a spray of reddening oak leaves in a copper bowl; a slum street. "You did all this? Nobody ever told me."

396

"They didn't know. And if they had known, why should they have told you?"

Standing in the sudden stillness that fell between them, something went soft in Claire. This woman had lived through passions of which she, Claire, still knew almost nothing. She had endured and had come through to create all this. As Jessie had come through also, in her way. And Claire thought, *Women survive*.

"What is it?" Mary asked.

"I feel sad," Claire said simply.

"Yes." Mary held out her arms. "Oh, yes! We could have loved each other, you and I."

Afterward, it became clear that if Mary had known her son was to arrive from Egypt, she would not have invited Claire to stay overnight. But Ned was not expected for weeks.

Shortly after breakfast an athletic young man came striding up the driveway carrying a travel-worn suitcase. Five huge dogs clamored all over him in exuberant and loving welcome. When the greetings were past, Mary made the introductions.

"So you're the American cousin. I remember you," he said.

"You couldn't possibly. I was only three years old."

"And I was eight. You cried because of my dogs. I had to put them outside, and I was mad."

"I don't blame you. You must have hated me."

"I did," he said. The top half of his face was earnest. The bottom half had a cheerful mouth and a square chin made gentle by a touching cleft. Claire found him extraordinarily attractive.

By the end of the first hour they had learned everything that was important about one another.

"I always wanted to be a doctor," Claire had told him, along with the facts that she loved animals, music and travel; she was a night person, very forgetful and hated to cook.

He told her that he loved dogs, music and old houses. Business fascinated him. But someday he wanted to write, too—serious writing. He despised "social" people and "class." He thought he would be at home in America because there was so much less of that sort of thing there.

"I like your accent," she said. "It's so neat."

"You're free and easy. I always think Americans are like that. But I've never known any very well."

"Your stepmother is American."

"Not really. She's been here so long she even speaks like an Englishwoman."

After a moment Claire said, "I shouldn't have come."

"Why shouldn't you have?"

"Because. The air's thick with things we mustn't mention. Chiefly, my father. Do you know what I'm talking about?"

"I know. Do you want to leave?"

"No."

"I don't want you to, either."

They bought a Wedgwood plate for Jessie in the village, bicycled to a pub for lunch, climbed the church belfry, read on stained-glass windows the distinguished names of military heroes. And they talked.

"My father doesn't know I found those photos," Claire told Ned. "I guess Mary thought he would stay on after the war."

"I remember hoping for her sake that he would."

"But there was Hazel! He couldn't stay. He's steadfast."

"My father was, too, in his own way. Are you shocked over what I told you about him, Claire?"

"Not *shocked*. But, tell me, has it made you feel you have to prove you're not like him?"

"I should wish to be like him in every other way. He was one of the kindest men I ever knew."

"Well, then, as for the other, it's no crime, Ned."

"A lot of people wouldn't agree with you."

"I'm a scientist. We look at things without judgment. My father taught me that."

"You're very proud of your father, aren't you?"

"He's a great doctor. They send patients to him from all over the country. It's so strange that I can't mention him here."

It seemed to Claire that she had never spoken as easily to anyone in all her life. In the next few, swift weeks, they toured the south of England in Ned's small car. Claire would always remember wet ponies in a downpour on Dartmoor, a dinner by firelight

in a room with a seven-foot ceiling. She would remember—and later they would laugh about it—hearing footsteps outside her door one night at an inn and hoping it was Ned. It had been.

"I had my hand on the doorknob," he said, "but then at the last minute I lost my nerve."

When he brought her back to London, he said, "You'll marry me, Claire."

"Is that a statement or a question?"

"A statement, of course."

The blood ran high in her veins. She felt light, triumphant, flirtatious. "How do you know I'll say yes?"

"The same way you knew I was going to ask you," he said, laughing.

They parted in London with Ned's promise to be in New York in the fall. The parting was a tearing. It crossed Claire's mind that it had probably been the same for her father and his mother, and she thought how strange and sad that was.

MARTIN observed the audience while he waited for his turn to address the conference. He wished that Claire were here in San Francisco. But she was still in England. Hazel was sitting with some other wives six rows back. Catching his eye, she smiled.

Now his name was spoken. He was being introduced. He stood to meet a few seconds of applause, and began.

"I shall make three points," he said, "beginning with the nutrient arteries to the midbrain. It is generally understood . . ."

In plain, crisp words he made his points, noticing that one listener's forehead was knotted in thought, another looked dubious, and a pair were nodding toward each other as if to say, Yes, he's got something there.

So he came to the end, and feeling a warm internal glow, he sat down to long applause. He had done well.

Later, in the lobby, Hazel cried, "I'm so proud of you, Martin! Even though I didn't understand a word."

They walked out into full sunlight. He was filled with euphoria. His work was truly bearing fruit.

"Martin, do you mind if I stop here for a moment? Marjorie

wants a Japanese doll and I saw one in a window. I can't for the life of me think of anything for Peter, though."

"A chess set," Martin said promptly.

"Oh, do you think—" Hazel was dubious. "He's only eight."

"I'll teach him. It will exercise his brain." For Peter, who was jolly and surely not unintelligent, had as yet not much ability to concentrate.

Martin stood at the shop's entrance and watched Hazel go in. After great effort she had lost ten pounds, and this loss revealed angles in her face which had been hidden by that roundness of youth. Yet perhaps he liked this more; it gave her face strength.

But still she smiled too eagerly, too timidly. Now she was thanking the saleswoman for the fourth time. Ah, Hazel, dear, loving Hazel, of what are you afraid? Do you sense something that lies too deep for you to understand?

And with a kind of shock he realized that for the second time he had married a woman who was unsure of her own worth. Might it have been because of some insecurity of his own? There was so much one would never comprehend, even about oneself.

Hazel handed him the packages. "Don't you want anything for yourself?" he asked.

"I have everything," she answered simply.

"You were looking at a tablecloth in the hotel arcade."

"The Venetian lace? It was awfully expensive, Martin. Can we afford it?"

"Yes," he said, "we can," and was pleased at the smile which came to her lips.

Later, from the terrace outside their room, he could hear her singing cheerfully while changing into a swimsuit. He had been concerned that she would regret having come on this trip, that her mind would be at home with the children. They were her center, but they were not that for him. He was impatient with them sometimes. Hazel never was. She was so patient with Claire, too! Once, not long ago, she had even spoken up when he had scolded Claire for something.

"I'm surprised," she had said. "You so seldom criticize Claire, even when she needs it. This time she didn't need it."

Suddenly now he remembered that. And he wondered whether Hazel thought he favored Claire over the others. Because in his heart he did, and he knew he shouldn't. He had such hopes for her! And up to this minute, every one had been fulfilled.

She was doing brilliantly in medical school, had even written a paper on genetics which might possibly see publication. She would qualify for the finest training, an internship at Fisk. After that, a neurosurgical residency with him, or perhaps her interests might lie in research? Whichever, there would be a place for her on his team, father and daughter; she would—

Hazel came onto the terrace. "Sure you won't change your mind about a swim?" she inquired.

"No, you go. At the moment I feel too lazy."

"Good. It's what you need, to feel lazy." She smoothed his hair.

"Go along with you," he said, "and work up an appetite for dinner. We're going to Trader Vic's."

He lay back in the lounge chair. The good warmth of the sun went through to his bones. How he loved it! Tomorrow they'd go to Carmel, and for a whole week he'd get up early and go down to the beach to look at the endless blue, the diamond dazzle.

But now, even while he watched two sailboats heading toward the Golden Gate Bridge, his thoughts were traveling back east. They'd made tremendous progress! After six years of effort they'd reached the Dobbs Foundation at last and were moving into high gear. The crucial contact had been brought about through Bob Moser, but the decision to make the grant had come because of Martin.

"I've gone as far as I can go," Moser had told him. "You'll have to put the idea across."

And he had done so. In one fateful evening at the Mosers', Martin had been able to convince Bruce Rhinehart, then president of the Dobbs Foundation.

First Martin had produced an estimate of the cost. Then he'd shown the rough sketch of the institute wing, dog-eared by now, which he always carried in his pocket. They had talked until midnight, Rhinehart listening all the time with attentive courtesy. Finally Bob Moser had said, "We've a long way to go, Mr. Rhine-

hart, and I hope you'll see the road ahead as clearly as I do. We—
that is, Dr. Farrell here—is one of the outstanding—"

Rhinehart, observing Martin's embarrassment, had put in
quietly, "Indeed I know of Dr. Farrell. His text on neuropathology
is the current standard." And he had turned to Martin. "I assume,
of course, you will expect to head the institute."

Martin had made a small gesture of assent.

"It would be a question, then, of our gambling on you."

"To an extent, yes. Although I would hope the project would
encompass a broader span than any one personality."

Rhinehart had asked Martin in what ways this institute would
differ from existing ones.

"Naturally every man has his individual methods," Martin had
told him. "This has been part of me for so long, this conviction
about encompassing mind and brain in one study— Yes, it's done
elsewhere, of course. But I have worked out my own ideas about
modes of research and patient care."

"Well," Rhinehart had said, "I'd like you to come before my
committee and tell them everything you have been telling me."

And so they'd be laying the cornerstone sometime next spring!

He was half drowsing when Hazel came back out onto the terrace. "Oh, did I wake you? You have a letter. You won't believe
it—it says Jessie Meig on the envelope."

He sat up instantly and opened the letter, which had been forwarded from his office. He read:

Dear Martin,
   No doubt you will be astonished to receive this. I thought it
better to write than to telephone. I'll be brief. Claire has returned
from Europe with shocking news. While in England she took it
upon herself to visit Lamb House. There she met young Ned Lamb.
They spent three weeks touring together and have now decided to
be married. He is to come to New York in the fall—has a job in the
offing. The wedding will be next summer after Claire's graduation.
   You need not answer this. I shall simply assume you will do what
you can to prevent this folly.

Sincerely,
Jessie Meig

"Whatever's the matter?" Hazel cried.

He crumpled the letter. "It's Claire. She wants to get married."

"I thought someone had died, you looked so stricken!"

"It's Ned, her aunt's son. She met him in England. Went to visit Lamb House."

"But he's a cousin, isn't he? How can they marry?"

"They're not. His real mother died when he was born. She—Mary—brought him up."

"I see. Well? Does it matter, then?"

He turned on her. "Of all the stupid questions! It's an insane folly." His vehemence appalled her. "I'm sorry," he said. "You didn't mean anything. But, oh, children can wreck things!"

He pressed his lips together and leaned against the wall. There would be grandchildren. They would belong to him and to Mary. Also to Jessie. It was unthinkable! He groaned.

"Oh," Hazel cried, "I've never seen you like this! But surely it can be worked out. You don't even know the boy, do you?"

"He's been raised as her son. That's awkward enough."

"Yes, of course, but much more so for Jessie than for you. After all, you only had a few days'—affair—and never saw her again."

Suddenly Hazel annoyed him. He wished she would go inside. "Let's fly home in the morning," he said abruptly.

"But we were going down to Carmel!"

"I don't feel like it. I've got a hundred things to do at home."

"You mean you've got to see Claire." Her lips trembled. Then he thought, She asks for so little. . . .

"Let's compromise," he offered. "Four days at Carmel. I really want to get back a little sooner, Hazel."

Her eyes softened. "Fair enough. Let's dress for dinner, shall we? And try to take your mind off things a little?"

They were eating chicken in coconut sauce when a couple came to sit at an adjoining table. The man hailed Martin. "Colonel Farrell! It is you, isn't it?"

"Why, yes," Martin said, hesitating.

"Floyd Dickson. Don't tell me you don't remember?"

"Of course I do. For a moment I couldn't think."

"Meet my wife, Dot."

404

"And my wife, Hazel. Dr. Dickson and I were stationed together in England."

"I was a crummy lieutenant. Used to hang around and watch the colonel stitch the boys together."

Martin sighed inwardly. He was in need of a quiet dinner tonight. But he inquired politely, "Living in San Francisco?"

"No. L.A. I've got a pediatrics practice there. Listen, how about pushing these two tables together? That is, if you don't mind?"

"Well, no," Martin said.

Scraping and shoving, the Dicksons settled down. "I hear you're making a name for yourself," Dickson remarked. "I met a fellow this noon who'd just come from your speech. He said you're the man back east! But seriously now," Dickson addressed Hazel, "you ought to make him have a little fun, too."

She smiled. "I try."

"Sure. Take a couple of months off. We went to Greece last year. Took the cruise around the islands. Beautiful, beautiful."

"I'd like to do that sometime," Martin admitted.

Mrs. Dickson assured him he would love it. "And the shopping's incredible," she told Hazel. "Oh, I adore traveling! Two years ago I almost bought a silver service in Copenhagen. But then I thought it probably wouldn't go with our dining room—it's French provincial. What do you think?"

"I really don't know," Hazel said. "I'm afraid I'm not very good at things like that." She fell silent.

And Martin thought how much he appreciated a quiet woman.

Then Hazel, feeling a need to be more sociable, remarked, "I've always wanted to see England, but Martin doesn't want to. I guess the men saw enough of it during the war."

"I'd like to go back," Dickson declared. "Dot here is wild about old houses and all that. Say, Martin, speaking of old houses, remember that place you used to visit near Oxford?"

"No," Martin said, startled.

"Sure you must! I drove you there a couple of times. Talk of old! That house must have been three hundred years old!"

Martin asked Hazel, "Would you like a salad? I forgot to order one. Waiter, two green salads, please."

Dickson turned to his wife. "You would have flipped over that place, Dot. I never got to go inside, though."

There was no malice in the man. He simply had no idea what Martin had been doing there.

"What did they call it again? Lion House? No, Lamb House. That was it. Wasn't it Lamb, Martin, where you used to go?"

Martin raised his eyes. The anguish in them must have communicated itself to Dickson, bringing a terrible comprehension.

"Maybe I'm thinking of somebody else," he said quickly. "I rode around with so many guys, you get mixed up." A flush, like a scald, rose from the man's throat to the hairline.

A queer silence fell over the table. Presently, in a flat voice, Hazel spoke. "Ask for the check now, Martin, please."

"No dessert?" Mrs. Dickson remonstrated. "You don't know what you're missing! The pineapple—"

But Hazel had already risen. "I don't want any," she said steadily. She walked to the door. Martin excused himself and followed her. They got into a cab. "Hazel," he began.

"I don't want to talk," she said.

In their room she took off her coat and stood leaning against a table. "So you did see her in England," she said at last.

"Yes."

"You made love to her. Not just one time. You stayed together."

"Yes."

She began to weep without changing expression, a fixed face, with streaming tears. "Why?" she cried.

"I came back, didn't I? Doesn't that tell you anything?"

"Yes. It tells me that you loved your children."

"No, no. It was more than that. I thought of you," he said.

"Oh, I believe that one! I surely do believe that one!"

"But it's true."

Hazel began to speak rapidly, with mounting pitch. "You were my whole life, Martin. You were what I lived for. And to think that every loving word you ever spoke to me was a lie! Oh, my God, I understand what that poor cripple went through! What sort of woman is this, anyway, that she couldn't leave you alone? Oh, I could tear her eyes out!"

406

"Hazel, I can only beg you to try to understand my conflict. My weakness. Weigh this against our years together. I've been a good husband, you know I have—"

"Claire's marriage," she interrupted. "No wonder you can't bear the thought of it!" She flung herself on the bed.

"Be reasonable, Hazel. Please. I'll get you some medicine, a pill, to help you get through this tonight."

"I don't want a pill. Do you know something, Martin? I hate you. Whatever I felt for you all these years is gone. It left me at the table in that restaurant. Just left me."

"You're frantic and I don't blame you. But can you try to put everything aside till the morning?"

"In the morning I'm going home to my children."

"All right, we'll go home, then. Now please lie there quietly while I go out for the medicine."

When he returned, she had undressed and was lying in the bed. Her eyes were swollen. "Is there anything I can do?" he asked. "Anything that can be undone?"

"I don't see what." She spoke quietly. "You never got over her."

"But I love you," he said, not denying the other. He sat down on the side of the bed. "Please, Hazel. Please understand. I never *wanted* it to happen."

"You couldn't help it, you mean?"

"No."

"That makes it worse, doesn't it?"

In the morning they packed their belongings and flew home.

Losses

CHAPTER ELEVEN

FOR two months gloom like a heavy shroud had lain on the rented house in Westchester. On a hot September evening Martin sat alone on the porch. He wished they were back in the city. At least there he would be able to walk over to the office at night and do some paperwork. Anything to get out of the house! But school would not open for another week, and Hazel had wanted to stay here as long as possible, obviously because she could hide more easily in this place where they were merely summer transients.

She was upstairs now, already shut away in their bedroom for the night. Martin had stayed up to let Claire in. She had two days off from school and was spending the time with them.

He left the porch, wandered into the living room, picked up a newspaper and put it down again. He had been trying to straighten things out. Oh, how he had been trying, since that ghastly night in San Francisco. Hazel would sigh. Her tears brimmed unexpectedly. Sighs and tears. He wondered how long a family could hold together like this. Certainly Enoch must sense something. He was old enough now to notice things. There'd been one quarrel when they'd first come back from California, during which Hazel had been in a rage, pounding her fists on the wall. He hadn't known she was capable of such passion.

He shook his head as if to clear it and got up. From the drawer of the desk he took out a folder. "The Institute," he had scrawled on the cover. This at least was direct and clear. Every detail had its purpose, whether technical or artistic. Across the entrance he wanted a single sentence to be carved in the stone. Searching, he'd gone back, as he often did, to the Greeks. "For where there is love of man, there is also love of the art." Hippocrates.

He had begun to enjoy himself, his tension loosening, when he heard Claire's brakes screeching on the drive. She drove too fast! Impetuous, charming Claire! Capable of stunning surprises, too. He was still not over the shock of learning that she had known about Mary and himself for years, since she'd discovered those photographs.

He opened the door for her.

"Hi, Dad, how's everything?"

"Fine. Want some coffee?"

"Please." She followed him into the kitchen. "I watched the cement mixers and all the rest of the stuff at the institute today, and I got sort of choked up, thinking that it's really happening at last, and you did it."

"I and a few hundred others."

"Oh, don't be modest!"

408

"Jessie always used to tell me that," Martin reflected.

"Anyway, it becomes you. You may be sleepless with excitement, but it becomes you."

Blind, blind. She's so happy that she sees nothing else. Happy over that fellow! He'll be arriving soon, Martin thought with a sinking in his chest, and I'll have to see him. He'd already landed a good job here, at one of the city's biggest advertising agencies.

"I did a delivery today," Claire was saying. "Dr. Castle was there, but I did it all myself. I felt great."

Martin sipped his coffee. Then, forcing cheerfulness, he said, "You're growing sure of yourself, are you?"

"Yup. No butterflies in the stomach. A little clinical experience really gives you confidence."

"For a woman who ranked number five in her class last June, I should think you'd have plenty of confidence."

She smiled. Would "genuine" be the right word for her, with the still boyish curls and the charming tilted nose?

Suddenly she turned somber. "Dad, Mother simply will not open her mind about Ned and me. It seems to me one ought to be able to come to terms with the past."

He murmured, "It's not that simple. You've revived old pains. It's not only the young who feel."

"Oh," she said quickly, "oh, Dad, I know. You and Mother think you're being asked to give up the peace you've made. Mary feels the same way. Ned wrote me."

"Well, wouldn't we?"

"Yes, but— Oh, I grant it would be easier to start clean with a new family and no skeletons in the closet. It's not ideal that nobody speaks to anybody else."

Suddenly Martin was very weary. I'm tired of thinking, he said to himself. Outside, a cricket had set up frantic, repetitious chirping. "Ah, well," he managed to say, "we'll solve nothing tonight. How about some sleep?"

Claire yawned. "I've been looking forward to these two days. I plan to spend every minute on the beach tomorrow."

He watched her go up the stairs. Superb product to have come out of so strange a marriage!

In the morning Martin woke to see Hazel sitting on the other bed in her nightgown, staring at him.

"How long has this been going on?" he demanded.

"Why? Can't I look at you?"

He got out of bed without answering. In the bathroom he scraped once over his face, a sloppy job, but it would have to do. He went into the bedroom and dressed in a suit and tie. Hazel was standing now. She seemed to have lost weight during the night, her eyes were so large.

"Hazel, how long will this go on?" he asked.

"I don't know."

"It's been weeks. I've said a hundred times how sorry I am. What else can I do? Tell me what you want and I'll do it."

"What I want you can't give."

"What is it?"

"I want it not to have happened," she whispered.

Martin threw up his hands. "You've got to stop feeling sorry for yourself, Hazel. You think you're the only one who's had any trouble? People don't . . . don't"—he stumbled—"dine on champagne and strawberries every day. That's not life."

She clasped her hands. "Champagne! It would be good to have a taste of that. Oh, you've given me bread and meat—"

"Bread and meat? What are you talking about?"

"I mean, you've given me a home and you're a good father. At Lord knows what effort! Oh, how my heart goes out to Claire's mother!" This must be the fiftieth time she's said that, Martin thought. "Why, I even felt sorry for—for Fern, Mary, whatever you call her," Hazel went on. "Isn't that a joke?"

Martin felt a queer weakness draining through him. It would follow him all day. At the hospital he would dread coming home, and yet look forward to it with the hope that maybe this day something might have changed while he was gone.

"Hazel," he said deliberately, "listen to me. We are here, a family, together. We've a whole future, years and years, I hope. Even though the past hasn't been what you wanted, can't you put it behind?"

"It's all ruined. I'm a second choice."

410

"You're not a second choice. I came back to you. But I can't spend the rest of my life with someone who is so miserable."

"Then leave! Go on, leave!"

"I'm not going to leave and you know it!"

"I don't care," she said, "whether I live or die."

"Ah, you've gone crazy!"

"Damn you! Do you hear? I don't care whether I live or die!"

He walked to the top of the stairs. "You're crazy!" he shouted. "And I'm sick of it!"

She slammed the bedroom door. The vibration shook the walls. "Hazel, open that door! I can't leave like this."

No answer. He looked at his watch. Seven minutes to catch the train. The hell! He fled down the stairs and out the door.

CLAIRE woke to the sound of Hazel's voice piercing through the wall. She was crying. Martin's voice came now, an angry rumble: ". . . the rest of my life with someone who is so miserable."

"Then leave! Go on, leave!"

Embarrassed and alarmed, Claire got out of bed, dressed, and went down to the dining room. Esther, the maid, opened the swing door from the kitchen.

"Will you have cereal and muffins, Miss Claire?"

"Yes, thank you, Esther."

A moment later Hazel came in. "I thought I heard you. I'm sorry I wasn't up to greet you last night. I wasn't feeling well."

"All right now?"

"Oh, yes." Her eyelids were red and her lipstick smudged. She wore a terry robe. "I've got a suit on under this. I thought I'd go for an early swim." She sat down decorously, clearing her throat. "Have you got everything you want?"

"More than I should have, thanks. These muffins! I'd be fat as a house if I lived with you!"

"You'll never be fat. You'll be like your aunt Mary." And as Claire looked astonished, she added, "Of course, I've never seen her or your mother."

"No," Claire said.

"Do you think you look like your mother?" Hazel persisted.

411

"I don't really know who I look like." Very odd, these remarks. "Are Marjorie and the boys gone for the day? The house is so quiet."

"Yes. Their last freedom before school starts."

"You've got marvelous children, Hazel. I hope I'll be as lucky as you."

"You've got time for children, haven't you? I suppose you'll want to wait until you finish your residency with your father."

"Well, Ned and I will have to work that out," Claire replied cheerfully. "You know, sometimes I think I have all the time in the world. Then some days it seems as if I ought to hurry up and do whatever I'm going to do."

"You're in your twenties, and I'm over forty," Hazel said.

"You don't look it."

"I feel seventy," Hazel said. She got up and walked to the porch door and stood looking out.

"Everybody feels old sometimes," Claire said gently. "We all have our days."

Hazel turned to her. "Oh, do you think so? Do you think people are fundamentally alike? I ask you because you're a doctor—or almost one. You must have had a lot of experience."

"Well, the differences can be amazing sometimes. I've seen mothers frantic over a minor cut, and then last week I saw a woman with two mongoloid children. She was so courageous! I thought, I don't know how you bear it."

"I would have liked to be a doctor," Hazel said. "Nursing was as far as I got and I loved it. Except," she reflected, "except I got too personal. Some patients just touch your heart. Cancer patients, especially. Sometimes I'd turn the light out after the night's last medication and I'd think how frightened they must be, lying there in the dark and wondering how much longer they had to live. But other times I think it may not be hard to die. Maybe when people have to leave, they're ready to leave."

"Why think about things like that?" Claire cried, almost angrily. "Do you often have thoughts like these?"

"No, no, of course not. I'm sorry. It is a stupid conversation, especially for a young woman in love."

412

Claire stood up. "I think I'll put my suit on. I've a great book and I'm going down to the beach."

"I'll meet you there," Hazel said.

They swam the length of the beach and back. Hazel was a strong swimmer and she slowed for Claire's benefit.

"You could be a pro," Claire told her as she spread a towel. She had brought binoculars. It amused her to watch boats crossing Long Island Sound. "Hazel, I've been thinking. Dad and you ought to have a vacation. Why don't you go to Europe this fall? Of course, I know it's hard to get the time."

"Oh, that's not a problem, for me, anyway. I don't do anything. I'm just Dr. Farrell's wife. I go to meetings of the wives' auxiliary and I'm treated with respect because I'm his wife. Otherwise I'm nobody."

"That's not so," Claire said. "You *are* a person in your own right. Your job is raising children, and they're fine children, too. You've just sunk into routine, Hazel. You have to get away."

Hazel stood up. "I'll get away." She put on her red cap, tucking the hair in. "I'm going in again. Coming?"

"Not now. I feel like reading."

Hazel walked into the water and turned over to float.

No life except through her husband, Claire thought. Thank goodness Ned and I are a different generation.

Claire read a few pages before growing drowsy. She turned over to let the sun bake her back. Last sun of the year.

Somewhere on the beach a dog was barking. "Oh, do stop!" Claire cried crossly. She sat up and looked out at the water. Hazel had been swimming parallel to the shore. Now she was swimming away from it. What was she doing? Claire lifted the binoculars. The red cap rose to the top of a swell, sank out of sight and rose again. No doubt of it, she was swimming out! Claire stood up and ran to the shore.

"Hazel!" she called. "Come back!" and knew that she couldn't possibly be heard. She squinted through the binoculars again. The cap and the arm were growing smaller, moving away. Good God, what could the woman be thinking of?

And suddenly Claire knew what she was thinking of.

414

She thought of plunging into the water and following. But she wasn't a good enough swimmer. She scanned the beach. There was no one in sight. Then she remembered the Mayfields, two houses down. They had a speedboat moored at a little dock.

She ran. A boy of fifteen or so was in the driveway. "Please!" she cried. "Mrs. Farrell! I think she's drowning! Please get the boat!" The boy stared. "Hurry! Please hurry!"

"Miss, I'm not sure I can run the boat. I only just learned."

"Try, please!"

The boy climbed into the boat and tried the engine. It sputtered and died. Claire got in. The boy tried again. Two minutes. Three. "There, I've got it!"

Claire pointed the direction. "There! Out there in a straight line from where I was sitting! Hurry!"

Clouds covered the sun and the air grew chill. The prow pointed to the sky, then fell as the boat rose and sank through swelling hills and troughs. Claire shaded her eyes, straining and peering.

"Sure we're going right?" the boy asked.

"Yes. Yes, I'm sure." Claire gripped the seat. "You look to the right, I'll look to the left." Claire had never known such terror, such absolute, sheer terror.

The boy, holding fast to the tiller, asked doubtfully, "Could she have swum this far?"

Claire looked back at the shore, where the houses stood no larger than scattered boulders. Her teeth were clenched. Panic churned her stomach. "Let's go a little farther."

The boat pitched like a roller coaster. "We've gone a mile and a half," the boy said at last.

"Yes."

"We'd best turn back."

"Yes."

They stared at each other, the boy's face scared and wondering. Claire began to cry.

"Was she—is she your mother?"

"My stepmother. Oh, God!"

The boy became practical and manly. "We've got to call the police. And the Coast Guard."

The boat tore back toward the shore, Claire still searching the surface. Nothing. Nothing.

I didn't see, Claire thought. All the time she was talking, this desperate resolve was inside her. Oh, Hazel, poor foolish Hazel, why did you? If I'm a doctor, shouldn't I understand? But perhaps no one can know what lies inside another. In the most ordinary people lie such secrets. Old childish hurts that make us what we are, visions of what life ought to give.

The answer is, of course, there are no ordinary people.

MARTIN knew clearly what was happening to him. He understood his own progression from numbness to the most awful pity and self-accusation (If I had gone back upstairs to talk to her that morning instead of going to work) through sleeplessness, until at last depression closed around him like a curtain.

His children turned to him at table. Their eyes asked, Why?

"Eat your vegetables," he would answer kindly, "if you want to grow tall like Enoch and me."

It wasn't fair to link Enoch with himself in the rank of adults. The boy seemed younger than his age. Martin tried to remember what he had been at sixteen, but was unable to. There are times when the past closes over like waves, is hidden and drowned.

Oh, drowned.

"You spoiled my doll's hair!" Marjorie wailed at Peter. "I'm going to tell Mommy!"

Shocked, Enoch looked toward Martin. But Peter spoke first, scornfully. "Mommy's dead, don't you even know that?"

"Well, when she comes back, I mean."

"She isn't going to come back. Don't you know what dead is?"

Yes, the dinner hour was the worst. Hazel's chair now stood between the windows, facing Martin. And he recognized his puckering mouth and racing heart as symptoms of panic. He sat quite still, knowing that in a minute or two it would ease. He must pull himself together. If only he had someone to talk to, but there was no one. He certainly couldn't talk to Claire. He thought of Jessie. Curious that he should think of her! Yet, once, there had been no mind more responsive to his own.

416

Tom Horvath ought to have been the one. Trust and loyalty lay between them. Kindly Tom would claim to understand, but he wouldn't. For he had never wanted very much. But he, Martin, had wanted everything: an exquisite love, exalted knowledge, the warmth of a family, all the color and music of the earth.

His hands bore down on the arms of his chair. Rain spattered on the roof. It dropped in gusts and churned the Sound. And he sat on, listening. Was there a motif of water in his life? Flood had torn him too early from his mother's womb and killed those other children. How had his parents survived their loss?

Hazel had loved water. Sometimes they'd walked on the beach in the winter; he, disliking the cold, had done so for her sake only.

I hate this house, Martin said to himself, and all this water. We'll never go near water again.

But once back in the city, he thought, Everything is loose, life has come loose. He would sit across from a frightened patient, listening and replying, but thinking all the while of his children. I robbed them of their mother. It was too much for him.

On a raw November afternoon, the telephone rang in his apartment. "Just to remind you," Leonard Max, the hospital's chief resident, said, "we've got the Devita woman in the morning."

Martin knew he wasn't prepared to operate. "I don't think I can make it. You'd better get someone else to help you."

"I can get O'Neill," Leonard said quickly. Too quickly? "Martin, maybe you should take a rest. Sleep late, relax, spend some time with the kids."

Falling, falling. "Yes, I could do that," Martin said.

Leonard was hearty. "You'll be back better than ever."

"Thanks, Len," Martin said. He hung up and went and locked the door. Then he pulled the curtains shut, so that the room grew soft and dark, and lay down.

For a week he feigned the flu. Claire kept telephoning, but he warned her away from his contagion. He simply sat, listlessly reading the news—all discouraging, nothing but strife.

Yet he couldn't maintain the pretense, couldn't stay in hiding. He would have to force himself, find something pleasant to do. Yes, that was it, find something happy. Surely there was something colorful and happy left. Christmas shopping, perhaps, before the stores got too crowded?

So, with a careful list, he set forth. He thought he would buy a sweater for Claire, but he wasn't sure of the size. In the store he looked at the sweaters for a long time, unable to make up his mind. The saleswoman left him for another customer. "Well, when you've decided," she said. "I really can't—"

Oh, go to hell, he shouted at her silently, and left without buying anything.

On the sidewalk in front of the store he realized he was terribly tired. His overcoat weighed him down. He must go home. He tried to hail a taxi, but they were all occupied, and he began to walk. Faces wavered as he passed. He tried to focus on them, growing queasy with the effort. He began to walk faster. Something was pursuing him. The thing was coming closer, reaching for his back. And at the same time he knew that there was nothing there, that he was having what the layman might call a nervous breakdown, or at least, the harbinger of one.

When he arrived at his apartment, he was panting. His chest felt squeezed in an iron fist. Red and yellow lights swirled before his eyes.

He lay down on the bed without taking off his overcoat and thought, I'm dying.

"You can't go on like this," Claire said.

Martin opened his eyes. "What are you doing here?"

"Enoch called me. He saw you and was scared."

"No need to be. I'm weak from the flu, that's all."

"Dad, you're not fooling anyone, so don't waste your breath. Sit up," she ordered. "Let's get your coat off. I'll get you a brandy."

He felt like a child. "Claire, I'm falling apart."

She took him in her arms. "Dad. Dear, dear. No, we're not going to let you."

"There are things you don't understand. You don't know why Hazel—" But something in his daughter's expression said she might know.

418

"I've an idea. She found out about you and Mary."

Martin sighed. He put his hands on his knees. "It was in California. We met a man I'd known during the war."

Claire said softly, "If I were a man, I would fall in love with Mary, too, I think."

The room was still. No sound came from the apartment. It was as though the household had suspended its life in wait for Martin. Suddenly anxiety came fluttering back.

"Ah, Hazel!" he cried. "I destroyed her!"

"No," Claire said. "She did it herself. Other people can't destroy you, unless you let them."

"I hear your mother talking."

"Well, she's got a lot of strength. And Hazel didn't, no fault of hers, God help her."

"You make it all sound very simple," he said.

"I don't mean to. Listen to me. You've been stumbling along with a load of guilt that's enough to break your back. But you were good to Hazel. You gave her good years."

"If I could undo it," Martin began.

"Well, you can't. You know what your trouble is? You think you ought to be a saint and you're only a man. Everything in your life has to be perfect, and it can't be."

Martin laughed. He hadn't laughed in months. "You've analyzed me pretty cleverly, I think. I hope you do as well with Ned."

"Does that mean you've decided to approve?"

"No, it just means I've decided not to fight it."

They sat for a while without speaking. "I wish it could be different—joyous and warm," Martin murmured finally.

"It's all right, Dad. For me things don't always have to be perfect."

He felt something soft and calming in his chest, strength pouring back into him. It was a fine tingling, a rising of hope. And just as he had known when he had been falling into sickness, now he recognized the first faint start of healing.

The door opened and three heads appeared around its edge. "Come in," Claire called. "Don't be afraid. Dad's feeling much better. He's going to be all right."

THE NEW APARTMENT WAS complete a month before the wedding and Ned had officially moved in. Claire spent a good deal of time there, too. One night, when Ned came in from work, he was pleased to see her already there.

"You're the only person whose face truly wreathes in smiles," Claire said.

"Idiot," he replied, kissing her.

"I've brought stuff to eat, sandwiches from a deli."

"When you said 'stuff to eat,' I thought you meant you'd cooked a dinner."

"Heavens, no! I can't cook, Ned. But I'll learn. In the meantime, here's potato salad, French bread and a beautiful melon."

"Leave that a minute and sit down. I want to tell you something," Ned commanded. His eyes were smiling with excitement as he grasped her hand and pulled her down. "Listen. Anderson called me in today and said we were going to the president's office. For a minute, I got cold. Jergen never sees anybody. Then Anderson told me what it was about. They're reorganizing the offices in Hong Kong, and Jergen asked Anderson to make a recommendation for the top man and—and, Claire, I'm the one!"

"I don't understand," Claire said.

"Me! Us! I'm to be head of the office! We're going to live in Hong Kong!" And he sat back with his face wreathed in smiles.

She was perfectly sure she had heard it all correctly. Still, the thing was totally unreal. She wet her lips. "Aren't you forgetting something? I've been given one of the most desirable internships in the world here at Fisk, and a neurological residency after that. So this can't make any sense to me, Ned."

"Darling, I know it must be upsetting to you. It's so sudden." He put his arms around her, his safe arms. She laid her head on his shoulder.

"Ned, you used to dream about being an investigating journalist, exposing wrongs, you said."

"Yes, I know, that was all very fine, but you have to seize your opportunities. And this is my opportunity. Darling, I'm sorry. You've been so efficient, working so hard and still getting this apartment together. I'm just sorry to do this to you."

"Well, then, do you have to?"

"A man wants to get ahead, Claire." Ned spoke softly. "A man needs to. I want you to depend on me. That's what being a man is all about."

She drew away. Depend on him? Yes, in a way, but—

"Claire, I'm not asking you to give anything up. We won't be there for more than four or five years."

"Four or five years!"

"Yes. You'd still be young enough to begin a residency then."

"You must be crazy," she said.

"Crazy? I thought you'd be thrilled for me, Claire. I'm the youngest man ever to head a foreign office for the firm."

"Oh, Ned!" she cried. "Of course I'm terribly proud of you. I do see what a fabulous honor it is. But what about me? I can't just put my work aside for a while and pick it up again later."

"You could," he said gently. "It's not impossible."

Dumbfounded, she made no answer. And he went on, "After all, you're not a man. You don't have to earn a living."

"Earn a living!" she cried. "I thought you understood me. Medicine is all I ever wanted, Ned. It's my—my life!"

"I thought I was your life. Your love and your life."

There was a silence. At last Claire said, "What shall we do?"

He turned on her. She had never before seen his anger. "I've been trying my best to explain! We'll go where I can carve out a future for us!"

At ten thirty they agreed to stop wrangling and Claire went home. But the next evening the argument continued. "Machismo, Ned," Claire cried. "That's what it is! Maybe one day you'll learn there's more to being a woman than just taking care of a man."

"Listen, Claire. Ever since I came to New York I've seen and thought—I haven't spoken out but I will now—you're letting your father plan your life! *He* decided you would be a neurosurgeon when you were some sort of a child prodigy and now—"

"Nobody ever said I was a prodigy. Don't make a fool out of me! Putting words in my mouth, or my father's."

The air quivered between them with the intensity of a summer storm. "I'm going for a walk," Ned finally said angrily. "I need to

421

get out. Maybe it'll clear our thoughts, being quiet for a while."

She heard the elevator descend. *Whither thou goest,* and so forth. Yes, but women were different then, and I am different; not better, only different. I am a doctor first.

She got up and put on a record. This need for music was a legacy from her father. Laying her head back, she willed herself into another place and time, while Respighi's "The Birds" rustled. Thousands of birds fluttered against a background of triumphant Sunday bells. The birds filled her head. So free, whirling through the windy sky! So free!

The door opened and Ned came back. He turned the record off. "Claire," he said, not looking at her, "we've talked it all out. We've gone as far, I think, as words can take us. For the last time I ask you. Will you come with me?"

She took a deep breath. "No, Ned. I can't."

"Well, that's it, then, isn't it?"

"Yes," she said.

"Well," he began, and stopped. He opened his mouth again to speak and closed it without another word.

CHAPTER TWELVE

Judy was eight years old, and she was going to die.

Martin had been keeping her alive for eleven months. He recalled his grief when he had first opened her skull and discovered the spreading glioma multiforme. She had asked him whether he would fix her up so she could skate again. He had given her an evasive answer.

He had left an opening in her skull, covered only by scalp, so that the growing tumor might move outward instead of farther in upon the brain. Soon they would have to operate again. And then one Sunday afternoon Leonard Max telephoned.

"Martin? I'm at the hospital with Judy Wister. The intracranial pressure's shot way up."

"I'll be right over. Call Perry, will you?"

"It's Sunday. He may not be home."

"Try. I always feel better with Perry for anesthesia."

Martin hated this operation. He was not like most surgeons, who managed to be dispassionate. It was not the way he was.

The child lay on the table under the lights. Leonard Max was ready. Perry Gault came in, too, and took his place. It seemed to Martin that he was panting, as though he had come in a hurry.

He picked up the scalpel and began. Blood came spurting into the automatic sucker. He cauterized the surface vessels. Now farther, knowing that the tumor was too deep for hope. How it had grown in these few months! Like a weed it had flourished, spreading roots and arms, branches. Hopeless. Hopeless.

Why are you doing this? Because until the last breath has left the body, you do whatever you know.

The room was unusually quiet. Perry stood beside the cylinders of oxygen, listening to the stethoscope, announcing, at regular intervals, the blood pressure. Occupied with his own exploration, Martin was still alert to everything else around the table. Suddenly it seemed too long since Perry had last spoken. "Blood pressure," Martin called. He looked up. Perry was standing there with an absentminded, dreaming look, gazing out the window. "Blood pressure, Perry!" Martin called sharply now. And at that moment he saw that the oozing blood was turning dark, turning blue.

"For God's sake," he cried. "Oxygen!"

Perry leaped. He turned one cylinder up, the other one down. Oxygen purred with a soft rush. He looked up at Martin with a strange, helpless look. "I can't get the pulse," he said.

"Adrenaline," Martin commanded.

"I definitely can't get the pulse," Perry said.

"Cardiac arrest!" There was a scurrying in the room. Someone began to thump on the child's chest.

"Two amps bicarb! Open the intravenous line!" The needle of adrenaline pierced the heart; it seemed like hours and was, actually, minutes.

"The EKG is flat," Perry said finally. "It's finished."

Someone was still working desperately on the chest.

"No," Leonard Max said, "it's no use." And then he added, "Perhaps it's a mercy." Martin didn't answer. In a familiar gesture he drew his gloves off and threw them on the floor.

The mother went mad. Her scream was the most terrible sound one could ever hear. Her husband and some other young man, a brother or brother-in-law, took her to a room. A nurse came running with a hypodermic. It was over, and Martin went home.

Later, in bed, he tried to reorder his thoughts. Had the child become cyanotic because of the surgical shock or had Perry in some way failed? He had sensed something strange about Perry. But everything had happened so fast.

In the morning Leonard Max asked, "Did you see Perry yesterday, afterward?"

Martin looked up. "No, I went straight home. Why?"

"Well, there was something odd about him." He sat down. "I think—I hate to say this—but I swear he'd had a couple of drinks."

"You know what you're saying, Leonard?"

"Sure I do! I'm not saying it to anybody else, Martin. I'm only telling you."

"Did you notice anything in the OR?"

"I thought—well, I thought he wasn't paying attention. The kid should have gotten more oxygen. He wasn't monitoring."

For a minute neither of them spoke. Martin tapped a pencil on the desk. He remembered Perry looking out the window.

"Yesterday was his anniversary; they were having a party at his house," Leonard said.

Perry was not a drinker, but at an anniversary party, surely he would have had a few?

"Of course, little Judy's days were few and cruel. When you consider, it's just as well," Leonard said.

"True. But not the issue exactly."

"I wonder whether we should say anything to Perry."

"Let's wait. Maybe he'll say something."

Leonard stood up. "Right. Nothing hasty."

PERRY said, "Tough about the little girl, Martin. But I guess it was no surprise to you."

"It was a considerable surprise," Martin said distinctly.

Perry's eyebrows rose. "I don't understand. You honestly expected her to survive the operation?"

424

"I certainly did, and maybe another one like it."

They were in an empty corridor, waiting for the elevator. "Perry, were you feeling all right yesterday?"

"What makes you ask that?"

"Because she went cyanotic. You weren't monitoring."

"The devil I wasn't! What are you trying to prove, Martin?"

"I'm not trying to prove anything. Don't get excited."

"Don't get excited! When you're practically accusing me of negligence, you expect me to—"

"I'm not accusing you of anything. I was only asking in order to clear up something in my mind."

The elevator came. It was crowded. The two men stood apart, and Martin regretted having spoken.

One morning not long after, the nursing supervisor met Martin in the lobby. "I've had a call from a lawyer, a Mr. Rice. He wants to see the record on Judy Wister. It looks like trouble."

So it's come, Martin thought. My first malpractice suit. He was quite prepared when a few days later Mr. Rice came to his office. He was a garish individual with oiled hair and a rasping voice. "What is it you want to know?" Martin began.

"Nothing about you, Doctor. Mr. and Mrs. Wister specifically exclude you from any culpability in the death of their child. The matter concerns the anesthesiologist alone. We want your testimony to the effect that he was negligent as a result of being under the influence of alcohol."

"Oh, no," Martin said. "I've known Perry Gault for years, and he's the best man in his field. He's completely reliable."

"That may be true, but the fact is that on this particular day he had been drinking. Mrs. Wister's brother, Arthur Wagnalls, spoke with Dr. Gault and smelled alcohol on his breath."

Martin raised his hand. "Wait. This is all unsubstantiated. The child's uncle is not an impartial person, after all."

Mr. Rice smiled. "We have an impartial person. The nurse who attended Mrs. Wister was present when Dr. Gault and Mr. Wagnalls were talking. Afterward, Mr. Wagnalls remarked on Dr. Gault's condition, and the nurse answered, yes, it was clear to her, too. She has already given a statement to that effect."

425

Martin, stunned, resorted to pencil tapping.

"Furthermore, the records show the girl became cyanotic. Anesthesia was quickly lowered and oxygen increased after you ordered it. Dr. Gault had not been monitoring the flow."

"What do you want of me?"

"I want you to be a witness for the Wisters in a suit for malpractice against Dr. Gault."

"No, no," Martin cried. "I want to be left out of this. I don't have time, I'm a busy man."

Mr. Rice stood up. "Then I won't take any more of your time now, Doctor. Think it over. You'll do the right thing, I'm sure."

PERRY looked large and clumsy in Martin's den. "I'm sorry to come busting in on you like this," he said, "but after dinner I thought, Why don't I go see Martin and talk it all out? You've heard they've served me with a suit?"

"I heard."

Perry leaned forward. "I'm going to level with you. I did have a couple of drinks. You know me. A little goes a long way. I shouldn't have gone to the hospital at all. I know I ought to have told you to get somebody else, but when you're a little bit dazed, you don't know you are. Martin, you're not going to testify against me, are you? She was going to die anyway." There were tears in the friendly copper eyes.

Martin was silent and Perry continued. "You can bet it will never happen again. Never. Martin, I'm scared."

Martin spoke very gently. "Take it easy, Perry. Things have a way of working out. We all want to help you through this." What was he saying? Words, smooth, easy words, meaning nothing. Just what was he going to do?

A week after that, the lawyer came from Perry's insurance company. He wore a nice dark suit and had a nice quiet manner.

"What is it you want?" Martin asked this second lawyer.

"We want you to testify on behalf of Dr. Gault," the lawyer replied. "There is no convincing proof the child died of anything but natural causes."

Martin passed his hand over his forehead. "I'm not cut out to

426

be a lawyer," he said apologetically. "I'll confess my head's beginning to spin with all this business."

"Of course. Let me get in touch with you in another few days, to go over specifics. I'm sure we can work things out satisfactorily." And with a pleasant smile, he departed.

The case seemed to fill Martin's life. The Wisters telephoned him at his home to plead. The mother wept. Well, he couldn't blame her! Perry's wife came to his office late one afternoon, redeyed and begging. Couldn't blame her, either.

One afternoon the hospital superintendent called him in. "There's talk that you don't want to work with Perry's lawyers," Mr. Knolls said.

Martin answered slowly, "It's not just them. I don't want to work with anybody. I want to be left out."

"Of course," Mr. Knolls said, "I can't tell you what to do. I've known you a long time, though, and I feel free to point out a few things you may have overlooked."

"Such as?"

"Perry's had twenty-two years here at Fisk. An unblemished record. The publicity of this affair, the emotional damage can wreck a man after all those good years."

"I know that."

"He needs all the help he can get now. Don't condemn him. It won't bring the child back, anyway."

Martin looked at him. "I know that, too."

"Well, then, I'll say no more."

Martin began hearing unpleasant things about himself at the hospital. "You're acting like a Boy Scout," he was told. "The guy had one extra drink. He shouldn't have come into the OR. But he's never slipped before, and he'll never slip again."

Purpose. Abstractions. A man's whole professional life versus a dead child who was going to die anyway.

"You'll be a great hero to no one but yourself, Martin. Perry's going to win the case. He's got prestigious people to testify for him. And that resident Maudley is scared out of his wits. He'll say what he's expected to say."

Cold, stony looks in the hospital now. He used to think it was

427

simple. One side or the other. At night he lay awake conducting internal dialogues while shadows flickered over the ceiling. The child was going to die anyway, remember that.

But if it hadn't been that child; if it had been a benign tumor, something easy and Perry had not monitored, what then?

So the long nights passed.

Finally one evening after dinner, he walked to the window in his den and opened it. Then he put the Reformation Symphony on the record player. For long minutes he stood listening, his eyes on the sky over the river. The music was a shaft of light, a great plea and answer. And in some crazy way it seemed his father's voice was mixed up in it.

Suddenly everything was very simple. He went to the telephone. Might as well call Perry's lawyer now and be able to sleep tonight. He picked up the receiver and dialed.

"This is Dr. Farrell," he said. "I'm sorry to disturb you at home, but I'll be brief. I've made my decision and it's a painful one. I simply cannot help you. I couldn't do it and rest."

MARTIN, having changed from operating clothes to street clothes, stood in the hospital lobby, waiting for Claire.

Young Simpson, he of the good cheer, called out, "Going back to the office so late, Martin?"

"No, waiting for my daughter. We've a party on the Island."

"Enjoy yourself," Simpson said.

As the man left, Martin felt the smile still on his mouth. It was remarkable how even the most casual proof of being liked and accepted could freshen and support him these days. As for enemies, you could hardly get through life, he supposed, without garnering some. And he thought regretfully of Perry, who, having won his case without Martin's help, now ignored him whenever they chanced to pass, and of other doctors, too, whose greetings were noticeably cooler.

He was reading the names of recent benefactors on a bronze plaque when his daughter appeared. He watched her before she saw him. Her face was grave; as soon as she saw him it bloomed into a smile. Real or assumed? he wondered.

428

"Reads like Dun and Bradstreet, doesn't it, Dad?" Claire said.

"I don't like this lobby," he replied. "It's pompous. The institute will have quite a different feel."

They went out to the parking lot, on their way to a party at the Mosers'.

"Up to the second story already," Claire observed as they passed the new construction at the end of the block.

"Right on schedule. Yes, we ought to be functioning a year from this month." And for the sake of some foolish dignity, Martin tried to keep the jubilation from his voice.

They got into the car and he took the wheel. Claire sighed. "I can't say I'm looking forward to this shindig."

"You're doing me a big favor. I like to show you off, you know. Besides, it doesn't hurt you to become known."

"Don't mind me," Claire said. "The fact is I'm starved, and I get cranky when I'm starved."

They drove along in silence for a while. Then Martin thought of something. "I forgot to tell you. You know that man from Salt Lake City I operated on last winter? The one who owns half a copper mine? I got a letter from him today. He wants to know how much we'd need to pay for an operating room at the institute. An entire operating room! Imagine!"

"A grateful patient," Claire said. "You've had loads of them."

They were riding now along a maze of highways. Martin felt a vague melancholy. Then, glancing over at Claire, he realized that the melancholy was because of her. There was something remote about her these days. No use asking her to talk about it, because she would refuse. *Just as I am unable to talk about Mary.*

The suburbs became the exurbs. There was restful space between the houses. Overhead, trees were budding so that the land was veiled in pale green lace. As Martin's car rolled up the Mosers' long driveway he saw hundreds of daffodils scattered over the lawn. "Another spring," he said. "Every year I'm glad I've lived to see it again."

It was warm inside the Mosers' house. The press of people, the fires under the great carved mantels, and the good Scotch produced this hearty warmth. Claire found a young couple whom

429

she knew. Martin watched her in her quiet dress standing among all the bright silk plumage. Distinguished. The authentic article, he thought.

Bob Moser came up to him. "Having a good time?"

"Very. It's a spectacular party, as always."

"I'd like to talk to you for a minute in the library."

They sat down. Moser seemed to be studying Martin. Finally he took off his glasses. "I suppose this isn't the right place for what I have to tell you, Martin. I had thought of ringing you on the phone, but one can't talk properly on the phone."

Martin waited attentively.

"We've been friends for a long time." His mouth made a queer twist as though he were about to cry. "I feel the way you must when you have to tell a family the patient has died."

Alarmed, Martin asked, "Is anyone ill? What is it, Bob?"

"I wanted to be the one to tell you. I didn't want you to get it by letter or however they planned to do it. You know Dr. Francis? Stanley Francis?"

"From San Diego. I've met him at meetings."

"I understand he's a good man. Kind of a duplicate of yourself, if I may say so, only younger."

"About five or six years, that's all."

"Yes. Well." Moser got up from the chair. "Martin, I haven't slept these two nights. It was decided—this is still confidential, of course, but the trustees had a meeting the day before yesterday and it was decided— Well, they've offered the directorship of the neurological institute to Stanley Francis, and he's accepted. That's it in a nutshell."

"I see," Martin said. "I see. . . ."

"New blood," Moser said dully. "That's the reason they gave. But it was yours by right. You're the one who dreamed of it; your patients gave funds for it; you set up the program. It was yours."

"Yes," Martin said, feeling faint. "Yes, it was."

"I tried!" Moser said. "I was two hours in there fighting for you. But you made enemies, Martin. What can I tell you? You threw it away." Moser spoke angrily. "You were a fool!"

"You think so?"

"I know so! My whole life experience tells me so. Look out for number one, it says."

"Maybe you're right. At this point I don't know."

"Yes. But I'd still go to hell and back for you. What are you going to do?"

"First, get my balance. My head's spinning."

"Want another drink? Brandy?"

"No, I'll be all right, Bob. Really. Just leave me. Please."

After he had gone, Martin got up from his chair and walked across the room to French windows that led to a terrace. Outside, he leaned on the balustrade, looking downward on descending terraces, an imitation of the Villa d'Este outside of Rome.

He stood in a trance of exhaustion, looking beyond the terraces to a field of rough marsh grass, out of which the peepers were trilling. They would still be there a thousand springs from now, long after the terraces had worn away. He thought, I ought to be full of hatred, but I'm not. Isn't that strange?

"What are you doing out here? I've been looking for you everywhere," Claire said.

"I've been smelling spring in the air," he answered.

"Why, what's the matter? You look white. Are you sick?"

He told her. She leaned against the wall as if she had been struck. "No! I don't believe it! I simply don't believe it."

"You can believe it. It's true."

"It's because of that case, isn't it? You betrayed the club, the good old boys." She began to cry. "Oh, Dad, I could murder, I could kill them all! It's yours! You earned it!"

I did, he thought. And it hurts. Like a knife, it hurts. Punishment, because I did what I know, *and they know*, was decent. Yet it doesn't seem as much of a punishment as I would have thought it would be.

"You know, I'm not as crushed as you'd expect," he reflected.

"Why? All my life I've heard about the institute."

"And it's come to pass, hasn't it? It'll flourish and I'll work in it, without the status, that's all."

"That's all? Well, I'm crushed, if you're not! Why don't you get out and fight?"

"You accept what you can't change. A good thing to learn."

"You mean *I* need to learn it?"

He answered gently, "I only mean it's a good philosophy."

Claire laid her head back against the stone. "What are you going to do?" she asked, as Moser had.

"Go home, for one thing," he answered.

"All right then, let's get out of here."

"Shouldn't we go in and say good night?"

"Ah, the hell with them," Claire said. She took his hand, and they went together across the grass.

Time and Tide

CHAPTER THIRTEEN

ALL that winter Jessie had been admonishing, "You're overworked. You don't even rest on your days off, what with running around on errands for those children of your father's."

Quite truly, Claire, like every other intern, was overworked. Yet that was to be expected. As for the children, well, ever since Hazel's death Claire had felt poignantly their need for hours of childish things: museums and walks and ice-cream treats. Martin tried to care for them, but it was hard. He had so little time and, never having been with them very much, his beginning attempts were bound to be awkward.

All this crossed her mind one morning while she stood in the operating room at the hospital, watching her father work. He had suggested she witness as much neurosurgery as possible, so as to get a head start on next year, when she would start her residency with him. As she stood among the group of residents and interns she felt a thrill of pride. Strip a man of title—as they had—but it made no alteration in his true value.

Afterward, she waited in the corridor for Martin. The nurse at the charge desk looked up. "Pretty soon we'll be seeing you up here every day."

"Next year."

"What a privilege to learn from your father! Nobody needs to tell you that, I'm sure." And taking her sheaf of charts, she went down the corridor.

A privilege, Claire thought. Not a day passed without someone, some nurse or intern or clerk or even her mother, reminding her of the privilege. She had begun to be tired of hearing it.

The smell of snow was in the air when Claire reached Madison Avenue later that day and began to walk quickly toward her mother's brownstone for their weekly dinner together.

In Jessie's house the lights were lit. Grateful light, grateful warmth, she thought as she went in. "Well," Jessie said, holding out her cheek to be kissed, "how are you? You look worn out."

"I am, a little. You're not, I see."

"I don't allow it. Nobody thanks you for it. Sherry?"

"Yes, please."

"What are you looking at? The jewelry? It's new."

"It's magnificent."

Jessie's taste in jewels was exotic. Tonight she wore jade in ornate gold filigree. "I know I attract attention. I will, anyway, so I might as well make a bold job of it." She smiled at her daughter. "Let's go in to dinner. Tell me what you did today."

"Very different things from what you did, I'm sure," Claire answered as they walked into the dining room and sat down. "I had the gynecology clinic, and I saw a young woman who had a botched abortion. She'll never have a baby, short of a miracle, that is. And I don't believe much in miracles." Suddenly she put the fork down.

"Claire, what's wrong?"

Claire felt the threat of tears. Lowering her eyes, she stared at the flowers on the center of the table. "Ned would have loved a child," she said softly. "How he would love a proudly pregnant woman waiting at home for him every evening!"

"Most men would, you know."

"I know most men would. There's nothing wrong with it. . . . So, he'll find somebody, if he hasn't already."

"I hope you're not too bitter, Claire?"

"You've been bitter often enough, haven't you?"

"Yes, but that doesn't mean I want to see bitterness in you.

433

Come. You're not hungry. Let's go into the living room and you can stretch out on the sofa."

Claire stared into the fire, which purred softly, like a cat. "Smells good, doesn't it?" Jessie remarked. "Cedar logs."

Claire didn't answer. Her head ached with the held-back tears, with weariness and the weight of things. "I want to go away," she said suddenly. "To India or Brazil, someplace. Anyplace."

"What? You don't want to train with your father?"

She began to cry. "No! But I don't dare tell him."

"I don't understand! Such a fabulous opportunity!"

"Yes, only I don't want it."

"Good Lord, whyever not?"

"Because I hate it. It's awful." Claire shuddered. "The shaved heads and the people who can't talk afterward. All the contrived cheer because somebody can take one step."

"Well!" Jessie cried, throwing up her hands. "When did you start to feel this way?"

"I don't remember. It just grew. I never really *thought* about it at all until I began to get into it."

"You wanted to please your father. You always have."

"No, I don't think I even thought that much! It just seemed to be the thing I was naturally going to do." And to her own dismay, Claire began to sob. "I hate Dad's work! I'd be no good at it. He's been so wonderful to me. And I've been so depressed because apparently I don't appreciate it enough."

"You ought to tell him," Jessie said quietly.

"I can't! He's counted on it for years. He's already had so many failures. How can I give him one more?"

"You're not obliged to compensate for his disappointments. Tell me what you want to do in India."

"Oh—go somewhere with one of those agencies that sends medical help to people who haven't got any. I don't want to be a medical great. I'd just like to bring primary care to people." And she began to cry again.

"You were speaking of Ned a while ago," Jessie said. "You still think about him."

"He treated me badly. *Badly!*"

"Why don't you just forget him, then?"

"A good question! Why don't I? I don't know. . . ." She sat up. "Should I have gone after him?"

"Certainly not," Jessie said stoutly.

They both sat looking into the fire. At last Claire's tears stopped. "I guess I'll go home," she said.

"No." Jessie came over and laid her hand on Claire's forehead. "Stay here. You'll get a better night's rest."

Silently Claire nodded. And like a little girl she followed Jessie up the stairs and into her old room.

A GREAT square desk covered with papers, medical periodicals and sundries stood between Jessie and Martin.

He still looks like a doctor, she thought. For the past two weeks she had been experiencing a confusion of emotions: stubbornness and pride, worry and embarrassment. Still, she reminded herself, she was doing this for Claire. For Claire she would take sword against monsters if need be.

"It's cost you a good deal to come here, Jessie. I want you to know I understand that."

"Quite so." Through Jessie's head went scraps of flitting thought: *It seems a century since we walked in Kensington Gardens while Claire in her yellow coat rode the tricycle. It seems yesterday since Cyprus.* She sat up and spoke decisively. "Claire mustn't know I've been here. This must come from you."

"She really hates the work that much?"

"Apparently so. It's tearing her down."

"When—when did she first realize this about herself?"

"How can anyone say exactly when anything happens inside one's head? It's tied up somehow with Ned Lamb, that I know. At any rate, it's been growing more and more."

"Why hasn't she ever told me?"

"She knew it would be a terrible wound."

Martin looked down at his hands. Jessie's eyes circled the room. On a shelf near the desk stood a photograph of a woman with a quiet face. Claire's description of Hazel had been remarkably accurate. Yes, he's had trouble enough, Jessie thought.

"Such a waste of her mind!" Martin cried abruptly. "She'd be doing the most rudimentary medicine. Does she know that?"

"Of course she knows it. It's what she wants."

"I had been counting on her. Looking forward to something very special! She, in a way, beginning where I, in not too many more years, will leave off." He tapped a pencil. "There's so much new. One would need five lifetimes to learn it all."

Jessie was silent a moment. Then she spoke. "I'm remembering something," she said softly, "that you may have forgotten. I'm thinking of you and your father."

And now Martin gave her a long look. "You're reminding me that every human being must develop in his own way."

"True, isn't it?"

"Yes. Yes. You always did get at the heart of things in a hurry, didn't you? You're right, of course. I'll tell her that I've been thinking it would be better for us both if she were to go her own way. I'll make it convincing."

"I thought you would."

"What about that—other affair? She never talks to me about him."

"Nor to me, until that night. It shocked me so! Claire almost never cries." Jessie stood up. "Well, call me if there's anything I should know. Otherwise I won't expect to hear from you."

"Of course," Martin said courteously.

He came from behind the desk and opened the door. She put out her hand. "I'll be going, then."

"I'm thankful you came. I had no idea, none at all. But I'll set her free—for India or wherever she wants to go."

For long minutes after Jessie left, Martin sat staring at the wall. This problem hurt so much! Never by one word had Claire revealed herself. Poor little soul!

Then he thought of that other pain of hers, the man-woman thing. She wanted Ned Lamb still! There was no sense in it, when the world was full of young men who would gladly have her.

He could see Ned and Claire: handsome couple! They had looked as though they belonged together. Her longing, if it was anything like what he had suffered, was dreadful. And remember-

436

ing, he actually began to feel a soft ache again, creeping, settling.

Suddenly he sat upright. He looked in his telephone book for a number and dialed it. "I want to book a flight to London," he said, "toward the end of the week."

FROM the hotel window Martin looked out on a steady rain. An English winter; he had forgotten. Thoughtfully he drank his coffee, still not sure he ought to be here. On the plane he'd had moments, thinking he'd made a mistake, that he would just turn around at the airport and take the next plane back. He'd had moments at home, too, in which he'd tried to extricate himself from his own undertaking. When he had called the New York office of Ned's firm to ask whether he was still in Hong Kong, all he'd found out was that Ned wasn't even with them anymore.

He looked at his watch. Too early. He sat on, brooding over a thing he had never dared to examine until now. It began to take shape. It grew so rapidly that he knew it had been lying there, stifled inside him, for a long time.

The desk called to say the rental car had been delivered. He went downstairs and took the wheel. A sudden enormous excitement possessed him. The last he'd heard, she was still living at Lamb House alone. What if—as long as he was going there to speak for Claire—what if he were to speak for himself as well?

The maid said, "There's only Mr. Ned at home. He's in the studio. Shall I fetch him?"

"Thanks. I know where it is."

For a moment Martin stood in the doorway, watching Ned, who was removing a painting from a crate. When the young man turned around, astonishment spread over his face.

"No," Martin said, "you're not imagining things."

"Well—well I—"

"I didn't expect to find you so easily. I rather thought you'd be in Singapore or somewhere."

"No, I've been home awhile."

They stared at each other. In their looks were anxiety and wariness, puzzlement and embarrassment.

"Come in. Sit down."

Martin took a chair, and Ned sat on a packing case. It seemed to Martin that he looked tired and older than one ought to look at his age. He began resolutely. "I want to talk about Claire. But first I have to ask you. Is there another woman in your life?"

Ned's expression was unreadable. "There's no one."

"Then that's one hurdle past. The next is, no matter what should come of this conversation, I want your word that my daughter will never know I've been here."

"You have it."

"Now the hard part. The fact is, she's still in love with you. She's miserable. She's never told me, but her mother knows."

Ned put his head in his hands. The room was very still while he sat there, not looking up. "I wish I knew what happened," he said at last. "I've asked myself and asked. I wanted to go to her, but she sent me away. Somehow I couldn't get over that."

"You could have written."

"Yes. We hurt each other so." He looked up at Martin. "I thought about her. . . . I'd take a girl out, and driving away, I'd see Claire's face. You know how it is?"

Martin said steadily, "I know how it is."

Ned flushed. "Where is she? What is she doing?"

"She wants to go to India."

"Not going to work with you?"

"No. She has very different ideas which I wasn't aware of. A failure of communication. Life seems to be full of them."

"What can we do now?" Ned asked.

"That's rather up to you, isn't it?"

"India," Ned repeated.

"Yes. She wants to work with the poor. How could you manage that if—if you two should straighten things out?"

"Oh, I'm a free agent now. I quit the work in Hong Kong. I was miserable there, thinking of her—" Ned cleared his throat. "I found I didn't really *like* advertising, anyhow. I'd always wanted to write. To write truly, I mean, without tricks. Claire knew."

"But you were so enthusiastic about the job—"

"Yes, well, you see, the kind of journalism I had in mind, reporting on conditions in slum schools, or saving the whales—

438

you don't just break into that whenever you feel like it. So I got sidetracked into advertising, making a lot of money, getting this great promotion, very flattering to the ego—"

"A man's ego," Martin said. "That always figures."

"Perhaps it figured too much with me. But now I've taken a chance and it seems to be working out. I go abroad on contract and report for newspapers and magazines. I don't need a great deal of money. I never did, even when I was earning it."

"Come to think of it, Claire doesn't, either. She buys a pair of shoes when the old ones have worn out." Martin smiled.

"I could go wherever she went." Ned spoke thoughtfully. "We could work our schedules on an equal basis."

"You're really ready to accept that equal-basis business? I'm not sure I could. But then, you're a new generation."

"Yes, sir, I have to remind myself of that sometimes, too."

Then Martin thought of something else. "I don't even know whether she'd have you, after all that's happened. This may have been a wild-goose chase, Ned."

"I'll go and find out. . . . But I haven't asked you about yourself, sir. I suppose the institute is open and running by now."

"It's open and running," Martin said, "but not under my hands." Ned's eyebrows went up. "That's another story." He looked around. "These pictures, they're all—"

"All Mother's. They've been out on exhibit."

Martin got up and walked around the room. Beautiful, he thought. Grace and love shone in these faces, that child. His heart hammered. "How is she?"

"Happy in her work, as you can see. Happier all around than she's been in a long time."

"Claire's told me that you knew about Mary and me. I thought, coming here, that maybe after all this time, she and I—" Something in Ned's expression stopped him.

"I'm not sure I understand your meaning."

"I think you do understand," Martin said.

"Oh, then, I'm sorry! You didn't know. . . . Mother's been married almost a year."

"Married!"

"Yes. Simon and she have known each other a long time. He owns a gallery; he's done wonders for her."

Married! He must have looked ghastly, for Ned added kindly, "Things can be a muddle sometimes, can't they, sir?"

"Muddle?" Chaos and storm, more likely!

Feeling weak, Martin sat down again on a packing case, thinking of that bright thread that had been woven through all the twisted patterns of his life. Married. She with the eyes and the dreams and the dark, lovely face.

He pulled himself together. "I'll have to be going. I've done what I came to do." He was about to leave when a man entered the studio. He was tall, with a pleasant outdoor face.

"Simon," Ned said, "we've a visitor from America. This is Dr. Farrell, Claire's father."

Simon shook Martin's hand. "I'm glad to know you. But you're not leaving?"

"I have to, I'm afraid. I only came for a word with Ned."

Ned explained. "Dr. Farrell came about Claire. I may be going to New York next week to see her."

Simon looked from one to the other. "So that's it. Why, I'm delighted!" His pleasure was genuine. "You see, I understand what it is to know what you want and not get it. Have you met my wife, Doctor? But of course, you must. Her sister. Forgive me."

"Quite all right," Martin murmured.

"Has Ned shown you her portrait? I had it done by Juan Domingo, a very fine artist. He's caught her to perfection, I think." He guided Martin to the far end of the room.

There she was, next to a table on which stood a bowl of flowers. Her dress was a subtle clash of ruby and flame, but all he really saw were the great, wondering eyes.

"I had this done ten years ago," Simon explained.

"You've known her ten years," Martin repeated.

"Yes. It took me that long to persuade her to marry me. But I'm a persistent man." Simon laughed.

Martin looked up and saw the pity in Ned's eyes. "An excellent likeness," he said, and moved toward the door.

"Mary will be here soon," Simon said. "Can you stay to tea?"

440

"Thank you. You're very kind, but I really can't."

They shook hands and Martin went out.

At the top of the rise in the road he stopped the car and looked back through bare trees at Lamb House. Well, he had come for Claire, and he had done his best. As for the other business, he could hardly feel. He was numb.

MARY came into the studio, where Simon and Ned were still arranging pictures.

"We had a visitor, darling," Simon said. "Your former brother-in-law. The doctor."

"Martin! Martin was here?" She looked at Ned.

He nodded. "He came to talk about Claire." Ned spoke steadily and she understood that this tone was meant to steady her. "I think, Mother, I'll go back and see her."

Mary sat down. "I'm just—stunned. I—seem to be shaking."

"Oh, you've worried your mother, Ned," Simon cried.

"She oughtn't to worry about me at my age."

Mary said, "Of course I wasn't happy about it at the beginning. Jessie and I . . . But I do think Claire's exceptional, and if you can work things out, why . . ." Her voice left her.

"Her mother didn't like me at all."

"Well, the father likes you, I could see that," Simon interposed. "An awfully nice chap, Mary! He took a great interest in your paintings."

Ned spoke lightly. "Naturally anyone who admires your work ranks on top with Simon." For a moment Ned and Mary looked into each other's eyes before she turned away.

"I'm going up to the house," she said. "That is, if you don't need me here, Simon?"

"No, no. We're almost finished. Go ahead."

She went slowly up the path. Suddenly, not wanting to go inside, she sat down on a bench and laid her head back. Suppose he had come last year before I married Simon? What then? Oh, Simon is everything that's steady and good and male. There's such peace now in my heart. But if Martin had come last year?

So many, many ifs! Tears gathered in the corners of her eyes and she wiped them away. She could hope; maybe it will turn out well for Ned and Claire. They must do what's right for them.

"I thought you'd gone inside," Simon said. He bent and kissed her. "Mary. Mary Fern. Are you pleased about Ned?"

"If it works out well for him, I will be."

"I've been thinking, would you like to go to America?"

"I don't know. They say it's so changed. Highways and tract houses—all built up."

"We'll go to California, show some of your work, and have a vacation at the same time. And stay in New York for a while."

"Not New York," she said quickly. "Let's just pass through it. I never liked New York."

"Whatever you say, as long as we're together."

NED and Claire were to be married very quietly on a Saturday evening at Jessie's house. There had been tacit agreement that Martin would not be present. Instead, he was to give a little dinner for the bridal couple at his apartment the night before.

On the afternoon of the wedding Jessie covered the mantel in the library with white flowers and silk bows. She hummed as she worked. She would not have believed that she could feel happy at Claire's marrying this young man; but her daughter's joy during these past weeks had canceled all regrets. She was fastening the last bow when the doorbell rang. "I'll answer, Nora!" she called.

She opened the door. The woman on the doorstep smiled uncertainly. "Jessie, may I come in?" asked Mary Fern.

JESSIE was curled in the wing chair. She must be lost in a room without a wing chair, Fern thought. "I didn't come for the wedding," she said. "I didn't even know this was the day. If I'm not welcome, Jessie, just say so and I'll go."

"Have I said you were unwelcome?" Jessie asked brusquely.

"No, but—well, you see, we're flying to California Monday morning.... And I was sitting at lunch just now ... I had such an overpowering sense of your presence. I thought I must see you, even if you were to slam the door in my face."

"Well, I didn't slam the door in your face." Jessie picked up a

442

basket of needlepoint that stood next to her chair. "I have to do something with my hands. I'm never able to sit still."

"Then you haven't changed."

"None of us ever do, do we?"

One could take that remark in many ways. Fern made no answer, and silently the two women sat. Presently Jessie spoke. "I'm told you've made a great success with your paintings."

"Yes," Fern replied simply.

"A pity Father didn't live to see himself proven wrong."

"He would have been proven wrong about you, too," Fern said gently. "Ned's told me about you. And this house is lovely. Mellow, like Lamb House."

"Hardly like Lamb House! You're still living there?"

"Still there. For me, it's home. Simon loves it, too."

"You're happy with Simon?"

"He's very good to me. He's strong and kind."

"That's not answering my question, is it?"

Fern threw her hands out. "Oh, Jessie," she said.

Jessie thrust the needlework away. "I'm sorry. I shouldn't have said that. I'm upset. You've upset me."

Fern started to rise. "I understand. I'd better go."

"No, stay! I wouldn't forgive myself if you left like this. Now that you've come, I must tell you that I'm not angry anymore. I don't hate you, Fern. I haven't for a long, long time."

Fern got up and walked to the end of the room. On a table in a corner stood a group of photographs; one was of Fern and Jessie's mother. For a long time Fern looked at the remembered face. At last she turned back to her sister. "You've relieved a pain that has been so sharp—so sharp, Jessie. You can't know."

"Maybe I can." Jessie stood and put her hand on Fern's arm.

Fern's arms went out and Jessie's head came to rest on her shoulder. Fern's hand moved over the curly head; her other hand lay on the misshapen little back. They stood, holding one another, while something slowly eased in the heart of each.

"It's so simple after all, isn't it?" Fern murmured. "Why didn't we do it before?"

"I don't know." Jessie wiped her eyes. "Sit down and talk to me."

They talked, while an hour passed, speaking of Cyprus, of everything and everyone except the man whose name would best remain unspoken.

Then Jessie said, "You'll need to go back and dress for the wedding. You and Simon be here at seven, will you?"

"It's been—it's been beautiful, Jessie."

"Beautiful. Bitter and sweet."

Yes, sweet to be together after so long, and bitter that it had taken so long.

THEIR plane was leaving for India Sunday night. Martin had already bid good-by to Ned and Claire, but it came to his mind that he wanted to see them just once more. They were, after all, going to the other side of the world.

At the desk in the Waldorf's lobby he was told that Dr. Farrell and Mr. Lamb were still upstairs. "Mr. Lamb and Dr. Farrell," indeed!

At the fourth floor he got out of the elevator and stood wondering in which of three directions to find the room. Across the corridor a man and woman were also hesitating, with their backs to Martin. The woman was tall. She wore a suit of thin wool the color of wheat. Her hand rested in the curve of the man's elbow. He knew her at once, even before he heard the unmistakable voice. "It's number eleven, I think," she said.

Turning just then, she caught Martin's look. Her glance swept down the corridor beyond him, swept lightly back and paused. He thought her lips moved, but perhaps it was only the quivering of his own vision.

"It's this way, Mary," her husband said.

The elevator came again and Martin got in. There was a roaring in his head. He left the hotel, feeling as if he had been struck.

"If we ever see each other again," she had said, "walk away. Will you promise?"

"Yes, I promise," he'd told her. And he thought that possibly the best proof he loved her was his wish that she be happy now.

Mary Fern. Mary Fern. A distant glimmer, fading and brightening. For how long? For always?

444

He had walked two blocks when a limousine drew up just ahead of him. A little woman, wearing a loose cream-colored coat, got out and dismissed the car.

"Jessie!" he cried.

"Martin?" She hesitated, then put out her hand. "How are you?"

"I'm fine, thanks. You're going in here?" he asked, indicating the apartment house before which they stood.

"No, walking home. I need the exercise, so I sent the car back to the garage."

"It's certainly a handsome limousine. And I like your coat."

"Rats! It's the same outfit I always wear. The same cape to cover the hump. Only the fabric and the color change."

Little Jessie! Tart, plucky little Jessie!

"Do you mind if I keep you company?" he asked her.

"Come along, of course."

They had gone a block when Jessie said, "You've been to see Claire, haven't you?"

"I went to the Waldorf, but I didn't see her."

"Because you saw Fern instead."

"Now how did you know that?"

"You have a faraway look. Didn't I always know when something was on your mind?"

"That's true. You always did." He was silent a moment. "I did you a very great injustice, Jessie. I've carried the guilt of it with me every day of my life."

"I'm sorry to hear that, Martin. In the last analysis you did me an enormous favor. I've got Claire because of you."

He looked down at her. Her face was alert and keen as ever.

"Did you know Fern was in New York?" she asked.

"No," he replied. "Did you?"

"No. Nobody did. But she arrived in time for the wedding."

"She was at the wedding?"

"Yes. She came to my house that afternoon. I'm so glad she did. We had a good, long talk."

Martin was astonished.

"The wonderful thing is that seeing her didn't hurt me as much as I would have expected it to. I suppose it's because I've made

445

something out of my own life. I don't have to feel like—like *nothing* anymore. You understand?"

"I think I always have, Jessie."

They walked on in silence for a while. Finally Jessie said, "I shall miss Claire terribly. You, at least, have three others."

"True. But she is my special child, my heart. You did a fantastic job, Jessie, bringing her up. I've always wanted to tell you."

"You had something to do with that yourself, you know. You were her hero from the start. How I suffered when she went to claim you! I had so wanted to keep her all for myself."

"You've kept her, Jessie. She loves you."

"Yes. But we won't be seeing her much at all anymore."

"It's lucky we're both busy."

"I didn't cling to her when she was with me, that's one good thing." Jessie sighed. "Oh, drat! I never could stand mournful people and that goes for myself. Here's my place." She held out her hand. "It's been nice. Luck, Martin."

"And to you, Claire's mother."

A LIGHT shone through the crack of Peter's door long after supper. When Martin went in, Peter was sitting at his desk. "Math again?"

"Algebra. I hate the stuff. And I've got to do better on the next test."

"There's no 'got to.' No one person is expected to excel at everything, Peter."

"Claire does. I wish I was smart like her."

"You are smart in your own way."

"Not like her," Peter said stubbornly.

"We're all different."

He laid his hand on the child's shoulder. And something of the tenderness he felt must have been conducted through his touch, because Peter looked up anxiously. "Are you unhappy, Dad?"

"No, no, of course not. Why should I be?"

"Well, Enoch says you'll miss Claire so much. Will you?"

"Yes, we all will, won't we?"

"But you will especially."

The boy's eyes, trusting and shy, rested on his father's face. And for the first time, Martin did not turn away from that reminder of Hazel, that quiet gaze. He cleared his throat. "Gosh, you're growing. The cuffs on that sweater are halfway to your elbow."

"I grew three inches since last year."

"We'll go shopping next Saturday morning. I guess you'll need practically everything, won't you?"

"Marjorie's been wanting things ever so long. Her dresses are too short, and her spring coat doesn't fit."

"Ever so long? Why didn't she ask me?"

"I guess she thought you were too busy."

Martin shook his head. "I don't know anything about what little girls should wear."

"You could just get what the other girls in her class have, couldn't you?"

"You're right," Martin said. The boy's kindness struck to his heart. Ever since their mother's death, it seemed these children had been gradually drawing together in an adult way. He smiled at Peter. "Well, we'll take care of everything. Now I suggest you go to sleep. It's late."

He went into his den. All the little objects in the room glowed in the light of the white walls. Suddenly he understood why he had surrounded himself with whiteness. That first room of hers— And he opened the closet, where on the top shelf, still in its English wrapping paper, dusty and brittle now, lay the *Three Red Birds*. Taking it down, he unwrapped it and propped it against a shelf. Tomorrow he would hang it up at last and face reality.

Had it, though, been all real? If they had lived together, sharing a roof, childhood diseases, plumbing bills and fatigue, how would it have been then? That, my friend, you will never know.

It was time for sleep. Hazel had always provided a piece of fruit for him at bedtime. Now Marjorie continued the custom. He sat back to enjoy it, a fine tart apple, a Northern Spy, he'd guess. The apples of boyhood: russets, greenings, Gravensteins. Wasps in sweet, rotting piles of apples on the grass. Baskets on the porch when Pa sickened and died.

447

When I die, my patients will bring neither apples nor tears to my house. Some of them will not even remember my name. "Some big doctor did the operation," they will say. But my father—how they loved him! They never knew how little he knew.

So one pays for everything. We know more, we can do more; but we are not the fathers to the sick that my father was, and they do not love us.

He had gotten his old diary out to show to Claire before she went away. It lay now on the table, opened at the frontispiece where he had written that quotation from Hippocrates, which, forgetting that he had known it long before, he had chosen again for the pediment of the institute. And he saw himself on the bed under the sloping roof of his room in Cyprus, writing with the book propped on his knees.

That Greek physician, alive in a time and place so different from this, had perceived the truth. The lustrous sky of Attica, Martin thought. He would go there yet, take his children some day and see it. "Yes, yes," he murmured, turning out the light. Then clearly, loving the sound of the old words, he spoke them aloud into the darkness.

"For where there is love of man, there is also love of the art."

Belva Plain

Belva Plain is a slender woman with warm green eyes who describes herself as an ordinary housewife. Well, she's not— quite. Housewife, yes. Ordinary, no. For Belva Plain, on her first try, wrote one of the runaway bestsellers of the decade— *Evergreen*. And with the publication of her second book, *Random Winds*, she seems destined to match her record. One reason for her success is obvious: she loves her stories as much as her readers do. "The morning after I finished *Random Winds*, I felt so let down," she says now.

"I didn't have my characters with me any more and I missed them."

Mrs. Plain was born and brought up in New York City but now lives in South Orange, New Jersey. She has been married to Dr. Irving Plain, an ophthalmologist, for thirty-nine years, and is the mother of three children and the grandmother of four. But although she is new to the world of novelists, she is not new to the art of writing. While her children were young, she wrote several dozen short stories that were published in major magazines. And finally, when her family had grown up, she found the time to write her first full-length book, *Evergreen*. Not surprisingly, in both her novels concern for family life is the theme that dominates. "The family is the bastion of any culture," she says in her quiet voice. "No matter what the troubles of the times are, the important thing is to keep a roof over the children's heads and keep the family together."

Mrs. Plain writes on a Monday-to-Thursday schedule, reserving the other days for her home and friends. "But sometimes," she admits, "I can't help it and I sneak upstairs on Saturdays to write." She's now working on her third book. "Let's just say it's another big, fat romantic novel, and it takes place in a foreign country." And then, a respite from writing? "Oh, no. I have ideas for two or three more books. I'll want to get started on them right away."

IN THE SIGN OF THE BEAR

A CONDENSATION FROM **NORTH BY WEST** BY

R. D. Symons

ILLUSTRATED BY ALAN DANIEL

PUBLISHED BY DOUBLEDAY
AND COMPANY, INC., NEW YORK

Far, far north, in the frozen wastes of the Canadian Arctic, a tiny child is raised by a band of Eskimos after miraculously surviving a plane crash. But as he approaches adulthood he yearns for his own people, in spite of the affection that has grown between him and the kindly Inuit hunters.

With only his loyal husky as a companion, the youth sets out for the unknown south. This is a story of faith and survival against the formidable odds of Canada's winter. Yet it is something more: the author's passion for the natural environment, here so sensitively evoked, shines through on every page of this memorable story.

1

The little plane sideslipped, stuttered, recovered, and droned on. The third time in ten minutes, thought Elspeth, and looked down once more as she had done so many times since they had left Edmonton. But all below was shrouded by the snow which was falling in feather-size flakes.

By her reckoning they should be well beyond Great Slave Lake, and below should lie the dull white of the late winter barrens.

She glanced at the pilot's head, less than two feet in front of her. His shoulders looked determined enough, and she checked the impulse to bother him with questions. Instead, she looked down again at her child. She wrapped the blue woolly blanket more firmly about the little thing sleeping so confidently in her arms, his breath rising like a thin mist from the gap she had left in the soft material.

How pleased his policeman father would be! He had so much wanted a boy.

She had hoped to have the baby at Coronation—a true "son of the north"—but Bruce had vetoed that. "Edmonton for you," he had said five months ago. And what he said was law to Elspeth. He knew the Arctic. But now she was impatient to see him again and to show him his son.

The roar of the engine ceased . . . then started again, but unevenly. In that brief moment of utter silence Elspeth felt a sudden premonition of disaster and, in spite of her resolution, she reached forward and touched that close, broad shoulder.

The engine spluttered, and died. The pilot turned his head.

"Off course," he said. "Sorry. Out of gas, I'm afraid. I'm going to make a landing. Hold tight, eh?"

Elspeth felt the machine shudder and heard the wind scream. Her last connected thought was more of a plea—Oh, God! Take care . . . .

That was all.

And somewhere in the Canadian wilderness between Coppermine and Bathurst Inlets, a small plane lay like a broken dragonfly, while slowly, flake by moon-white flake, the snow obliterated the last traces and the shattered parts became one more well-kept secret of the featureless landscape.

THE OLD COUPLE huddled low in the lee of the great rock. Here was a little patch of harsh, frozen ground which the falling snow could not reach. They had not been able to keep up with their Inuit band, so they were left a little oil, some dried meat, and a tattered caribou robe. The food was gone now and they awaited the end, huddling close, more from companionship than for the benefit of the feeble warmth they might share—for death is a lonely thing even when pain leaves, as it does at the last.

The sound of the falling plane seemed no more to their dull ears than the wingbeats of a white owl. But the crash of metal on rock alerted the old man. He stood up and then knew that his wife would not rise with him.

Stooping painfully, he laid the dead woman down on her side, then moved feebly towards the plane which lay, grotesquely bent, among the snowy rock humps.

He was not frightened. He recognized what he saw as one of the flying *komatiks* of the white man; and now he searched for what he might find. A dead man. He grunted. A dead white woman, young and evidently healthy, for she was fat. Then he saw that she was not so fat, but that she had her arms locked tightly about something. On his knees now, he felt and pulled.

Now it was in his arms, and with a sense of disappointment he realized that it was not a bundle of food, for how could dried meat wriggle and cry out? He was about to drop it in the snow, for, with the mother dead, the child, too, must perish. But then he tripped on a

454

duffel bag of sorts. He thrust in his arms and felt two cans—white man's food. And not frozen yet, since the bitter cold of deep winter had passed and the sun now showed above the horizon a little more each day.

Laboriously carrying the baby and the cans, he made his way back to where his dead woman lay, noticing that the patch of over-hung ground where they had sheltered narrowed at the back between the rocks. Perhaps it led to a bear den. An old one, for his dim eyes could pick out no tracks, and at this season a bear should be stirring again—unless it was a she with cubs.

The child cried now, and the old man thought of food, as he had not thought of it for many days. What kind of food would be in the cans? And how did the white man get it out? He bashed a can on the rock but the metal only dented. Then he found a sharp piece of stone and, using another larger rock, pounded it into the top of the can. He was rewarded by a slow trickle of something thickly liquid.

Carefully he tasted it. So sweet it was, like the caribou milk he had taken after he had killed a nursing doe! He drank a little and then, smearing a finger with the stuff, he pushed it between the baby's lips. The crying ceased and the little lips sucked ecstatically. Again and again the starving old man, knowing that he was at the end of the long journey of life, fed the small man whose foot had not yet taken the first step. Through the blackness of that night, while the soft snow fell, the ancient and the infant slept together, the one too old to care for the morrow, the other too young.

IT WAS NEARLY NOON when they awoke. The snow had stopped, the clouds were breaking, and the air had the damp chill of late March.

The child was crying again and the old man opened the other can very slowly, for his strength was dwindling. But this can, a different shape, yielded only some pink dust which smelled like a summer's day and was so dry that he could not stomach it. As for the child, it cried harder than ever when he tried to force some between its lips.

The old man squatted, slightly rocking the little thing across his knees. And as he peered with his nearly sightless eyes, a smell made his nostrils twitch, the musky reek of an animal. It came from the narrow fissure in the rocks behind him.

The child held close to his sunken chest, he slowly squeezed between the rocks and found himself within a den where the reek was stronger and the air held a steamy warmth. Whether the occupant was a he- or a she-bear, it would not be such a lonesome place for a child to die as out there. He placed the baby, blanket and all, beside a great shaggy flank of coarse, yellowish-white hair and retreated.

Later, when he curled up beside the body of his wife, the low sun was stretching pink fingers across the tundra. The rays played briefly upon the old man's face, and his lean cheeks and wrinkled forehead were suffused for a moment. He put his arm across the old woman's shoulder and pressed her close. *Ayolarama*, he thought sleepily. It is the end.

2

Nook was a mighty hunter, and Nook had boasted to the Company clerk that he would bring a fine white bearskin to the post if he could get a supply of ammunition and other necessities on "jawbone", for his fall hunt might be a long one.

The clerk demurred. There had been too much credit given out to others the fall before. It was high time more furs came in. But he wanted a polar bear rug for his mother in Winnipeg, and although it was against the rules, he advanced the goods on his own credit.

Now, several weeks later, Nook was far to the east, with his few necessities packed on the backs of his loose-running dogs. Travelling was easy, for the summer had been warm, melting much of the snow.

On the caribou hunt of the previous fall, after the first light snow, he had seen a bear track. With winter imminent, a she-bear (he knew it by her sign) would have been fattened on the tundra berries and her coat prime; nevertheless, he had abandoned the track and gone back to the hunt with his people, for that was custom. But he remembered, and this fall his brother-in-law would hunt caribou for him, while he pursued bigger game.

He camped that night by a small rivulet, now dry, below a height

of land he remembered. The few dry twigs he had gathered hissed
and spat in a small fire. Nook knew he was close to where he had
seen the track almost a year before. She-bears denned late if they
had borne cubs during the winter darkness, and since he had found
no cub tracks the previous year, she should certainly have a cub this
season. Only one, Nook thought, since the berries had not been
abundant, nor had marmots, for two years past. In time of great
plenty, a bear often had three cubs, although two was the common
number. She should not be far away. Nook called his dogs about
him and composed himself to the half-sleeping, half-waking rest of
a hunter.

HE WAS RECALLED to full wakefulness by the croak of a raven, and
his heart rose. Ravens seldom stray far from some hunting animal,
since it is largely upon their leavings, or the mice they disturb, that
these birds sustain life. Something was near, that was certain.

Without haste—the hunter's betrayer—Nook munched his dry
meat. His dogs looked on hungrily, their jowls drooling, but they
could be fed only at the end of their day's work.

Carefully, Nook lashed his packs to the dogs. Flour; salt; dried
meat; tea; sugar; his tinderbox and ammunition were kept in the
fold of his parka lining. He slung his rifle over his shoulder, tucking
its soft scabbard into his belt. Then he talked to the dogs and stepped out in long easy strides towards the ridge, now outlined in dark
blue against the saffron sky.

He had gone barely half a mile when one of the dogs dashed
forward, stopped at the foot of a small hillock, its nose to the
ground, and began to scratch. It was soon joined by the others, all
tumbling about in a flurry of waving tails. Reaching the spot, Nook
found himself staring at a recent bear sign, dark with the pulp of
autumn berries. The ravens had not lied, he thought.

Nook looked beyond the hillock to a jumble of grey-black rock
which formed the shoulder of a ridge. There he saw a pale patch
which he first took for a belated snowbank, but as he watched, it
moved slowly to the right, and he made it out to be a bear. At that
distance he could not tell if it was alone.

To his right a little watercourse, now dry, zigzagged down the slight rise of ground. Calling his dogs, he strode into the gully, noting with satisfaction that its sides became higher as he progressed towards its source among the black boulders.

When he clambered up the bank and peered over the top, there was the bear, thirty yards away, rooting among the stones for beetles, grubbing out tubers or lemming broods. He unslung his rifle and waited. Then he saw two cubs gambolling among the scarlet stems of fireweed. The bear turned, her nose towards them, and at that moment Nook pressed the trigger.

His dogs broke into a chorus of staccato barks, and as he rose and approached the bear, rifle ready, they bounded forward and surrounded the dying animal. One of the cubs stood up, and whimpered. Nook raised his rifle and the cub fell. The young meat would be good, and these two would soon perish without their mother.

Now the dogs drew back, puzzled, looking from the second cub to Nook; for this was no cub and it gave out the man smell. Nook rubbed his eyes. What was that little creature on all fours, dragging a piece of something that looked like ragged cloth?

He approached slowly, then laughed, as he recognized the little creature as a human child, perhaps a year old, but like no little person back in his village, for its hair was red and it would have been naked but for the strip of torn and soiled blanket it clutched.

He swept the child into his arms, his hand hardly feeling the quick bite from the boy's tiny milk teeth. Taking a length of sealskin line, Nook quickly trussed the little boy and, oblivious to his whimpering sobs, started skinning the bear. He noticed that her dugs held little milk and surmised that the cub and the child had for some time been more dependent on berries, roots, and perhaps even meat.

He placed the bear's bloody skull high on the rocks, for as an ancestor she was entitled to this attention. Then he skinned out the cub and packed the skin, wrapped around the meat, on the largest dog.

Back at his camp he turned the dogs loose. They would return to the bear carcass and eat their fill. He would not need them the next day anyway, for he would have to trim and flesh the hide and fold it into a shoulder pack. While a stew simmered in his black kettle he untied the child, speaking softly and avoiding, with a laugh, the little hands which clawed at him and the mouth that tried to bite. Holding him firmly, Nook filled his whalebone spoon with gravy, blew a few times to cool it, and pushed it between the close-clenched jaws. At first the child tried to spit it out but finally, won by the delicious taste, he began to swallow the broth greedily.

THE INUIT CAMP was a small one of only a dozen summer tents. These formed a little circle on a piece of flat land separating the beach of a narrow salt-water inlet from the boulders which rimmed the low tundra. Beyond the inlet the pack ice was freezing together, and it would not be long before the dark salt water became a frozen hunting ground for seal and walrus.

Snow had fallen before Nook's return, and the brown and scarlet of the tiny shrubs, dun grasses and low-growing arctic flowers just over-topped it. Where the wind had blown off some slopes, they looked like scattered bits of carpet; where it had left the rock faces bare, the low escarpment resembled an abstract design in black and white.

The little tents of caribou hide, held up by forked sticks, were a smudgy stain on the white scene, the smoke of cooking fires rising darkly into the bright, clean air. The autumn caribou hunt had been a good one, and the drying racks were full of meat. Many of the women were already shredding the dried meat between smooth stones.

Nook and his hunt were the talk of the camp. The Old Ones said it was not good that a white child—and raised by a bear at that— should be with the Inuit, the People. There had been an Indian child once, an old crone remembered, a young savage; *he* had been found on a hunt that went too far to the south, to where the trees stood on end like posts. The Inuit had cared for him, and what had *he* done? Brought a bad sickness to them from which many, and the small bearer himself, had died in great pain . . . .

"Each generation must learn its own lessons," the shaman said. And after he had looked at the entrails of an unmated caribou cow, he added, "Let him be tested, for I see no wrong here."

First the shaman looked long and hard at the dirty rag from

which the child refused to be parted, until he came to the marks woven with faded blue thread in one corner, thus: ΛΛ. This he drew thrice in the snow, while the people strained forward to see. Then he plucked three hairs from the boy's head, plaited them with dry grass from his wizard's bag, spat on them, and tossed them into the air. Whirling like a shuttlecock, the little bundle hurtled down and landed on the piece of cloth in front of the child. He crowed with delight and began to play with the bundle, tossing it high.

Still not completely satisfied, the shaman walked three times around the group of onlookers, one hand over his mouth, shaking a rattle and groaning. Then with a sudden yell he stopped, fumbled in the bag hung around his neck, and threw his magic walrus tooth directly at the child. It grazed the boy's cheek and fell with a thud behind his right shoulder—the shoulder which activates the arrow-hand. Now the shaman picked it up and studied it carefully: it had landed with the rune side up, the side carved with the strange marks that only a shaman can interpret.

Slowly he turned to the people, his face a mask. After a moment's silence, he spoke: "Let the child stay with the Inuit. The bear is an ancestor, and there is a purpose. Till *he* chooses, he stays.

"The magic grass says so. See, he clutches it and is not afraid! The walrus tooth says so. The rag of strange wool says so, for do you not see for yourselves," he pointed to the marks in the snow, "that he walks in confidence to our tents and later perhaps to other tents, in peace?" And he began a chant which was old when the Inuit were young:

> "I will take care not to go towards the dark,
>   for I will go always towards the light."

So the boy stayed. He learned to speak as people speak and to stand upright; soon, any memory of the cave and the bear passed, and he thought Nook and his plump wife were his parents. They had been childless and made much of him.

But sometimes one of the other little boys would put a finger on the white scars which crisscrossed the pale skin of his forearms. And secretly he would sometimes touch the same kind of scars on his

460

shins, and frown and try to remember. And once, when a hunter had killed a bear cub and brought the small, bleeding body into camp, the boy had stood looking till his chest ached and then suddenly burst into tears, a thing no Inuit child would do.

But he did not know why he had done so, and was ashamed.

THE BOY became part of the band of caribou Inuit who lived mostly inland. Their hunting grounds were rarely visited by strangers and in what little contact they had with the post at Coronation, the child was not mentioned, for it would be better, the shaman had told them, to keep it to themselves. He reminded them that the white man was unpredictable. Only fifteen years before, two Inuit had killed a white shaman, a priest, near the Copper River, from fear only, for he was the first white they had seen and they had misinterpreted his purpose. Soon after, a tall man with yellow striped pants, together with three more warriors like himself, had come and said they must not interfere with whites at any time; for the whites were powerful and under the protection of a great banner, such as flew at Coronation. And they said that under the banner all killing of men could be punished by hanging, but because the two Inuit had not known these things, they would spare them. But this was a hard thing for the Inuit to understand; if the banner forbade all killing, how could its servants hang men?

Moreover, the shaman concluded, there had now been, for several years, a yellow-leg man at Coronation, and it would be best if he did not know of the child, for fear there might be an accusation of theft—which the banner might think even worse than killing. And who among the whites would believe how the child had come to them?

Silence would be better.

They called him by a long name all made into one word, which means: "He came by way of a Bear Ancestor," this strange boy who could cry as their children could not. They complained only when they were hurt or hungry; not like this one, who became disturbed for nothing! But mostly they shortened the name to Nanuk, which means "a bear".

The boy loved to run and jump and play with the other children but after play was over, he often sat by himself, silent-looking, always looking towards the day. And always so eager and happy when the village moved south into the tundra to hunt the caribou.

Sometimes on these hunts they went as far as the tree-stick country, but not if Indian sign was around. Indians were savages who attacked without warning. Surely there were deer enough for all!

NANUK WAS three years old when the white man came. The village saw the stranger while he was still far off. The low winter sun threw his long shadow and that of his dogs almost to the camp, and they knew him for a white man: an Inuit would travel in company, and his dogs would be drawing a high-sided Alaskan sled.

The stranger halted his dogs some distance from the camp and approached with long strides. In halting Inuit he told them he was from the coast. They had already guessed that he was the yellow-leg man from Coronation.

He asked many questions. He wanted to know if they had found the carcass of a flying *komatik* during their travels in the barrens. One had been lost, he said, for almost three years. In trying to find it, he had visited all the bands of people for miles around and they, at this village, were the last. But no, the people said, they had found no such thing. If they did, they would try to send word to Coronation, but sometimes they were far away for as long as two years.

The policeman stayed with them that night, and was preparing to leave next morning, harnessing his dogs by moonlight although it was already late. Nook and some others stood watching him, and as the white man turned to bid them goodbye, a small boy came from behind the group and approached him shyly, staring. It was not until the little fellow had grasped him boldly by the stripe on his breeches that the policeman noticed him.

He looks white, he thought, and started to push back the boy's parka hood, catching a glimpse of what might have been blue eyes, just as the youngster backed away. The policeman was framing a question about the child when he saw Nook and his woman exchange a long, peculiar look; misinterpreting the crafty, sideways glance, the white man killed the words on his lips and began to fill

463

his pipe. Then he offered his tobacco pouch to Nook, who put a wad in his mouth and passed it on.

Moonlight plays strange tricks, the policeman thought, and sometimes so do white men in native camps. Often he had seen near-white children among the bands—the result of an indiscretion or perhaps wife-lending. He was pleased he had not inquired further, for he had no wish to offend.

Now he picked up his long whip, spoke to his dogs and, stepping on the back of the sleigh, cracked the whiplash and was gone. But as he listened to the whine of his sledge runners, and as the sky to the south began to brighten, he felt uneasy. He felt that something was left undone, and his thoughts were drawn willy-nilly to the woman he would never see again.

"Time for a transfer," he said aloud, and his lead dog answered with a low whine and increased the pace.

3

Nanuk was fifteen the year they had to go farther east than usual to find caribou. For some reason the animals had swerved from their usual migration route, and the Inuit lost a great deal of time before finding their feeding grounds.

Nanuk was already taller than many of the villagers, and still growing rapidly. But he was much slenderer of bone than they were and his height was more in his legs. The lad was no fool, the Old Ones agreed. He had a way with dogs that no show-off young Inuit could match, and no one of his age could handle the fire stick and bow so well. He was an apt pupil, the shaman found, and he understood many things which puzzled other boys of his age. He was also much more content to listen to the Old Ones, and asked many questions.

He went off much by himself. "Let him," said the shaman. "He has much to find behind his eyes. Already his ancestor spirit tells him that he is not a true Inuit. See how he walks! We do not swing our arms that way."

Though the Inuit hunted late that fall, penetrating farther towards the stick country than usual, mild weather meant the ground was still bare—even well into November.

Late one afternoon, Nanuk became separated from the other hunters as he followed a fine caribou bull he had wounded with an arrow. It had plunged south, towards a thick patch of trees, and he followed it for over a mile but did not press it close, knowing that before long it would lie down. Then its wound would stiffen and he would get another shot.

He left the open country in which they had found the herd, threaded his way through a close growth of young spruce, and came into the open again. Nanuk could not see the caribou, but heard a raven croak farther south and knew his game was there. When he did come upon it, it was dead, sprawled in a hollow where stunted willows grew. He could still hear, faintly, the shouts of the hunters behind him, as he carefully skinned his prize, using the good steel knife Nook had got him from the Company. As he worked, Nanuk felt a flake of snow on the back of his neck, another on his hand. He looked up. The sky was dark, speckled with the white spots which now came thicker and faster. He could no longer hear the voices of his friends. Then came a gust of wind, followed by another, and he felt suddenly cold.

By the time he had finished his job it was dark. A fierce wind tore at the scrub willows, and the snowflakes had become as small and sharp as sand. He could see no farther than the length of a whiplash in any direction. But Nanuk felt no fear; hardly annoyance. No Inuit is impatient, for weather is beyond changing. He would have to wait out the storm, that was all. He had a small tea pail at his belt, he had his knife and his bow. He had meat in plenty and the Labrador shrub grew in abundance here, so he would not want for a hot drink. But he would have to make a fire drill, using a piece of straight spruce for the upright, with his bow for power and a piece of half-rotten wood which lay underfoot for tinder.

It took him some time to make his simple instrument, working in almost total darkness, but his fingers were sensitive and he felt his way. The caribou skin, propped by a few sticks, made a windbreak, and he rotated his stick in a piece of punkwood under its shelter. He had a handful of dry moss and some small twigs ready, and soon there was a little puff of smoke, the punkwood glowed, and a fire no bigger than his hand crackled. He gathered deadfall to keep it fed.

As he finished his strip of broiled venison, his tea pail boiled over and the pungent and aromatic steam curled up around his face. Suddenly he started. Something brushed his shoulder and a cold nose was thrust against his. It was Ahneek, his favourite among Nook's sled dogs—the big yellow one with dark patches around his eyes and on his flanks. The dog looked north into the blizzard and whined, but, "No," said the boy, "we camp here tonight," and threw his companion a rib bone.

THE STORM LASTED all the next day and into the night, while Nanuk made shift to keep his fire going. On the second morning he woke to the whining of Ahneek and, as he ate, the dog walked back and forth, looking always to the north, then turning to push Nanuk with his nose, making little yelps, which the boy disregarded. During the night he had tried to think out something which had long disturbed him. Nook and his wife, the shaman, and all the Inuit had been very good to him. Yet always there was an urge within him which said he must leave them. For what, even now, he did not know. To find another people? Where? Not north, surely, for few lived there; east and west he knew, but that too was Inuit land.

South? He knew nothing about the south, but it was the land of the highest light, the light that always seemed to beckon him, towards which his spirit strained.

Why? And why did he yearn for another people?

Had it to do with his colouring? His features? So different from the other children of the camp, who resembled their parents. He was not like Nook or his wife and he knew in his heart, from hints, from looks, from the teasing of other children, that his beginning was not as theirs. His name, even . . . the name meant something like the Sign of the Bear . . . the Ancestor.

He was puzzled by the conflict within him. But an inner voice said: Now is your chance to find out. Already you are well on your way. Follow the light. Let the day be your guide and go towards it.

What could be there? Would there be big trees like those lying on the northern beaches—brought, it was said, by the great river to

466

the west? There were Indians, he knew, but it could not be they who drew him on; indeed, he would have to avoid them if he went.

If he went?

The thought of turning north again gave him no pleasure, although he loved Nook and Nook's wife. For years he had thought of her as his mother, but now he could not. That the Inuit would look for him he did not doubt. But the storm had destroyed his tracks, and he had been warned not to go too far into the scraggly timber. They would hardly look for him there. And if they did, he told himself with a sudden flash of resolution, they would not find him.

Nanuk tucked his knife carefully under his parka and rolled up the blue rag with the strange marks on it. He could never part with it, though he did not know why. He would rather have lost his fine knife. And even as he touched the rag he felt that it was what tugged and strained towards the unknown south, and he felt a tingling of his fingers which spread through him till his heart thumped.

He picked up his bow and his fire stick, wrapped a generous length of caribou side-ribs in the skin, and called Ahneek. Together they stepped out, their faces to the growing light in the south. Ahneek whined once or twice and made to turn back, testing the north with his nose. But each time he finally turned and caught up to the trudging boy, and soon he was content to pad easily by his side.

4

Nanuk was weary. For three days now, he and Ahneek had walked from long before dawn through the short, fitful day, camping each night by the sliver of moon which cast a pallid light over the snow.

Today the pull of sleep came early. The muskeg moaned and all the little stick trees shivered as if naked. Far and far they stretched in spidery webs between pool and frozen pool, between tussock and lichened rocks where the snow partridges clucked, while all around the cotton grass danced and quivered. At dusk, Nanuk lay down in the dry, bristly tussocks, Ahneek at his side. The boy lay wide-eyed, facing the sky, and tried to count the stars. But more and more came out to wink at him and he sighed at the impossibility of the task. Soon, boy and dog were asleep.

THEY AWOKE in darkness and Ahneek yawned, then stretched and got to his feet, nose to the southeast, as though his own yellow eyes would bring the sun over the black rim of the world. Slowly the horizon paled and the night became palest saffron, then as pink as the flesh of an arctic salmon. At that the boy rose too, and began to stretch the cramp from his bones. He would make no fire. It was not so bitterly cold and having slept later than usual, he felt the need to press on.

They had been walking for some time and the sun was well up before Nanuk became aware of a change, a softening of the southern horizon, as if a light film or vapour was rising and falling. As he paused to look, a faint southerly breeze began to patter through the low shrubs and made the sedges whisper; and with this movement came a sweet scent, like smoke.

The two walked on till the short day was well-nigh over, and Nanuk began to be hungry. They had come far, yet seemed little nearer to that strange smoke—if smoke it was. But then as the light paled and the ptarmigan fell silent, Nanuk thought he sometimes saw a dull, red gleam to the south.

By the time darkness covered the land, and the first wolf howl split the silence, the glow had increased, crouching behind the far distance like some skulking enemy. The boy looked for a place to camp.

NANUK HAD HOARDED his supply of frozen meat, eating little, sharing the bones with Ahneek and augmenting it with the partridge berries which grew on the hummocks of the winter barrens. He saw little game. The caribou would not be in these woods till the midwinter cold forced them from the open tundra. But once he had flushed a covey of ptarmigan that had been feeding on a patch of partridge berries. Tomorrow, he thought, as he resumed his journey, he would try to find such a spot again and set some snares for the white birds.

When it came on to snow again, the boy knew it would be wise to camp soon. He was drawing close to the red glow now and suddenly he noticed a thin spiral of smoke coming out of the ground. He turned towards it, leaving the scraggy trees behind and crossing a large, open muskeg. The smoke was rising from a crevice in a small hummock. Coming closer, he saw, almost at his feet, a hole with blackened edges from which came a ruby glow. He smelled the sweetness of burning peat, so like the smoke from tundra fires, and heard the soft hisses as the flakes of snow settled quietly and turned to steam. On the far side of the muskeg, he could see dozens of larger craters with rising smoke which hung like mist. The glow rose and fell; black became orange and turned to black again.

As the darkness deepened, so the glow became brighter. Occasionally larger, yellow flames flared up, as tussocks of heavy grass caught fire, illuminating the blackened trunks of small spruce. Some still stood upright; others leaned drunkenly sideways as the slow peat fire consumed their roots, burning away their footing; still others were already prone.

Now the soles of Nanuk's sealskin boots were becoming warm, so he stepped back, dragging Ahneek with him. He was just in time. A large piece of the peat he had been standing on gave way and sank with a sound like a sigh, ending in a crackle as its surface vegetation burst into flame. As it had been doing for years, the fire would devour the uncounted miles of muskeg, but so slowly did it probe and crawl that Nanuk could camp safely within fifty yards of the peat bog's edge, and sleep in comfort, for the smoke warmed the air.

HE CAMPED there all the next day. The snow let up before noon and he heard the clucking of ptarmigan off to the right. They were feeding in a patch of berries but flew off at his approach. He had taken the long sinew from the back of the caribou he had killed, and now he separated it into its tough threads. With these he fashioned two snare loops and set them carefully among the low plants.

He returned to his fire, and as he sipped some bitter but strengthening Labrador tea, he heard the birds once more. About an hour later, as snow began to fall again, he returned to his snares. Only one ptarmigan had been caught and he quickly throttled it, then put the two snares in his parka. It was not worthwhile to reset them, for the full-cropped birds would roost somewhere under the snow till the skies cleared.

NANUK AWOKE to a cloudless sky, his body warm but heavy beneath a deep covering of snow. The short-lived storm had passed and now the moon hung low in the west. Over the muskeg a low, thick blanket of smoke hung, obscuring it so completely that it might have been a lake. All was still, from the dog at his feet to the farthest point his vision could reach, and shivering, Nanuk rose, shaking off the clinging snow. He threw some wood on his peat fire, filled his pail with snow and set it to boil, breaking in the Labrador bush leaves with their russet undersides, like dry leather. He had only half of his grilled ptarmigan left, the last of his food, but he savoured the cold meat, eating slowly.

Nanuk's mind felt troubled that morning. He had dreamed of Nook's warm tent of caribou skin, of the flat, smiling faces, the smell of warm bodies and food cooking and seal oil. He was lonely, as he had never been before. He and Ahneek alone lived in this world which frightened him with its silence and threatened him with its flitting shadows. He had heard the shaman speak of the spirits of the trees—which were to be avoided, as Indians were to be avoided.

He almost resolved to turn back, but he had walked too many weary miles for that. No; the dice had been thrown and he must abide by their decision—just as the Old Ones always abided by the position of the ivory counters when they gambled.

To go back was more dangerous than to go ahead, for surely the tree belts were becoming thicker now, the trees pressing closer, and in their shelter must be game. Where there is game there must be people, and if they could live, so could he.

Yet even these thoughts brought no comfort. He had no words for what he felt, but it was as though he was empty inside. Under his ribs, inside his limbs, behind his eyes—all was empty. So empty that when he bowed his head and held his face in his hands, only dry sobs racked him. He felt Ahneek come to his side, pushing under

470

his arm with his nose, uttering little grunts of understanding, till the boy threw his arms about his companion and buried his face in the cold, frosty fur. Then the dog licked his face and soon Nanuk's heart warmed, and filled with resolution. By the tears he knew once more that he was not an Inuit, but still he walked in the Sign of the Bear. He had medicine around his waist. He had feet which could take him as far as he wished—and a companion who would be faithful unto death, who felt no fear, who even now scratched at the snow, eager to set off.

Nanuk rose stiffly, knowing that never again would weakness overcome him; where he had been a boy he was now a man, and he was ready for any challenge.

THEY HAD HARDLY got into their stride when a hooting sound startled them, and they stood quite still, listening. It came again: three, four long hollow notes, followed by a living silence. Again and again the eerie notes sounded across the flat, bristly land.

Fear caught at Nanuk's throat. Was this one of the malignant spirits for which his new resolution was prepared? Perhaps one of the cannibal spirits of which the Inuit speak only in low voices, one of those which draw the soul from a body as it sleeps and leave it a mad, gibbering thing . . . . But a sudden thought allayed Nanuk's fears. These spirits were believed in by the Inuit; therefore they must be avoided by them. But he was not an Inuit—already he was sure of that—and if he chose not to believe, then the thing had no power over him; for him, it did not exist. Besides, he was in a strange country, so why should there not be strange creatures?

He walked on, every sense alert but not in fear, only in curiosity, his sealskin boots making little noise. Ahneek was as noiseless, and to an onlooker the two would have seemed to be drifting ghost-like, rather than marching—so silent, so almost unseen were they in that dusky half-light between the moon's setting and the sun's rising.

They stopped at the edge of a thick, dark grove of swamp spruce, and once again came that hollow voice, now overhead. Nanuk, searching the trees with his eyes, saw a shadowy form perched near the dead top of the nearest one. "Hoo, hoo," it called again and

471

the boy looked right into staring yellow eyes, burning with the reflection of the first rays of light.

This could be no evil spirit. An animal of some sort, he thought, and an animal meant meat. Quickly he strung his bow, quicker still he adjusted an arrow and took aim.

The shaft caught the creature full-body and scraping through the branches, it thudded to the ground and lay still. It was only a bird, though of great size; an owl, Nanuk guessed, for its taloned feet and round face were much like those of the white owls of the tundra, though their voices were not so frightening. Much cheered, he picked it up and on they went, swinging far to the west to work around the smoking muskeg.

As noon approached, Nanuk found that he could once more bear to the east, and by the time the sun set, the pall of smoke was behind his left shoulder. When they stopped for the day, Nanuk skinned and broiled the owl, carefully salvaging each drop of melting fat in his tin pail. The bird's feathers he stuffed into his sealskin boots for added warmth. That night, he would patch their worn soles with pieces of caribou hide.

5

That week was one of walking, camping, gathering berries, and snaring the now rare ptarmigan. The last two days, Nanuk was reduced to cooking small portions of lichen. Bitter as it was, it augmented the wild tea, and had saved many a hunter's life.

As they travelled south, the snow became deeper, no longer lying in drifts but evenly spread. It puzzled Nanuk, for he had thought that closer to the light, there might be less snow. He did not know that the fall was heavier in the forest than on the barrens.

They were coming into bigger timber now, with spruce in the hollows between the low rock outcrops and gnarled birch on which the bark hung tattered. He had pulled some of this bark away and found it to be oily and easily ignited, and from then on always contrived to carry some of it in his parka for kindling fires.

For two more days, Nanuk looked in vain for tracks. Then he

472

came upon a little pile of cones on top of the snow, from which small footprints led to a pine tree. Ahneek ran to the tree, put his front paws high against it, and began to whine as a little creature with a bushy tail chattered at him. It looked to Nanuk like a ground marmot of the barrens, but smaller and darker with much more tail. Soon it was joined by another and he managed to kill both of them.

Tucking the little animals into the flap of his parka and replacing the arrows he had used in his skin quiver, the boy pushed on, Ahneek at his side. But he soon found that his meagre fare had weakened him. He stumbled more often and was slower to regain his balance.

The next day, walking down the slope of a smooth, high outcrop, he felt himself slipping in the snow. His feet flew out from under him and he landed heavily in a deep crevice, hitting his head. He lay for a moment, stunned, then everything below him heaved and he was thrown sideways. He became dimly aware that Ahneek was barking and growling at once, a thing he rarely did. Then the dim light was blotted out, as a rank, sickening scent came to his nostrils, and his left arm was seized by some enormous, hairy thing which bore him down.

He felt himself being dragged along between the steep walls of rock; clumsily he reached under his parka with his good arm, fumbling for his knife. When he got hold of it, he stabbed upward with all his strength, felt the blade drive deep, then a gush of hot blood struck him full in his face, almost choking him. Spitting it out, he became aware that he was in the open, at the foot of the ridge. His arm was free and all around was noise: thudding and stamping mixed with whines and hissing growls.

Ahneek, bloodstained, held grimly to the ear of a great brown bear, which slashed at him with long, cruelly curved claws. Blood was everywhere, and the bear's roaring.

Nanuk stooped for his knife and, legs bruised and trembling, moved back to where his bow and arrows should be. He found them but all the arrows were broken. Hardly knowing what he was doing, he grasped a heavy stone and, staggering under its weight, approached the two animals. Desperately the bear lashed out at Ahneek, while the dog dodged this way and that without losing his hold. Stepping close, the boy brought the stone down with all his might on the bear's snout. The animal roared and shook its head, blood gushing from its broken jaw, almost shaking off Ahneek's grip.

Then with one more desperate lunge, the bear tore free and turning from the dog, made for Nanuk, who was clambering up the rocks. But it was weakening from loss of blood, and the boy was able to scramble away. Ahneek rushed in again, and seized the bear by a leg. Round and round they went, the dog avoiding those awful front paws, the bear's head sagging lower and lower.

Nanuk, who had gained the crest of the outcrop, now felt such a stab of pain in his left arm that he looked quickly at it. Blood was running down into his mitt, but the arm was not broken, so he grasped the knife more firmly and had begun to descend when quite suddenly, the bear's limbs sagged and it fell. But only when a last shudder had passed over the creature's body did Ahneek let go.

Staggering away from the bear, the dog fell on his side and Nanuk knelt by him, scrutinizing his wounds. There were deep claw slashes along Ahneek's ribs and flanks and one swollen hind foot had lost two toes. When he touched it, Ahneek trembled and whimpered.

Turning over the dog's heavy body was not easy with one arm, but the boy accomplished it, and found to his relief that Ahneek's other side bore only a couple of superficial cuts. Nanuk then fetched the caribou hide, and unrolled it by Ahneek, managing to drag him onto it, and packing snow under him so that the dog lay comfortably.

NOW NANUK had to get a fire going—a slow and painful process, for while he could use his wounded arm a little, he had not sufficient strength in it to press heavily enough on the upright stick while he operated the bow with his good arm. He had to put the full weight of his throbbing head on top of his hand, and then press with all his might. Finally, a little puff of smoke rose and the punk-wood glowed, as he laboriously piled dead twigs and watched them catch, followed by chunks of resinous branches, until the blaze shot high.

Next, he had to turn his attention to the bear before it froze. He

474

wanted the skin, and he also needed some meat. Weary to the bone, his gashed face sore and bloody, the boy set his teeth and drove his knife through the tough skin. It would be but half a hide or less; he could never turn over the dead weight to get at the other side. But it would make a fine robe to lie on if he could manage to carry it.

Pulling the last of the hide away, he turned to Ahneek and could have shouted for joy to see that the dog was sitting up and licking his flank. Now, in spite of the throbbing pain of his arm, Nanuk hummed a little as he stretched the hide flat, close enough to the fire to prevent it freezing, and then cut long slices of meat from the bear's rump, first removing the two-inch layer of fat which covered it. Both meat and fat he sliced into smaller pieces, which he laid on the snow to freeze. He would have a good supply for the next few days, but a supply limited by what he could carry.

As he set two pieces to broil for his supper, his thoughts revolved around his lucky escape. Truly, he walked in the Sign of the Bear, the great beast which the tribes held in such reverence. And the bear had died, not he, for the beast of the cave could not withstand his spirit. Or was it really *his* spirit? The Inuit spoke of evil spirits which, if not appeased, could destroy the spirit of man. But might there not be one great Good Spirit, mightier than they, who protected people, who gave to man the power to overcome? He felt no presence of evil in these woods. Why, he thought, should people fear the unknown? Or was it that if one walked through fear, then fear had no power?

How he wished the Good Spirit could, would speak to him . . . ! Perhaps even now it *was* speaking, through his own mind . . . and perhaps he would find the answer at his journey's end.

IT WAS GETTING much colder, so that night Nanuk made a rough shelter of forked sticks and spruce boughs, open to the fire's warmth. Then he considered the matter of his wound and Ahneek's injuries.

A resinous piece of deadfall blazed up, the gum spluttering as it melted. With that, the boy remembered that Inuit women used the gum to treat wounds: it was one of the things they brought back when the band hunted far to the south.

Nanuk rose and went to the spruce trees. Their trunks were

476

bright copper in the firelight, and several large globules of the balm hung from gashes about the height of his shoulder, made by a caribou rubbing its antlers. With his knife he pried off several lumps and returned to his shelter.

He held a piece of the resin to the fire on his knife blade and when it began to soften, laid knife and all on a piece of bark, painfully stripped off his parka, and examined his arm. The tooth marks did not appear to be deep. Caribou hair, forced through his parka, had made a mat which stopped the bleeding. He dabbed the area with the sticky gum, hoping he was doing the right thing. He had seen worse wounds than this heal rapidly, and he took it for a good sign that his arm felt hot and feverish.

Replacing his parka, leaving his left arm out of the sleeve, he turned his attention to Ahneek, plastering the worst wounds with the gum—but lightly, for he knew the dog's own tongue would be the best medicine; that, and food and rest. Then, dead tired, the boy threw big chunks of damp deadfall on the fire, banked it up with ashes, pulled the bear hide over himself and fell asleep.

He woke within an hour. Great gusts of nausea seized him, and he had to rise and go to one side, and was violently ill. Perhaps he had eaten too greedily of the bear meat, he thought, or was it poison from his wound which caused this rebellion of his stomach? Exhausted, he returned to his bed and slept.

Towards morning he began to dream. He tossed about and thought he woke once or twice, yet he could not be sure. Strange visions danced and gibbered before his eyes. Balls of fire came between him and something for which he seemed to search on hands and knees. Voices, too, spoke to him from little trees which danced a jig in and out among the rocks. Something roared and smothered him and he tried to raise a feeble arm; but the arm was hot, full of knives, and it would not obey. Then he was walking, walking, but he could not feel his feet and he kept stumbling . . . .

NANUK HAD LOST all track of time when he came to. It was dark and very cold: the fire had apparently burned out. Ahneek was standing over him, rumbling deep in his throat, and the boy half turned and flung up his good arm as if to ward off danger. But the dog stooped and licked his face, then stared again into the velvety blackness.

Weakly, Nanuk crawled to the ashes of his fire. Some embers remained and from his parka, the boy took a piece of birch bark which he coaxed into flame. As the small fire caught, he heard a muffled movement from the darkness beyond the faint outline of the bear carcass. Then he saw a pair of yellow eyes; and another. Ahneek let out a growl that was more like a roar, and jumped forward stiffly. The eyes disappeared like a flame blown out.

So, the wolves had found the kill. It was not a good thought. Wolves were cowards, but a weak man and a crippled dog . . .? He replenished his fire, and when the sticks had caught, threw a branch with what strength he could in the direction of the wolves, sparks flying in an arc.

All was quiet but soon they heard a howl from at least a mile away, answered by another, and yet another. They were safe for the time being, and if he kept the fire going well, Nanuk thought, they would be for the few days that would give them both strength to continue on their way.

IN THE END, the travellers stayed over a week in their snug camp between the humped rock and the sheltering spruce. During that time Ahneek occupied himself for hours in licking his wounds, which looked pink and healthy. Nanuk's arm had swelled horribly, but he knew nothing of blood poisoning and so accepted the discomfort cheerfully enough.

On the fifth day, when he removed his parka by the warmth of the fire and started to lay more gum on the swollen wound, Ahneek pushed his hand aside and began to lick the sore. The feel of that pink tongue was soothing and soon matter oozed from the wound. The boy wiped it off with a handful of dry moss, and his arm felt much relieved. Nanuk replaced his parka, and after that, exposed his arm daily to Ahneek's healing tongue.

Daily he also increased the amount of food he ate, and daily he had to stumble among the trees in the bitter cold, to gather twigs and dry limbs. Fire was life now, and as he began to wander farther afield in his quest for fuel, he felt his strength increasing.

The day before leaving camp, Nanuk went over to the bear's carcass. He wanted something to show, should he ever have to tell the story. With his knife, he cut off the great claws from the beast's front feet, and then he began to make careful preparations for continuing his journey. First he made shafts for new arrows, then a new fire drill, choosing his material carefully. Then he mended the arm of his torn parka with some lengths of sinew, piercing holes with his knife point and using a small piece of caribou hide for a patch.

Next day, he would complete his preparations, but that night before he lay down, he inspected his arm and found that the swelling had subsided, and new pink skin was slowly spreading. Nanuk felt very thankful to the Unseen Power which worked even as he slept.

IN THE MORNING, he dried out his sweat-dampened boots, hanging them well above the fire on long sticks, and while they hung, dried and fluffed out the owl feathers before replacing them. He also dried a double handful of moss to take with him should he have to camp where none was available.

He wanted to take the big piece of bear hide, so he cut a long, narrow strip from one side of it for binding. Then Nanuk wrapped a good store of the sliced and frozen meat in the hide, folding it over and over. With the strip he bound the pack together, leaving two long ends to put over his shoulders and tie at the back.

Replacing his knife carefully in the blue rag he still carried next to his skin, he picked up his bow and arrows, and started off with never a backwards glance, Ahneek limping at his heels.

6

That day, they came to a frozen river which crossed their path from southwest to northeast, where it took a sharp bend; from that direction came the roaring sound of a rapid about half a mile away. Along the riverbank, the treetops were swathed in white frost which had gathered on them as the waters below had steamed in the cold

479

before they finally froze. Nanuk judged by this that the river ice would be none too thick.

He made camp in the shelter of an overhanging bank and gathered enough wood to last till morning. Then he and Ahneek ate. After caching the supplies high in a tree where they would be safe from marauders, Nanuk banked a fire and settled down for the night with Ahneek on a bed of spruce boughs.

When they woke in the pale morning light, a mass of pink fog was rising beyond the bend, and a few fine wisps hung over the ice before them. Nanuk took a stout branch to test the ice ahead as they started for the opposite shore, a hundred yards ahead. The strength of the current had prevented freezing until the last really cold days and as they reached halfway, the boy felt the ice bend beneath him. Then he saw a narrow, open channel before them, the dark water rushing northwards, and they stopped, then turned back. As the ice began to give way beneath them, Nanuk held the branch parallel to it, to hold him up if they went through. The boy was sweating when they reached firm ice again but at the shore he turned southwest, Ahneek beside him, and they followed the loops and bends of the river, looking for a safe crossing. But they could find none and finally camped just after dusk.

That night the frost strengthened. So bitter was it that Nanuk built two fires a few feet apart. As they lay, the boy and dog could hear the trees above the bank popping like rifle shots, while the ice below them boomed and muttered. They slept fitfully and awoke chilled. Little crystals of ice clung to Nanuk's eyelashes and to his parka hood, and Ahneek's jowls were heavily rimed.

The boy decided to continue down the west bank of the river until the increasing cold safely froze the ice. He would be working a little west but as the river flowed now, he would at least be making his way south.

For two more days they pushed on, sometimes clambering painfully over rocks and fallen trees, or climbing the riverbank and threading their way through the brush and timber. It was clear and sharply cold, and the steam from their breath hung like smoke in their wake. The sun hung low in the south, making narrow ribbons of blue shadow run over the snow from the base of every tree. No squirrels chattered now, and the snow was unbroken for miles.

At night, lying in their tiny world, warmed by the glow of a fire, the two cared little for the black, fathomless depths around them; overhead the sky was so charged with brilliant stars that it made a bright canopy above the sombre tops of spruce. Then, one night, the stars were dimmed by the green and pink of the northern lights, which played and swung so close that Nanuk felt he could touch their trembling curtains with his fingertips. He knew this as a sign for some let-up in the bitter cold; and next morning, to be sure, the frost eased. The two companions broke camp and stepped forth almost gaily, trotting like children, Ahneek snatching at the snow with his jaws and tossing it up to sparkle like a shower of diamonds.

The trees stood pure and unsullied against a cobalt sky shot with a few fleecy clouds, gold and faintly pink. Only the river below was half obscured by a film of frost-fog, blue-grey beneath the shadowing banks. The boy was sure of his directions. When he had the sun to guide him, he used it; when skies were leaden he knew the south by the lie of the snowdrifts, by the trees' lighter south and darker north sides. In the predawn darkness and after sunset, he had the stars and the moon, and when these were obscured, instinct held him on his course. Never having been frightened by adult tales of failure, he hardly thought of it.

THE CROSSING Nanuk finally chose was about forty-five miles from where he had first tried to cross the river. It was considerably narrower here, the banks lower and more heavily clad with willows. He scraped a small patch of ice and, looking down, could see no flow of dark water beneath. Even the rocks were frozen firmly to the bottom.

Such ice could carry a herd of caribou, so he started confidently across but was soon walking in much deeper snow. He reminded himself that it was now midwinter and the heaviest snowfalls lay ahead. He would have to contrive some snowshoes.

They stopped for a moment on the far side of the river, looking back, Ahneek pressed close to Nanuk's side. Their tracks had made blue slots across the snowy channel; the crossing seemed an achievement, a marker on their journey.

Satisfied, they climbed the bank through a heavy fringe of timber, then came to more open ground again. There Nanuk saw a dozen sagging poles set in a circle with their tops meeting, and plunged forward in excitement. This was the pole frame of a hunter's lodge, the kind his own people sometimes used, covering the poles with skins.

He kicked the snow away and found long-dead ashes. No one had been here recently but the lodge must have been put up by Indians, he thought, and resolved to proceed with caution. He must now be within the hunting ground of the savage tribes which had no love for the Inuit, and Nanuk did not wish to be caught off guard.

Heading south, he passed several more sets of lodge poles, some partially collapsed, but it was a much greater surprise to come upon a small log shack.

He had never seen a shack, but he recognized it as man's work by the trimmed logs and the cut poles of the earth-covered roof. Weeds grew on the roof, as he could see by the brittle fronds which shivered above the snow covering, and a round black thing like a small log stood up near the centre.

The cabin door was ajar, and the rising wind made it creak on its rawhide hinges. Nanuk entered, looking carefully about. There was just enough light for him to make out a rough table of poles, a bunk of the same—although he had no idea what it was—and a rusty tin stove, like one or two he had seen among the Inuit. "Here we stop," he said aloud to Ahneek.

From a thick growth of willows at the back of the cabin, Nanuk gathered some twigs. An armful of split wood already sprawled on the dirt floor inside and soon smoke was pouring from the pipe on the roof. The only other thing in the cabin was a blackened lard pail which he took to fill with water from the small, deep creek he had seen beyond the willows.

The pail was a real find and he used it to boil up a stew of bear meat while he made a brew of spruce tips in his own little tea pail. He had made this drink before; though he had never heard of it, from chewing the tips he instinctively guessed that spruce should not be poisonous. What he did not know was that this was just what his system required to remove the last traces of the infection from his arm. He sipped it slowly till his body glowed with warmth.

The sun had long set when the late moon shone in, touching with silver the two who slept so soundly on the floor.

NEXT MORNING, the dawn broke feverishly, as liverish wisps of cloud scudded across the sun, foretelling high winds and even more bitter cold. The air became foggy, and soon the horizon was obscured. By evening, snow was coming in gusts, lashing around the cabin. That day, Nanuk and Ahneek had rested. In the morning, the boy would start to make some snowshoes.

After gathering a good supply of wood for fuel, he looked for spruce boughs which were sound but not too stiff. These he cut to length for the side bows, two to each shoe, then steamed the front ends to give the toes the proper upward bend, so they would not catch on every obstruction. He notched these ends for the sinew which would bind them together, and pared down the hind ends so that they would fit snugly to form a long heel. With his knife, Nanuk slotted the bows to let in the crossbars which were about nine inches long and having inserted them, drew the fronts together, lacing them tightly with strips of hide as he had seen Nook do. Then he bent them enough to join the heels and when they came together, lashed them tight as well. Now he had to make holes for the final fastening and, using his bow to rotate a nail he had found, he drilled at intervals all around the wooden frames. Through these holes he would thread laces of caribou hide for the webbing.

He spent the next day weaving these webs, and the strong wrapping which kept the bars from spreading. Finally, he rubbed bear fat into the webbing and set his somewhat crooked snowshoes to dry.

THE TWO DAYS' delay had strengthened both boy and dog, but Nanuk's eyes felt sore from the glare of the sun-dazzled snow they had been traversing. Before they set off again, he stopped to carve a pair of goggles from a piece of birch bark, leaving slits for his eyes and attaching a rawhide string to each side.

Ahneek could now put his lame foot to the ground with only a suggestion of a limp; and the boy, seeing this, decided that the big dog could carry his pack. He lashed it to Ahneek's back with the binding piece, and they started out, looking like a respectable snowshoed hunter and his well-packed dog rather than a pair of wanderers.

Daily now, the forest thickened. They were in the heart of the taiga, the boreal forest. Even the muskegs showed patches of arctic birch and red willows only half covered by the deep snow. In one such area, the black spruce were only a foot or so taller than Nanuk and grew almost as thick as rushes. Once they saw a tiny owl which Nanuk could have taken in his hand. But it was too small to eat and he passed it by with a smile because it looked so comical as it turned its round head towards him.

Every night the boy searched for a good camping place on the higher ground where large spruce spread their cone-heavy limbs; here it was easier to find firewood, and the shallow snow could be scraped away to expose a soft duff of rotted needles upon which he could make a comfortable bed.

He killed a squirrel or two during these milder days and once, a big black and white woodpecker with a red crest which yakked at him from a dead tree. Otherwise he saw little sign of life beyond the remains of an old wolf kill from which an ermine scuttled. By its bones, he knew it had been a caribou, and he felt heartened, for he had not seen a sign of those animals since his journey began.

THEY TRAVELLED for another month, while the woods became denser. Now Nanuk began to see signs of man; some cut stumps indicating a camping place, a blazed tree, the remains of a deadfall.

The bear meat was long exhausted, and for many days now, the boy had seen no ptarmigan. He had made do with squirrels for himself and Ahneek, and with lichens, but there was little nourishment in them. Though he did not know it, he was far south of the winter pastures of the little northern deer, for which he looked in vain.

Then one morning he came to an open muskeg and saw five animals watching him. Even at a distance of perhaps three hundred yards, he could see how fine and fat these woodland caribou were. They had recently lost three of their little band to the Chipewyan Indians, and were restless. Snorting and stamping, they wheeled in a flurry of kicked-up snow, and were soon lost to sight.

The sun reached a little higher each day now and after another cold snap in the middle of February, there was a change—a light, soft breeze which made the snow begin to glaze in the open. Lumps of snow fell from the trees where squirrels could be heard chattering to each other. Nanuk shot several with his bow, but he longed for something less stringy to eat.

More broad-leaved trees began to appear, though still in their winter nakedness. Many open, grassy muskegs wound through the forest, threaded by small creeks, their sluggish waters frozen solid. In places, beds of cattails followed these narrow channels, their spear-pointed tops shivering. Fascinated by all he saw, Nanuk contrasted the mass of line and colour with the austerity of his old home on the barrens.

Twice he crossed the tracks of some big beasts which must have had longer legs than caribou, for though they sank much farther in the deep snow, they seemed not to flounder; and he found places among the willows and alders where one had been browsing on twigs well above Nanuk's head, for there hung tufts of coarse hair, almost black. Whatever they were, they did not travel in herds.

Nanuk killed several strange birds among a group in the spruce above, where they sat and peered at him. The first one that he shot fell with a thud, but the others did not take flight. He downed three more, then missed the fifth shot, his arrow striking a branch. As though disappointed that the show was over, the remaining three launched themselves on short, rounded wings and disappeared into the gloom of the forest.

He later dressed the birds, and found dry spruce needles in their crops—their flesh bitter with the flavour. When one day he learned that they were called "fool hens", he could understand why.

7

A few days later they crossed a toboggan trail which had perhaps been made a week before, and followed it a short way. When he came to a place where the toboggan had halted and snowshoe tracks went off to one side, Nanuk guessed this was an Indian trap line; a tuft of grass hung in a willow fork also indicated the position of a set. Nanuk did not investigate further, for another person's traps are as sacred to an Inuit as to a Chipewyan. But he knew he must soon meet the savage Indians whom the Inuit feared. Though he did not know how they spoke or if he would understand them, he supposed he would be able to speak to them by signs. By now, he was more curious than apprehensive.

And when Nanuk finally did see a Chipewyan camp, it came as no great surprise. Ahneek had been whining about for at least an hour before they broke through a thick tangle of willows to stand and look towards a little cluster of smoke-stained lodges. The camp was set in a grove of jack pine which topped a sandy ridge, and they could see people moving about and the smoke from their fires.

With Ahneek by his side, Nanuk moved slowly forward. Suddenly, with a chorus of yapping barks, a group of lean sled dogs left the tents and rushed towards them, half menacingly, half in play. Ahneek answered with a roar and ran towards them. They met halfway, the big yellow husky and the mongrels, all stopping as one in their several places. The leader of the Indian curs finally stepped forward, stiff-legged and wary, to within a few paces of Ahneek. He was Ahneek's height, but less heavily built, with a grey, battle-scarred muzzle. Also stiff-legged, his bushy tail tightly curled over his haunches, Ahneek turned sideways, ears and mane erect, lip curled.

Nanuk strode nearer, as three men from the camp approached at a jog trot. Both dogs moved at once, silently, and in seconds they were in the blurred rough-and-tumble of a fight, the others looking on, ready to back the winner. The Indians began to lay about them with sticks until the animals parted, while Nanuk seized Ahneek by his harness.

Honours even—with the odds perhaps in favour of Ahneek—the two animals stood panting but no longer enemies. Assured that his friend was not hurt, Nanuk looked up to face the Chipewyans.

The man in the centre was the oldest. He wore patched, faded blue pants and a hooded parka of glazed moosehide, the sleeves heavily fringed, the hood trimmed with wolverine fur. Around his

486

waist was a frayed sash in which a sheathed knife was stuck. His companions wore hooded coats of blanket cloth, once white but now grey, and cross-striped with black and red. The men were leaner and taller than most Inuit, with faces less flat, eyes larger, and cheekbones prominent; their leanness of face was accentuated by their shoulder-length hair. They smelled of buckskin and willow smoke.

The centre man stepped forward and spoke in a series of guttural clicks, evidently asking a question. Because he spoke first, Nanuk took him for the headman of the village and politely extended his left hand, the heart-hand, as he made the only reply he could.

Touching his chest with his right forefinger, he said, "Inuit."

The three stared and began to talk among themselves, their faces dark and scowling. The chief stepped closer, and while Nanuk, his heart beginning to pound, stood straight and unflinching, the Indian lightly touched his blond, downy cheek, then pointed to the snow.

"Inuit," said the boy again. He removed the worn piece of caribou hide which covered his shoulders and held it out to them. They gathered around with grunts of recognition, one pointing to the north. Then one of them spoke haltingly in another tongue with an upward inflection, and Nanuk heard the word "Eskimo" for the first time in his life. But he did not understand and so remained silent.

Ahneek came to his master's side, growling slightly, and the Indians drew back a little. But when Nanuk took the pack from the dog's back and laid the piece of bear hide next to the caribou skin, the three men stared hard and put their hands over their mouths. One exclaimed questioningly in Cree, "*Wha! Mishi Makwa?*" at which the boy, mistaking the question for an Inuit word connected with fire, brought from his parka the fire stick.

The Indians exclaimed again, taking the stick in their hands, turning it and smelling the charred and blackened point. One of them pointed to Nanuk's snowshoes and laughed, showing white teeth. Another came close and touched the bow which hung from his shoulder; then, smiling, the Indian pointed first to the little stick then to the bow, making sawing motions with his right hand. Again the three covered their mouths, their eyes bright with interest.

487

On an impulse, Nanuk plunged his hand into his parka and brought out one of the long curved claws he treasured, handing it to the chief, who exclaimed and seemed pleased. He made no move to return it, but stood looking from it to the long scars on the dog's side; so Nanuk half turned to show his parka, all roughly patched on its upper arm, and pointed to it. The Indians again talked among themselves, indicating in turn the boy, the dog and the claw.

Then the chief, apparently happy with his gift, made the motion of eating, at which Nanuk nodded vigorously, and the four, with Ahneek following, started towards the smoking tents.

By now, a little crowd of people had gathered in front of the tents, some young men and a few ancients in front. Several shawled women, full of curiosity, had left the lodges to watch, their children peeping from behind their full skirts of faded print. They all made way as the chief approached with his entourage, the stranger in their midst. He stopped by a tepee before which a fire smoked, and his wife left the large black pot she had been stirring to fetch several battered tin bowls and crooked spoons, as well as a thick, round flour cake which they call bannock. The chief indicated the steaming pot and the men squatted as Nanuk filled a bowl with coarse, dark meat. He pointed at it and then looked inquiringly around.

One man said, in the clicking speech, "*Mooswa*," and indicated an enormous set of antlers lying by the lodge; not long and skinny like a caribou's but broad and shovel-like. Could the antlers and this meat come from the animals whose deep slots he had seen? As if guessing his thoughts, the man who spoke Cree got up, went to a tall willow, and began to break twigs as high as he could reach, indicating a browsing animal. Nanuk smiled and nodded in understanding.

The stew was good and they all ate heartily. By the time the meal was finished, Ahneek came to lie just behind Nanuk. The other dogs had followed but as they came close to the fire, the women had driven them off with sticks, using harsh words. But Nanuk's hosts made no move to drive off Ahneek and by a tacit understanding, the boy and his friend were not parted.

The Indians now produced tobacco and began to fill their pipes.

There was tea also, hot tea sweet with sugar, into which the men stirred some white fat from a pail. The stars were coming out as the last tin cup was drained and the chief, whose name was Exkees, indicated the conical lodge, which he entered, followed by the two travellers. The chief pointed to some skin robes and, taking one, the boy chose a spot by the lodge wall and lay down.

He was weary, yet he could not sleep. The old, familiar bustle of people moving about and speaking softly; the nostalgic smell of tobacco and human bodies; the whimper of a child, the crooning of its mother; all these brought back memories which came and went, fluttering like the little snowbirds of the summer barrens.

He thought of Nook, thickset and silent, of Nook's wife, who had mothered him, of the long stories told by the Old Ones. And when a drum was thumped softly in a neighbouring lodge, he thought of the shaman's quavering voice as he sang of the spirit world, and Nanuk was suddenly homesick.

GRADUALLY the women and children got used to the tall, silent youth who spoke by signs. All the children wanted him to make them fire sticks and little bows; and it was they who taught him his first words of the Déné—or Chipewyan—language. He learned fast, for children are patient teachers, and though he never got beyond a halting speech, he knew enough for everyday purposes.

Nanuk's stay opened his eyes to many things, and especially to the fallacy of the Inuit belief that the Indians were savage and cruel.

They happily included him in their activities; once he went on a moose hunt with a party of them and thrilled at the sight of a great bull they brought down, using their large rifles. Its antlers were a disappointment, though; at this season, they were no more than two furry bumps on its forehead, the growing replacement for the wide rack the beast had shed earlier. Nanuk felt the bulbous nose and rubbery lip, which he was later to taste as a delicacy.

They had smaller rifles for killing birds and in the camp, Nanuk saw many other strange pieces of equipment which the Indians, pointing east, let him know had come from the white man's store at a place called Brochet. They spoke often of the whites and their ways and he would listen, trying to understand.

Just behind the camp was a large lake where the Indians fished. After cutting a hole in the ice, they pushed their nets underneath with a long spruce pole. When it had gone full length, one of their dogs would scratch and bark at the pole's far end—invisible under the ice—and a man would use his ice pick to find it and push it along again. This they repeated till a long net hung in the water below the ice. To each end of the net, the men attached long strings which they left coiled and anchored securely on the ice surface. The next morning, they would pull the string at one end, remove the fish from the net, and reset it by drawing back the other string. At this season the catch was not great; still, it was a welcome change for Nanuk to eat whitefish or lake trout, the latter as pink as the salmon of the Inuit.

But the first time he saw a woman light a cooking fire with a little lump of stick, not so long as her finger and with a red head, Nanuk jumped back, for it looked like magic. Then she showed him some in a tin box and, by signs, bade him take one and draw it across a piece of rough canvas. It flared, and he stood staring at the little flame till it consumed the stick. He dropped it then, and they both laughed.

Indeed these people neither looked nor acted like devils at all, and were not unlike the Inuit—except in features. In most things, they were more like them than he himself was . . . .

DAILY THE LIGHT grew and the sun became a little warmer. Having started his journey before the winter solstice, Nanuk had not been obliged to put up with those weeks of total darkness he had known each winter from childhood. He had gone towards the light, and it had not failed him! The thought filled him with awe. Could it be that the sun was the Great Spirit of good? Was that why the closer you got to it, the bigger the trees, the more numerous the game? And what greater wonders would he see as he went farther into the light?

He felt restless, anxious to be gone, but his Indian friends said, "Wait. The moon of storms is upon us. Wait till the wild goose flies north."

There came a day when his hosts beckoned him to come, and he followed. Each hunter had a bag of traps over his shoulder and several had small rifles.

They had walked barely two miles along the north shore of the lake when they came to a large bed of reeds and cattails surrounded by hard-packed drifts. In the centre of the wide marsh were several frozen ponds where a number of dark mounds of half-rotten vegetation stood like little three-foot tepees. Nanuk followed the chief, Exkees, to the nearest mound and watched him chop through its wall with a hand axe and carefully place a trap within.

He indicated to the boy that these were the lodges of small animals whose skins they would sell at the store, and he pointed east again.

While he spoke, Exkees drew the soggy water reeds and bits of broken rush back into place, patting them down so that the water below the muskrat house would not freeze. Then they set off for the next mound.

The Chipewyans finished their trapping in two weeks, during which Nanuk proved himself useful, for he was an expert skinner and could stretch a pelt as well as any. Many of the little skinned bodies were hung on the meat racks to smoke dry, but Nanuk found the fresh ones extremely tasty.

The muskratting had been better than usual that year and the little band credited the presence of the Inuit. Exkees boasted of his own good sense in treating the boy well, saying, "Long ago, the Inuit were enemies to be killed at once. But it is good to think twice, for how can one come to know a dead man? Moreover, a hunter who has killed the big bear of the barrens is not to be trifled with, for the spirit of the creature is strong in him." And Exkees touched the curved claw he wore at his throat.

NOW THAT the muskrat pelts were cured and baled up with the winter catch of lynx, fox, and ermine, the camp would soon move to the place called Brochet, many miles to the east. It was also the place of the Company, which the boy took to be another name for store.

But he did not want to go east. These people were kind but they were not his people and the south called strongly to him again. He had lingered too long, as the homeward-bound hunter lingers too long where fur is plentiful.

There came a morning of warm sunshine and blue sky, across which the first early skeins of geese and cranes began to pass, their necks stretched to the north, the gabbling of the geese mingling with the metallic, grating calls of the cranes. Then came a wedge of great white swans, their fluting calls adding a softer note to the wild clamour. Nanuk followed them with his eyes, his face uplifted, calling silently on the bird spirits to tell Nook and the wife of Nook that all was well with him.

Soon the skin lodges came down, and everything was lashed to the toboggans. The cringing dogs were harnessed and hitched, the whips cracked, the cries of "Mush!" echoed among the trees and the whole company started off in single file, Exkees in the lead. At the margin of Reindeer Lake, the toboggans would be cached and they would camp till the ice went out. Then the canoes would be taken from their pole stands among the brush there, and the families would paddle across to Brochet with their fur catch, to loaf and trade and make their short summer trips along the waterways; until with the early snows of winter they would turn their dogs' noses once more to their hunting grounds, as they had always done.

At the end of the first day's travel, they set up camp beside a small stream, and during that night Nanuk made his decision. He must go south, not east.

In the morning he told the Chipewyans his intention, but they were not pleased. The chief tried all his powers of persuasion, while his daughter, Xhitsoo, a girl of about Nanuk's own age, peeped coyly out from her father's lodge. Exkees suggested that perhaps Nanuk wished to find a wife—but why go farther? Were not the daughters of the Déné as beautiful, strong and useful as those of the strangers to the south? Moreover, now that Nanuk could converse a little in their tongue, would it not be better to stay? It is a weary thing to learn new words and new speech. And they had adopted him into their band. Was he not like a son?

Nanuk had been aware of Xhitsoo. Her eyes were large and soft as a caribou fawn's, her hands small and exquisite. He had followed their deft movements as she stitched and beaded the moosehide moccasins he now wore. He had felt drawn to her, and thoughts had run hotly through him at such times, disturbing him, blotting out the real purpose of his quest. But she was not of his people, and perhaps the spirit within him would later war with her spirit.

At the boy's long silence, the chief stopped smiling and Xhitsoo withdrew her face from the tent flap. With a sudden impulse to bring the matter to an end, Nanuk reached into his parka, detached one bear claw, and brought out the remaining six. These he held out to Exkees, and was rewarded by seeing his face relax into a smile. The chief took the polished claws—within which would surely be a part of the bear's spirit—gazed at them, and said, "It is well then, Inuit." Pointing south, he added, "There lies your way. Go across the small creeks to a river. Follow that and you will come to a camp of the whites. Go in peace."

So once more, Nanuk and Ahneek set off. They looked back only once, from a low rise nearly half a mile from the camp, and Nanuk saw his friends for the last time. He waved at them, but could not be sure that an arm was raised in return, or only to ply a dog whip, as they followed their loaded toboggans in single file—moving specks which soon dwindled to nothing.

8

The rest and food had fully restored Nanuk and Ahneek, and they made a long march that day, over ground soggy with melting snow in the open, yet still holding deep drifts at the edge of the timber. The new moccasins soon became wet, but Nanuk had packed them with moose hair and as long as he kept walking, his feet were warm. That night and at each camp, he would have to dry his moccasins and rub his feet well, as he had seen the Indians do.

Walking next morning with the cool scent of the spruce in his nostrils, the boy saw a tiny bird swaying at the tip of one of these trees, singing in such loud, clear notes that he smiled. When it flew to the ground, Nanuk saw that it had a white circle round its eye and a narrow patch of ruby red on its crown.

Life and movement and subtle smells were all around. The willow bark was red with sap, the poplar buds fat with sticky balm, and everywhere the snow crust settled lower in the heavy brush and in the lee of the big trees. In one wide opening, he had spied a mass of white, like a late snowbank, which suddenly erupted into wheeling and twittering snowbirds—the little songsters that nested in hundreds in the arctic. Now he knew where they disappeared in winter—towards the sun, like him.

Nanuk had brought some dried muskrat, a strip of moose meat, and two frozen whitefish with him. He had fed one fish to Ahneek the night before and now cooked the other for his breakfast.

Towards noon they crossed a large muskeg with a low hump in the centre; on it, a number of brown grouse were hopping and dancing, and Nanuk crawled towards them, under cover of some light brush. He managed to shoot two with his bow and arrows but the rest flew off, with a dry drumming of wings, to the safety of the woods.

The next day, they came to a lake with many arms and crossed on the southwest one. It was still frozen, though they had to wade through water for a few strides at the shore line. A small river flowed from the far end of this arm, hurrying south as if leading them on. Surely the land of light could not be far now! The river seemed to offer an easy route, but after one day of following its crooked course, Nanuk wearied of it and they struck across country, straight south again.

In two or three days, they came to another river which appeared to run fairly straight towards the south, and since its banks were heavily wooded, they took to the ice rather than struggle through the brush, walking all day between low banks of willow and poplar backed by tall spruce.

NANUK AND AHNEEK between them had eaten the grouse, and the moose meat was almost finished; he would have to find game or fish soon. The Indians had told him that within two weeks, the fat, sucker-mouthed fish would be running, and had given him a three-pronged fish spear. He had also asked them, by signs, if there were rabbits in this country and they had shown him soft and silvery rabbit-skin robes, explaining that sometimes there were many, but that about two years before, they had begun to succumb to the rabbit sickness and all through the past winter there had been none. But they had heard that a few were being seen again farther to the south. Now, before they camped for the night, Nanuk followed a track through some willows, sure that it had been made by a hare. In the half-light, he came upon more tracks, and so set three snares.

It was starting to get colder when he made camp and by the time their fire was going, it had come on to snow. Nanuk took off his wet footgear and set it to dry, rubbing his chilled feet with handfuls of the marsh grass which grew in clumps among the willows, its tops free of snow. Then he and Ahneek shared the last muskrat, and turned in under a rough brush shelter. But both felt cold and damp and the day broke dimly after a miserable night.

Wet snow lay quite deep everywhere, and the bushes hung down curved with its weight, the tips of their limbs touching the ground. Somehow Nanuk got a fire going, then once it blazed up, he went to his snares, pushing aside the drooping willows. One snare was pulled tight on a snowshoe rabbit, but it had been half eaten by some night prowler—probably a mink. Disappointed, the boy returned to his fire to broil what was left of the rabbit.

When they set out again, the new snow made the river ice better going for Ahneek but worse for Nanuk, as it slid under his feet. He saw no more rabbit signs and put this down to the snow; in fact, those he had encountered represented only an isolated colony, just beginning to increase—such had been the severity of the myxomatosis, and the keen competition among predators for the new offspring.

Now the snow began to fall thicker and thicker, clinging to Nanuk's eyelids, gathering on Ahneek till he looked like a woolly sheep, blotting out the shore-line timber to either side of the river.

Nanuk raised a mitted hand to brush the snow from his eyes and suddenly he stepped off into space, to gasp and struggle in a current that whirled him among rocks and broken ice—a current that roared loud enough in his ears now, though he had not heard its warning sound in time, muffled as it had been by the heavy snowfall.

Ahneek caught the boy by his parka hood, making desperately

495

for the shore, but the current overcame his efforts and began to drag the two of them downstream, bumping them between spume-covered rocks. Several times the boy's head went under, for he was heavy from the water beneath his parka. In the end, Ahneek lost him.

Nanuk tried to swim, but his feet went down and there was no room for his arms amid the hurrying ice. He thought, in an odd, detached way, that he must be close to the river's mouth—where it flowed into a lake. There was often a rapid at such a place. With that thought, his head struck something and his mind went blank.

NANUK CAME to among some willows on the riverbank. He was lying on a portage trail that was marked by a tall spruce lobstick. He must have passed the marker for the other end of the portage in the snow; it would have warned him of the rapids.

The snow had almost stopped but he was unutterably weary and shivering with cold. He looked for Ahneek but saw, instead, a dark face bending over him, and heard the Chipewyan speech from close by. He could smell smoke and knew there was a fire. Another Indian was approaching, with his arms full of spruce boughs.

Nanuk felt the darkness coming over him again and fell back, as several hands seized him, and he heard voices in guttural talk, then realized the Indians were removing his wet clothing. He felt the heat from the fire, then a heavy robe was thrown over him and he drifted into an uneasy sleep in which he called for Ahneek.

The next thing he knew, a warm tongue was caressing his cheek and he opened his eyes to see his dog standing over him, wet and shivering. Then someone came with hot broth, lifted his head and put the bowl to his lips. It was fish soup and he thought, "Well, the suckers must be running now!" The liquid warmed his stomach and he felt it crawl to his very toes. Nanuk sighed, lay back, and slept.

9

The little Chipewyan nurses' aide turned quickly towards the bed where the white youth, who could not speak English, was sitting up and staring around him. Pneumonia had left him haggard and weak.

Where was he? What was he lying on, so far from the ground? What were the bars behind his head, and that bottle thing with the long tube hanging from it? Warily, he started to get off the unfamiliar bed, but the aide took him by the feet and lifted his legs back.

He croaked something in Inuit and she replied in the Déné. She told him he was in the white man's lodge at a place called Lac La Ronge; that a party of her people, camping at Mink Rapids, had taken him to the nearest yellow-stripe, who had sent him here by plane three days before. It was his chest, she explained, and put a brown hand on her own bosom, coughing. But the white shaman would make him well.

He understood the general drift of what she said, and nodded. Then, "Ahneek?" he said, in a voice he did not recognize as his own, which seemed to come from far away.

The aide shook her head and he tried again, stumbling over the word for dog. She smiled then, and pointed out of the window where Ahneek lay in the spring sun, lonely and still. Now the girl stepped into the hall and called a name, and a red-headed orderly entered. In English, the aide said, "Will you watch my patient a little while? Don't let him get out of bed, eh?" and disappeared.

The orderly went to the window and saw the little aide go to Ahneek, who turned his head and pricked his ears towards her. She spoke softly in her own tongue, smiling and extending her hand. Ahneek rose, wagging his curly tail, nosed her hand, and the girl and the big dog began to mount the front steps. When they entered the room, the young orderly eased out, keeping wide of Ahneek, who bounded to the bedside and ecstatically greeted his master.

Dr. Summers had instructed that the husky be left strictly alone, after Pete, the orderly, had tried to tie him up. The dog had taken up a position on the little patch of grass in front, ignoring man and beast. Only the Chipewyan aide, Madeline, could go right up to him with his evening bone, and he would get to his feet like a gentleman, touch his nose to her hand, then take his supper gently from her.

The doctor had also ordered that when Nanuk's fever broke, his companion should be brought in. "The boy knows no one," he had said, "and seems to speak only Inuit and a bit of Chip. He'll be frightened when he wakes, but the dog will calm him. It's a lucky thing that young Ballentyne put the dog on the plane with him. According to the Indians, it was he who dragged the lad ashore. They said the dog wouldn't leave him, and none of them wanted to lose an arm—nor did Ballentyne, I dare say!"

THE INDIANS had taken Nanuk to Sandfly Lake in a blanket litter, and delivered him to Constable Ballentyne of the RCMP, who was to them not only the law but the government. Just before their party arrived, the spring packet had come in by plane from Brochet to be forwarded to Prince Albert, and with it a note from Corporal Fielding, reporting the rumour of a young white man who spoke no English, who had been in old Exkees's camp at Wolverine Lake. But no one knew his proper name or where he came from.

Constable Ballentyne had sat long at his desk that night, punching his typewriter keys by the "hunt and peck" method. His finished report to the superintendent read something like this:

(1) About noon of April 22, 1945, Beaver Tail and four members of his band, Johnny, Isadore, Old Fox and Atanuk (Chipewyans), arrived from Mink Rapids, approximately twenty-seven miles northeast this point, bringing an almost unconscious man, well wrapped, together with his clothing, and a large yellow husky dog, evidently the victim's property.

(2) Isadore's statement (in English) was to the effect that the previous day, April 21, the band was moving camp to Sucker Lake and arrived at Mink Rapids for noon meal. While they were cooking, a large, wet husky approached from the willows, then turned back into the brush of the riverbank. Following the dog, Isadore came upon what they thought was a dead man. He called for Atanuk and they brought the body to camp, finding it to be a youth of about seventeen, who still lived. They gave what aid they could and the victim came to for a few minutes, then relapsed into unconsciousness.

(3) Reconstructing the accident, they think the youth had been travelling south on the river ice and had encountered the rapids unexpectedly, owing to very heavy snowfall at the time. He had evidently been swept downstream, suffering injury

from rocks or ice on the way. Apparently the dog had dragged him up the bank, as was shown by tracks in the new snow and ragged tears about the man's parka hood, evidently made by the dog's teeth.

(4) They kept him in camp overnight, but as he was still breathing next day (April 22), they made a litter and the five of them brought the victim to my detachment.

(5) *Action taken.* Since the plane from Brochet was still here, I persuaded the pilot to take the victim to St. Paul's Angelic Hospital at Lac La Ronge.

I also sent the husky, which might be a clue to victim's identity. The dog does not understand English commands, but the Chipewyans warned he might be vicious if attempts were made to part him from the young man. The victim's parcel of belongings was sent also.

(6) *Reason for action.* The following description of victim and list of possessions led to my belief that he is of pure white blood but has lived among the Eskimos until the last few months.

Name—Not known.

Height—Five feet eight inches, slim.

Age—16–18 years. Beard beginning to show.

Colouring—Fair. Blue eyes, red hair. Freckles.

Marks—White scars (old) on arms and lower legs. Large bruise on back of head. Healed wound from animal bite on muscles of left forearm, evidently not attended by doctor.

General state—Victim in shock. Pneumonia feared. Talked in apparent delirium.

Speech—Inuit, with a few words of Chipewyan. Spoke Cree word—*mooswa.* No English.

Possessions—All old and badly worn except:

Chipewyan-style moccasins, recently made.

Fire drill and bow, Eskimo style. Also tinderbox marked in Déné syllabic characters.

Case knife, similar to those traded to Eskimos for seal-skinning.

One bear claw in parka. Too large for black bear, but could be barren-land bear from few dark hairs still adhering to it.

A *few strands sinew,* look like barren-land caribou, and a small piece of untanned hide of same.

A *ragged length* of what might have been a blue woollen blanket, with two letters interwoven which read VY. Blanket appears to be camel hair. Evidently of white make.

Pack carried by dog, made of a rolled-up piece of hide of same type of bear as above, containing a few scraps of dried meat. Fastened to animal by rawhide thongs.

Dog. A large Eskimo husky, obviously devoted to victim. Since latter repeated the word "Ahneek", I tried it on the dog, who responded. This Eskimo name, I believe, means "friend".

Recommendations.

I believe the victim will be able to give an account of himself in the Eskimo speech, and therefore suggest an Eskimo-speaking white or Indian be sent to La Ronge to interview him.

References.

Please refer to report from Corporal Fielding at Brochet dated April 20, 1945. There would seem to be a connection here.

Copies to: Corporal Fielding, Brochet,
          RCMP, Lac La Ronge.
        Senior Medical Officer, St Paul's Hospital,
                Lac La Ronge.

Constable Ballentyne signed the report, dropped it into the "out" tray for the next plane, yawned, and went to bed.

10

Superintendent Bruce Young leaned back, filled his pipe, locked his hands behind his head, and gazed at the ceiling, towards which the blue smoke was curling and eddying.

It was sixteen lonely years since he had lost Elspeth, his wife. Sixteen years in which he had thrown himself into his work with a sort of savage fervour—and those years had taken their toll, even as they had led from promotion to promotion.

Now his mind went back to his first northern posting, the drab little detachment at Coronation. How bleak it had been without her, since her plane went down in the tundra, somewhere between the Mackenzie River and Hudson's Bay.

He had loved that country—the great spaces, the sense of freedom; the knowledge that he, a lone constable of the mounted police, was helping to roll back the map of Canada, establishing the rule of law among the almost unknown tribes of the interior. Unlike the coastal bands, these caribou-hunting nomads of the barrens were shy, suspicious, and not easily known.

He shifted restlessly, then relit his pipe, remembering how love had turned to cold hate for a land so vast, so secretive, so quick to blot out for ever those who trespassed on its lonely silence. But he hadn't turned tail. The Old Man had offered a transfer on compassionate grounds and he had refused. His, he felt, was the grim task of helping in the search for that plane. But as the months went by, the search planes and patrols had been dispersed; and all he could do was inquire ceaselessly on his long patrols, wearing himself down, losing weight and becoming more bleak of face as time went on. He could no longer remember exactly how many patrols he had made, how many camps he had visited. Every post, every company store, every mission had been notified, but not a word or a hint had emerged from that sullen, frozen desert.

Now his eyes dropped to Constable Ballentyne's report, lying loosely shuffled on his desk: here was a boy of sixteen who had come from the north . . . from the barrens. But he was white, red-haired—and freckled! He had seen Eskimo kids who looked white, even some with a tinge of red in the hair. But freckles? That he had never seen on an Inuit—or even a part Inuit.

Elspeth had been freckled . . . . He banished the thought. He must think objectively, like the policeman he was. The young fellow apparently spoke no English; only Inuit. But what of the piece of blanket the constable had so carefully described? Those initials, VY. . . . He donned his pea jacket then, and stepped across to his quarters.

502

Going to an old-fashioned escritoire, he fumbled about for a moment and came up with a packet of letters tied with string. Taking out the top one, the last one, dated Edmonton, February 1929, he began to glance over it, his hands trembling: ". . . and Aunt Emma says his name must be Vincent. I think she's afraid we'll call him Sonny or Junior. She even wove the initials for Vincent Young into that blanket she sent from Kingston. Oh, I forgot to tell you that she sent a lovely blanket—camel's hair and what not—you know how mad she is on weaving. Says it helps her to *express* herself! And she'd woven those initials *right in*—so they can't be changed! I suppose after that, we'll just have to call him Vincent, after his grandfather. . . ." Vincent Young! VY!

His mind reeled as he stumbled over to the phone. Then, "This won't do," he said aloud, and sat down to fill his pipe, concentrating on packing the tobacco neatly, striking a match with care.

Only when he had full command of himself did he pick up the instrument, and, "Get me Sergeant Wilde," he said in his usual crisp voice. "Sergeant? Can you have the plane ready by three o'clock? . . . Yes? . . . Good! I have to go to La Ronge.".

IN THE CRAMPED SEAT of the little plane, Superintendent Young opened his briefcase and took out a sheaf of papers. He was trying to piece things together but knew he mustn't jump to conclusions. What if this were some half-breed boy who'd got lost? But then where would he—or his people—have got that blanket?

He closed his briefcase and looked down over the now greening bush country: the tamaracks in the dun swamps faintly emerald, the poplars misty with pearly catkins, the dark spears of the spruce pointing to the sky, rank on rank. Whiteswan Lake was a blue ribbon to the east; Trout Lake, Mecymot Lake and its winding river below him. To the north was the island-dotted expanse of Lac La Ronge and, coming ever closer as they lost altitude, the white walls and red roof of the Anglican hospital.

THE SUPERINTENDENT was facing Dr. Summers over a cup of coffee. "Well, Doctor," he said at last, "what do you think? I want to see this lad, but not till I hear what you have to say. What I have told you so far is just a guess, and I don't want to build on it. I'd rather treat it as a straight police case. I speak Eskimo like a native, you know, or I might have sent someone else."

"I can tell you one thing," the doctor said, "the boy is pure white. And he's not shamming—he doesn't know a word of English. I'm firmly convinced he was brought up in the wilds by natives—whether Eskimos or Indians, it's up to you to find out. I know neither language. But it's perfectly obvious that he'd never even seen a proper bedstead until he came here. He was frightened of it! His legs are a mass of small scars—tooth marks of some sort. I don't know to what extent natives allow their youngsters to rough-and-tumble with dogs. The scars are bigger than one would expect from small pups, but by the look of them, they've been on him since he was an infant."

"Well, what about this husky that's with him—would he have made those scars?"

"No. The dog can't be that old."

"What about the boy's wounded arm?"

"Animal of some kind, a few months past. I'd say a wolf or a bear. Could be some connection with the bear hide—and the claw he had with him."

"Did you see the piece of blanket mentioned in this report?" Young asked.

"Oh sure. Looks like a bit of crib blanket to me. Made of fine wool. Seems it was his 'medicine', as they say. He doesn't want to part with it. Holds it a lot, like . . . well, you've seen a little kid dragging a teddy bear around? It's a security thing."

The policeman rose. "Thanks, Dr. Summers. I'll see him now."

As SUPERINTENDENT YOUNG entered the boy's room, a big yellow dog rose from beside the bed and advanced on stiff legs. But at a word from him in Eskimo, the husky settled down again.

The boy was sitting up in bed, staring at him with wide blue eyes. Madeline, the aide, rose from her chair, rolled up her knitting and moved towards the door.

"Please stay, Sister," said the superintendent.

Smiling, she sat down again and began to ply her needles.

504

Nanuk was thin and pale, and his freckles stood out sharply on skin now even whiter with the pallor of illness.

Young gripped the foot of the bed with his hands, then controlling himself, he smiled. The boy smiled back.

My God! Was this Elspeth looking at him? But no, he must push that back. All redheads had a similar look—they were a type.

"Do you like this place?" he asked in Eskimo, hardly knowing how to begin—he who had questioned hundreds. "Are you afraid here?"

"I am not afraid," replied Nanuk in the same language. "The Indian girl"—he indicated the aide—"brings me good food. But I would like more meat.

"It is good to speak Inuit again," the boy went on. "Are you another white *angakok?*"

"No, I am not a shaman," and the superintendent came around the bed to stand by Nanuk's shoulder.

The boy looked him up and down, then gazed at the badges on his uniform and the gold stripe on the police breeches. "Now," he said, "I see you are a yellow-leg warrior. I have heard of them. They can hang people," he added.

"And have you seen one before?" The question came rapidly, for he seemed to be with Nook again, and could feel again a child's hand on his leg. A child with blue eyes—but that was not uncommon among the Inuit, and the light had been bad. . . .

The boy wrinkled his brow. "I do not remember," he said.

Young went on, "Do you know of a man of the Inuit called Nook?"

"Nook? Why, Nook is my—no—the man in whose tent I lived. But that was long ago. Before ever the snow came."

"Did you get lost, then, on a hunting trip?"

"Lost, Father?" The superintendent started at the word, but he knew it was common among the Inuit, as among the Indians, for a young man to address a respected elder as Father. "Never is an Inuit lost. No. I had to leave. The spirit said so, for I had to follow the light. They were not my people. I did not know who my people were. But now I know. They are your people, whose eyes are like the sky and their skin pale."

"And how did you first come to Nook and his band?"

"I do not know. Perhaps Nook found me. He is a mighty hunter. Perhaps it was the doing of my medicine which I have always had," and from under his pillow the boy withdrew a piece of threadbare blanket, freshly laundered but badly stained. "This is my medicine, and it bears the marks of a lodge." He indicated the letters, but held them upside down and the superintendent saw what he meant. "And I have come to the lodge," added the boy. "I had to find it, for there would be my people. It is a much greater lodge than I expected."

"And what did your medicine say you would find in the great lodge?" pursued his questioner.

"Not my medicine, Father. It was the spirit who told me. It said, 'Go to the lodge of your own people and find there the man who is your father'," and the boy gazed long at the face so close to his.

Years of training restrained the superintendent. Not too soon, his mind told him above the clamour of his heart. He must go slow for both their sakes.

The boy now lay back upon the pillows, his face flushed, and the aide rose.

"The patient must have his medicine now," she said. "He will have the fever again, so please leave if you don't mind."

The superintendent stepped back. He felt a cold nose in his hand and, looking down, saw the big husky close to his thigh.

He spoke quietly to the dog and, turning, left the room, his mind racing.

"SO, DOCTOR," Superintendent Young concluded, "I didn't dare go further until I was absolutely *dead* sure. See what I mean?"

"Yep," grunted Doctor Summers.

"Now, if I could send a message to Aklavik . . ."

"You bet. Good girl to help you, too," said the doctor. "Half-Indian. Just give these *metis* a little training and you can't beat them. Come along!"

Summers was proud of his building and modern equipment, but even more so of the staff he had trained so patiently. He loved the north country, which he invariably spoke of as "she". Now they entered a small room where a dark-haired girl sat by a radio set.

"Oh, Julie—take care of Superintendent Young, will you?"

The girl nodded brightly.

"Get me Aklavik if you can, please," Young said. "RCMP."

She twirled some knobs, and her voice sounded loud in the little room. "La Ronge calling. . . Come in please. . . . Over! Hello? Superintendent Young for you."

She handed him the earphones, slid from the stool, and he sat before he spoke. "Young this end. Reference Nook. Caribou Eskimo band, Coppermine area. Got it? Check reports, patrols back to 1929. Loss of plane carrying Mrs. Young and child, March 1929, and subsequent search patrols to 1933, with special reference to native hunter Nook. Repeat please. Over."

He heard the voice at Aklavik repeat and turn over.

"Thank you. Now, can you check the following two files? One: Any report adoption of white child by native since 1929. Two: Any reports of natives lost since 1944 if files still open. Can you let me have this information over this station tomorrow noon? Over."

Yes, they could, the voice said, and the superintendent rose.

"Thank you, Julie. Let me know when they call back tomorrow, will you? If I'm not right here, I mean."

He returned to the doctor's office. "Just put in my call. Might turn something up."

"Good," exclaimed Summers. "Now I want you to get a decent night's sleep, so take two of these in a glass of water, and to bed with you! You're in Ward Three. If you need anything, buzz the nurse."

In spite of the pills, Young slept badly. He dropped off quickly enough, but the boy's pleading eyes kept coming between him and something. Then the boy's mouth would open but no words come. Now he was in a plane, looking down, the earth rushing towards him, and a voice—Elspeth's voice—above the shriek of the wind, "Oh, God! Take care. . ." And there she was. He tried to touch her but could not. He tried to count the freckles on her face but she dissolved then and he saw her no more.

He woke sweating, switched on the light and reached for his pipe, which he lit with unsteady hands, and lay looking at a text on the wall with the words, "Behold, I make all things new."

507

After a few minutes of deep thought he put down his pipe and lay back, switching off the bedside lamp.

He slept heavily this time.

WHEN HE WOKE, the spring sun was streaming in, and looking through the open window he could hear the birds. An aide entered with a tray.

Later, as he shaved and began to dress, he was strangely at peace. He looked in the glass to brush his thinning hair, and noticed how grey he had become. Well, forty-five wasn't young any more.

Elspeth would now have been thirty-eight. . . .

Julie called him to the radio room just after twelve, and Aklavik reported the only two mentions of Nook were, first in his own report of a patrol in 1932, when still a constable. Quote: "At camp of caribou Eskimos seventy miles southeast Coppermine River. One Nook questioned, who seems to be chief hunter. No signs of plane seen by this band." And in a December 31, 1944, report from Constable Burkett, Coronation. Quote: "On the 27th instant, Mr. McLeod, Hudson's Bay post manager, stated, 'Solomon Atseek, local native, heard rumour from Bathurst Inlet seal hunter about a member of caribou Eskimos, now in winter camp—the adopted son of one Nook, who had been missing for some weeks.' Await instructions if any, otherwise will check on regular spring patrol before breakup."

That was all, but it was enough. When he had questioned Nook, he had been within touching distance of his own son! Why had he not turned back when his mind had been uneasy? Why do we choose to ignore such feelings as had nagged at him that day, after he had left Nook's camp? He supposed that he had already accepted the total loss of his son by that time, and the feeble questioning of his heart (his "hunch" if you like) had not been able to break through the barrier which kept his rational side separated from his emotions.

Yet how wondrous are the ways of God, he added to himself; for he *had* known his own flesh and blood when first he entered the boy's hospital room.

VINCENT WAS SITTING in a chair by the window, the hospital dressing gown hanging loosely on his lean figure. Ahneek stood by him; and at Young's entrance, the two turned their heads towards him.

There was a moment of silence, then, "You are my son, Vincent," said the tall man at last.

"Yes, I know," replied the boy, and Ahneek stepped forward and pressed against the superintendent's thigh.

"How did you know?"

"Am I not one born in the Sign of the great Bear? How else did I come to leave the place of tents and come here? The sign is very strong in my heart, yet the sign is not the spirit—I think it only shows the way of the spirit. It brought me from the land of dark to the place of light.

"I shall live with you and learn your speech and many other things. I hope one day to be an *angakok*, healing all manner of illness. And I hope you will tell me of my mother, for I know she does not live now. When I can, I shall go to Nook and the wife of Nook who cared for me, so that I may be forgiven for leaving them as they grow old.

"And Father, Ahneek knew you even as I knew you. That is why he presses against you, for he perceives the same spirit in both of us."

THERE WAS REJOICING in the tents of the caribou Inuit. The long secret was out at last, and they had received thanks and many presents and greetings from Nanuk. When the yellow-leg from Coronation had come and told them that the boy had found his people and his father, the camp was astonished—all but the shaman.

Now he addressed them as they sat smoking new tobacco through the long, bright night. "Did I not say he was to follow the light? I knew he had to leave. That is why I told you not to spend overlong in search, and why the snow spirits came to cover his tracks. Had he not passed the test of hairs, the test of the tooth?

"I knew then that I spoke to fools, but I am old and I am patient. What are years, say? They are but moments that pass as the caribou herd passes. But the years are also for counting the time, and there is a time for this and a time for that, according to the passage of

509

years. It was not the time for you to speak of the child when he was small. And so I told you.

"Now is another time, and it is well, O Nook, that you spoke to the yellow-leg who came among us yesterday. Now that the boy has accomplished what was required, it is greatly to his profit—and ours," he added.

"And now if I tell you that the youth we called Nanuk will return one day as an *angakok*—a shaman curing all ills—then neither will you believe me. My words will be like the rising of a fish in water—a little ripple soon forgotten.

"But the spirits have also told me that by dawn there will be dried fish, some oil and the fat from a caribou's kidney beside my tent. For it is a hard matter to commune with the spirits and make divinations for your sakes, and keep more than a thousand secrets."

R. D. Symons

R. D. Symons was born in England in 1898, and privately educated in a country household in Sussex where casual visitors included such illustrious neighbours as Rudyard Kipling.

At the age of sixteen his sense of adventure took him to Medicine Hat, Alberta. Apart from his wartime service, Mr. Symons spent the rest of his life in the Canadian West, working as a trapper, cowboy, gamewarden, naturalist and artist.

In his middle years, R.D. Symons and his wife built a ranch in a rugged part of northeastern British Columbia, where he had literally staked a claim. Eventually ill-health forced him to give up

ranching for a relatively simpler existence in Silton, southern Saskatchewan, on the shores of the fifty-mile-long Last Mountain Lake. Here he began writing about the pioneering way of life he had earlier known, in such books as *The Broken Snare* and *Where the Wagons Led*. Our present selection, *In the Sign of the Bear*, is one of two novellas contained in his popular *North by West*.

Mr. Symons died in 1973, at the age of seventy-five, after a long battle with leukaemia.

EE112